A Tale of Love & Bones

DAUGHTERS OF THE KEEPER

BOOK ONE

ALLIE MADDOX

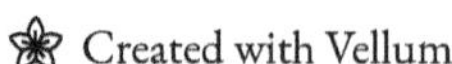 Created with Vellum

To all the girls struggling, I see you, I hear you.
Come get lost in this world.

AZUDORA
NORTHERN CAMP
KAANOS MOUNTAINS
GODLESS MOUNTAINS
GRAVENEAR TERRITORY
easthallow
FORSAKEN WOODS
fallholt
gilded forest
feral sea
midburgh
dunworth
BAREBOURNE
elwyn
REDMOND
SOUTHERN CAMP
SATURNINE BAY
whitshore
ISLINGTON OCEAN

Bria

I'm having the dream again.

Strolling down the sun-kissed hallways made of polished limestone, I drop my hand, letting my fingertips slide down the smooth surface as I walk. I take my time and admire the landscape through the large windows. The gardens stretch wide, filled with muted pastels of spring while servants flock to the markets down the steep, rolling hill.

Outside of the window I see him. My father is sitting in the garden, legs stretched out beneath him as he holds his tea. His long fingers grasp the handle of the teacup, and though it looks like an average cup, I expect it was overly priced. A young girl runs up to him, her blue-black hair bouncing in long waves around her shoulders, her smile beaming. She says something to him, and he laughs before she takes off, running back toward the house. He looks up at me then, through the window and smiles, his bright white teeth gleaming. I can see his eyes crinkle the way I love, scrunching until only a glint of deep blue can be seen beneath. The sun sprinkles golden sparkles across the glass of the window and deepens the gold curls around his head.

Then suddenly, everything is shattering. A loud cracking echoes in my ears, rattling all the bones in my body. The perfect limestone and glass erupt into shards, falling like jagged snowflakes all around. The look of horror etched on my father's face is heart-wrenching and I see him reach for me through the waterfall of debris.

Waking with a start, I sit up quickly. Sweat soaks through my nightshirt. The pillow beneath my head is damp, the blankets twisted around my limbs. Nausea roils through my body, bile building at the back of my throat, but I swallow hard, forcing it back down. Kicking away the sticky sheets, I push off from the sweat-streaked mattress, padding softly but quickly to the bathing chamber off my room.

The morning sun is just starting to peek through the windows as I pass, the curtains not fully drawn. I shove my hands into the basin, letting the icy-cold water that's leftover drip over my fingers, filling the bowl of my hands before tossing it onto my face. The shock of it jolts me out of the dream state. Gripping the sides of the small vanity, I peer into the mirror, catching my own reflection. It's jarring. The deep cobalt blue eyes of my father stare back at me, sending a shudder crawling down my spine. I finger my hair, matted from the sweat of the nightmare—the same gold locks he sported, though mine are stick-straight, not a curl to be seen. I scowl at my reflection. I look too much like him.

I shake off the feeling, unwilling to stay locked in a horrid memory for too long. They will all be awake soon and I should get going.

I look around the room. A tiny bed lies in the center of the small space, sheets tossed and tangled in disarray from yet another night of thrashing through the waves of nightmares. The dark, damp stain of sweat is still visible on my pillowcase, a nice reminder of my fitful night's sleep.

There's a single window that overlooks the small village, the northern camp. I walk over and lean against the frame. It's cool to the touch, a chill that seeps into my skin through the long sleeves of the thin nightshirt. I scowl at the frost clustering on the long blades of grass outside, sparkling like frozen gemstones.

It may look beautiful, but I hate the cold.

This is not my home. Not where I came from or where I grew up. No. I lived so much farther south—the town of Elwyn, along the southern coast of Azudora. The last place I saw my father alive. The last place I held my mother and sister. Where the winters never bore snow, just cool breezes. Where flowers bloomed year-round and there was no chill that made your bones ache. Where fields and meadows gently curved like lazy rivers.

But here I stare at the sharp edges of black mountains capped in glistening ice and snow. The northern camp is nestled in the Kaanos Mountain range, as far northwest as you can get in this world. If anything lies beyond the mountains, we are unaware. No one ever travels that far, the routes through the mountains too treacherous. I need to dress in thick, itchy wool or fleece and require fur-lined gear just to keep a semblance of warmth in my body here. I wish to go back to Elwyn, to my home, no matter how impossible I know that reality is.

But why dwell on it? I'm here now, aren't I? I narrow my eyes and lift my middle finger at the frigid landscape. Fucking snow.

Pushing off the splintering wooden frame, I stretch and straighten my spine. Grabbing the clothes I left out, I slide on a thicker pair of leggings and pull a long-sleeved cotton shirt over my head. I own one pair of older, thin shoes I use for running. I may hate the cold, but running keeps my mind at ease—keeps me sane—and keeps the fire inside dimmed.

It's early enough that no one is awake yet and I'm able to slip through the old building and out the front door before taking off. My body knows where to go. I turn around the side of the inn and up the closest route into the mountains. I start to slow, letting my lungs adjust to the biting air outside. It burns and tightens my chest, but I kept pushing, letting my legs carry me up the winding path. The pounding of my feet, the heaviness of my breathing, and the rapid swish of my arms all fall into place to bring me back into my body.

The nightmares are getting worse, and I think about them as I run. More of my father and now my sister keeps appearing. The ones of my father have been there for years, but seeing her? That was new. I'd honestly forgotten the last time I saw her was outside with him until that dream brought it all back.

I shove out the memory and keep going until I hit the small plateau that marks my turnaround—a short trek up and back that usually takes a half hour to complete. It's enough to keep my body nimble and my endurance up. Both things I will need in the near future.

When I make it back, the fire in my room is running on fumes but the water buckets I left next to it the night before are warm enough. I fill the clawfoot tub and slide in, letting the lukewarm water do its best to soothe my aching muscles and wash the cold out of my bones. Just another thing to miss: having servants fill a steaming bath for you whenever you want. I would kill for a hot, scalding tub of water.

Striding to the dresser, I open the top drawer and frown. Only a handful of items look back at me. Not many choices these days. Long gone are the mornings where I could peruse armoires of resplendent dresses made of the finest silks, assisted by my maid Elia to adjust the bodice and ensure the layers of skirts cascaded gracefully. Instead, I drag out a long tunic once an evergreen color—now faded to worn sage—and fleece-lined leggings, thicker than the ones I use for running. Do I even own anything that isn't a worn earth tone or black? Unlikely.

Leather chest armor lies on top of the dresser with deep scratches and gouges along the surface, the age of it apparent in the loose buckles and fraying straps. I lift it, pulling it over my head as I have each day for the last five years. Well, four and a half. The first six months here I spent sulking like a child about my fate and drinking myself into oblivion. I tighten the straps and snag the bandolier next, strapping that on as well and pushing the hilts of the daggers to make sure they are locked in tight. Tugging on thick, heavy woolen socks and lacing up my leather boots, I wonder how much longer this will last. How much longer will we remain rebels, the resistance movement against the Crown?

Fully dressed, I realize I might as well get on with it. Everyone will be rising by now. I snatch my old leather gloves and fur-lined cloak off the bedside table and stalk out of the room, closing the door swiftly behind me.

This section of housing had been a cozy little inn before the rebels took over the town. Now, I live in a small room on the second floor, up a steep set of creaky and tired stairs. The rest of the higher-ranking members of the rebel faction dwell in the rooms along the hall. Mine is set back from the stairs, tucked in the darkest corner of the inn.

Passing the other rooms as I saunter down the hallway, I listen to the faint noises of others readying for the day. Drawers open and close, water splashes, and boots scuff across the oak floors. The familiar sounds are soothing, and I take them in as I weave the long gold and bronze strands of my hair together in a braid across my shoulder. The dampness seeps into my tunic. I should have dried it more before leaving. I'll be grateful if it doesn't freeze when I step outside. My face scrunches at the thought of that icy fucking air and I hope the thick fur of my cloak will at least keep me a bit warm on my way to the library.

As I make my way down the stairs, the old wood cracks beneath me with each step. Then a voice, rich and soothing, hits me before my boots land on the floor to the main room.

"I was hoping to see you this morning, Bria," the voice croons.

I look up to see Evander leaning back in a wooden chair, his booted feet crossed on the seat of another. Strong arms hook across his broad chest, making his biceps bulge. His position is the picture of leisure and comfort, contrasting with the armor and weapons he boasts, looking both out of place and right at home at the same time amid the rebel camp.

I quirk a brow and continue walking toward him, reaching an arm across him to grab a chunk of bread from the meager breakfast array. The cooks do what they can with what they have available, but it is winter here. And despite their summer and fall harvests, we usually start to run low around this time of year. Though spring will be here before we know it.

"Where have you been?" he asks, gazing up at me through thick lashes.

"I've been busy," I respond. He knows full well what I've been up to and why he hasn't seen me in days.

My mouth turns down as I stare at the bread in my hand, wishing it were a warm scone, flakey and scattered with chocolate. Smothered in fresh butter. Those were my favorite. I feel my mouth watering just thinking about them, but the bread will do for now, even if it seems to crumble like ash in my mouth when I take a bite.

Straightening myself, I dare to ask Evander what he's up to today. He still makes me uncomfortable, even to this day. It isn't a bad uncomfortable and never has been. But it's a dangerous one, nonetheless.

"And where might you be headed to this morning?" I question, trying to remain nonchalant. And likely failing miserably.

He smiles, revealing the deep dimple on his left cheek. His molten brown eyes have a beautiful intensity to them, flecked with deep gold. Long, sooty lashes sweep across his lids. He tugs a hand through his chestnut hair, pulling stray pieces from his eyes before speaking. It's longer up top and no matter how he slicks it—slightly to the side and back—the unruly strands always seemed to fight free. The casual motion makes me shift on my feet, too aware of his beauty.

"I'm on patrol today. Helara added more security after..." Evander trails off and quickly averts his gaze. No need to finish *that* sentence.

"Right," I reply.

Helara, our fearless leader and Captain of the northern camp of rebels, recently received word from our southern camp that scouts were spotted nearby. They were tracked and killed, but still. They were only miles away from where my mother and sister are hidden. A chill skitters across my skin, puckering the flesh of my arms at the thought. It means our time is running out if the king's scouts made it that far. They are finally closing in after five years of hunting us.

He glances to the window beside him, a thin layer of frost decorating its edges. Then those eyes slide back to me. "And who has the pleasure of your company on this lovely day?" he drawls.

I stand mere inches from him, so I scoop an apple off the table and move back a few steps, placing my back against the wall as I watch him.

"Cato today," I respond, unable to keep my eyes from rolling back in my head. The thought of the shrunken old man and the way he drones on forces an audible sigh from my lungs and my hand flies to cover my mouth. Cato had been good to me, always. But some days I have more patience for him than others.

The bark of his laugh echoes in the room, deep and hearty, his eyes glistening with humor. I bite down into the apple to keep myself from smiling too brightly in response, chewing with a smirk tugging at my mouth.

Evander kicks his feet off the chair and stands, stretching his broad shoulders and making the leather armor creak with the effort. Then, moving quickly, he closes the gap between us in three strides and snatches the apple from my hand. His eyes remain on me as he sinks his teeth into the shining garnet skin with a snap before tossing it back. My hand darts out to catch it, a honed reflex. My body moves quicker than my mind in that instant, grasping the fruit without ever dropping his gaze.

His eyes widen and the corner of his mouth turns up. "Well, your training with Garrith has paid off, to say the least."

Indeed, it has. For years, I've joined the others to train in the evenings with the former soldier and his men. Though, in more recent months, Helara requested I take more intensive sessions with him. They were grueling, exhausting my body daily, but I grew as a fighter in those months.

Few in the camp knew of my destiny, what I was being groomed for. It was kept quiet, the information only relayed to a select few, mostly those who knew me before I'd come of age. But Evander had known me then, known when it had happened. And it shows in the curve of his smile now.

Gone is the thin and weak eighteen-year-old girl that arrived at this camp five years ago. The girl that stands in her place is changed. Her body is stronger, muscles long and lean from learning to fight and trekking the mountain paths on early morning runs. I can kill with sword or dagger, more agile than most of the men in the camp. And my mind is sharper too, thanks to honing my magic over the time with Cato.

"Just a little," I remark with a wry smile. He holds my gaze and I sweep my tongue over my lower lip, my mouth suddenly too dry.

I become increasingly aware of the burn in his eyes as they drift over me, dipping from my eyes to my lips and following the trail of my tongue. The heat from his body sets mine on fire when he stands this close, his face inches from mine. The earthy smell of the worn leather armor mixes with the crisp citrus of his soap, and I breathe it in, the smell lingering in my nose. I wonder if he can hear the deep thud in my chest. I resist the urge to wipe my now clammy palms on my pants. Does he have any idea the effect he has on me?

The door slams open behind him, cracking the wooden panels of the wall. The sharp wind that sweeps in is biting. Evander doesn't startle or even move at the sound, but I see the smirk he wears as I snap my head to the door. My focus had been wholly on him—on the way he smelled, the way his full lips smiled, and the way his eyes raked over me. I'm yanked from my reverie to see the dark figure in the doorway.

"Ev. Time to go." Quinn crowds the frame with his massive body. A crossbow is strapped to his back, quiver brimming with arrows. He's armed to the teeth, daggers decorating his chest, and a sword gracing either side. Only a fool would think that the rebel warrior doesn't have at least three more weapons in places unseen. Quinn is intimidating to most, but he has a soft side, despite his terrifying frame. He nods to me, his eyes narrowing as he glances between Evander and me.

"Good morning, Bria," he says, his voice softening when he speaks to me. It's a far cry from the rough tone he gave to his best friend just now.

"Quinn." I nod back.

Evander stares at me a beat longer and I meet his eyes, the intensity still there. For a moment, I feel lost in the deep brown, but Quinn clears his throat behind Ev as he stands in the icy doorframe—a warning to get moving.

"See you later, Bria." Ev's smile doesn't falter as he turns on his heel to leave.

He grabs the midnight cloak off the back of the chair and slings his crossbow over his chest. He strides to the door before glancing back at me with a flash of teeth.

My stomach drops with that smile and the thought of how close we just were. But I see Quinn staring, his hazel eyes darting quickly between us, noting the interaction with furrowed brows. He does not look pleased. He grasps Evander by the shoulders and shoves him brusquely through the door and into the frigid morning. The door slams shut behind them and I remember to breathe.

"What exactly do you think you're doing?" Quinn demands as we trek across the small green toward the stables.

"I have no idea what you're talking about," I reply, keeping my tone cool.

"Like hell you don't," Quinn shoots back.

I skid to a halt a few feet short from the building and look back at my dear friend. I let loose a heavy sigh. "Did you see her today?" I ask, knowing full well he will be pissed at me for saying it.

Quinn snorts. "You're acting like a child."

"I would argue—a *child* doesn't feel this way at all." A smirk twitches on my lip as I speak.

"You know she has a purpose here." Quinn's eyes darken, his voice lowering. "You cannot distract her from it. No matter your...feelings," he finishes with a disapproving look.

I throw my hands up in feigned resignation, palms facing out. "Who am I to get in the way of destiny?" I counter sarcastically, though my face falls as I think about the meaning behind Quinn's words. "We don't know that it's her."

Quinn shrugs as he pushes past me into the stables, the earthy air within warm with the scent of hay. "We don't know that it isn't."

I follow closely behind him, letting his words sink in. Bria is thought to be the prophecy. Well, one half of it anyway. And we treat her like she is—those of us who know, at least. Hell, most of my job here at the camp has to do with protecting her as one of the few who know her destiny, keeping her true identity a secret while maintaining security of the entire camp. We are to keep her hidden, even from the rest of the rebels, until the time comes. It's still difficult to recognize her as this girl who can change the world. Who *will* change the world. We were all so close for years before the attack in Elwyn, playing together, growing up side by side, and now living this rebel life together.

When my father took me to the king's court after the attack, I know Quinn was devastated. He thought I was gone forever. To be fair, so did I. I look toward him now, remembering all he did to help me, to give me a place in this camp and give me a new life—one worth living. He's never resented me or judged me for all the evil things I did in the capital. And there is plenty to hate me for. I owe him.

"You're right, Quinn, I'll be more careful," I concede, moving to grab a saddle from the rack on the old wall.

Quinn gives an approving grunt, taking his own saddle to the dapple-gray stallion at the far end and readying the horse. Silence settles in as we adjust straps and lead the horses out into the chill morning. They shake, letting their dissatisfaction with the cold be known, but they'll warm up soon enough. We have a decent ride ahead of us this morning and the movement will help keep the cold at bay.

We mount our horses and start toward one of the steep paths leading out of the small mountain village. Another trip to see how far the king and his people are getting, how close they are to finding our quiet camps and the precious daughters of the prophecy we conceal within them.

CHAPTER 3

Bria

As the door slams shut, I flop into the seat Evander occupied, still warm from his body heat. I take another bite of the apple and try to ignore the sinking feeling in the pit of my stomach. Evander is attractive, there's no doubt about that. He has always been handsome, devastatingly so, even when we were young. It's almost unfair how he and Quinn have been blessed with such looks. Though, I know I'm not supposed to notice, not supposed to be affected by his beauty, since my family is from wealth and his is far from it.

My father was an earl and my mother was a lady from a nearby city. Evander, however, was born to a soldier and a seamstress, not exactly someone I was ever allowed to consider as a potential suitor. As children, it was less of an issue, and we were allowed to play daily with one another. All the children were, as long as we recognized that when it came down to it, there was a difference. And Evander's father always made sure he knew that.

His father...I grit my teeth at the thought of the man. My hands grip the apple tightly and my nails dig into the flesh, the popping followed by a sticky juice running down my arm. Aamon had been my father's right-hand man, his captain of the guard.

When I close my eyes, Aamon's image is clear, vivid. He's a hard man, tall and stoic with dark eyes and onyx hair cropped tight to his head. He had never been very talkative, never showed much affection to his wife or son. Evander bears little resemblance to the man, aside from his large stature and the long, straight line of his nose. In both physicality and demeanor, he takes after his mother, a stunning woman with the same chestnut hair as Ev that fell in waves about her shoulders. Olaphina had always been kind to me growing up. She was kind to everyone. Evander is so much like her, and so unlike the man who raised him. The man who took them away.

Savoring the sweet taste of the apple on my tongue, I picture Aamon. When we make it to the king's court at last, to the capital, I will kill him. Thoughts of taking my blade and driving it into his abdomen take over. Watching the life drain from his face will be the exact revenge I need. I suppose I could use my magic to kill him—it's always an option —though it will take a lot more out of me to do so. I could choose to summon monsters from the shadows and have them rip him apart with their long, black talons. Shred him with their wicked teeth made from nightmares. But no matter how I kill him, he deserves to see my face when he dies. To see the face of my father.

Aamon betrayed all of us and serves in the same position he once had for my father, now for the king. After all, he tried to deliver some of the most powerful magical people to King Braddock. And for that, the king showed extreme gratitude, rewarding Aamon with the righteous job, even if he was unsuccessful in his attempt to capture my sister and me.

When I turned eighteen, my gifts began to show. Coming of age does that to those with magic in their blood, though it doesn't happen to everyone who comes from magic. Nowadays, it seems fewer people have any powers at all. But those of us who do, have a hell of a time when it starts. The closer you crept to that fated birthday, the more magic flowed into you, coursing through your body like a raging fire with no beginning and no end. It came on naturally but controlling it could be difficult. It required practice and training to keep your emotions from getting the better of you. An angry outburst, a painful injury, even a broken heart could send your gifts haywire.

Which made hiding those gifts even more trying. My parents

worked tirelessly to keep their own gifts as well as mine hidden from all but a few servants in the home, those who were closest to us, those who worked with me and would see as I struggled to gain a grasp on them. But somehow, Aamon caught word of what I could do, learned of the dark magic within me.

Armed with that knowledge, he chose to sell my family out instead of help, to go to the king and tell him what he knew: that my parents had magic in their blood, and so did their daughters. And furthermore, that our servants whispered of the prophecy. Magical bloodlines were dwindling and dark gifts like my own had not been seen in ages, spurring talk of who we may have descended from.

Aamon is the reason my father is dead, the reason I'm separated from my sister and mother, the reason all of this is happening. And what he did to Evander and Olaphina was worse. I may not know all the details of Evander's years in the capital, but I know enough to say Aamon's life is not one worth saving. And I am sure his own son agrees with that statement. Evander and his mother are too good for this wretched world.

I stand, arching my back until the resounding crack of my bones echoes in the room and I toss the core of my apple into the bin with a sigh. Pushing the chair in, I walk out of the inn and into the cold morning, sucking in a breath and groaning as the icy air catches in my throat once again. Miserable mountain town.

Looking up, I can see the library a short distance away, across the other side of the village green. My boots crunch on the light layer of snow, patchy with gaps of dark ground underneath pecking through the glittering white.

A frown sets on my lips as I think of my sister. Nimai doesn't have to put up with the cold. She resides in the southern camp, even farther south than our hometown of Elwyn. And I would bet it's warm and sunny there today, especially with spring so close. I pull my cloak tighter around my body, fighting the chill in my damp hair that feels as if it might freeze the end of my braid straight off.

The library will offer a reprieve from the cold. When I approach, I lay my fingers on the strong wooden handles of the doors and let them wrap around the ornate surface, carved with a delicate touch and so much more sophisticated than the entrances to the other buildings here. Aside from the temple, that is, but no one goes there anyway. I inhale deeply, readying myself for what waits beyond the doors because honestly, I'm just not in the mood today. But I step inside the old building anyway. The smell of musty books fills the air, and I'm hit with a gust of warmth emanating from the roaring fire on the far wall. Thousands of old tomes line either side of the great room and the ceiling soars overhead. The high windows let in the early morning light, pouring golden sunbeams across the room.

"Early riser today. Are you eager to keep learning, Prophecy?" The withered old man appears in front of me, and I startle.

There is no need for it. And I hate when he does it.

"Show off," I spit, narrowing my eyes to a glare. "And don't call me that."

"Hmmmm," Cato hums. "You're in a mood today, it seems."

He walks to a nearby table littered with books, clearly laid out by him in anticipation of my arrival. Despite his age, the man moves smoothly, so quiet he is nearly imperceptible. His gait is more a glide than a walk. I wonder if that has to do with the old magic in him. I also wonder how old he really is. Given how magic slows the aging process, and he's a ripe old geezer, I gather he might be as old as time.

Following behind him, I strip off the heavy cloak and gloves, tossing them onto a chair and pulling back another to slump into. Cato silently moves into the seat across from me and slides a book toward me. I pick it up, studying the dusty cover, worn and gray.

Eyeing the odd title, I tap my nails on it. "*The Art of Bones*? I thought we would be continuing to work on the shadows."

"You've mastered the shadows, dear girl. The creatures you can summon and control give even me nightmares." He shakes his head, pure white hair falling around his face, a deep roadmap of wrinkles. "And I haven't had a nightmare in over one hundred years." He frowns at the thought, and I laugh at his genuine display of discomfort.

I still remember the day he showed up at the rebel camp requesting to see me. He had been drawn to me, drawn to the dark magic that lies within me, though he was vague about how he found me. I suspect Helara knows more about it than she lets on.

Over the last several years, we've spent countless hours together. He taught me how to use my magic, how to draw upon the shadows and bend them to my will, how to cloak myself in the dark mist that swirls around my body. And how to keep it contained, to restrain myself and manage my emotions so I can remain undetected in a land where I am hunted.

Magic is nearly gone, and what is left remains hidden, thanks to the king. His anger and fear got the better of him years ago and eventually he began a crusade to find all those with magic to ensure he would never be defeated, and that the prophecy could never be fulfilled. Instead, he allowed his priests and high priestess to be the only ones who wielded magic in the name of their true god, Vaohr. It's all bullshit.

Somehow, he's never found Cato. Probably because the man can shield himself from sight and manipulate the air and space around him. One of the last remaining old magic wielders—a relic in this changing world.

I know there are others out there, people hidden by their families as long as they can manage. Though I have no idea how many still exist. I'm assuming, for the most part, when someone comes of age, they end up sold out like we were. Eventually ending up in the hands of the Crown. But back when magic reigned, it came from the gods, blessed upon the land and the people residing there. Passed down through blood, it thrived for generations. Though now, with the gods gone, it dwindled, and we are hunted. All of us.

Sitting back in the chair, I cross my arms over my chest and survey the old man. "Okay then, get on with it."

He purses his lips and watches my face for a reaction as he speaks. "As I am sure you are aware, Nimai's birthday approaches."

Keeping my features neutral, I respond, "Yes, in two weeks. Probably for the best, given the reports Helara has been receiving."

"Indeed," he agrees. "I will need to travel to the southern camp before she comes into her gifts fully. She's going to need training, as much as we can give her before we go after Braddock."

"Hence the bones?" I question, looking at the book that lies in front of me.

"Yes. You must master the bones before I leave," he explains. "I'm going to make us some tea. Get to reading." With that, Cato rises from his seat without a sound and glides out of the room as if lifted by an invisible breeze.

I settle into the chair, trying to get comfortable on the hard wood, and lift the book again. The pages are brittle with age, and I turn them with a gentle touch, afraid they will crumble to dust between my fingers. I love reading, but this is more for work than pleasure. Still, I open the book to begin learning all I can about bones. Whatever that means.

Reanimation. Raising the dead. That's what it means, as I soon find out after perusing the pages. Cato returns at some point with tea, but I'm lost in the text. I vaguely notice him set the cup down and disappear from the room. The warm steam curls around my hands as I continue reading page after page about armies of the dead raised to help in battle but reanimated for only a short period of time —skeletal warriors who can wield a longsword, zombie soldiers who can kill with a mace. As long as their soul has departed, they can be brought back, no matter the state of the body or bones they once inhabited.

They could be controlled. My blood runs cold at the thought. I could bring the dead back to life. At least, that seems to be what Cato is suggesting with this book. This is a power I didn't know could exist or had existed at any time. According to the text, it's a rare power, only possessed by a select few across the centuries. Including Lilith and her descendants. No one had told me the extent of Lilith's' powers, trying to keep me in the dark lest I turn out not to be the prophecy.

As I read, the light in the room shifts overhead. Other rebels filter in and out of the library across the day, but they know better than to interrupt me. They may not know who or what I truly am, but they are all aware I hold a seat next to the captain and am likely doing something important. At some point I realize the room is darkening, and Cato comes back to the table with a lantern, the oil glistening from the flame above.

"How?" is all I ask, placing the frail body of the book gingerly on the table in front of me.

Cato waves a hand over my tepid tea and steam begins to emanate once more from the cup. Lifting it to my lips, I inhale the spicy scent before taking a sip and letting the honey-tinged liquid pour down my throat—one benefit of his manipulation of air, I suppose.

Cato smiles and his entire face crinkles with the effort. "You've read the answer to that, my dear girl."

"Fair enough," I concede. "Then why? Why me?" I say, trying my best to remain stoic as I clutch the warm cup in my hands. I brace for the answer I know will come, yet hope anyway—always hoping—that maybe, the answer will change.

It never does.

"Because you are a descendant of Lilith, daughter of the Keeper and goddess of death. You possess the side of magic that resides in darkness and death. You can manipulate the shadows, bend them to your will and create a world of nightmares. You can draw magical energy from others, and with that energy, you can reanimate the dead," he explains.

"It's a bit morbid, no?" I snark, my mouth turning upward. Despite the morbidity, I've welcomed the dark magic over the years.

"I suppose it is," he muses, his smile sardonic.

I tap my pointer finger on the dusty book. "Where did you get this? And how long, may I ask, have you been hanging on to it?"

My brow arches as I wait for his response—the mentor who's been keeping this little secret from me all this time.

"It's from my...personal library," Cato responds, casually pretending to swipe lint from his midnight-blue tunic.

"And you waited so long to tell me...why?"

"Because you have quite a temper and an exasperating sense of ethics that tend to get in the way of things."

A snort escapes my nostrils, and his eyes flick to me, twinkling a soft gray-blue, almost silvery in the light of the lantern.

"Nice," I reply, my lips curling back from my teeth.

"For someone who is supposed to save our world, you sure are a pain in my ass," Cato says, forcing a laugh to burst from my lungs. He isn't wrong. I've never made things easy for him.

"Rest up because tomorrow, we try." Cato stands and turns from me before I can object, vanishing into a silvery mist.

Rolling my eyes, I call into the mist, not even sure he can still hear me, "You're dramatic as fuck, just for the record." I push up from the table and gather my things. Turning to leave, I see the book and snatch it, tucking it into the pocket on the inside of my fur-lined cloak. Needn't have anyone else in the camp figuring out what we were discussing. Not for now, at least.

CHAPTER 4

Bria

I leave the library to find it's well past supper time. Pulling the thick hood up over my head, I trek back out into the freezing air. Though my hair dried hours ago, I feel much colder after spending the day by the cozy fire of the library.

Warriors made of bones dance through my mind as I pass the pub where the rebels and soldiers are drinking after a day of training and patrolling. Lost in thought, I look up at the sounds of clinking glasses and laughter coming from the building. I pause my steps as one of the soldiers opens the door to enter the bustle and the joyful noise bursts from inside.

Evander is sitting by the front window, drink in hand and leaning back in his chair, his feet casually kicked up as per usual. Quinn sits across from him next to a captivating girl with long fiery hair curling around her. Ashbel is laughing, her emerald eyes dazzling, even from here. I make an attempt to duck my head, but she catches sight of me through the window and jumps up, waving.

Damn. I'm not in the mood to go out drinking with anyone tonight, but Ashbel beckons me inside. I push thoughts of bones and death to the back of my mind, determined to focus on the living tonight. As I open the door, it's a barrage to my senses: loud music and laughter, the smell of alcohol and sweat mingling, and heat. Glorious heat. My fingers are stiff and nearly numb already from the short walk.

Ash meets me at the door, pulling me into a tight embrace. If her intention is to suffocate me, she's succeeding. Her hair still holds the sweet fragrance of vanilla from her day in the kitchen and the scent makes me smile. She always smells delicious.

"Where have you been all day?" she squeals, grabbing my hand as she leads me back to where they have been sitting. We make our way through the throng of people relaxing after a long day.

"I was studying with Cato," I reply, allowing Ash to guide me around the clumps of rebels milling about.

"Well, that sounds atrocious. You'll be needing a drink," Ash answers firmly as we arrive back at the table.

Evander pulls his feet from the remaining chair, his head lifting to look at me. I meet his gaze, his eyes reminding me of hot cups of chocolate we would have on special nights as children. Warm and inviting. The flecks of gold only make them more so.

"You have no idea," I respond, taking the open seat next to Evander.

"Is one of you going to get your lady a drink?" Ash demands, her eyes a striking green as they dart between the men. "Or is chivalry dead?" she asks, her voice taking on a teasing but firm tone.

Evander lets out a deep laugh that rumbles in my bones, while Quinn rolls his eyes and pushes back his chair with a loud scrape across the floor. "Of course. Where on earth are my manners?" he quips before prowling away.

Titles mean nothing anymore. Where you came from is merely a talking point here. But Ash still likes to tease about my former status, especially since I'm the only noble in the rebel camp. But we are no longer forced to abide by our status like we had been at a young age. And we never would be again.

"How was Cato?" Evander asks as I get comfortable, removing my cloak and gloves, stretching the chill out of my fingers.

"Oh, fine," I reply, not sure how much information I should give the group just yet about my newfound gift. "It was mostly just reading today."

"Sounds wretched," Ash cuts in, her lip curling in disgust. She enjoys reading, but mostly romance. Give her anything else and she won't last more than a few pages. "We were just talking about their patrol today," she informs me as Quinn returns with a mug of ale.

I thank him and take a sip of the cool beverage, the foam brushing my lip with familiar and delightful floral notes. For quite some time my friends were hesitant to offer me a drink, fearing I would slip back into the dark hole of depression I sank into upon our arrival at the camp. It took months of me pulling myself back together and focusing my attention on my training and magic before Ash and Quinn finally realized I had no intentions of drinking myself to death and I had just been in the midst of a breakdown. A short-lived stint of allowing the despair of my fate and the warmth of whiskey drag me under before I came around and started acting more like an adult. Now, no one pays any mind to offering me an ale or a glass of whiskey. There's no fear that I'm going over the edge again.

The men start back in on their recounting of the trip as I sip at my drink. They were gone most of the day, only returning an hour ago. Quinn sits with his back straight in his seat, arms crossed in front of his chest while Evander lounges back in his chair, rolling the sleeves of his tunic up to reveal toned forearms.

The two have shed their armor after their shift and now sport more relaxed clothing. I let the conversation lull me, listening to the back and forth of my friends, feeling at ease. Evander tosses an arm behind my seat, the heat from his arm warming my back, the calluses from his fingers brushing across my shoulder. I chew on my lower lip, consciously reminding myself not to lean into him. Were it not for the fabric between his fingers and my skin, I might just melt into his touch.

"Wait, what did you say?" I snap back, trying to focus on what Quinn is discussing. I realize that, yet again, I had been so distracted by Evander's touch—by him—that I tuned out of the world around me for a moment.

Ash eyes the hand on my shoulder, one brow arching as she takes a sip of her drink. I glare back, ignoring her wordless query and instead turning my attention to Quinn. She knows me too well and I'm aware there will be a conversation in the near future about my behavior toward Ev.

Quinn's hazel eyes look pained. "The whole village was gone. Wiped out. But they must have found someone there who was of use to them."

"What makes you think that? The king has killed off villages before, especially if he thought they were linked to the rebellion," Ash offers.

"They were sending a message," Evander adds in a low voice, staring down at his drink. I note the warning glance Quinn shoots him when he speaks.

"What? They'll hear about it soon enough. Word travels pretty fast around here if you hadn't noticed," he scoffs.

The rebel camp is comprised of only a few hundred people, and we function as a unit. From what I understand, the southern camp is similar. It's necessary to keep the peace, or that's how Helara sees it, at least. She wants transparency, wants every person here to understand their role and be here willingly. She believes it's the only way to make this work. She keeps no secrets in the camp. Aside from me.

Quinn nods his head in agreement. "Ev is right. They were trying to send a message. The bodies were..." He looks down before finishing. "Ripped apart, torn limb from limb."

"Shit," Ashbel curses, knocking back the remainder of her drink and clasping the empty mug tightly, her fingers white with the effort.

"They hung them from the trees on the outskirts of the village, the symbol of Vaohr burned into the bodies. Branded." Evander continues, "The whole community was burned, including their fields. There were no signs anyone made it out alive." He rakes a hand through his thick hair, pulling it away from his face.

A quiet spreads, nestling down between us, thick with the words we are all thinking but no one dares speak. No one but me.

"Magic," I say, the word catching in my throat. "They found someone with magic. What other reason would they have to send a message like that?"

Evander tightens the hand around my shoulders, running his fingers down my arm. It's a soothing gesture but my skin still prickles in response.

"Yes, that's what we think." I can feel his eyes on me, and it takes everything in me not to look into them, keeping my own focused on the drink in my hand.

Another person like me, hunted down. It hurts and it's terrifying, and I know if I look into his eyes and see pity, I will fall apart right now. And maybe he would be there to help me pick up the pieces, but I can't let that happen either. Instead, I look out at the group of people enjoying their night. They laugh and dance like there is no rebellion, like there are no bodies strung up in trees, like people are not being chased and killed for being different—tracked down and captured because of what runs through their blood. Like we are not fighting a war we may not win.

It's times like these that I want to run to the capital and turn myself in so no one else can be harmed. But I know that type of thinking is useless. Being a martyr won't get us anywhere. Even if Aamon and King Braddock have me, they will still track down the rebels and kill them for taking me in the first place.

"This is a problem for tomorrow. Tonight, let's drink," Ash says, slamming her palms on the table before standing and gracefully moving herself back through the throng of bodies to the bar.

I watch her slide between people and somehow land herself next to a handsome soldier while grabbing more drinks. He is a younger man, newer to the camp, and I'm not yet familiar with him. They are too far for me to make out what they are saying but I can guess the mood of the conversation by watching Ash's body language. It shifts when she talks to him, and she tosses her bright red curls back from her shoulder and tips her head back as she laughs. The girl has confidence. And why not? She is simply stunning, curvy in all the right places, and has an outgoing personality to boot. Men always have their eyes on her.

Evander clears his throat as he witnesses the same encounter. "Well, we know Ash will be busy tonight."

I stifle a laugh, choking back my drink and covering my mouth with a hand.

Quinn spins quickly to see the interaction and lets out a low whistle. "Cade." Gritting his teeth in a grimace, he turns back to the table.

Evander laughs louder then, unable to keep the humor he feels at this arrangement to himself. Ash evidently hears his booming laugh from across the room, as it results in a look that makes Ev curse and toss back the rest of his ale.

I jab his ribs with my elbow. "Knock it off. She's going to get pissed."

Laughter brims in my voice and Evander doubles over from the stab to his side. He grabs his stomach with his free hand and continues to chuckle to himself. Quinn remains facing us, not wanting to brave the wrath of Ash. Smart. He's far smarter than either of us right now.

I see her peel away from Cade with a lingering look back at him before she makes her way to us, a fresh batch of drinks in her hands. Cade's gaze follows her even though he remains with his companions. I see him continue to drink, one eye locked on Ash the entire time. I quickly knock back the remaining ale to avoid looking directly at Ash. I can feel her irritation brewing. She sits down and points her piercing eyes at Evander.

He grabs the new mug from her and takes a sip, speaking before she can lash out at him. "I just feel bad for the kid. He's not going to know what hit him, Ash."

A wide smile spreads across Ash's face, her teeth gleaming. Predatory. Quinn shakes his head at her, pulling his own mug toward him. "He's a baby," he says with distaste.

"Precisely what I need tonight," she responds, the smile remaining on her face as she tosses her curls to the side. Cade shifts in the distance, trying his damnedest to see her from where he stands. "They are so eager to please," she purrs.

At that, the entire table erupts with amusement—a welcome reprieve for all of us. If even for a moment, the horrors occurring outside the borders of our camp are forgotten.

We continue to drink and talk as the night wears on. Evander winds his arm around my shoulders once more, his fingers trailing along the side of my neck, sending a pleasurable sensation up my spine and across my arms. We discuss our days and reminisce about childhood like we always do when we drink, dredging up memories of sneaking off to the beach to swim by the moonlight when we were supposed to be in bed, chiding Quinn for his reputation as a heartbreaker, and recalling fond memories of those we left behind.

And as we talk, Evander's fingers curl around a tendril of hair that escapes my long braid. He twirls it about his finger and my body responds traitorously each time his finger traces the shell of my ear. The tiny tugs on my hair make my stomach tense. I try to blame it on the ale but know I'm making excuses. To my relief, though, no one else seems to notice, the alcohol blurring their senses.

After another round, Ash makes a half-hearted excuse to leave, and Cade nearly trips over people to escape behind her. Quinn looks to Evander and reminds him that they are on patrol again in the morning, then stands, stretching his back with a loud grunt.

I figure this is the end of the night and I should be getting back as well. Evander finishes his drink and removes his hand from behind my chair, fingertips lightly grazing along my neck, causing the hairs on my arms to raise and butterflies to dance in my stomach. It feels like he is making every attempt he can to touch my skin, though I know that seems silly. He likely has no idea that he keeps touching me or the effect it has.

When Evander glances down at me, his eyes are a bit glassy from the alcohol but alert nonetheless. And focused entirely on me. I swallow, surprised by the intensity of his gaze as he stretches his hand out. Taking it, I let him pull me to my feet, a shock vibrating through my body at his touch. The motion brings me so close him. Unbearably close.

Quinn gives a gruff command of "let's go" and I quickly drop Evander's hand, grabbing my cloak off the back of the chair and following dutifully.

We walk back to the old inn in the cold, cloaks tight around us, though we are all kept warm from the alcohol running through our blood. As two of Helara's commanders, both Evander and Quinn reside on the upper level of the inn along with me. Ash lives on the lower level near where she works in the kitchen, though I wonder now if she's returned to the inn tonight or to another lodging with Cade. The thought makes me smile as I'm sure Ash is having a good time, and I shove aside the small pang of jealousy that comes with the smile. The one that bubbles up over her ability to lead a somewhat normal existence here. And my inability to do so.

As we pile into the building, Quinn holds a lantern high so we can see our way up the stairs to our rooms. He grunts a rough goodbye and pushes open the door to his room near the top of the stairs, barely passing the flickering light to Evander as he stumbles into the dark, making me wonder just how much he had to drink. Evander and I continue down the hallway, walking at a slower pace now that Quinn is gone. I want the walk to last but am surprised when Ev slows his gait as well. I'm stretching the time to my door, savoring the closeness when we are forced together by the narrow gap between walls.

Evander's hand brushes against mine and my breath catches as he caresses a finger up my hand and back down again. It's such a small movement to cause such a strong reaction in me, my whole body becoming hyper-aware of him. I don't dare move my hand away for fear he'll stop as we near the end of the hall, the doors to our rooms looming across from one another.

I turn to say goodnight and Evander wraps his hand tightly around mine. The light from the lantern casts shadows on his face, yet I can still see his eyes. They look darker than usual, almost black as he stares into mine. He raises my hand to his lips and brushes a soft kiss against the back, letting his mouth linger.

"Goodnight, Bria," he breathes against my skin, never breaking his gaze.

A fluttering starts back up in my stomach, and I somehow manage a quiet "goodnight, Ev" before he releases my hand and I slink through the doorway into my room.

As I close it, I see him standing there, illuminated by the lantern, looking like a fallen angel. Beautiful. I force myself to push the door shut and lean my back against it, my heart racing in my chest.

I stay there for a moment, hanging on to the feeling of his lips on my hand. So soft and supple against my dry and calloused winter skin. His breath so warm and sweet. I catch myself thinking of what his lips might feel like on other areas and raise my hand to my mouth, smothering the smile that blossoms from the wicked thoughts.

"Idiot," I say aloud to no one but myself. I'm a fucking fool to even think that anything is possible between us.

Especially because of the prophecy. I'm destined to save the world, to be a weapon. Not to flounder after a man, no matter how drop-dead gorgeous he may be.

I push away from the door, scowling at the foolish thoughts

running rampant in my head before stripping off my clothes. I slide on a nightshirt and climb into the small bed, then hook an arm around the pillow and pull it close. It's warm beneath the blankets, and tonight I have no trouble sleeping—probably the aftereffects of drinking a few beers and talking easily with my friends. No matter what it's from, it is a welcome gift to drift off so easily. Even if I spend the night dreaming of the stark white...of bones.

CHAPTER 5

Evander

I lower the lantern as she shuts the door, smiling to myself and sliding into my room across the hall. When I first arrived at the camp a little over a year ago, Bria wouldn't even speak to me. She would set me with a seething glare any time I walked into a room and if looks could kill, I wouldn't be standing right now. We may have been friends since child-hood—all of us—but it was my father who betrayed her family. Betrayed *her*. My father is to blame for the death of hers.

I had taken her behavior in stride. Or at least tried to. I didn't push for her to listen to me or try to explain myself in those early days. I just lowered my head and let her be. This was her camp, her home, and her people, and I was the son of a monster. The monster who ripped her world apart. I owned those actions as if they were my own, taking every dirty look and curse word she threw at me.

It wasn't until Quinn and Ash became fed up with Bria's misguided anger and sat her down one night that she acquiesced. They explained what occurred over the four years I was gone, the years I spent in the capital with my father. And while Quinn and Ash spoke with her, Bria had looked at me with pity in her eyes. I had remained silent through-out, having no problem with her anger despite how it pained me. But she softened toward me after that, turning back into the girl I knew before it all.

Once, she asked me why I never told her myself, why I never tried to explain and endured the shitty treatment. But I shrugged and told her that she needed an outlet for that anger, and I was glad to play the role for her, happy to accept any fate she deemed appropriate for me. I remember the puzzled look that spread across her face that day.

Both of us changed so much in the years apart. We had hardened from our individual burdens, our journeys. We were children no longer and had been forced to grow up in harsh, difficult ways.

Though, I couldn't imagine the suffering she experienced daily and was in awe of how she kept going. Despite what I endured, I'm still not sure I could have survived *that*, could keep surviving like she does. Anyone else would have broken by now with the pressure—broken just by thinking about their future—yet she thrives with the weight of the world on her shoulders.

Pulling the tunic over my head, the memory of my earlier conversation with Quinn filters in. My face contorts with a grimace as I recall telling him I would be more careful. Because that's not what I'm doing at all.

I was lucky Quinn was distracted by the mind-numbing ale tonight and tormented enough from the village we found to drink like he did. It's rare for him to let go or lose any sense of control over himself. And if he hadn't tonight, I would be facing yet another lecture in the morning. For distracting her. For touching her.

I'm not quite sure what came over me, but I couldn't help myself. Maybe drinking made me a bit bolder, but it's not like that was the first time we've all been drinking together. I think I'm just sick of waiting. Sick of pretending that I don't care for her. That I don't want her.

That loose strand of hair was like a ribbon of silk between my fingers, and I longed to run my hands through her hair. To free it from the braid and let it cascade down her toned back. To fist my hands in it and yank her head back... I let out a groan at the depraved thoughts running through my head before I need to sink into an ice-cold bath, then throw myself face-first into the bed, stifling the noise with the pillow. Turning my head to face the window, I gaze at the half-moon that shines through the parted curtains and will myself to sleep.

I close my eyes tight, hoping for darkness, but all I see is Bria.

CHAPTER 6

Evander

I blink my eyes open to a sharp rapping on my door. Throwing back the blankets and rising from the bed, I tug on a pair of trousers as I pad to the entry. I pull it open, leaning on the door with one arm and rubbing my bleary eyes to reveal Quinn's dark and massive form, already dressed for patrol.

He eyes me. Taking in the bare torso, tousled hair, and groggy look I give him, he lets out a chuckle. "You're late, hurry up," he says, turning to disappear back down the hallway.

"Fuck." I stand in the empty doorframe for a beat, leaning my head against the wood even though I know I have no time to do so.

The door across the hall calls to me, begging to be opened so I can see her before I leave for the day. I doubt she's still sleeping. Bria is up before the rest of us most days, usually off on a run to keep her gifts in check around so many people who don't come from magic. If they saw the nightmares that girl could produce, all pretenses would be gone. Even *I* have only witnessed small bursts of her power—not the true beast that dwells inside.

I drum my fingers on the wooden frame, trying to shift my focus away from her. We have a long day ahead of us and my mind needs to be focused on patrol. Quinn and I are going to check on another nearby village, just a few hours' ride from here. Helara has been keeping tabs on where the king's scouts are going, which villages are still thriving, and how close the scouts are getting to our rebel camp in the mountains.

We didn't tell Bria and Ash the entire story about the village last night, both refraining from saying how fresh the massacre was. We couldn't have arrived long after the attack as the smoke had still been billowing in the air. The scent of burned flesh was lodged in my nose for hours after we left. I squeeze my eyes shut and can still see the bodies in the trees, the blood crystalizing as it hit the freezing air.

Quinn had immediately begun to cut them down. My friend's face had been blank as he surveyed the scene and wordlessly worked on the ropes with his dagger. I aided in the effort and Helara is sending others back there today to burn the bodies. The ground is too frozen to allow for a proper burial, but she won't leave them there, not like that.

Who knows what lies ahead of us today—more carnage? Or will we find this other village still undisturbed? I suppose it matters whether they have stayed loyal to the Crown or not.

I leave the doorway and begin readying for the day hastily in an effort to avoid another unexpected visit from Quinn. When I descend the staircase, the breakfast room is bustling with the others, grabbing something to eat before their busy days ahead. *Shit.* I really am late this morning if all these people are up already.

I walk swiftly past the table of commanders, nodding but not making a point to stop, that is, until I see Helara at the head of the table. Her charcoal hair, dusted with silver, is pulled high atop her head, wound in an intricate bun. The sleek style reveals her skin, a deep bronze, and she looks regal in her fine armor—more like a knight of olden times than the rebel leader she actually is. She shifts her focus to me now and her eyes narrow. My posture deflates and I make my way over to her side, kneeling by her chair.

"Commander Foster is waiting for you," she says in a quiet voice, hands folded on the table in front of her.

"Yes, Captain. I'm running a bit behind, I apologize," I state, leaving my arm draped across my raised knee. I train my eyes on a spot next to where my lowered knee sits, pressed into the hard floor.

It's not as though she requires us to be so formal, but my training as a soldier both back home and in Easthallow drilled it into me. This is just who I am now—a soldier awaiting command.

"I am meeting with all the commanders today. After you return from patrol, you both need to meet me in the hall," she declares, cool and straight to the point.

"Yes, Captain," I answer and rise to my feet, the conversation over. Managing a small bow, I turn to take my leave, delighted to get away with such an insignificant interaction this morning.

"And, Commander Lansing," she drawls, "*Don't* be late." Her eyes remain on the table full of people, not turning her body back to me as she speaks.

I bob my head in acknowledgment anyway, though she can't see me. A flush of embarrassment spreads across my cheeks as I continue toward the door. Ashbel is arriving with a tray of tea for the commanders as I pass, and my face betrays me. I note the concern in her eyes but as she opens her mouth to speak to me, I slip out the front door. No need to let Ash—or anyone else—know I was just shamed for sleeping in.

"You could have warned me they were all downstairs!" I spit out as I bring the stallion outside in line with Quinn's. The horse's mahogany coat glistens in the sun, fresh from a recent grooming.

Quinn shrugs. "Where's the fun in that?" he retorts, chuckling as he takes off down the steep path out of the village.

Irritation grips me and I huff, leaving a cloud of white mist in the frosty air. I stare at his back as he speeds away from me, then kick my heels into the horse to catch up.

CHAPTER 7

Bria

I rose early again this morning from the nightmares that tore through my sleep, keeping me from any true rest last night. Though this time, the nightmare involved only my sister. She had been so young, only thirteen, when we were separated. But even then, she had the darkest hair I've ever seen—ebony, but so lustrous it appeared tinged with blues and purples. Her eyes have always been green, like our mother's, resembling moss fresh with morning dew. In the dream, she was just as I remembered her, but older, more mature. Nimai was graced with the same soft features as me—round cheeks but on a more slender and taller frame, a lithe body more on the skinny side as a kid. My mind was playing tricks on me, showing me a girl who had grown into her figure, a beautiful young woman that bore a striking resemblance to my sister. What I imagine she would look like now, but with fear in her eyes. And she had been screaming, a blood-curdling sound that ripped my body into consciousness.

It was the worst nightmare I've experienced yet. It felt vivid. Real. And it left me with a fierce bout of nausea that had not let up until my run this morning, where I emptied the contents of my stomach halfway up the path. Maybe I did have too much to drink last night, come to think of it.

"And what has your attention today, dear Prophecy?" Cato's voice draws me back to the present. Gods, I'm tuning out far too much lately. Too much in my own head.

I don't even have the chance to scold him about the nickname before he continues, "Focus on the bones, Bria."

Shit. The bones. I'm supposed to be working on reanimation right now and instead I'm zoning out. The nightmares are really getting to me.

"Right," I say before turning my attention back to the graveyard in front of me, blaming my absent mind on the pressure of my role.

We are on the edge of the village today, far from where anyone might stumble upon my session with Cato. No one ventures out this far and none of the roads leading out of the camp would take them in this direction. We are alone on this quiet morning.

The frigid air holds the crisp smell of snow, and I'm certain there will be a new dusting of snowflakes coating the ground by the end of the day. I understand why this part of my training needs to be outside, but I miss the warmth of the library and the crackling fire. My toes ache from the cold as it seeps through the leather and wool protecting them and I long for this to be over.

"Use your mind to move the energy into the ground," he coaches.

I close my eyes, gathering the bright light inside of me, calling it to the center of my core. It warms my body from the inside out, freeing me from the teeth of that biting cold. I feel the tingling start in my hands and my palms begin to itch as the flames of energy grow, spreading through my veins. I concentrate on the feeling, the burning. It doesn't hurt but I need to move the energy quickly or the heat will become uncomfortable rather quickly. Beads of sweat pop to life along my brow despite the chill, signaling that my body is ready.

"Focus, Bria," I can hear Cato softly speaking, though he sounds far away now as I pull on my gifts.

Fire roars in my ears, muffling his voice, and I sink to the ground, my knees colliding with the frozen dirt. A twinge of pain radiates through my kneecaps and up through my hips, but I barely register it. Slamming my hands into the earth, I let the heat pulse, let it build. I push the wave of energy from my core through my veins and to the tips of my fingers, the process burning a trail through my body.

"Sew the bones together," the command whispers through the thrumming in my ears.

I feel the earth shudder beneath me. Unable to keep my eyes shut, I pry them apart just a little to see the ground split in front of me in an upheaval of dirt and bones that spills from the snowy gap. Quickly, I snap them closed once more and do as Cato said, I visualize the bones. Ivory limbs tinged with pale yellow stack upon one another, forming a fearsome monster.

Sitting back on my heels, my eyes flare wide, and I know. I know that the flames are there. Cobalt and sapphire fire reflect the skeletal warrior in front of me. It's there. It's real. I'm struck with awe at what I've just accomplished, gasping at the sight. The skeleton falters, stumbling forward a bit.

"Shit!" I yelp and scramble backward when I see it move. The bones clatter before me in a heap, splintering with the impact.

Cato claps his hands together in delight. "Well done, dear Prophecy. Well done!" he exclaims, showering me with praise.

But I sit there shocked, panting from the effort. "Stop calling me that," I growl out through shallow breaths before slumping all the way back on the cold, hard ground. I look up at the gray sky and listen to the faint laughter coming from Cato.

He lets me lay there for a few moments, heaving air into my lungs and staring into the sky. Fucking bones. I can't fucking believe it.

"You're going to need some rest after that," he remarks, stretching out a hand to help me up from the where I lie. "We can practice again tomorrow." I take his hand and stand, my legs shaking with the effort, threatening to give out on me at any moment. The fire within is no longer a roaring flame, now a mere flicker of energy. My body feels as if I have run through every peak of the Kaanos Mountains and back, slack with fatigue.

The pile of shattered bones stares back at me as Cato speaks. "We used your own store of energy today, so you need to build it back up. This would be easier if you were willing to pull energy from something living," he explains, a clear disdain for my choices in his tone.

"I said no," I bite back.

The old man wants me to learn how to pull energy from others so that I can hone the skill of draining energy to raise the dead, but I refuse. There are no other people around with magic aside from him, so how could I even do that?

Cato lets out a "tsk" and throws his hands up in exasperation. I'm not an easy student, but he need only put up with me a few more days before he will be rid of me. Nimai will be far better behaved. She always has been.

We walk back to the village together, slowly now, as my drained body barely manages one foot in front of the other. As we near the door to the inn, I feel the first flake of snow fall on my face and am happy to be back, delighted to get out of the cold now that my body is cooling off from the burst of energy. The surge of heat always leaves after my energy stores are depleted, leaving me cold and tired.

Cato walks inside with me and finds Ashbel to tell her I need food and to make sure I spend the day recouping. I want to tell him to shut up and that I will be fine on my own, but I appreciate his explanation as I don't know how much longer I can remain upright after this. Having Ash to help is probably better than me collapsing in my own bed, tired and hungry.

Ash listens to the crouched figure with her arms crossed before she shoos him away and helps me to her room. I melt into her soft and worn sofa and close my eyes while she covers me in a warm woolen blanket. I feel her tuck an arm around me, sliding her body next to mine, and I drift into a deep sleep, pulled down by exhaustion and the smell of vanilla.

CHAPTER 8

Evander

We hear screaming far before we can see the outline of houses in the small village. Still remaining behind the cover of thick evergreen trees in the forest, I dismount in one swift motion. Quinn's feet are already on the ground. We quickly tie the horses, and I draw a dagger, sliding it from the sheath across my chest. Crouching low, Quinn and I rush to the edge of the forest.

As the village comes fully into view, a blinding white light shoots from near one of the houses. The man in the path of that light is struck and flies back into the ground, a plume of smoke rising from where his body lands. One of the king's scouts it would appear, from the royal blue peeking out from under the man's armor, the symbol of Vaohr emblazoned on his chest. Quinn's eyes widen and slice to mine, mirroring my stunned expression.

"What the hell was that?" I shout, more a statement of distress than a question. I know Quinn has no answer for me.

"I don't know, but we better go find out." Always one step ahead, Quinn is already on the move.

We creep around the side of the nearest building, the downed scout only about fifty feet away from us now. His tunic is singed around the edges of a hole that burns in his chest. It must be at least a foot wide, if not larger. There's no way anyone could have survived that. The familiar smell of searing flesh floods my nostrils, and I have to stifle a gag. Most of the village buildings are visible now as I look around, trying to remain hidden from view. It's a small town from the looks of it—there can't be more than seventy-five people living here.

Quinn signals to me and we split off. He darts around the far side, and I round the corner near me, full grasping the gravity of the situation in the village center once I can see it all. I count nine more soldiers. If Braddock's men are here, scouts must have reported the location of this village to the king, meaning they suspected the inhabitants were harboring someone with gifts. It's the only explanation for the burning hole in that scout's chest. No mortal weapon could have inflicted that kind of wound, could have done that kind of damage. That was magic. And if the Crown assumed magic, they would have sent enough soldiers to keep the villagers from putting up a fight—comply or die.

Or so he thought. But Braddock was wrong by the looks of it. These people *are* putting up a fight. A handful of women race across the village green with a cluster of children attached to them. Some are slung over shoulders or gripped in their arms while others tag along, holding on to skirts so they don't fall behind. From what I can see, they are trying to gather the children into their small temple— attempting to barricade themselves inside, shield them from the onslaught. It's a smart move. From this vantage point, I see they have maybe two dozen men and women attempting to fight back which is distracting most of the scouts and soldiers. The villagers are armed with whatever they were able to find, and it's apparent. A few dull swords and daggers are in the mix and one of them even holds a shovel. Probably a farmer. The fields around this place are enormous. The whole town seems to be quite able to sustain itself. And these people are desperate right now, just trying to survive, to protect their home, to protect their own.

Those with weapons are engaged with the soldiers, but these are civilians far outside the reaches of the capital of Easthallow or the bustling cities of the south. There are no lords or ladies here, no earls or dukes with a wealth of land and an army in tow. They are untrained and have never seen battle. They have likely never killed another man. They have nothing on these skilled soldiers. And they are going to lose.

I watch the small cluster of children desperately sprinting across the green in front of the temple. And it appears now that they have caught the attention of a soldier. One of the women ushering them is grabbed. She screams for the children to run as another villager hurries to her aid, sword drawn. I hope he makes it to her because there is no way for me to run that distance with enough time to save her. It's utter fucking chaos and something nearby catches my eye. It's another soldier, notching an arrow, readying himself to kill. And he's aiming at the children.

My eyes narrow on him, blocking out everything else around me. My sole focus is getting there in time. I need to. I break into a sprint and close the space in seconds, rushing him before he can fully turn around to see what's causing the sudden noise at his back. He's positioned on the outskirts of the village and likely thought no one would be flanking him. And no one should have been.

My body collides with the man. No—*boy*, I think, as disbelief spreads across his young face. He can't be more than sixteen. His skin is dark, his eyes bright and naïve. No signs of age or stress have touched that face yet. Gods, he must have just recently completed his training. Why did they send him out here?

Pain reverberates down my spine as our bodies slam onto the frozen ground and roll. Despite the shock, the boy is well-trained. He quickly rights from the surprise ambush and is back in his body in an instant, landing himself on top of me as we tumble to a halt. Dagger in hand, I stab at the young man, the blade finding a home in his shoulder with a sickening rip of flesh. He cries out but manages to land a fist square along my jaw. My head knocks back, jolting my neck as blood sprays from my mouth into my eyes and clouds my vision. The sharp pain spreads through my jaw and I swallow the metallic tang of blood that slides down my throat. I stuff my hand between us to yank another dagger from the sheath along my chest as we grapple, and when the boy pulls his body back to land another steel fist to my face, I drive that blade into him. I thrust it into the soft flesh of his side in the gap of his armor and yank it toward me with a twisting motion, grunting with the effort of tearing through his muscle.

The boy stops abruptly, staring down at me as his eyes go soft and glassy. Warm blood pools around my hand, and I can feel more than just liquid pouring out of him and onto my body. I don't look to see the contents as I tug the dagger free. Instead, I focus on pushing his body from me and pull the other blade from his shoulder. Inky blood gathers around the wound instantly. The boy's body slumps to the ground, his eyes empty now. I stand, straightening my back and wiping the blades clean on my pants before tucking them back into their homes in my bandolier.

"Gods help you," I whisper to the boy. Each kill is easier than the last. Some people say it never gets easier. I am not one of those people.

I glimpse Quinn as I turn away from the soldier. He has his hands full fighting off three men at once, another running to their aid. Cursing, I draw my crossbow and notch an arrow. Taking aim at the one running, I exhale fully, releasing all the breath from my lungs before freeing the arrow into the wind. It meets its mark, connecting with the man's throat in a bursting crimson wave that erupts from his neck. Before the body drops to the ground, I'm tossing the crossbow on my back and bounding across the space to Quinn. The muscles in my arms and back flex as I draw my longsword and my legs carry me swiftly despite the heavy armor and weapons. By now, the other soldiers are aware of my presence, having seen their brother in arms downed by my arrow. The closest one whirls on his heel, swinging his sword at me, allowing Quinn some sort of reprieve from the onslaught.

Dodging the first strike, I jab, slicing through the fine leather armor around the man's thigh. But he comes at me again, unphased by the seeping gash in his leg. His footwork is masterful, but so is mine. That's the beauty of fighting the king's men—I'm better. I'm not just being cocky, I was trained by the man in charge of them, brought up by their captain of the guard. My whole life, I lived and breathed becoming a soldier. The only other person I've known like that is Quinn and he's humbled me. Since the first time we sparred as boys, he'd proven he was better, a natural warrior, born to be in battle.

But this man in front of me right now? He is no match for either of us. I'm too agile for him to keep up. We dodge and thrust, each landing a few blows to the other, but he's tiring quickly. I keep one eye on

Quinn throughout the fight, though I know he can hold his own. He has the reputation of being notoriously brutal and has killed far more than he's let on. Presently, he stands ready to land the final blow on his last remaining opponent, the other currently staining the grass next to him a deep shade of burgundy.

Unexpectedly, my opponent's sword pierces my upper arm, carving down the side and releasing a gush of liquid heat. I curse and spin on the man, landing a downright blow, my sword brilliant in the sun as it cleaves through his neck. The soldier's head lands with a thud and rolls toward Quinn.

Panting, Quinn barks out a morbid laugh. I look up at him and can't help the low laugh that erupts from my own lungs at the ridiculous sight. I didn't intend to behead the soldier, but it worked. Quinn claps a hand on my shoulder, his face covered in blood, his ebony hair streaked with it and falling from the knot at the nape of his neck.

"Are you alright?" I ask, scanning his face and body to ensure none of the blood is his own.

Quinn nods. "Fine. Your arm isn't though." He gestures toward the wound from the soldier.

"It's nothing," I say, brushing it off.

It isn't nothing, but I can deal with it once we get back to the camp.

Carnage lies around the small village. The inhabitants managed well enough, killing the five other intruders in addition to those Quinn and I took out. Though, from the looks of it, they lost quite a few of their own in the process.

A thin, middle-aged man around my height strides over, his long legs quickly eating up the grassy expanse before us. He amply professes thanks to Quinn and me, expressing his gratitude for our support in the attack. I'm just glad we happened upon the village in time. They would have fallen to the king's forces had it not been for us and we are all well aware of that fact.

A younger man stands slightly to the side and behind him, keeping his head down, blond hair falling over his forehead. His skin is a golden tan like my own usually is. The kind of color that comes from too much time in the sun. They are absolutely farmers—the older man is the one I saw armed with a shovel. The two sport the same bright blond hair and I gather the boy is his son, given the protective stance he takes up in front of him.

"Why are you here? Did you know we would be attacked?" the older man asks, his eyes darting over the leather armor we wear, the armory of weapons tucked around our bodies. No royal crest, no symbol of any kind, no inkling as to who we are or where we came from.

"We are part of the northern rebel forces," Quinn explains to the men. Most know that Helara and Reinhardt had split up the rebels after the Uprising. Most know that we still survive but finding information on either camp is difficult. I know that firsthand. "Given what we saw here, it appears as though you and your people are not sworn to the Crown," Quinn continues, looking to the older man for confirmation.

He lifts his chin, responding to Quinn, "We have reason not to be."

I keep my eyes focused on his son, tossing my head toward him as I wipe droplets of sweat from my brow and call, "Would that have something to do with you?"

The question is pointed at the boy, and he knows it. His head tips up and piercing blue eyes meet mine over his father's shoulder, glowing with an icy fire. He straightens himself to full height as he fixes that frigid steel gaze on me. I swear there is a faint white light emanating from his fingers, but his father shifts to shield him before I can get a good look.

"Please," he begs with a soft look toward Quinn and me. "He's only nineteen, gods know what the high priestess will do to him."

I know what the high priestess will do to him. I know the exact details of what she will do. I lean my weight into the hilt of my sword, the tip perched on the hard ground. "He's gifted," I remark. It isn't a question. I saw that white ball of fiery light and I'm willing to bet it came from this boy.

"Y- Yes." The man stretches his thin arm out behind him, tucking his son further back. It's a fruitless effort as his son is nearly a head taller than him, putting him around Quinn's height if not taller, but the sentiment is felt. He wants to protect his boy, at all costs—including rebelling against the Crown and the priests to keep him safe.

I look beyond to the bright patch of grass in the village green. The remaining survivors stand clustered together, whispering and staring back at us, aware that the conversation occurring is important, even if they cannot hear what we are saying. They hid this boy for at least a year from Braddock and his men. They're a tight-knit community willing to die for their own. The temple door opens, and tiny heads peek out, eager to rush from the threshold, but are held back by the adults all waiting with bated breath to see what will happen.

They can't stay here, I know that. When the soldiers and scouts don't return to Easthallow, they will send more. King Braddock will stop at nothing to get the boy, knowing he is gifted. And the rest of the village...well I know how that will go too. And I'm not going to see them burned or murdered for protecting him. I'm not letting that happen.

"You are coming with us. All of you," I say to the man. "Go pack your necessities, gather as many horses as you have and get a move on."

Quinn shoots a glance at me, eyebrows raised, but doesn't utter a word. The man thanks us again and hurries back to inform his village of the impending travel, shoving his son along in the process. They will come. None of them will want to wait for the return of the king's men. There is nothing but death for them here.

The boy glares back at me with those glowing eyes and I resist the urge to shudder, his gaze sending spiders crawling up my spine. That white ball of firelight did a lot of damage, and he's still on edge from the fight. Even I'm not stupid enough to provoke him right now.

"Don't say anything," I warn as Quinn opens his mouth to speak.

"Oh, I won't...but Helara might." He stares at me, his dark features flecked with blood.

He's right. She won't be happy with this unannounced delivery of civilians.

"By the time we make it back to inform her of the attack, more scouts could ride through. There's too much risk in leaving them here. Especially him." I nod my head toward the boy walking with his father back to the rest of his family.

He's too young and the thought of the king taking him and using him, of the priests and the high priestess getting their hands on him...I grit my teeth. I can't stomach the thought.

Quinn shrugs and heaves his sword into its sheath. "Let's get going then," he responds and starts toward the group.

I watch him walk away and suck in a deep breath, steadying myself. I brave a glance back at the bodies behind me and see the beginnings of snow starting to fall, intricate diamonds fluttering down to land on the blood, so dark red it's almost black now. I close my eyes to block out the image and turn to follow.

CHAPTER 9

Bria

When I finally wake, it's dark outside the window. Only slivers of tangerine and salmon are left above the horizon, quickly bleeding to black. Ash is reclined next to me, feet tucked underneath her body, her orange-red hair tied back in a messy bun to keep it out of her face. My feet are pulled across her lap, resting in a cocoon of the soft fabric.

She notices my stirring and sets down the book she's reading on the old side table, chips of paint scattering from the edges of the wood. Her emerald eyes gleam, only made brighter by the deep pine green of her dress. White lace peeks from the bodice, a transition of texture from the luxurious velvet. This dress is my favorite because of the way it brings out her eyes and contrasts so nicely with the fire of her hair. I've never questioned why Ash still wears her dresses. It just makes sense for her, even if I'm always dressed more casual in leggings and tunics.

Everyone in the camp is expected to learn how to wield weaponry, though some more adeptly than others. Working in the kitchen has meant Ash needed only occasional training, so she can wear them most of the time. She prefers to and I understand why. It reminds her of home, of the life we lived before coming to this camp. I long to wear a beautiful dress again, to feel the fabric trailing around my ankles. But

I've become accustomed to the more practical clothing of the rebels over the years. Plus, a dress would make my cache of weapons a lot less accessible.

"How long was I asleep for?" I question, groggily rubbing my eyes.

"About three hours or so now," Ash replies, rubbing my feet through the rough woolen socks. "How are you feeling?"

"Still exhausted."

I pull my arms from beneath the blanket and stretch them above my head, pain shooting through my muscles from the motion. I grimace and shake out my arms. "Have you been here the whole time?"

Ash scoffs. "No. I would have stayed with you, but if I missed dinner preparation the others would have known something was going on," she explains. "I made sure you were comfortable, and I slipped out for about an hour to go to the kitchen. Madalena is doing my cleanup, so I'll be forced to take over her breakfast prep in the morning thanks to you." She lets out a small laugh and squeezes my feet as she speaks.

"Thank you," I manage as I drag myself to a seated position beside her, crossing my legs comfortably underneath me, though I feel my knees protest and recall their collision with the frozen earth earlier today.

"I've never..." Ash chews on her lip but keeps her focus on me. "I've never seen you like that, even in the beginning when you first started using your gifts. You were so drained," she finishes hurriedly, as if she's forcing the rest of the words out on this one breath.

I have never known Ash to be timid or hide her true feelings about anything. So, for her to hesitate... I know she thinks this is serious. Concern plays across her face.

"I'll be alright," I assure her. "It's just going to take time for my body to adjust. I'm using a lot of energy right now." My body will become accustomed to the new power, even if right now my muscles ache as if I've been to battle, and I feel like I've been awake for a week straight. I've been down this road before, though it's been a few years. But right now, I just need to make sure Ash doesn't worry too much. She doesn't need to take on my problems as her own. Everyone here has enough on their plates.

Ash pulls the blanket further over us, covering our laps before she speaks again. "Are you going to tell me why?" she questions, smoothing a hand over the soft blanket. Her deep emerald gaze is piercing and there's no escaping it. Even if I tried, she would push.

I drag a hand down my face and pinch the space between my eyes. It isn't exactly something I want to share yet, but I tell Ash everything. There are no secrets between us now and there never were, even when we were children. Ash's parents were employed by my father's estate and her mother worked in the kitchen, often taking Ash with her to learn. We were raised side by side in the same home, nearly inseparable.

I look up at my friend, trying to read her face as I delve into the story of my newfound gift.

"I'm working on the art of bones," I start, watching as Ash's auburn brows furrow. "Raising the dead," I clarify, and her eyes widen. A sea of emerald stares back at me as I continue to tell her all about what I've learned with Cato over the last two days. She listens, apparently mesmerized by the story. That's something I love about Ash: she always wants to hear about magic. She isn't scared by it or put off at all, but intrigued. She makes me feel less like a monster and more like a wonder.

"It takes a great deal of energy to do it, and I have to pull from myself, from my energy stores," I finish, waiting patiently for her to take in all the information I just threw her way.

Ash blows out a loud breath from her lips and sits back, crossing her arms over her chest. "Well then," she says, a smile tugging the corners of her mouth and crinkling her eyes.

"Bria Saldhene, the Mistress of Nightmares. It has a nice ring to it, though a bit macabre for my taste." She barely gets the words out before breaking into a fit of laughter.

"Oh shut it." I shove her arm gently but am unable to control the girlish giggle that escapes my lips. It may be a ghastly power, but it's mine.

"It is shocking but also a bit marvelous when you think about it. I mean, it's rare, you said—right?" she questions.

Thinking back to the dusty book Cato gave me, I let it really sink in. "Yes, very rare. The text from Cato said only Lilith and one of her descendants had the power to do it."

Ash nods, understanding what that means. Understanding how powerful that makes me now.

"How long do they last? The living dead?"

"Right now? Only a few seconds, but as I build up my energy stores, I should be able to make them last longer. And if I pull energy from"—I pause, scrunching my nose at the thought—"other sources, Cato thinks it will make it easier on me."

Ashbel knows all about the training I received from Cato on pulling energy and how I feel about it. I loathe the idea of taking anything from another person to aid my abilities. And it isn't as if we have a whole host of people with gifts here at the camp. It's only Cato and me.

"Bria. You could turn the tide of a battle." Her words are hushed as she thinks of the future.

We haven't spoken of Nimai's impending birthday and what it means for me, but her thoughts echo the ones flitting around my mind —what her birthday means for the prophecy, what my gifts mean for it. If Nimai comes into power as everyone is expecting, we will soon be readying for the battle Ash speaks of. And that is a terrifying prospect to have hovering over you.

I distract myself by playing with the loose threads along the edge of the blanket. I twirl one between my fingers. My mind wanders to Evander—his hands in my hair, twirling and tugging on the strands, the faint brush of his fingers against my neck, the heat of his breath on my skin. My stomach tightens and I can feel the heat rising up my neck and into my cheeks.

"Let's not think about it now," I suggest and gesture to the unmade bed, a tangled mess of stark white sheets against a violet bedspread, pillows askew.

I turn raised brows toward Ash and state playfully, "I would much rather hear about your night."

Ash picks at her cuticles, a terrible habit she's developed over the years, especially when she's thinking or uncomfortable. She rips a small sliver of skin off with her teeth. Perfectly straight squares of ivory peek out as the rose of her lips widens to a wicked grin.

"Oh, it was fine." Her teeth are still showing despite the noncommittal response, hand waving the comment away as you would a nasty nuisance of a fly in the summer heat.

But I know better than to accept her feigned disinterest in the topic. "Liar," I chide, my spirited tone tinged with truth.

Ash just leans further back, kicking her legs up and laying them across me, pushing her back to stretch across the arm of the sofa.

"Cade was…insatiable," she responds, her grin widening again. "He genuinely might have the deftest tongue of any man I've ever met." She closes her eyes, clearly reveling in the memory of the night before.

I can't help it when my mouth drops open at the comment. Not from the brash nature of what she said, but considering the fact that she had been with a fair share of men, this was truly a compliment.

"So, do you plan to see him again? Maybe tonight, even?" Ash sits up with the question, bringing herself back to the present and looking at me.

"Perhaps," she replies, brushing a finger across her lips. "Though maybe you should give him a try." The response comes with puckered lips and a raised brow.

I choke out a laugh. "You're joking."

"Why not? You haven't let yourself enjoy anyone the entire time you've been here. It's been almost five years, Bria. Gods, you're going to dry up down there if you go any longer," she teases, waving at my lower half. "Good thing you can reanimate the dead because you may need to."

The raucous laughter that erupts from us both has my sides aching. She absolutely knows how to make me relax and laugh when I need it.

My experience with men is limited compared to Ash's, though I'm not completely unaware of what goes on beyond closed doors. There was a handsome young man back in Elwyn, the son of a wealthy merchant. Cedric. We often found ourselves at parties and gatherings together, our families traveling in the same circles. Over the years we made quite a habit of stealthily sneaking off to the gardens or finding each other and tucking away in a quiet study.

"Have you even kissed anyone since Cedric?" It's as if Ash is combing through my thoughts as they occur, and she knows I haven't.

She found us once when delivering more food to the ballroom, working with her mother during one of the many parties my family threw. I can't even remember what that particular event was for, we had so many. But that night, she was on her way back to the kitchen when she heard noises coming from the study. And upon opening the door, Ash caught the two of us tangled together in the corner, tongues deep in each other's mouths. I remember how she stopped, her jaw dropping as her eyes drifted to where Cedric's hand was mysteriously missing, lost somewhere up the inside of my skirts.

I could still vividly recall how her mouth quickly snapped shut, replaced by pursed rosy, red lips holding a smile. She then apologized for the interruption and whisked herself from the room, leaving me an embarrassed mess. The next day, I had taken a ration of shit from her for not telling her just how far things had gone with Cedric.

Heat rises back into my face at the memory of him. "No. Of course not." There was no point.

He was my first but also my only. She was right that I've kept away from anyone else since finding out about my destiny. It had taken time to move on from Cedric after the attack on my father's estate. I cared for him, loved him. And I don't know what became of him after that day—whether he died like so many others in the attack or lived, whether he still works for his father or has joined up with the soldiers in the kingdom. All I know is he's never showed his face at either of the camps. He is no rebel. And that means there is no future for me with him.

I have a purpose here. I'm in the camp for a reason, and it isn't love.

"I think it would be good for you." She pauses, thinking. "Maybe you could think of it as battle preparation if that would make you feel better about it. Get a little tension release beforehand?" Ash smirks and pokes me with her toes, her feet still laid across my lap.

"When you put it that way..." I say, letting the whites of my eyes show.

She shoves her toes further into my stomach and I grunt. "Fine, I'll think about it," I concede, throwing her feet off my body.

Ashbel jumps back and squeals. "Let the hunt begin!" she cries, eager with the prospect of finding someone for me to sleep with. It's absurd and we both know I'm fronting and unlikely to take her advice, tempting as it may be.

"What about Ev?" Her question comes as a surprise, and I don't mask my expression quick enough. She notices the smile wipe from my face at the mention of him, and based on the look plastered on her face, she was well aware of the reaction it would bring.

"Why would you even ask that?" I hiss back. "I would never suggest you sleep with Quinn, though I'm sure you would." The comment isn't meant as a slight to her or Quinn. In fact, Quinn is quite attractive, in spite of his dark and terrifying frame.

But Ash understands the meaning in my words and continues, "As would any woman who has eyes." She's not wrong. "Bria, normally I would understand your hesitation, not wanting to ruin a friendship. But for you, does it really matter anymore?" She looks up at me as she asks, her eyes glassy, her thoughts likely also drifting back to the looming birthday and what it means for me.

"I suppose not." I avert my gaze, letting my eyes fall back to the fraying blanket.

"Quinn told me that you two were...a bit close yesterday morning. And I saw it myself last night at the pub." Ashbel must note the sadness in my tone and is trying to bring me back, to keep the conversation light.

I smile at the memory, no longer bothering to keep my face neutral. She's onto my feelings for him. Quinn's eyes had been fierce when they darted between us yesterday and apparently he was worried enough about it to warn Ash of the interaction. It's irritating but he's also a good friend, trying to keep Evander away from a monster like me.

"We've both seen the way he looks at you, Bria. The hunger. He looks like a wolf that hasn't eaten in days. Though Quinn is *very* against it. We don't seem to see eye to eye on this topic, to say the least." The exasperation in her voice lets me know this has become yet another topic for the two to argue about. They are always arguing.

I try to shrug off the comment. "I think Quinn might be right on this one."

Though my mind keeps replaying Ash's words. *The hunger*. Could she be right? I thought there was tension between us last night—a feeling that was slightly suffocating, almost making the air thicker and harder to breathe. But does he feel that tension too? Does he feel the way they both seem to think he does?

I shake my head and my stomach growls loudly, a definite objection to the hours I've gone without eating today. Ash snorts at the sound.

"Fine, let's go get you some food. I put aside some things earlier so we can go eat in the kitchen," she says in answer to my disapproving stomach. She stands and points a finger at me. "But I'm not letting this go," she warns and turns to leave the room.

We walk the halls of the inn while chatting about her day and the drama that always seems to unfold behind the doors of the kitchen. They know everything that goes on around the camp, picking up bits and pieces from the commanders when they eat, not to mention some of the other girls are definitely sleeping with a few of them. Ashbel lets me know that the commanders are meeting with Helara this evening, hence the quiet that's taken over the halls of the old inn. There is no one in the main hall, no sound of laughter or clinking glasses and silverware. They are all tucked away in the private meeting room. Evander and Quinn had not returned from their patrol by the time Ash finished her dinner shift. Though she assures me they must be back by now, I still find myself worrying, my chest tightening with anxiety at the memory of the burned village they spoke of. They are both phenomenal fighters, trained for years by Aamon, but even that knowledge does nothing to squash the nervous butterflies thrashing around in my gut and ribs.

Ash pushes open the door to the kitchen and the warm smells of rosemary and fresh bread waft out to meet me. I'm ravenous. I pull up two stools the kitchen staff use at the prep stations while Ash gathers the dinner she put aside for us. She brings over a loaf of the still-warm sourdough bread I smelled when we walked in along with some sliced apples and a wedge of cheese with a dark rind. She pushes a jug of fresh cider toward me, and I pour the honey-colored liquid into two tall glasses.

We sit and talk while we eat, and the hours pass. There is always something we can find to discuss. You would think by now we would have run out of topics, but there is rarely a moment of silence between us. I feel my energy starting to come back, that small ball of heat curling in the pit of my stomach once more.

CHAPTER 10

Evander

I watch as the sun slips behind the ominous black mountains, the last of the golden light fading fast. We've barely made it to the edge of the rebel camp before darkness starts to drown the world around us. And it's a good thing we made it—the last thing we need after today is to be defending these people again from wolves and bears, or whatever else lurks in the woods beyond our camp.

Quinn has gone ahead to speak with a few of the rebels, to ask for assistance with supplies and helping the villagers while I make sure everyone gets fully into the camp and the horses are stabled for the night. On the ride back, we discussed where to lodge them before speaking with Helara, thinking that if we had a plan, maybe she would be less irritated with my insistence to bring them along.

The temple seemed like the best option. Given the *feelings* toward the priests and high priestess in the rebel camp, the temple sits unused, no one daring to step foot in it on principle. It's a substantial building, constructed by the old inhabitants as a show of their allegiance to the king, fake as it was. It now sits rotting away. The symbol of Vaohr had been torn from the front of it long before I arrived here. Probably one of the first things they did. Tomorrow, Helara could determine where she wants the refugees to go. We have plenty of homes and cottages with space to spare and a few that remain open completely. But tonight, at least they will have warmth and a roof over their heads.

The town that we've taken on as the northern camp was nearly abandoned when Helara arrived years ago after the Uprising, the first revolt against the king. The few remaining inhabitants were gifted, and she moved them to the rebel camp in the south once Bria came to live here. Those people had been left behind by their families and friends who took off for fear of retribution, fear of what would be done to them if the Crown found out they were associating with magic. Living beside them. *Breeding* with them. My jaw tenses at the thought of anyone thinking those with magic in their blood are worth less. Cowards.

We traveled back with about fifty people tonight, at least a dozen of them children. Thankfully, none of the children were lost during that ambush. Before leaving their small town, Quinn and I tried to give them a short time to grab necessities, but we hadn't dared linger too long. Mostly they'd gathered clothing, blankets, and some food—nothing more than what they could carry on their backs. It took us only a few hours to get to the village this morning, but the trek back was tedious. Having only ten horses in their village, most of them walked, letting the children ride to keep pace. It took us hours longer.

Tomorrow will begin a whole new life for these people.

Once most of the newcomers are settled, I seek out the thin man and his son. Ronan and Silas. I made it a point to learn their names along the way and hear what happened to them to provoke the attack. Silas had ventured from the village a few mornings prior, planning to hunt before dawn fully set in. Instead, he found himself squaring up against a bear. A big one, from the sound of it. Fear got the better of him, igniting that white fire in his veins, and his power erupted in that searing flash of otherworldly light. Little did Silas know, a scout was nearby and witnessed the explosion of energy, the release of fear from his body. Silas was embarrassed when he told the story, feeling like a foolish boy, but I knew better than to accept that. He couldn't be blamed for what happened only a year into learning to control his magic. I knew enough from my mother and Bria to understand the impact that emotions like fear could have on a person's magic.

Their family was safe now, nestled into the temple along with the two younger girls born to Ronan and his wife Tessa. Time would tell if the fifteen and seventeen-year-old girls would emanate the same power held by their older brother. Perhaps they would have different gifts, or none at all. Ronan claims to have no power but his family once did. Only dormant magic resides in his veins, like my own. Tessa either has none or she is an expert at hiding it—no flames licked the edges of her irises.

Now, Silas and Ronan are coming with us to face Helara. Quinn and I lead the way back to the inn to meet the captain of the rebels. We were supposed to have returned hours ago but given our entourage, we are much later than she's expecting. She will be wondering where her missing commanders are and may already be in a sour mood because of it. I'm hoping that returning with Silas, and possibly two sisters who may have magic, could help ease the annoyance Helara is sure to exhibit with my break in protocol.

There's no time to go back to our rooms and wash the now caked and flaking blood from our skin. No time to examine the wound that sears along my arm, the pain biting into the flesh whenever I move it. There's still time to clean and bandage the carved flesh before the sick of infection sets in and the grain alcohol in the kitchen will do just fine for that purpose. I make a mental note to go there after we speak with the captain, though I wince at the thought of it. It's going to hurt like a bitch.

We stride into the inn, the main room eerily quiet, a single sconce still lit and flickering. The room opens to a dining area on the left where we take most of our meals, filled with large tables of dark wood. The hall ahead leads to a parlor and the kitchen area. Beyond that lay the rooms of the rebels who work the inn. To the right of me is a closed door, the meeting room sitting on the other side of the solid oak.

I let out a curse when I observe the closed door and the quiet air that's thick around us.

The meeting is already underway, and we will be walking in late. Meaning all attention is bound to be on us. Quinn's eyes dart to me, narrowing before he stalks forward and pushes open the door. Light from within pours out into the dark main room, framing me in the doorway. Me, with a face flecked in blood, the clotting wound on my arm evident to all who look. And they *all* look.

The interior of the room is brightly lit. Bronze sconces line the walls and a pleasant fire burns in the corner of the room. The windows on the other side are drawn in dark curtains. All but two of the high-backed black chairs are filled along the long table in the center of the room. The faces filling those chairs stare back at me in shock, necks craning to get a good look at us before turning—almost in unison, as if all pulled by some invisible rope—to look toward Helara. She's staring at Quinn, his dark features somehow made deeper from the dried crimson on his skin. Her eyes then slice to mine, taking in the state of our clothing and skin, the exhaustion that plagues our features. I watch as she takes note of the men from the village. Silas and Ronan remain a step behind and to either side, flanking me. The captain quickly folds her hands in front of her, adjusting and stacking her spine to the regal posture we expect of her.

The leader of the rebels.

"Commander Foster, Commander Lansing." She nods in acknowledgment to Quinn and me respectively without making a single comment on our tardiness or appearance. Quinn steps forward at the greeting, his stance wide and balanced, shoulders and back broad, hands clasped behind his back as he launches into the story.

"Captain Hartgrove, our apologies—"

Helara holds up a hand, quickly cutting Quinn off before he can make any excuses. "Tell me what happened Foster."

Quinn clears his throat, "We arrived in the small village this morning on your patrol orders when we happened upon a band of soldiers mid-attack." Helara's gaze doesn't stray as he recaps our morning.

Quinn continues, depicting the events of the day with military precision, brief and to the point, giving salient details and covering the rest succinctly. She shows no flicker of emotion when he describes the blinding white light that seared a hole in a man. As Quinn finishes, he dips his head and steps back in line with me, one hand now resting on the hilt of his sword.

"Well?" she questions, shifting her focus to me.

Fuck.

I take a step forward as Quinn had, adopting the same confident and wide stance. "Had we left them, more would have come. The scouts reported Silas to the Crown days ago, having seen what he was capable of." I pause before continuing, "Captain Hartgrove, he's only nineteen, he's barely more than a child, just having come into his gifts."

Silas scoffs behind me as the comment hangs in the air. That little shit needs to control his ego. I ignore him and carry on. "We have them set up in the temple for tonight, I hope that is alright."

"It's a little late to be asking me Lansing," she pauses and takes a deep breath. "Very well." She's not pleased with me, definitely not thrilled that I so brazenly overstepped in my decision today. But Helara knows my history with the Crown, and she understands my reasoning more than most.

After all, she is the rebel savior. At least that's what the rest of Azudora calls her. She's managed to extricate and protect so many from certain death over the years since the Uprising. Her anger toward me likely won't last more than a few days and she's keeping her cool right now in front of the other commanders instead of laying into me. I figure it's mostly because of Silas and Ronan's presence, but I'm grateful for it either way. And once she sees what the boy can do, she won't be angry at me any longer.

"You're all dismissed." She waves a hand at the rest of the seated commanders, and they rise to leave the room, casting irritated glances at Quinn and I as they go.

"You two need to clean up. And tend to that wound, Commander Lansing." Helara's voice is stern as she points to my arm. "You will both come see me at breakfast and we can finish debriefing then."

Helara looks to Ronan and Silas next as she pushes the high-backed chair from the table, rising to her full height, her hair coiled in the usual charcoal topknot.

"Welcome to our northern camp. I will escort you both back to the temple. Tomorrow we can discuss more of what your time here will look like, what will be expected of you and your people. But tonight, you will all be needing some rest after the day you've had." Her smile is pleasant and genuine as she addresses the men.

Quinn and I step to the side, allowing our captain to take her leave with the villagers. Ronan clasps each of our hands as he passes, murmuring soft words of gratitude. Silas remains wordless, his blue eyes smoldering, but nods with a sneer across his face as he follows his father out of the room.

He's still vexed by my comment—calling him a child—I assume. The boy exudes a cockiness and naivety that I have no time for. His father seems like a good man, a solid person who will be an asset here in the camp. But I have a sinking feeling Silas is going to be a pain in my ass.

CHAPTER 11

Evander

Quinn and I walk the short distance to the kitchen together. It's late now, and I assumed the kitchen would be as deserted as the main room and dining area are. But as I push the double doors open, I'm pleasantly surprised to see Bria and Ash sitting together, knees touching, deep in conversation.

Bria is facing the door, one elbow resting on the table next to her, propping up her head. Her normally straight hair falls to the side, sliding over a shoulder in waves of precious metal glinting gold and bronze. Her eyes are heavy with fatigue, the long lashes brushing against her cheeks like she's close to passing out. My heart skips a full beat when I stare at her, struck by her beauty all over again. It doesn't get any easier, and I swear she just gets better with age.

I only glimpse her relaxed like that for a moment before her head snaps up when she catches sight of us, so focused on her conversation with Ash that she must not have heard the doors to the kitchen open. Ash spins around to face us after seeing the wide-eyed look of surprise spread across Bria's face.

"What happened?" Bria cries out, jumping up from the stool and nearly knocking it back with the force.

She runs toward me, not sparing a glance at Quinn, which makes my heart surge in my chest. She grabs my arm and yanks it toward her to examine the wound before I can protest. Pain from the movement stabs through me, and I grind my teeth together to keep from screaming.

Ash, however, rises calmly and walks to the corner of the room, grabbing a decanter of something, likely whiskey, and four small glasses. She carries them to the table and kicks a stool out for Quinn.

"Sit. And get talking," she commands as she begins pouring the amber liquid into the glasses.

"We got to the village just as they were under attack." Quinn obliges her as he strips off his sword and daggers and unbuckles his armor. Dragging himself to the stool, he drops his cache of armor and weapons on the floor next to him and slumps down. He runs both of his hands through his obsidian hair, pulling it out of the disheveled knot before letting them fall to the table.

Meanwhile, Bria pulls me by the hand to the corner of the room where Ash had retrieved the alcohol. I let her guide me, the warmth from her hand comforting and reassuring. And as she turns to grab a glass bottle of grain alcohol, I tug loose my sword and unhook the bandolier from across my chest.

Quinn picks up the whiskey and shoots it back, hissing at the burn before jumping into the remainder of the story for Ash. I stop listening as he tells her of the fighting in the village and the king's men. He's going to tell her how many we killed and how many villagers fell to the Crown today. Ash tips the decanter and pours more into his glass before taking a sip of her own as she listens.

I don't want to hear any more of it. I want to leave today in the past.

I look at Bria, knowing just her presence alone is enough to distract me. She stretches up on the tops of her toes to reach a cloth on the upper shelf, her short frame barely making it. Her feet are bare, despite the cool floor in the kitchen. Her hair cascades down her back as she lifts her arms and I have the sudden urge to run my hands through it again, to grab a fistful of the golden strands. The loose tunic she wears drops to the side, revealing her bare shoulder—a sliver of creamy ivory.

Quinn is giving Ash information about the boy. About Silas. I hear his name but I'm wholly focused on that harmless patch of skin that has me raging with want. Bria turns hastily, the rag in her hand, her cobalt eyes shining as she looks at me.

"He has magic?" she asks quietly with expectant eyes. Quinn and Ash continue talking in the background.

The hope I see in her makes it all the more pleasing to inform her that the boy does, in fact, possess power. And a lot of it.

"Yes," I say, smiling back at her. The eagerness in her tone is endearing. "His name is Silas. I'm sure Cato will want to meet him tomorrow. He will likely want you to meet him as well."

Her grin widens, her button nose scrunching and making her round, rosy cheeks a deeper shade of pink. Bria's excitement is palpable —I can feel the heat rising off her body and she nearly bounces on her toes. She grabs the glass bottle and unscrews the top, but I notice the wince and the way she gingerly sets the top down on the counter, her hand lingering above it for a moment.

Before I know what I'm doing, I reach out and grab her hand. Grasping it in my own and inspecting it, I flip her hand over and look for any wound just as she had done with my arm.

"What's wrong?" I ask, letting the concern I feel play across my face.

"It's nothing," she responds but doesn't remove her hand. "It's just sore from today. From training," she explains hurriedly.

I stare at her, wondering what kind of training she means. Definitely something with magic to leave no wounds but keep her in pain like this.

I slide my thumb across the back of her hand, rubbing small circles over the pale skin. "You need to rest. You're tired and in pain."

She snorts at me. Actually snorts, and fuck if it isn't the cutest thing I've ever heard. "I'm not the one who almost got carved to pieces like a fucking turkey," she counters, but the smile remains. Her eyes almost twinkle as she says it, the glittering behind them a sign of her magic, the same way Silas's eyes have that burning glow to them. I've witnessed the burn in Bria's before, but only occasionally.

I look at my arm. The wound has clotted over but is still in desperate need of cleaning.

"Get on with it then, Commander Lansing," she teases, feigning impatience and tapping her bare foot on the floor. But the tone she takes does nothing to squash the desire rising in me. It only fuels that fire.

"Yes, my *lady*," I reply, watching as she rolls her eyes with the jab at her old title.

I unfasten the clips and straps of the leather vest, removing the armor and placing it on the counter beside us. Grabbing the neck of the tunic and pulling it over my head, I let out a hiss, the stretch of my arm pulling at the edges of the fresh wound. The crystal amulet around my neck drops back onto my chest, the light of the room catching on it.

I toss the tunic to the ground, not caring where it ends up because I only care about her. She's staring, her bright blue eyes boldly roaming over the bare skin of my chest and lingering over the amulet before dropping lower, making me happy I've been training with Quinn lately and it shows in the ripple of muscles. I'll train every fucking day with him if it means she looks at me like that. She tugs the side of her bottom lip between her teeth, bruising the soft flesh and sending a wave of excitement through my body.

She blinks, no doubt realizing she's staring, though I have no problem with it. In fact, I ache for her to keep staring at me like that and am disappointed when she shifts her focus to the wound ripping down the flesh of my arm. It's maybe six inches long. Deep, but not hitting anything major.

I raise an eyebrow and tilt my head to the side, throwing her a flirty smile, letting her know I tracked her gaze. A flush rises to her cheeks as she catches my grin, her eyes still glittering, and she releases her lip from the grip of her teeth.

"It isn't that bad, is it?" I know it's bad, but it isn't a wound I'm going to die from.

"It's not great, but you'll live, you idiot," she chides, gathering the linen cloth and soaking it with alcohol until the smell permeates my nostrils. "And I'm sure you'll be back out there training or on patrol tomorrow," she adds, setting her lips in a firm and irritated line.

I show a flash of teeth, grinning back at her. "Ahh, you know me so well."

Letting out a soft chuckle, I reach for the glass bottle, taking a long swig of the obscene liquid and wincing before turning to lean back against the counter. I wrap my fingers around the side, steeling myself for the pain.

Across the room, Quinn and Ash are discussing the villagers and where they will be housed. But my ears, my eyes, my whole body is tuned in to Bria.

She moves in front of me, so close I can feel the loose fabric of her shirt brush the bare skin of my torso as she reaches up and presses the cloth to my arm. Squeezing my eyes closed, I brace my body against the stinging sensation and tighten my grip on the counter, my fingers digging into the hard surface.

"I'm sorry," she whispers.

Her other hand touches my chest. I feel the warmth of her skin and open my eyes. She still holds the cloth to my left arm, pressing it into the wound, but her other hand moves to grasp the ancient amulet around my neck. Her fingers are long and slim, her nails cut short as they curl around the crystal. I pull my gaze up to meet hers.

Beautiful. Stunning. Breathtaking. Take your pick because all of those words describe her. Those deep blue eyes are set on mine, making it hard to breathe. Hard to think. I swear they are glittering more now, almost as if there are blue flames locked inside.

"You still wear this?" she asks, her voice low, quiet enough that the others cannot hear our conversation.

It's a symbol of the Keeper, of Lilith and Kiara, of the prophecy. A gleaming orange globe of sunstone, orbited by a pearly white moonstone, fused together with a silver circle—the crest of the god Uldnoir, adopted after he left his mortal body and this world.

"I've never taken it off. Even in the capital," I admit. Bria knows my mother came from magic, that she was an avid believer in the gods of old. But this is not just a symbol of the Keeper, of the god whose power lives on in Bria. It's also a reminder of her fate.

I don't dare speak as she traces her fingers lightly from the amulet back to my chest, moving them gently upward and trailing them along my skin, leaving a path of heat in their wake. Her hand slides up the side of my neck and I relax my grip on the counter, letting her touch me in any way she wants.

I swallow, hard, over the lump forming in my throat as she weaves her fingers into my hair, scratching her nails against the short strands around the nape of my neck.

She tugs the side of her lip back between her teeth, her eyes luminous. I want to tug her lip with my own teeth, to feel the lush skin between them. I yearn to drag my tongue along them, to taste her. I know that once I taste her, I'll never get enough, never be satiated. That I'll take her perfect, untainted soul and make her mine, and that she'll be the redemption for my sins in this life. My body burns and I need her closer, the small bit of space left between us too much to bear.

I reach my hand toward her, letting my fingers barely graze her waist, though I want to pull her into me, to haul her on top of the counter and devour her right here in the kitchen. She sucks in a short breath when my fingers touch her and the tension between us ratchets up a notch.

"Everything okay?" I hear Quinn's voice and drop my hand from her, clenching it into a fist as it falls to my side.

Mother. Fucker. I could punch him square in the face right now and he would deserve it, my knuckles are itching for it.

Her hand falls from my hair, and she turns quickly, murmuring something about fetching bandages for me. I slump back against the counter and blow out the long breath I was holding. I watch her briskly walk across the room and through the doors.

My gaze slides to the others and I'm met with vastly different expressions from my friends. I groan at the sight, not sure I want to know how much they saw. I take another swig of the nasty liquid before asking.

"What?" I snap, cracking the knuckles on my hand to release the tension.

Quinn stares back, his mouth a firm line of disappointment. No surprise there. But Ash is smiling, her teeth gleaming in that predatory grin she has. Ash has never been one to stay silent. About anything. Even when we all would prefer she did.

"I'm just glad she's taking my advice. Finally," she croons, taking a sip of her drink.

Quinn's eyes go narrow at this, the hazel deepening and darkening with her words. "What advice?" he grinds out.

Ashbel's smile grows, a flash of white. She sits back with her drink and takes a long sip before answering him. "The advice that she doesn't need to be lonely all the time. She should try to enjoy herself more often."

"Lonely? How could she be lonely?" Quinn seems genuinely confused by what Ash is proposing. "She enjoys herself plenty. She has training and running, she's fine."

"Really Quinn? Her father is gone, she's separated from her mother and sister and has been for years. They are the only people she knows with magic aside from Cato. She lost Cedric..." Ash trails off, her smile fading as she speaks.

"But she ha—"

"Yes, I know she has us," Ash interjects, finishing the sentence for him, irritation beginning to form in two small lines between her brows. "We've all been subjected to death and destruction. You've both witnessed horrors, the slaying of innocents, even had to be involved in it." She sends a pointed look at me with the last bit, referencing my time in the capital. It stings but I let it go. "But you have each had moments of happiness as well. You get to have days off, you can fully relax, and even have the pleasure of another person. Bria never gets to experience that. She never gets to do anything she really wants to do."

"She seems perfectly happy to me. She has a purpose, she has friends." Quinn seems as though he's trying to grasp what Ash means and is coming up short. But I understand.

I look at Ash so she knows I'm on her side in this, but speak to Quinn. "It's not the same Quinn. You have no idea what she goes through."

Quinn scowls at me now. "Oh, and you do? I think it's ridiculous either of you think she's lonely. Bria is dealing with bigger things right now. Who are we to know if she wants that, even needs that in her life. She definitely doesn't need to be wasting her time pining over someone like Cade. Or even you, Evander." The last part is said in a low voice, a warning speared across the room at me.

"What she wants to do with her life should be up to her. It's never her choice. She's forced to be what everyone *wants* her to be." The gleam in Ash's eyes is daring Quinn to fight her, to give her a reason to unleash her anger on him.

Quinn is incredulous. "What we *want* her to be?!" He's nearly shouting at her now. "She's the gods damned prophecy, Ash! She's not some earl's daughter anymore, looking for love or a husband or a good time." His face is flaming, whether from the alcohol or the rage, I'm not sure. Maybe both.

But his words hurt more now than ever, and I drop my head to my chest. "We still don't know that, Quinn," I force out, feeling my heart heavy and leaden.

"No," Ash counters, her finger running along the rim of her glass. She won't raise her eyes to meet mine. "He's right."

That feeling in my chest tightens and my jaw clenches. I push the words past gritted teeth felling like I might be sick. "What do you mean he's right?"

Ash and I have always been on the same page about this. We don't *know* Bria is part of the prophecy. Helara always assumed she was, as did Bria's parents once she came into her gifts. It was the reason for separating the girls after the attack. Her sister and mother were sent to one camp, Bria to another. They were not to be around one another until her sister turned eighteen, until they knew of Nimai's own gifts—keeping them safe and separate until the time came for them to reunite, to gather their forces and revolt.

The prophecy tells of two sisters, the sun and moon, light and dark. And Bria is the dark. No one has exhibited magic like hers in decades, and none nearly as powerful, even those in her own bloodline. But there had still been a chance. She had yet to show all the magic that Lilith possessed. Or at least that's what I thought.

Ash finally raises her eyes to look at me, though the fight is gone, replaced by a glassy sheen of sadness. "She's raising the dead, Ev."

Well, fuck. She doesn't need to continue. I know what that sentence means. We all do.

If Bria is able to reanimate—to raise—fallen soldiers...she is now the most powerful woman to exist since Lilith. Her unique skills and dark abilities now nearly fully resemble those of the woman she descends from—dark like the nightmares that creep into your mind as you rest, dark like the shadows that lurk in corners, that slide along your spine when you walk over a grave. Not evil, but the opposite of light. The gifts from the Keeper of Life and Death, the descendent of a god.

I drop my gaze from Ash, not wanting them to see the look of defeat, to see the agony I know she is also experiencing from this revelation. Instead, I silently gather my gear from the counter and stalk to the table where they sit. I pour myself a generous glass of the whiskey before tossing it down my throat, letting the pleasant burn warm my body from the inside out, letting it push away the ache in my heart, just for a moment. I hate that no one told me, not even Bria. Slamming the glass back on the table, I turn on my heel and storm out of the kitchen.

CHAPTER 12

Bria

When I return from the cellar storeroom, Evander is gone. Ashbel and Quinn appear to be arguing about something, but that isn't surprising. I hurry into the room and place the bandages on the table in front of them, throwing my hands up.

"Where did he go?" I ask, annoyance lacing my question.

"To bed," Quinn answers shortly. He doesn't look at me, keeping his head angled down, staring at the glass in his hands.

I want to ask why—why they let him go when he was so clearly wounded, why they were arguing and stopped when I entered the room. But I have that feeling in the pit of my stomach, the one that tells me I'm to blame for whatever went down in this room while I was downstairs.

"Which is where we all should be," Ash says, rising from her chair and gathering the dishes from the table.

I watch the two of them for a minute, Ash busying herself, avoiding a conversation, and Quinn continuing to stare at his drink, swirling the melted amber around in a circle. I may not have been privy to the conversation that occurred in my absence, but their behavior tells me enough. They are no longer in the mood for company, or at least not mine.

Not even bothering to say goodbye to my sour friends, I grab the bandages and slowly make my way up the creaking stairs. The exhaustion returns now that I'm not thrumming with adrenaline and it's seeping into every pore, weighing me down. The hallway laid out in front of me feels so long, never-ending it seems, as I walk. But as I near the door to my room, I set the bandages next to Ev's door, knocking softly before slipping through the entrance to my own room. No matter what happened, he's still going to need them tonight and I'm willing to bet whatever sent him out of that room in a hurry will keep him from going back to get them later.

As I ready for bed, I think about his arm and the deep wound. It was clean at least, and I know infection will have no home in his flesh. But I hope he binds it tonight. I wonder what I did to make him leave so abruptly. Did I push too far? Was I too bold in the way I touched him? Probably.

Ash certainly thinks Evander is interested in me, but I'm not so sure now. How could he be? I'm a walking corpse, a nightmare set to leave a path of death and destruction in my wake. I can't blame anyone for wanting to avoid that. To avoid me.

I drag myself into the bed, not bothering to change my clothes, the fatigue enveloping me as I pull up the thick blankets. I succumb to the embrace and let my thoughts drift to Nimai again—of her blue-black hair, the way she appeared in the last dream. At some point my thoughts shift to Evander—the slice in his arm, the slightly tanned skin of his chest flecked with the smooth pink skin of scars. They bounce back and forth, surging between Nimai and Evander as I try to fall asleep. And just before I do, I feel warmth flooding through my body. Pinpricks of heat run along my spine and tingle in my palms, making them itch. Magic surges through me as my thoughts whirl into dreams and the weariness finally takes over.

CHAPTER 13

Evander

The moon is still visible through the clouds when I wake that morning, though it's light is fading with the coming sun. I stretch and move from my bed to the bathing chamber. There is a heat throbbing in my arm, but I know it can't be from infection. Bria thoroughly cleaned it. It's also not as painful as it was last night, more a dull feeling now.

There had been a soft knock on the door last night. I heard it but by the time I threw the door open, she was gone. An empty hallway stood before me with only the bandages she left on the floor. I used them to bind the wound tight for the night but hadn't bathed before falling asleep. The smell wafting from my body this morning is unpleasant, to say the least, and my eyes water when I raise my arms.

Gods. I fucking stink.

I also forgot to leave my water buckets by the fire last night. Usually, some of the rebels that keep up the inn will fill them for us if we are out on patrol or working all day, though if not, we just trek outside and fill them ourselves. But a trick I learned early on from Quinn and Bria was to let them sit by the fire all night. It allowed for a quicker bath in the morning, not having to wait to heat them. So here mine are, sitting in the cool washroom, and I have no patience for it this morning. I dump them in, filling the tub with chilly water before sliding my body in. It's uncomfortable but I don't need to stay in long. I scrub the now-crusted blood off myself and my mind drifts back to her—the feeling of her hands on my chest and in my hair, the closeness of her body, the lavender scent of her soap... She's all I can think about lately and gods is it frustrating. I remove the bandages carefully, peeling back the layers of gauzy material, and start examining the wound. But my breath halts, and I drop the bloody bandages to the floor when I catch sight of my arm.

The carved flesh had been gaping last night, an open, jagged slice through skin and into muscle. Now, the sides are closed, nearly fused back together. Only a thin line of the interior flesh is still visible. It's nearly healed.

Impossible. There is no way a wound that size could have healed so much in so little time, no matter how tightly I bound it overnight. I dunk it back into the water, letting it soak my skin, and scrub at it with a cloth, ignoring the stinging pain it causes. But nothing changes.

Fuck. Me. Because whatever this is, it's not normal.

I hurriedly dry myself and snatch the remaining bandages from the nearby vanity, winding fresh material back around my arm and wracking my brain for what could have caused the healing. I used no bizarre salves or balms on it, took no tinctures, though it isn't as if we have real healers here anyway. Not any with magic that could do something like this. Was there magic in the sword that bastard used against me? No. It wouldn't have healed me if the sword was tipped in anything or blessed, and the priests don't dole out their magic like that, certainly not to a lowly scout or soldier. I'll have to ask Bria or even Cato later today if I can find them. I have to meet with Helara this morning and I can't be late. Especially after yesterday. I'm in enough shit as it is already.

After dressing, I strap the bandolier back on my chest, sheathing the wealth of daggers and setting my swords in their home at my waist. I might not need the full arsenal today as I don't know what Quinn and I will be assigned to do, but it's better to be prepared. Though we will probably be starting training for the new arrivals.

I arrive downstairs before the others and help Ash with the trays for breakfast. She makes an attempt at conversation, but I have no interest in discussing last night with her. Or Quinn, for that matter. Better to pretend like it didn't happen, let them keep their opinions to themselves.

They know I flirt with Bria, that I've always found her unbelievably attractive. I'm not sure there is a man alive who doesn't, and I've gotten in my fair share of brawls over her throughout the years. Not that she knows that, but not once did I try to hide that from them. Quinn was aware I had feelings for her when we were younger, but I gather he thought I let go of my attachment some time ago, perhaps when I was in the capital or even before, when she was with Cedric. But just because a love is unrequited doesn't mean it disappears.

I tried to keep it hidden—the longing to touch her, the pain I felt when I saw her exhaustion and how drained she was from the training. The sickness in the pit of my stomach when I thought of her future and what she had to do. How her destiny was not only horrible, but how it had nothing to do with me and never would. I had managed to keep that to myself until last night. But given my outburst, the way I slammed down my glass, and stormed from the room? Now they probably have an inkling of how I feel about Bria.

Helara and Quinn descend the stairs to the main dining room together a few moments later. They're already deep in a discussion about the prior day. The regal captain greets me cordially before gathering a few bites of food and moving into the privacy of the meeting room. Quinn comes up beside me and we follow silently.

Once settled in the room, Helara takes a sip of her steaming mug, the bitter smell of her tea trailing through the air. She launches into a recap of the meeting with the commanders. From what she asserts and what the other commanders have reported, villages like the ones we found over the last few days are starting to fall to the king. The Crown's forces are getting closer by the day, closer to finding our mountain hideout. Our time is running out.

The village we visited yesterday was the farthest north the king's scouts have been seen thus far. Though, Commanders Grayson and

Finnegan checked the communities that lie directly east and south of our camp and declared them untouched. No one lives any farther west than where we are located. Only the Godless Mountains and Forsaken Woods remain in that direction.

"He's closing in on us. It's only a matter of time now before he decides to send scouts into the mountains." Helara shows no trace of fear in her voice, just facts. The captain knows what we are up against better than anyone else.

She faced the king before. And she failed. She is doing everything in her power to keep that from happening again. Years before, Helara had been one of the leaders in the Uprising. When King Braddock began waging war against those with magic, when the people figured out just what he was doing, they rallied against him. Now, she is biding her time until the prophecy can be fulfilled and help her in that quest.

My mother regaled me with all the old stories when I was a child. She told me everything she could about ancient magic and the old gods. So I'm well aware of the history—how those with magic came to be hunted like this and how we ended up in this war to begin with.

Centuries before, gods walked Azudora in their mortal forms: Uldnoir, the Keeper of life and death; Rhezenar, the Current of water and wind; and Caarae, the Incendiary of earth and fire. They came from the Forsaken Woods, though I'm sure the area was called something more pleasant before. The Woods were said to be the life source of magic, the forest brimming with powerful creatures and crystals. Every drop of magic that lives in Azudora came from that one place, the creation of all that is powerful in this world.

The three gods were cherished, ethereal beings who blessed those wherever they traveled. Their blessings contained a fraction of the power they held, doling out the ability to heal, to manipulate water, to forge fire, or transform air. There was no limit to the gifts they bestowed and those who came to reside in the Woods with the gods were strengthened by the magical land around them. The Ancients, they were called— those men and women who bound themselves to the gods, protected them and lived with them, devoting their lives to keeping magic thriving. Others flocked to the Woods as well, witches yearning to harness the power of the forest and work with the magic of the gods. They lived like that for ages from what I understand, only a few of the Ancients leaving the protection of the forest to live among the mortals. But those bloodlines they created were the most powerful around. Magic lived in their blood and was passed down through generation after generation, both from the Ancients and others who were blessed by the gods.

Eventually, Rhezenar and Caarae left the Woods and made homes among the mortals in other areas only known in the faerie tales. To be honest, I wish the lands the books told of really existed, that Melandrea and Stratho, the communities they built, were real and we could find the old gods, but they truly are gone. Uldnoir remained in the forest though, never wishing to leave his magical home. Until the old King of Azudora sought him out. King Edwin ruled nearly two centuries ago and defeated every other ruler who dared defy him. Uldnoir had no interest in our politics, only wanting to keep peace between those with magic and those without, trying to make the world a better place. So Edwin was free to overthrow everyone in his path to ultimate reign. But even when he achieved it, he still feared threats to his power, to his crown.

Edwin sent soldiers to find Uldnoir, the Keeper, and return him to the capital of Easthallow, where the king resided. Because what king could be bothered to make a pilgrimage on his own? Even to a god. He wanted power, as much as the Keeper could impart upon him, to make Edwin the most fearsome leader Azudora had seen. But the Keeper declined the request, choosing to stay in his magical wood, not feeling Edwin was worthy of such power.

Uldnoir had to have known what denying Edwin would do. He was a god, after all.

When Edwin sent his soldiers back years later, they were armed with more knowledge than before. He had found witches from the Woods and turned them to his side, taking in all the information he could about how magic worked and how to harness it. Edwin ordered those soldiers to march upon the Keeper and his people, with blades and spears tipped in emberstone, a powerful crystal that came from the Forsaken Woods. It was the only element that was thought to injure the mortal form of a god. Though, no one had yet tried. There was no reason to harm the gods, given all they'd done for us. But Edwin wanted power and he was willing to stop at nothing to obtain it, including claiming the power of a god as his own.

As the soldiers neared the Forsaken Woods, the Ancients rose to save the Keeper, wanting to keep magic safe. To keep their god safe. But Uldnoir refused, commanding them to stand down as he cleaved his magic in two. He ripped the power from his body and molded it into two mortal forms—his daughters, Kiara and Lilith. The light and dark, the sun and moon, life and death. The Keeper sent his daughters off, casting them to the farthest reaches of Azudora and saving the power Edwin sought before he was killed by the soldiers. Perhaps if he'd kept his power, his mortal form would have perished beneath the emberstone spear but his magic—his soul—would have lived on. But after tearing it from his body and creating his daughters, there was nothing left. The Keeper perished in that forest that day and many Ancients were taken by the soldiers.

And when he did, he uttered the prophecy that told the future of our world, that these daughters would die one day and come back again, stronger, more powerful. That the second coming of his daughters would right the world once again, that they would restore the balance of magic. The words spoken as he died were laced with magic, tying the fate of our world to his daughters. And that second coming is Bria and Nimai.

Something happened after that day when the Keeper fell. Something that kept the Incendiary and the Current from seeking vengeance on Edwin, though no one seems to know what that something was. No one could set foot in the Forsaken Woods afterward. I asked. Quite a few times, in fact, if we could travel there. My mother repeatedly told me it was impossible, that the Guardians who protected it would kill any who stepped foot on the soil of the forest. And that they would continue to do so until the daughters of the prophecy returned to their home.

Edwin went on to declare the old gods false deities. He proclaimed Uldnoir, Rhezenar, and Caarae frauds and thieves. In the years he spent determining how to kill the Keeper, he created his own religion, his own fake god—Vaohr—to shift the focus of the people. He announced that those three had stolen Vaohr's power, that all the magic they had came from Vaohr and that Edwin himself was chosen to return that power to the one true god. He planned it all out before killing the Keeper. Edwin promoted men to priests and kept one ancient magic wielder, a witch from the sounds of it, as his high priestess. They had scoured the earth to learn how to harness magic from the earth, from crystals, and from people.

And they were successful. They imprisoned those with magic, used the Ancients and others until they were nothing more than skin and bones, the magic and life energies drained from their bodies. The king and the priests used the harnessed magic to keep the kingdom in line, to ensure that everyone in Azudora knew who the rightful wielders of magic were. In the beginning, those with gifts were told they would be blessed by Vaohr if they returned their magic to him, if they devoted their lives to the temple.

It worked for some time, through Edwin's reign and that of his descendants. It wasn't until Braddock's father, King Phaelen, was nearing the end of his time as ruler that word began to travel of the dungeons. They were filled with the bodies of powerful people, reduced to vessels that they had abused for their own gain, their need to control. Phaelen worked tirelessly to create a level of distrust for those with gifts throughout the communities of Azudora. Not only that, but he began punishing anyone who protected them, anyone who dared keep powerful people from Vaohr and the Crown. Slowly but surely, people began to turn on one another, seeking good favor with the Crown and the priests. Talk of the old gods, of how magic existed because of them, fell away from our lives and memories.

Phaelen laid the conditions Braddock needed when he took over the role of king—fear, confusion, the need to believe in something. People were desperate. It's why so many came to his aid when he officially declared war on those with magic. In his mind, they had plenty of time to turn themselves in. The families knew what ran in their blood. So if they had not come to the Crown, to Vaohr, by the time he became king, they were hunted.

It was all to keep Azudora safe, he'd claimed, to keep intruders out and show devotion to the fake god. What intruders he possibly meant, I didn't know. The Godless Mountains lie beyond the Forsaken Woods, on the western border of Azudora and the Feral Sea expands to the east.

No one travels farther north than the Kaanos and the southern border is filled with ocean cliffs. Gods only know if anything lies beyond those seas, what threats Braddock could fear when Azudora is all we know. But fear is a powerful motivator, and it has worked better than expected in Braddock's favor.

Quinn and Helara continue their discussion, but I'm too lost in my own thoughts now. Too focused on the past to remain in the present. How Helara kept going and pushed forward after all of this was awe inspiring. She'd lost family to the priests and the king, just like so many in Azudora—parents, siblings, aunts and uncles, friends...left to serve Vaohr and never returned.

The rebels were naïve at the time of the Uprising, and they'd misjudged the king's forces. Helara and Reinhardt were the only two captains who survived that battle. They didn't realize the magic Braddock was capable of with the priests at his side. And when the rebel forces hit Easthallow, they were nearly wiped clean. Forced to flee to maintain the meager numbers they now had, they'd been driven to the outer reaches of Azudora, to live in hiding amid recent years.

The rebel numbers have grown during our time in hiding and now we have hundreds in the camps and others in the villages, just waiting for the call. I may not have fought in the battle like Helara and Reinhardt, but I remember the fallout—the push from the priests after that battle to gather as many people as possible with powers to the capital. That was when my father turned on Bria. And when he turned on my mother as well.

"Have we any word on Nimai?" Quinn probes and my mind slides back to the conversation at hand when I hear her name. Bria's sister. The other half of the prophecy.

"No, nothing yet," Helara responds, her brows pinching together. "The last we heard, she still had not exhibited any indication of her gifts. I should be hearing from their mother in the next few days, as her birthday approaches. Cordelia is keeping me informed," she finishes.

The stress of being captain has worn her features over the years. Her face is powerful, a strong beauty emanates from her. But there are fine lines around her eyes, around the corners of her mouth and nose. The two lines between her brows seem to be permanently etched into her deep bronze skin from the unceasing worry.

Quinn looks at me pointedly before continuing, as if challenging me to interrupt. "You've heard of Bria's new…gift?" I remain silent, waiting to hear what the captain has to say about it.

She nods, a small motion, before taking another sip of the steaming liquid. "Cato reports on her progress daily. He mentioned she was doing extremely well and would likely master the skill within a few days." Setting her cup down gently on the table before her, she continues. "Which is in our favor since he will be taking his leave shortly to travel and support Nimai in her own training. He wants to be there before she comes into her gifts."

Everyone had known before me. My chest tightens but I force myself to speak past the hurt.

"And Bria will be on her own from there?" I say finally, looking to the captain, trying to mask my feelings from her.

"Until we attack, yes." Helara's eyes are dark, and I'm certain she perceives my concern for Bria going forward without any guidance.

She sits up a bit straighter and folds her long fingers on the table. "She will be informed of all strategy meetings going forward. Though, ultimately, she will do as she wishes when we go to battle. There is nothing anyone can do to contain her once she starts. Nor her sister, if we are correct in our assumptions."

"How much have you told the others?" Quinn questions, leaning back in his chair slightly.

Helara gives a slight flick of her wrist, waving away the question. "Nothing more. They are aware we hold the prophecy but are unaware of who it is or where they are located. It's safer this way. For both girls. Once we see what Nimai is capable of, we may discuss informing the rest of the commanders."

The northern camp had been lucky to have no traitors among them in the years secluded up here in the mountains. The southern camp had not been graced with the same luck, though they managed to weed out the issues and deal with them as they saw fit before any information ever made it back to Braddock or the priests. Captain Reinhardt runs a tight ship in the southern camp, and he is not as forgiving as Helara. The only person that ever obtained any information about this mountain town was me.

"If there's nothing else," Helara offers, looking up for confirmation, "I should go see to the villagers. Ensure they settle in and begin training as soon as possible. We are going to need all the help we can get." With that, she pushes back the chair and rises, her hands flat against the table.

Quinn and I follow suit, and as we make to leave the meeting room, Helara stops me with a hand at my elbow.

"How's the wound?" she queries, turning my arm a bit in her hand as if she could see the gash through the shirt and bandages. "Will you be able to help today with training or should you take a day to rest?"

"I had been meaning to mention that to you this morning," I begin, running my hands over my jaw.

How was I going to explain what happened? How the wound nearly disappeared overnight for no clear reason? It had to be magic, but from where?

Helara's eyebrows rise, a look of genuine concern coming over her face. "Do you need a healer?" she questions, worry lacing her words.

She isn't about to risk an injury to one of her finest soldiers so close to the battle that may very well save all our lives. I should be happy that she cares enough to show any concern for me. It's not something I've been accustomed to from those above me.

I swallow. "It's healed."

She observes me closely and Quinn swings his head to stare, eyes narrowing. "Bria helped me clean it last night and...I'm not sure what happened. But this morning I went to inspect it and change the bandages..." I throw my hands up. "Captain, the wound is healed," I finish quickly, looking to Quinn, whose eyes are now deep baths of hazel.

"Well, that's interesting, isn't it?" Helara rubs a finger across her lips. "You should ask Bria. You said she helped you in cleaning the wound?" I nod. "Perhaps her magic has shifted once again, though it feels off. Healing was not something Lilith was known for." She hums, deep in thought. "It was, however, something Kiara did very well."

She steeples her fingers together and presses them to her lips. "She is powerful, that's for sure. So much more so than we expected."

"Indeed," Quinn replies in agreement, looking at me with warning in his eyes.

As if I didn't already know.

"Find them, today if you can. The sooner we know what caused it the better," she orders, shifting on her feet to continue out the door. "Garrith should be in the green with the villagers, I'll come check in on you all later."

Quinn and I leave the meeting room behind her and set off in the opposite direction, heading for the front door. I stop just outside the entryway to the inn, the cold hitting me like a wall of ice. Grabbing the leather gloves from my belt, I scan the area and contemplate where Bria might be today.

"I should probably go find Bria. See if she knows anything." I tug at the worn leather, weaving my fingers together to push the gloves tight.

Quinn rolls his eyes at me and begins stomping away, the snow crunching loudly beneath his boots.

"Just leave it alone. There's clearly magic at work and it had to come from her or her sister. Maybe even both of them. Does it really matter?" Quinn is a good deal ahead of me now, his shoulders hunched in irritation. Is it because I mentioned the wound to Helara?

"I didn't ask to be *healed* Quinn," I call after him, quickening my pace to catch up. "I'm not even sure she can do that. You heard Captain, Lilith was no healer. And how in the gods could Nimai have done that? She's miles away." He keeps moving, ignoring my attempt to discuss it. "What exactly is your problem right now?" I snap, staring at the back of his dark frame contrasting starkly against the fresh white of the newly fallen snow.

Quinn stalls and rounds on me, his lip curling in an agitated snarl.

"Leave it be. Let her train and don't pull her focus." His teeth are clenched now, and the words are forceful. "The whole kingdom of Azudora relies on her, Ev. The fate of the world does."

"I'm not pulling her focus. And I know the world is relying on her. *Gods*! None of you ever let me forget, nor do you let her," I start, but Quinn isn't done laying into me.

"You've been here for a year, Ev. I've been here for five, watching over her, keeping her out of trouble. Keeping her safe, for fuck's sake. I haven't spent all these years, all that time, to see her start questioning her path in life. To see her *think* she can live any semblance of normalcy." He shoves a finger in my face, leaving it only an inch from my eyes. "She's not normal, Ev, and you would be wise to back the fuck off." He pauses, blowing out a deep breath before resuming his tirade. "Find. Someone. Else. She doesn't need to stroke your ego." His eyes narrow on me then. "Or anything else for that matter." And with that, Quinn turns and begins stalking away from me.

I'm taken aback by the harshness of his tone, and it takes a minute for me to respond. "You're a real prick sometimes, you know that?" I yell after him, my voice sharp. I have to speed up to nearly a jog to catch him.

He barks out a forced laugh. "Ha! I may be a prick, but at least I'm not thinking with mine."

My hands ball into fists, fingernails piercing the skin of my palms. "What is your issue with this? Why *are* you so against anything happening with Bria?" I'm close to raging by this point.

I understand her purpose, understand why Quinn may not want her distracted. But I'm not some fool who has no idea what her fate is and his anger seems misplaced toward me.

Quinn's pace slows to a halt. He hears the anger—the pain in my voice—and he turns back to face me.

"Because, Ev," he starts, shaking his head, remorse tightening the line of his mouth and turning his eyes to glass. "I've seen you at your lowest. I don't want to see you back there. She can't give you what you're looking for. You may not want to believe it, but I'm looking out for you just as much as I'm looking out for her. This group, us, it's all I have left." His voice cracks the tiniest bit, but he pushes on. "If you do this, if you let yourself fall for her like an idiot, then..." He trails off, leaving the sentence, laced with doom, to hang in the sharp, icy air.

I know what he means. He has been trying his best to protect me this whole time. He's not just being an ass to me, but trying to be a good friend to both of us. Quinn worries that if I open my heart to Bria, it will be broken. Broken in ways beyond repair. I try to keep my face neutral, pushing my lips together while he's speaking, but he can tell. I see the way his face falls when realization dawns.

"Gods," he breaths, watching my expression. "You never stopped loving her, did you?"

I shove past him, not answering, and leave his question lingering. He falls into step beside me, and I feel the tension in the air between us so thick it's suffocating—the knowledge that I never stopped loving her, not for a day. And the understanding that I will break when fate comes for her. That I will never be the same.

CHAPTER 14

Bria

I drop to the bed and fling my body backward. Today was spent the same as the last five. I rose early, before the rest of the inhabitants in the inn, for a morning run, letting the freezing fucking air wake me up and fill my lungs before practicing with the bones and Cato. I stayed in the chilly graveyard each day as the sun arced across the sky and spent the evenings visiting with Ash, talking in her room. I spent the nights dreaming of Nimai. As her birthday draws closer, she is becoming an ever-present part of my nights.

I've been avoiding the others. Especially Ev. Ash had been kind and understanding when I explained how I felt about him. I told her all of it. I told her that I wanted him. Badly. And that being close to him, being around him, made it so much harder. That I didn't want to do anything stupid, not with so little time left. I was determined not to hurt him, and surprisingly Ash agreed. So, it was just easier to steer clear of him for now. The feat was only made easier by the new villagers. They needed a great deal of training as most of them had never held a weapon before, let alone fought anyone. And Evander and Quinn have been busy with long days of training.

It's allowed me to focus on my own training, to throw myself into mastering reanimation. Cato will be leaving in another day, and I need to spend as much time as possible with him.

After the first session, I woke the next morning to find my energy stores entirely refreshed. It was odd for sure, but since then it's continued to happen. The reanimating has been draining me far more than any other power I've wielded but I wake up and can manage to practice again the next day. I've still declined to pull energy from anyone to practice—I fear what draining energy from Cato would do to the old man—but I did manage to make the skeletal warrior move more today. So I am making progress, nonetheless. Even without the additional boost.

I think back to my earlier session and close my eyes, letting the memory sweep over me. I imagine the long line of stark white bones against the gray sky. How the skeleton bent at his knees and waist to pick up the long blade I had placed in front of him. How he turned it over in his hand, the joints in his wrist and fingers seamless with each movement. The fluidity with which he wielded the weapon—*I* wielded it. Me. Because it was my mind that controlled the warrior.

The idea of that makes an unabashed smile burst across my face. The accomplishment of today has me giddy. With more energy, who knows how many dead could be raised, how many could be commanded? Perhaps an entire army of the dead will follow me into battle, I muse.

My stomach growls loudly, interrupting my thoughts, and I spring from the bed, suddenly ravenous. In an effort to avoid Evander, I've been waiting until after dinner to go eat with Ashbel. My stomach has protested every day, angry at me denying it food when it's worked so hard with the bones. I stroll to the washroom and clean up before leaving to find Ash. After scrubbing the dirt out of my nails from digging my fingers into the partially frozen ground, I throw on a loose sunflower-yellow tunic and a clean set of warm leggings.

Padding down the hallway, I feel the cool wood of the floor on my bare feet, but it doesn't bother me in the least. I'm always warm now. The energy inside me is constantly pulsing and vibrating, the warm ball inside my core spreading throughout my body, though the glow is dull now after a day of using my magic and burning through my stores. The heat remains, and I imagine there are tiny heat footprints left behind me as I walk the halls.

I come to the end of the stairs and make my way across the main dining room, empty aside from two commanders sitting in the corner, deep in conversation. I make a point to smile at them, a small greeting, and keep moving. I catch a glimpse of Ash ducking into the parlor down the hall and follow. We've occasionally taken meals or drinks in the parlor with Evander and Quinn in the past, wanting privacy from the rest of the crowd, but we have been eating in her rooms as of late. Maybe Ash decided to set up our dinner in there for tonight, warm and cozy by the fire. That would be nice. But as I come to the doorway, my body stalls, unable to take a step into the room. My legs just stop working.

Evander's face is drawn with exhaustion, short bits of stubble breaking out all over his chin and neck. He looks anguished as he sits leaning forward, hands falling between his knees. Straight locks of chestnut hair fall in his face and creep over his eyes. Quinn sits across from him, reclined in a cushioned chair, the back rising above his head. His hazel gaze is lost, staring at something unseen, some memory in the back of his mind.

The room feels tight, their stress palpable as I halt in the doorway. None of them are speaking and I wonder what they were talking about before I got here that made my normally easygoing and comforting group of friends so visibly distressed.

Ash turns from the chair she's standing beside as she hears me approach. Her gaze is pleading, begging me for forgiveness, gleaming emerald pools filled with apology. She hadn't meant to ambush me like this, with Evander. I force a small smile and brush her arm lightly as I walk past, positive there is no ill intention from her.

No. Something bad happened for them all to be sitting here, and I intend to find out what it is.

I meander into the room to find a free chair and my body tenses as I pass Evander. He's so close that I could easily stretch out my fingers and drag them through the tousled mess of silky locks. I feel his eyes lingering on my back as I move to the empty seat by the fire, curling my legs under as I climb into the overstuffed chair. It's snug and warm from the heat of the flames. No one speaks as I adjust myself in the seat, tucking my bare toes beneath me.

Brushing my fingertips along the crushed velvet arm, I stare down at the chair, a faded sky blue, likely a beautiful color years ago. "Is it Nimai?" My voice crackles with nervous energy, and I focus on a single brass button sewn into the arm, circling it as I wait for a response.

"No," Ash assures me. "Of course not, Bria. Why would you think that?" Concern blossoms in her voice.

I release the breath I was clutching on to, pushing it out deeply from my aching lungs. "I've been dreaming about her. For the last few nights," I admit, still hesitant to look at any of them.

"As far as we know, Nimai and your mother are fine," Quinn begins, his voice deep and quiet. "A few of our soldiers were killed while out on patrol. Their bodies were on the road just past the village we evacuated. Put on display with the mark of Vaohr burned into them, like the ones from the other day."

"Another warning," I respond, and Quinn drops his head into his hands, nodding.

He drags his fingers through his shoulder-length hair, the ebony strands free from the usual knot he wears. Ash sinks into the chair next to me, skirts spilling over the arms in a pool of burgundy. She's watching Quinn closely, analyzing his features. Only Evander looks at me. His molten eyes watch me with a curiosity and intensity I never knew possible. I swallow, meeting his gaze.

"Have you told Cato about the dreams?" he asks, his voice gentle and husky.

I shake my head, feeling strands fall from my braid with the motion. "I'll mention it to him in the morning."

Evander nods, though he continues to stare. I shift uncomfortably and stretch my back, suddenly very sore from the day and wanting a reprieve from his gaze. As I twist in the seat, the tunic slides up and I feel the warmth of the fire on my bare skin. I look back, noticing his eyes flick to the exposed flesh, his jaw flexing.

A flush creeps into my cheeks, heat flaming them, and my chest tightens as he drags his eyes back up to meet mine. The issue isn't his reaction to a small show of skin. It's that I *wanted* the reaction from him. I stand quickly, lifting myself from the soft velvet, and say a terse goodnight to the group, swiftly gliding through the halls to scavenge some leftover dinner from the kitchen before heading up the stairs to my room. I'm eager to leave my solemn friends and the weight of Evander's stare for now.

CHAPTER 15

Evander

My mind is racing with what to say to her. I want to speak to Bria, but how? I need to know about my arm, to see if she has any insight into what may have happened. And I have been avoiding her since the conversation with Quinn, fairly certain she's been doing the same since our encounter in the kitchen.

But tonight, the look in her eyes, the sorrow when she spoke of Nimai, it was too much. The fear she's experiencing, constantly worrying about her mother and sister and their safety, must be truly awful. And the dreams she's having. The nightmares. I just need to see her.

While I bathe, I think about what to say, scrubbing at the dirt and grime that collected along my skin from training, letting it flow away in the warm water. The smells of citrus and lemongrass infiltrates my nostrils. I take a deep breath of the clean scent as I exit the bath and examine my face in the mirror. The stubble along my jaw is starting to creep down my neck. I look tired, worn down. And I am tired and worn down. I scratch at the rough hair, thinking I can put off shaving until tomorrow.

After drying off, I yank on a pair of loose black trousers and a matching tunic, then sit on the edge of the bed, steeling myself to go across the hall. Hopefully, by this time, everyone else at the inn will be in bed, and it will be quiet in the halls. I can visit her unnoticed. Not that it's forbidden like it might have been back home, but I know Quinn doesn't want me speaking to her. Even if I seek answers about my arm. Neither of us needs the drama that would follow if rumors of a late-night visit made their way back to him. Or Helara. It may not be prohibited in the sense of titles, but Helara has a hands-off rule for those of us protecting Bria. Mainly me and Quinn.

Gathering courage around me, I step out from the room and into the dark, still hallway, waiting a moment to listen for any stirrings, but all is silent. I close the space between the rooms in a few smooth strides, letting my hand fall in soft raps against her door. I brace a hand on either side of the frame.

And wait.

CHAPTER 16

Bria

It's late, and I lie in bed waiting to be whisked away by exhaustion, but sleep is still far from my reaches—irritating me to no end. I'm debating whether I should go back downstairs and see if Ash is alright when a quiet knock fills the room, a soft echo that disrupts the lurking silence.

I sit up abruptly, curious as to who could be at the door, then look at the clock and note it's past midnight, nearly one in the morning now. Just as I was thinking of her, it might be Ash coming to check on me or even apologize for earlier. Not that she needs to, but I saw the guilt in her eyes when she was unable to warn me that the men were with her this evening.

It wasn't as if I *couldn't* be around Ev. It was more that I *shouldn't* be around him. That I don't trust myself anymore to not act impulsively and give in to my desires. My looming fate is doing nothing to stifle that impulse control.

Thinking that's probably who it is, I move toward the door and swing it open. It's not Ash that greets me, but Evander. There he is, hands pressing hard against the sides of the doorframe. His head hangs down as he gazes up at me through the whisps of warm brown hair falling in his eyes. He's lit by the soft glow of the sconce in the hallway, looking devastatingly handsome.

"May I come in?" he asks softly. That husky tone from earlier is still present. He's tired, run down from days of fighting and training.

"Of course." I step aside, allowing him entry to my room as I close the door behind him.

Evander strides in, his legs taking up so much more space in each step than mine, until he reaches the bed. He sits on the edge, leaning slightly forward and rubbing his hands together briskly in thought. Something is bothering him. I follow, positioning myself beside him and tucking my feet under, crossing my legs. There are no seats in here, just my small bed, an end table, and the dresser that holds the few clothing items I own.

He turns to face me. The bit of a beard he's sporting ages him but makes him look rugged and somehow even more attractive than usual. I can feel my heart hammering in my chest just from looking at him. Why is he here?

"I need to ask you about my arm," he says, answering the thoughts swirling through my mind.

My brow furrows in confusion. His wound had been bad but not *that* bad. "Did it worsen? Do you need me to call a healer for you?"

Shit! I don't even know where we would get one, the furthest town is hours away.

Evander chuckles. "No, Bria. It's quite the opposite."

Rising from the bed, he tugs the tunic up over his head, the amulet thudding back down on his toned and tanned chest, his skin almost copper. It's like the kiss of the summer sun never fully leaves his skin, leaving it a deeper shade than mine. His stomach is a road map of ridges, outlining the tight abdominal muscles that flex as he moves to place the tunic on the bed. My eyes roam greedily over his body, eating up every inch while I can, a flush creeping up my neck and chest. He turns his body fully toward me, so his left arm is visible, but the wound is gone. A long pink scar runs in a jagged line down the outside.

I gasp, pulling my legs from underneath me. Before I know what I'm doing, I've crawled the short distance to him and stopped, kneeling before him. Looking at the mark, my jaw falls open in awe. The sword had carved a deep gash in his skin. I saw it just days ago, felt it. Now it's nothing more than a scar.

I raise my hand to his arm and run a single finger down the smooth pink skin, puckered in the center. Evander shudders and I look up at him. His eyes are smoldering with such severity I feel I may suddenly burst into flames from the heat of his gaze.

"Was it you?" he questions softly.

I swipe my tongue across my bottom lip, grasping for words. "No," I murmur, moving my focus back to his arm, "At least, I don't think so."

My eyes shift from the scar back to the taught muscles of his stomach, the roundness of his pecs. I move my hands to his chest, pressing them against his hard body as I remain kneeling on the small bed in front of him. I muster the courage to glance at him, lifting my gaze to meet his.

Evander steps closer, his thighs now flush with the side of the bed. I realize my hands are still on his chest but don't move them. *I should move them*, I think, but he doesn't shake me off or step away. The way he stares makes me wonder if he feels the same thick river of tension undulating between our bodies.

"I'll-I'll have to ask Cato about it. Tomorrow," I stammer out. "I don't think Lilith had healing powers. No. I know she didn't, this can't be from me." I am puzzled by the scar and I'm rambling now, barely able to form words with him this close.

"There's no one else here with magic, aside from Silas. And he hasn't touched me," he states, and I nod. Somehow, it had to be me who did this. "Tomorrow," he agrees, his eyes wandering to my neck and collarbone, making me very aware of the old, thin shirt I had tossed on to sleep in. Not to mention it only lands midway down my thighs and the neckline is stretched out, dipping low. It isn't exactly an outfit meant to be seen by anyone.

His arms hang loosely by his sides, but slowly, so slowly, he moves them to my bare legs, never breaking eye contact with me. My breathing becomes heavy as his fingers trail along the edge of the shirt, sending a tingling sensation through me. Evander slides under it and I gasp at the feel of his rough hands as they move up the sides of my thighs to rest on my waist. I press my thighs together, clamping them tight to stifle the pulsing starting in my core, the tension throbbing between my legs. The anticipation building inside me pushes away any thoughts of the scar and anything but him.

Evander stills, leaving his fingers resting along the bare skin of my hips, waiting to see how I react. It only takes a moment. A moment for the shock of finally feeling his touch to fade before I'm winding my arms around his neck and twisting my fingers into the silky chestnut strands of his hair again, still damp from bathing. He tugs me closer, splaying his hands along the small of my back and leaving our bodies flush against one another. I can feel the thudding of his heart in his chest, see the rise and fall as he breathes as heavily as I do.

I tilt my head to the side, taking in the lush curve of his lips and the short stubbly beard that makes him unbearably handsome. When he smiles at me, the dimple on his left cheek is still visible through that stubble and I bite down on my lip between my teeth. His smile is striking.

His eyes burn deeper, molten, and he leans in, the soft velvet of his mouth brushing against mine. Everything stops. Nothing matters now, in this moment, except for him. There are no more bones on my mind, no more wars to be waged. Just us. Just now.

I inhale the scent of lemongrass wafting from his body as his mouth presses into mine. He digs his fingers into the flesh of my back as he holds me tighter. I feel his tongue flick over my lips, and I part them in response, welcoming him, reveling in the sweet taste of his mouth. Of his tongue. Deepening the kiss, I allow my body to melt into his, fisting his hair in my hands. I wrap the smooth strands around my fingers and tug his head into me, craving more.

Feeling as though I could devour him, I pull the edge of his lower lip between my teeth. Evander lets out a low noise, almost a growl in response, and I fight the urge to smile at getting that reaction out of him. He grinds his body into me, releasing his grip on that hunger a bit more. His kiss becomes fierce now, his tongue thrusting into me and tangling with my own. I can feel the hardness of him pressed against me and it sends a fresh wave of arousal through me, drenching me with the thought that he wants this just as much as I do.

It's intoxicating. Finally kissing him and letting myself go like this.

His hands wander, caressing over my back and down to my ass as he continues to kiss me. Slicking his mouth against mine and digging his fingers into me in the most delicious way. I let my own hands wander in response, moving from his hair to his shoulders and chest, gliding over those hard ridges of muscle.

Unexpectedly, Nimai flashes into my mind. The image is sharp and agonizing, sending a searing sensation through my skull. I rip back from the kiss, grabbing my head between my palms and gasping, trying to catch my breath but feeling like I cannot get enough air into my lungs. I fall forward onto my elbows, my knees pressing into the hard mattress as I try to gulp down air.

Nimai is screaming, her face contorted from some sort of torment. Pain rages through my body, surging through my veins, and touching every inch of my skin. I dig my fingers into my hair, grasping as if I could peel back the skin of my skull and release the feeling.

"Bria!" Evander cries out and lunges onto the bed beside me. He grabs me around the waist, his grip strong as my body thrashes against the torture. As he hauls me into his lap and wraps me in his arms, the image of Nimai flickers and lifts. Gone as abruptly as it appeared. But the pain lingers, a whisper of what it was just seconds before. My hands are still squeezing my temples, my eyes clamped shut.

Evander is holding me tightly, as if my whole body is going to break apart into pieces, shattering from the impact from the vision. "Bria," he soothes, but I can hear the terror in his voice.

I press my face into his chest, the amulet he wears cool against my skin. I can smell the herbal citrus of his skin, not the searing, burning smell that came with the vision. I pull a deep breath into my lungs, filling them with the scent of him. I let my hands drop from my face and wrap them around his neck, burrowing further into his body. I let him stroke my hair in slow, sensuous movements, allowing my own body the time to relax.

I'm not sure how much time passes before the pain really fades. It happens slowly, as if it is receding from my fingernails and toes all the way up through my limbs, leaving a lingering burn along my back before it vanishes entirely.

"I saw her again," I begin, my breathing starting to regulate and steady once more, my face still glued to his chest. "But it was different."

Pulling back from his body, I gaze into his brown eyes, my own stinging with the fresh tears I try to hold back—tears from the terror I feel at seeing my sister's face like that.

His brows pull together, concern blooming. "What do you mean, different?" he questions.

"I could feel...pain. Horrible pain. Hers, I think. I don't know." I shudder, recalling the debilitating sensation. The burning sensation.

Evander's eyes soften, the brown and gold seeming to melt with the change of expression. "Are you still in pain?" he wonders, bringing a hand up to caress the side of my face as if he could see the source of it if he just looked hard enough.

My mouth tilts up in a smile at the gesture. "I have a killer headache now, but mostly I'm just tired." I yawn as if in response to the words and my eyelids begin to sag. The fatigue of the day coupled with the vision is depleting.

Evander shifts, turning so he can lay my body back on the bed. Briefly, he is poised above me and despite the exhaustion, desire courses through me, my breath hitching as I take in his naked torso.

His lips tug up in a smirk, noticing my reaction to him, but he keeps moving, pulling back and swinging his legs to the edge of the bed. His feet thud lightly as they hit the ground and he reaches for his tunic. He's leaving. But I want him to stay, need him to stay. I'm always alone, have been for the last five years, and his closeness fills that emptiness in my chest.

Reaching out to touch him, I splay my fingers over his arm, grasping lightly. His eyes shift to my hand then slowly up to meet my face. I'm sure he can see the pleading in my wide eyes. I tug on his arm and the smile returns, his dimple reappearing as he raises a brow in question.

"Please," I begin, barely able to project my voice above a breathy whisper. "Please...stay."

Evander slides wordlessly into the bed beside me and grasps the edge of the down-filled blanket, covering our bodies. I roll onto my side, facing away from him, and tuck my body back into his. He's warm and comforting as he curls himself around me, sliding an arm across my middle and gently pulling me closer. His breath is soft on the back of my neck as he nuzzles his face into my hair. My body relaxes even more into him, muscles unclenching, fear and concern melting away. Evander's touch is soothing, calming, and feels...right.

Finally, he speaks, his words floating across my neck in a light breeze. "You *need* to tell Cato tomorrow." Though his tone is kind, there is a firmness to his words. He's concerned and he wants me to listen to him. "About all of it, Bria. The dreams, the visions of Nimai, whatever happened with you that healed my arm. He needs to know."

The vision is bothering him. I sense it as he tightens his grip on my body. And why wouldn't it? It's bothering me, it's concerning me. The closer my sister's birthday gets, the more vivid the images of her become. I *feel* more. Like there is some invisible thread tying me to her. And if the prophecy is true, if we really are part of it, then maybe there is.

"Mhmmmm," I murmur back, enjoying the feeling of his embrace. I let his touch and smell wash away the fear that is creeping into the back of my throat, making my eyes begin to water once again.

He kisses the back of my neck, lips skimming along my exposed shoulder where the old shirt has slipped. I feel a shiver ghost over me and want the kisses to continue, to let him erase the fear that is eating away at me. But sleep is pulling me down, begging me to succumb whether I want it to or not.

"Goodnight, Bria." I barely hear the whisper brush across my ear before I allow myself to be dragged under.

CHAPTER 17

Evander

T he feeling of her body pressed against mine is the first thing I notice before I even open my eyes. And when I eventually do, I take in the golden waterfall of hair that cascades over the arm arranged beneath her, the length of her slender neck—ivory skin gleaming in the early morning light. She's still sleeping. Breathing deeply. Easily.

It's a stark contrast to the heavy panting of last night when that agony wracked her body, made her convulse like someone being tortured. I squeeze my eyes shut and wince at the memory. I've tortured enough people to recognize that kind of suffering and it worries me more than I'd like to admit.

I've understood for some time now that she was different, powerful beyond measure. But to me, she was always a friend, someone I wished could be more. Last night was the first time I witnessed what the threads of fate were doing to her, how destiny was devouring her and twisting her into what the prophecy needed her to be.

I can't bear the tightness in my chest when I think of her fate. Instead, I focus on her. On Bria. I shove away the thoughts and take in her sleeping form, still tucked in tight to my body, her back flush against my chest. And I vow to myself, here and now, to do so for as long as we have left.

Looking at her now, I know. I know that I'm lost already. I've waited so long for her, and I'm not coming back from this. I'm not coming back from her.

As I lie there gazing at her, I don't want to wake her. Unfortunately, neither of us are the type of people who can be missing for long. We will both have others looking for us if we don't get going soon. People will notice.

Feeling the thin slip of fabric under my fingers, I move my hand under it, grazing up along her hip until my hand reaches her stomach. I lazily drag my fingers across her abdomen until she starts to stir, relishing the smooth feel of her skin under my hands, indulging in the freedom to touch her as I desperately want to. I nudge my nose against her ear, a light tickle across the soft lobe before burrowing my face into the expanse of her hair. I gently kiss the nape of her neck. She starts to squirm, her body pushing against me, and I smile. Maybe waking her isn't all that bad, though it's causing my already hard cock to ache with need. I draw my tongue across the same space, up the soft side of her neck to her ear. She lets out a soft groan and twists her body around to face me, eyes bleary with sleep.

"And what exactly do you think you're doing?" she questions, her voice hoarse. A smile pulls at her lips, her head still resting on the pillow beneath, enrobed in a tangle of blonde.

I grin. "You needed to wake up," I murmur, captivated by the brilliant sheen of her hair, the blue fire smoldering in her eyes. *Perfect*, I think.

"Mmmm," she agrees, stretching her arms above her head.

I want to stay in bed with her all day, to finish what we started last night. I stare at her, willing her to stay and ignore the responsibilities of our days, to ignore the looming darkness over our lives even though I know we can't.

"You're right, we'd better get going," she says, slipping out of bed before I can protest. But I wonder if she's thinking the same.

I reach for her arm as she stands, but she quickly evades me. Disappointed, I slam my fist onto the empty sheets beside me and let out a groan. I hear her chuckle as she softly moves to the dresser and begins digging through the measly contents for clean clothing.

"You need to go before Quinn comes looking for you," she offers as she rifles around the dresser. "I'm not quite sure how you would explain this." She gestures to me, still lying in her bed.

She's right. I slide a hand through my hair, pulling the loose strands out of my face and sit up, tossing my legs over the side of the bed. Snagging the tunic from the ground, I stand and tug it over my head, pulling it down to rest at the top of my trousers. I turn to find her leaning against the dresser, watching me intently, her clothes forgotten in her hands.

My heart skips when she looks at me like that and I take the few steps across the room until I'm standing before her, thighs flush against hers. I place my hands on either side of her, trapping her against the small dresser, and her throat bobs. Knowing I can affect her the same way she does me makes it hard not to carry her back to bed. Or better yet, just turn her around and bend her perfectly tiny frame over this dresser. But then neither of us would leave this room. Instead, I lean down and brush a soft kiss across her lush rose lips. And when she presses her lips back into mine and I feel the flick of her tongue, I have to peel myself away while I still can.

Because I would stay with her until the end of time if I could.

"I'll see you later, Bria," I whisper into her hair, pulling fully back and smiling as I turn to leave.

As I'm about to close the door, I hear her voice once more. "Thank you, Ev." The faint whisper barely reaches me. I pause before nodding my head and leaving, pulling the door shut behind me. The soft click echoes through the barren hall.

A smarter man would have peeked out prior to taking his leave so as not to cause any suspicion among the commanders. But I'm in a daze as I traipse across the narrow corridor. My head swirls with the scent of lavender from her honeyed hair, the floral taste of her skin, everything about her taking over my senses. I shake my head as I enter my room, as if I could physically shake off the thought of her. But I can smell her on me as I ready for the day, and I don't dare wash it away. I want to carry her scent with me until I can see her again.

CHAPTER 18

Evander

Quinn and I stand with the rest of the commanders on the village green that morning. The air is brisk and there is a fresh layer of snow upon the ground, the bright morning light setting it to sparkle. Despite the chill, the first buds of spring are beginning to burst from the trees, pushing up from the snowy ground below. Spring will be a new beginning. For all of us.

With less than a week before Nimai's birthday, Helara has everyone working tirelessly. Most of the commanders have been training groups of the villagers in preparation for battle. I'm still not convinced there is enough time in the world to get some of them ready. But if there is even a slim chance they can hold a weapon, maybe strike down one of the king's men, she wants them to be trained.

Since Quinn and I are the only commanders who know of Bria's connection to the prophecy, we are assigned elsewhere—tasked with readying horses and supplies for the trek to the Forsaken Woods. The plan is for us to escort Bria in a few days and Nimai will meet us there after her birthday, along with Cato and the girls' mother, Cordelia. Cato is of the belief that Bria and Nimai will need to reunite in the magical forest to access the full potential of their powers. It's a theory, but if it works, we can all begin the final stretch of this rebel journey. Whatever that holds.

"Maybe Ash can help us with packing up food and supplies," Quinn suggests once the captain finishes doling out duties to the rest of the men.

I shrug, deep in thought, and follow Quinn through the crackling snow. How could it be less than a week away? I'm stuck wondering if there is a way out of the prophecy. Could it possibly be wrong? Perhaps Cato has interpreted it incorrectly, perhaps Nimai will be even more powerful than Bria. Perhaps she will be the one to save everyone and Bria can be released from her duty.

"You're especially quiet today." My friend's voice bursts into my thoughts, shattering the hopeful wall I was precariously constructing in my mind.

I shake my head. "It's nothing," I lie, ignoring the concern in Quinn's eyes as I push past him into the inn.

Setting my sights on the kitchen, I trudge down the hallway. If there is anything I can do to save her when we go to battle, I'll do it. No matter the cost.

CHAPTER 19

Bria

When I arrive at the graveyard, I'm surprised to see Cato already there, and not alone. The young man beside him is tall and slim, covered in lean muscle. He looks enormous standing next to the hunched old man. I imagine I will probably look like a child standing next to him. *Gods* he has to be Quinn's height, at least six foot three, if not taller. And to my measly five foot two, he feels like a giant.

As I near, I can see the familiar burning in his eyes. My own have a touch of flames, but this boy's eyes almost glow with magical fire. The searing blue is outlined in a burning white ring. I marvel at how the villagers were able to keep him hidden for the last year. It's impossible to look at him and not see the magic within.

I smile at him, a genuine expression of my happiness at being around another individual with power. The only person I've been near with any magic for the last five years has been Cato. I can feel the heat, the energy emanating from him, and it makes my heart squeeze uncomfortably. That feeling, I've missed it so much it fucking hurts.

Both of my parents descended from magical bloodlines, my father from Lilith and my mother from Kiara. The sisters of dark and light. Though not actual sisters, the two goddesses were cleaved by the ultimate god, Uldnoir. Their bloodlines haven't been difficult to trace as none ever bore more than one child. None until my parents. It made it easier to spot that Nimai and I could possibly be the children of the prophecy. My parents worked very hard to keep their magic hidden over the years, but there was no way to contain that energy, the celestial vigor that smoldered within. At least not when you were around another who also burned with magic.

The fact that my parents had even met was astonishing. Pulled together by fate, their paths in life intertwined with one another. I wonder if they would have done anything different, had they known—known that the fierce love that they felt for one another would result in the children of the prophecy. That their own flesh and blood would be cursed from the day they were born.

"I believe you've heard about Silas by now," Cato sings out when I approach, the excitement uncontained in his voice.

I can't help but grin in amusement at his eagerness. "Indeed, I have. It's a pleasure, Silas," I say, extending my hand to the boy in a welcoming gesture.

Heat radiates up my arm when he touches my skin, and I still. *Magic*. I watch as Silas does the same, his eyes widening, the white-blue overtaking them in an otherworldly glow. Energy wells up inside him, an innate response to the power in me.

Cato chuckles at the boy's expression. "Powerful, isn't she?"

"Y-yes," Silas stammers, still holding my hand in his own, his eyes boring into me.

Cato watches the interaction with some sort of rapt fascination, his lip twitching. "Yes," he cackles. "This will do just fine."

I tear my hand free of Silas's grip, to his clear dismay. He looks crestfallen at the loss of contact, and I turn to Cato, questioning the peculiar comment.

"What will do just fine? What the fuck are you talking about, Cato?" He has a reason for bringing Silas here, that much I understand. A reason to let him know just who and *what* I am. And I deserve to know that reason. He seems too thrilled at the energy radiating from us, at the spark that ignited with our touch. I cross my arms as I wait for a reply, feeling an odd urge to be closer to Silas, to touch his warm skin again. To feel that rush of energy.

Cato sucks his teeth before responding, as if weighing the benefit of telling me. "The mouth on you," he says finally, rolling his eyes in an exaggerated expression. "As you are aware, dear Prophecy" —I grit my teeth at the expression but bite my urge to mouth off and let the old man continue—"this is the last day I can spend with you. I must depart tomorrow to be with your sister."

"I'm aware," I spit, impatiently waiting for the geezer to get to the point already.

He smirks at the irritation growing and spreading across my face. "Ahhh, how I will miss your temper. And that sharp tongue." He's just prodding now, trying to get a rise out of me. "You have mastered the bones nicely, young Bria. But due to your...ethics" —he waves his spindly fingers out toward me as if hurling the word as an insult—"we have been unable to see your true potential."

I set my face in what I imagine is a very sour expression. "We have already talked about this," I snarl.

Silas is still staring at me with what appears to be anger flaring in his icy blue eyes. Is he angry with me? No. That can't be it, there is no way he could be angry at me. He's just met me.

Cato notices it as well. "Delightful," he mutters, intertwining his long, crooked fingers with apparent glee. I plaster a confused expression on my face. "He's already picking up on your emotions. He's young enough and novice enough in his powers that making a connection will be easier than if he had years of training under his belt."

When I glance over at Silas, I can see my confusion mirrored in his expression. He's experiencing anger because I am. And that doesn't make any sense.

Cato pushes forward with his explanation. "Bria, as much as you do not want to admit it, you are the most powerful woman to walk this earth since Lilith. You exude an energy unlike any other." He points to Silas. "He can feel it, can sense that, and is drawn to you." A flush bursts across Silas's young face at the indication. "Others will as well, and you can strengthen them."

This is definitely not what I expected. Though, I assume this new attribute can assist me in rescuing those with magic, those ill-fated souls rotting away in the dungeons of the castle. If I can strengthen them, I may have a chance at helping them after all.

As understanding blossoms in my face, Cato's skin, deep with the grooves of time, wrinkles up in a sly smile. "And he can feed your power," he adds.

"What?" I'm unable to contain my surprise at this notion. The old man is senile, I'm sure of it now, because he knows how I feel about this. So forgetting this key detail, in his ripe old age as the first man in existence, is the only explanation for his massive lapse in judgement right now.

"Your energy stores are depleted after raising one skeletal warrior. How exactly do you plan to fight off an entire army?" He tosses the question out there, knowing full well I have no chance of answering it.

I can't fight off an army. Even if I can strengthen the prisoners, the rebels don't come from magic, at least not any of the ones in the northern camp. I have no ability to protect them, to give them aid in battle other than the shadows and bones.

Cato is happy to answer his own lingering question. How the old crow loves to hear himself talk. "You're going to pull energy from him. Let him feed the fire within you so that you can raise more dead, cast more shadows. *Do more.*" Silas's brows shoot up at this. Clearly, Cato had not fully informed the young man of his expectations prior to this meeting.

I begin to shake my head, golden locks falling over my shoulders and shimmering in the sunlight. "I don't—" I start, but Cato holds up a hand in protest.

"You *must,*" he says tersely. "Or we shall all perish, dear Prophecy. I've indulged your refusal long enough." His eyes are colder now, quietly conveying that there is no choice in this matter. I have a momentous job, more so than any other on this earth aside from my sister. "It is important you learn how to feed your energy stores appropriately," he finishes, surveying my face for understanding.

I steady myself, drawing up to my full height and flicking my gaze to Silas. He looks a bit shocked, his face contorting as he tries to keep up with the conversation, tries to understand exactly what is about to happen to him. I wish I knew more so I could warn him.

Appropriately. I worry what he means by that part.

I give Cato a curt nod—a slight, almost imperceptible movement, but he registers it, his mouth turning up once more in a fiendish grin.

"Wonderful!" he exclaims, clapping his hands together at securing my commitment to the task. "We don't want you killing the boy, after all," he says lightly with a toss of his hand toward Silas.

Silas throws his gaze toward me, apprehension flashing into those icy blue eyes.

"For fuck's sake, old man!" I yell, wanting to scowl at Cato but trying instead to keep my face warm and inviting as I look back at Silas. I reach my hand out to him again and he grabs it, tentatively this time. "I'm not going to kill you, don't let this old fool scare you." I let the burning in my core well up and pour out of me, releasing a rush of heat down my arms, into my fingertips, and letting it curl around his hands. Silas's face relaxes almost immediately, and he straightens his back, nodding to me. His hand grips mine so hard I have to hold back a wince.

I thoroughly hope Cato knows what he is doing. I really don't want to kill this magical man I've just met.

CHAPTER 20

Evander

After spending the day packing, our bags are now stuffed with supplies we might need for the trip to the Forsaken Woods: breads wrapped in cloth, ripe apples, pungent cheeses, and salted meats, all prepared to withstand the travel ahead of us. We've filled containers with water, gathered extra arrows, and stocked up on weapons. Only once things were completed did Ash excuse herself to help with dinner preparation.

Tonight, we are eating with Helara and the other commanders, discussing strategy for the upcoming battle. The villagers are showing some progress and there are a few promising prospects among the group. *There may be some hope for them after all*, I think, listening to the reports.

Once the updates are complete, I take my leave of the group and retire to my room, a bottle of whiskey in hand. Sharpening my daggers, I recline on the bed, legs crossed over one another, letting the slow burn of the drink warm my body as I focus on the task.

Each time I pull the steel blades across the sharpening stone, the scraping noise fills the room and sends a ghostly shiver down my spine. But I continue, contemplating what beasts, human or other, may await us on the trip to the Woods. A sharp rap breaks through the grating and my eyes dart to the door as the knob turns.

I half expect to see Bria's petite frame standing before me, outlined by lustrous golden hair. But Quinn steps into the room, staring back at me. Disappointment strikes and I sigh audibly, not bothering to conceal it.

Quinn lets loose a harsh laugh. "Expecting someone else?" he drawls, quirking a brow as he closes the door behind him. He turns to lean against the hard wood, crossing his arms over his chest, the corner of his lip turned up.

I smirk, not ready to let on to what occurred between Bria and me—not ready to let him in and face his wrath just yet. "No, but anyone would be a welcome sight compared to your ugly face."

Quinn grabs his chest in feigned agony. "You wound me," he says with dramatic flair.

"What do you want?" I ask, the words peppered with laughter.

Quinn shrugs, his hazel eyes turning darker. "You seem off. I wanted to check on you."

Continuing to sharpen the blade, I ignore the deep stare from the dark figure at my door. "I'm fine. I told you that." Guilt sours my stomach with the thought of lying to him about Bria.

He taps his foot on the ground, not one to beat around the bush and clearly, I'm trying his patience. "We leave in two days, Ev. We need to bring Bria to the Forsaken Woods. To see if her power is strengthened by the magic of the of the forest and whatever lives there." He's running through a plan that I am already aware of. A plan I helped to create. But I listen anyway, figuring there's more, and sure enough he keeps going. "Captain wants us to bring Silas along with us." He eyes me warily.

The new information catches me off guard and I look up, searching Quinn's face for answers. "Why? Is she concerned about the recent attacks?"

King Braddock is unaware of Cato's interpretation of the prophecy, his consideration of the Woods as a crucial part of the girls' powers. The king hasn't sent anyone near the Woods in years. Not that the magic, nor the magical beings that reside there, would allow him or his people anywhere near it if he tried. Kings long before him learned the hard way about the Guardians and were torn apart in the process. Perhaps she wants to send the boy as additional protection for Bria, given his searing power.

"No," Quinn begins but there is trepidation creeping into his gaze, and I brace for whatever knowledge he is about to impart. "It appears as if the two—Bria and Silas—have some sort of connection. Captain doesn't want them separated, for now," he finishes, rushing out the last sentence and steeling himself for my reaction.

"What kind of connection?" My teeth grate together at the mere thought of any connection she could have with someone else. "What the hell is that supposed to mean?"

Quinn blows out a hard breath and brings a hand to his face, dragging his fingers roughly over his eyes and down to his chin in exasperation. "Yeah, I didn't think you would take this well. It's why I let Captain know I would tell you about the change in plans."

I grit my teeth harder, somehow not chipping a tooth in the process and begin again. "What do you mean they have a *connection*?" I ask, my voice registering more like a growl.

"I'm not exactly sure," Quinn admits. "I wasn't there for the talk with Cato. Apparently, Captain went to check on them since it was Bria's last day of training and now she seems adamant that the two not be apart." I stare at him, taking in every word. "Something about her needing him to feed from. Feed her energy or whatever." The last sentence is hushed, as if he doesn't quite want me to hear what he says.

But I hear every word.

"*FEED FROM?*" The words rip from my mouth, lashing across the room at Quinn.

I slam my dagger into the mattress next to me, the thudding sound tearing through the room. Quinn doesn't flinch from my rage. No, he was expecting this reaction, but even seeing that doesn't quell the fury rising inside me. *Who is this boy? And more importantly, why does she need him?* I hate the idea of her needing him, of her needing Silas to feed her energy, to pull from him.

Quinn tosses up his hands, a gesture of defeat. "Who the fuck knows, Ev. That's all the information I have."

"He's a gods damned child! We don't need to be protecting another person on this trip." Fuming now, I can feel color flourishing along my neck and creeping up to my cheeks.

When Quinn drags a hand through his dark hair, it loosens a few strands from their binding, framing his face in ebony. He speaks slowly, choosing his words carefully so as not to further the ire coursing through me.

"Listen, I don't disagree with you, Ev. But we've been given our orders."

The words roll around in my head as I try to make sense of them. But none of this makes sense, not a bit. There are people out there with magic, with the ability to pull power like this, but I hadn't known Bria was one of them. Hadn't expected this to happen. I know enough about what the high priestess could do and does do, but this sounds different, more intense and intimate, in a way. It makes me question if this means Silas is some part of the prophecy as well, some link that Bria needs. The thought only stokes my anger.

I can sense Quinn's eyes piercing through me without having to look back up at him. He's likely watching and planning for what I might do next in my fit of fury.

"I understand." It's the only reply I can manage. The muscles in my neck tense with the effort of forcing the words out and I cast my eyes down to look at the blade thrust into the mattress. I draw my finger across the leather-bound hilt and yank it from its resting place before shifting my concentration to sharpening once again.

"You're jealous of a child. You realize that, right?" he quips, attempting to lessen the blow of the news. But I set a scorching gaze on him, and he tosses his hands up in defense. "Would a drink help? We can head over to the pub if you'd like?" He's trying, and I can't fault him for that. But I want to talk to Bria, not him.

"I bet you could even find someone to keep you company tonight. I've heard some of the new girls have proven to be rather...friendly."

"No," I snarl, grasping the sharpening stone. I hold it so tight I think it might shatter beneath my fingers. Quinn may be trying to cheer me up, but that's the last thing on my mind. I haven't been with anyone here in the camp. I haven't been with anyone since *she* came back into my life.

"Fine, suit yourself."

Quinn pushes himself off the door and it groans under the pressure. He's annoyed with me but also knows when to leave it be, knows when I need to be alone. He shoves his hands into his pockets and looks down to where I sit on the mattress.

"Ev, just plea—" he starts, but I'm in no mood to hear it.

"Don't pull her focus," I seethe. "I get it, I'll leave her alone about it," I say, hanging my head. I don't look at him because I know it's a lie and I have no intention of leaving her alone.

Quinn shakes off the statement, taking a few steps toward me. "I wasn't going to tell you to leave her alone. I know you won't even if it's in your best interest that you do." He hesitates before speaking again and when he does, his voice is low, and I hear a touch of sadness seeping into his words. "I just wanted to say"—he pauses before continuing—"whatever this is, this *connection* between them... It has to do with her magic, Ev. It's not her fault," he finishes, remaining there, his gaze trained on me.

But I stay silent until he finally stalks out of the room, leaving me in a pit of my own rage and jealousy.

CHAPTER 21

Bria

The moon is hanging high in the sky, a bright glowing orb, when I arrive back at the inn late that night. From the looks of it, the full moon will likely hit right around Nimai's birthday. Funny that the descendant of the sun and all things light and bright will have the full moon grace that precious day. Though it feels like yet another connection between us, another sign of the prophecy. That the full moon, the phase that symbolizes transformation, would be present for the day she comes into her gifts fully.

Shadows whirl around me and I am at peace in the dark, in the night. Maybe it's something I can thank my blood for, thank Lilith for. The darkness calls to me, it calls to the magic in my blood, and I welcome it.

The inn is tranquil when I step inside, a surprise considering how close we are getting to battle. Everyone has already retired for the night, and I amble down the hall to Ash's quarters. It's later than I normally visit her, and I know there is a chance she's already in bed, but I desperately want to tell her about my day. About Silas.

Cato and I returned to the library after training and stayed long into the night discussing the future—what might happen with Nimai and the prophecy in the coming days. He's of the opinion that Nimai healed

Evander the other night and restored my energy for the coming days, that I channeled her blossoming power without either of us even being aware of it. Kiara had been gifted with healing and Cato believes Nimai and I have been communicating via dreams and visions, that the connection between us is growing—taking root as she comes of age. I glossed over why Evander and I were together when the vision hit, and what we were doing, for that matter. But given the smirk I saw on Cato's lips, I was grateful he asked no further questions. He didn't appear to have the same reservations with us that Quinn showed, which is intriguing.

Instead, he urged me to pay more attention to what I saw during the visions, to listen and look—that they might give insight into how my sister is faring, and how her powers are manifesting. I plan to tell Ev the next time I see him, perhaps ease his concern over the wound a bit. And if I'm being honest with myself, it's a good excuse to go to him again.

After knocking softly on the door with no response, I turn the knob to find it unlocked. Ash is sprawled on her bed, fully absorbed in the book resting in her hands. She looks up, a bit shocked to see me standing there.

"I didn't even hear you!" she exclaims, sitting bolt upright and tossing the book beside her. I love her pure and vibrant smile and her eyes that always seem to glimmer like gemstones.

"I wasn't sure you would still be up," I say, my eyes making their way to the bedside table, where I see two half-empty glasses of liquor. They drift to the bedding beneath Ash, a disarray of cream and violet. Ash is dressed in a thin, white nightgown and my brows raise in question.

"You're not interrupting anything," she answers, without me needing to say a word.

I laugh, pointing out the glasses and the bed. "It's late enough that you've already had a visitor and sent them away? I'm sorry, I can let you rest."

"Mmmm, there was no need for him to stay," Ash responds, a glint in her eyes. "Shut up and come sit with me." She pats the bed and I walk over, climbing onto the bed to lie next to her.

"If I weren't so tired, I would have a problem lying on your dirty sheets. Was it poor Cade yet again?" I ask, aware Ash has been seeing him regularly for the last week or so since their first encounter.

"It was, but I think maybe it's run its course. I want to go out for a drink tomorrow night, see what the new villagers have to offer," she says, throwing me a wink.

The prospect makes me uncomfortable, and I think of Ev and how much I want to see him. But with so little time left, I also want to enjoy the time with Ash, to spend as many moments as possible with the family bestowed upon me by the fates.

"Wonderful idea," I respond, my lips lifting into a smile at the sheer delight reflected in Ash's expression when I agree.

We lie together talking into the early morning hours. I recount the day with Cato and Silas, finding it difficult to put into words the way the energy pulsed from Silas when I was near him—how he was visibly drawn to me and how I could feel it in my soul. How we had this instant connection, and I knew that he would follow me anywhere if I asked. Including into battle.

But siphoning his energy had proven challenging, leaving both Silas and I depleted at the end of it. I need to check in on him tomorrow, ensure he's alright after today. I had focused that ball of energy that surged in my core and instead of flinging it outward toward the graves, I had pulled it in, reaching out to touch Silas, holding his hands in my own and continuing to pull—sucking the pure white glow from his body into my own.

I recall Cato urging me to slow, to hone my focus. And it quickly became apparent why he had warned about me harming Silas. It would have been easy to breathe in every last drop of magic from his body. I could have left him a shell of the man he once was. And he would have let me do it. But Cato had reeled me back in, forced me to look at Silas while I pulled so that I could monitor his well-being, ensure he was safe and unharmed.

I had stared into those icy blue eyes while they locked in on mine until I felt as if my body was brimming with white-hot liquid. Ready to erupt, I had dropped his hands, slamming my body to the ground. When my fingers dug through the frozen dirt, the energy propelled forth, coursing like a raging river of flames through my veins, my bones.

Light had burst from my hands into the earth and not one, but *ten* graves exploded all around me. The shards of stone had rained down upon the ground and littered the fresh snow.

Ash's eyes are wide, deep pools of emerald as I explain how the warriors moved and she pushes up to rest her head on her arm, enthralled by the story. I tell her how I can close my eyes and see each one of them, see from their vantage, tell her how the world melts away around me when it happens. It's so different from how I cast shadows into nightmares, creating creatures with sharp talons and fangs to strike fear into the minds of others and attack. With that, I focus solely on myself. Those creatures are conjured from my mind. These warriors are different, they move like they live. And it requires far more energy than I have to keep them standing and wielding weapons. Silas helped with that so much more than I'd expected.

He had dropped to the ground beside me when I'd finally released him. Cato insisted he was fine when we finished and I apologized profusely, feeling wracked with guilt when I looked down at him. His sinewy body was formed of tight, lean muscles, the kind you only get from a life of manual labor, and he had been a useless heap on the ground.

But Silas would hear none of it. To him, he was mine. To use as I saw fit. As uncomfortable as that thought was, we were linked through our magic. I could sense it, even if I didn't completely understand the how and why of it yet.

"Bria," Ash says breathily when I'm finished. "This is amazing." She's beaming now, captivated by the revelation.

I chew on my lower lip and at this rate, I feel I may put a hole right through it with my discomfort. "Helara wants him to join us when we go to the Woods. She's insisting he stay with me."

Ash's face breaks into a giant, radiant smile. "I mean, I like this idea of your little pup following you around all the time. But the real question remains...how is he on the eyes?" She's being crass, but I struggled to convey the connection between us and that's just how Ash is. So, I suppose this is warranted.

"He's young. He has these light blue eyes that look touched by ice, a strong jawline." I imagine the young man looking up at me from the ground with such adoration across his face, like I was the only person he could see. "He's quite tall...and handsome." I look pointedly at Ash, who is barely containing her glee. "And you're going to leave him alone."

She lets out a hearty laugh, her body shaking from the force of it. "From what you've said, I don't think he'll be showing any interest in me," she responds, tilting her head to the side, fiery curls falling over her shoulder.

I contemplate how to better explain the connection to her, what it is exactly, but I don't even fully grasp it yet.

"It's not like that. It's..." I trail off, not finding the right words to express what I feel for Silas. Not love, or adoration, or even lust. But an attachment nonetheless, an understanding of one another that I've not felt from another person. Not since I had my parents torn from me years ago. Deep in my soul, there is an awareness that this man understands me, my purpose. My destiny. And he is going to do whatever he can to help me, to protect me.

"Such a shame. The way you talk about that power in him..." Ashbel pushes out a long breath, the hint of a whistle coming along for the ride. She feigns fanning herself as if she might swoon. "It sounds hot."

Not quite the way I would describe it. And while he is an attractive man, pleasing to look at for sure, he's not Ev.

My mind now wanders to Evander, and I realize that he may have come to my door tonight. Looking for me. Those damned butterflies thrash in my stomach when I let my mind sift through the images of last night—and this morning. Had I not been hit with that awful vision at such an inconvenient time, what would have happened?

I swallow forcefully. I know what would have happened. And though I'm aware Evander has been with women before, and likely many of them, I've only been with Cedric. He knows about Cedric, saw us together plenty of times. But we never speak of him, no one ever speaks of him to me aside from Ash. Does Ev know just how inexperienced I am, and does he even care?

A smile creeps across my face when I realize how Ash has this way of turning my thoughts from the dark impending future I hold to things much more pleasurable. She does so without me ever even noticing the shift until my mind is elsewhere. Ash is able to quell the fear that rises in me, the fear that's becoming so constant these days. I'm fortunate to have her as a haven for my feelings. She accepts what I have to do but never treats me any differently. And for that, I am immensely thankful.

We talk until neither of us can hold our heavy lids open any longer and then we sleep, side by side, hands intertwined. Both painfully aware this is one of the last nights we have in the camp, one of the last nights we have together. Neither knowing what will occur within the coming days or weeks. No one knows how long it will take for Nimai and me to be ready for battle, for Helara and Reinhardt to rally all the forces they can muster, but it won't be long. They've been preparing for this for years.

They've waited years for this. For us.

CHAPTER 22

Evander

Sleep evaded me as the night had worn on. Any time I drifted, my slumber was interrupted by thoughts of Bria. I had tossed, thrashed in the sheets when I closed my eyes and was blinded by images of her—her and Silas. Sensing it was jealousy at work, I fought every instinct I had to go to her. Fought the urge to break down her door and finish what we started last night. To claim her as *mine* before that boy could do anything more.

I know it's ludicrous, beastly even, to think that way. But there is something about her. I have trouble containing myself.

To make matters worse, the fitful sleep caused me to rise early. And against my better judgement, I do go to her. While the moon is still a shadow in the sky and the inn is hushed, I cross the hall. But no one answers when I knock, and when I push the door open, I find her room empty, her bed still made.

She didn't sleep here, and the realization sends me reeling.

I observe the dull ache that burgeons in my chest as I slam the door. Sconces rattle along the wall, the impact making the one at the end of the hall sputter. *Where the hell is she?* I should have left that twit of a boy in the village, let him be taken by the king.

Gathering my things in a storm of fury, I nearly run from the inn, not waiting for Quinn before I set off to the stables. Helara requested we scout the first leg of the trip to the Woods today and be on the lookout for any signs of the king's men. Our group is set to leave tomorrow. With Bria...and Silas. A day and a half ride, with the two of them. Though if she lets us all take our own horses, maybe we can move quicker. Maybe I can be rid of him quicker.

My thoughts envelope me as I toss the woolen blanket and saddle on the stallion, fitting the leather straps into their homes and tightening them. Leaning my arms on the saddle, I press my palms firmly into the hardened leather and let my head fall, hair slipping forward in tendrils around my eyes, tickling the bridge of my nose. I work to slow my breathing before mounting the horse, not wanting to bother the animal with my storm of emotions.

Inhaling in the warm, earthy smell of the stable helps steady my exhalations. She's made no promises to me. Not to anyone, for that matter—aside from the prophecy, her destiny. But even that isn't a promise, isn't something she desires. She was born into that ill-fated path. It's foolish to feel this way, to be letting my emotions get the better of me. And to be lashing out.

But the closer we creep to battle, as the clock wears down, the more I urge time to stand still. To take in as much of her as I can. Breathing in, my eyes closed, I can almost smell the lavender of her soap, feel the warmth that seeps from every pore of her body and seems to filter through my own, all-encompassing. I shake my head, attempting to free the images from the clutches of my mind, but it's fruitless.

There have been other women, plenty of them back when I was in Easthallow, who were pleased to spend the night with me. But I have never felt like this with anyone but her. Never been overwhelmingly jealous of anyone but her. Those women were pretty, some beautiful even, but not once did I consider them anything more than company. I'd been scratching an itch, patching over a hole that lay agape in my soul. And I'm beginning to realize that Bria fills that hole, fills it with her energy until I feel as if I might burst.

When I pry my eyes open, I glimpse Quinn staring back at me from across the stables. He's leaning on the old wooden slats and his legs are crossed over one another, hands shoved deep in his pockets. I had been so lost in thought, so consumed, that I hadn't heard him enter.

"How long have you been there?" I manage, dropping my head back to rest on the saddle. The leather is cool beneath my skin, a welcome change to the heat of rage and jealousy that ripped through me mere moments before.

"Long enough to guess your mood." The deep timbre of his voice is barely audible as it travels across the space.

There's no chance Quinn is going to allow me to spend the day pining and I press my forehead harder into the leather. But he's giving me some time, a quiet space to release the pressure building in me. I listen as he pushes his heavy boot into the solid wood behind him, launching forward from the wall to move toward me.

"So, if you're all done with your bullshit, we should be on our way." He slings the saddle over his own horse, not looking at me while he speaks. I have a feeling he's fueling the rage on purpose. Pissing me off and trying to get it out of me rather than let it fester.

"Fuck off."

Quinn's face breaks into a full smile, and I fight the urge to reciprocate as we mount the horses and make our way out of the camp.

Bria

It's a strange feeling when I wake to the dark of Ash's room, realizing I have nowhere to be. Cato should be off by now, trekking with a few rebel guards to our southern camp. I have no more training to complete, though I'm sure Garrith would give me a one-on-one session if I asked nicely. He's likely tired of training the villagers who lack skill and would be happy for a more worthy sparring mate. Though I'm only more worthy of that role because he made me that way.

In the five years since I arrived in this small camp set in the depths of the Kaanos Mountains, I have yet to have a day off. How bizarre it feels to lie here with no agenda ahead, no one waiting on me, no training or tasks that need my attention. Of course it finally happens when I can barely enjoy it, when battle is looming over me like an ever present storm cloud of fucking doom.

I roll to my side, deciding that lying here is far better than finding something to do. I'm met with a sea of fiery red curls spread out along the violet sheets. Ash has one arm thrust under her pillow and one flung out toward me as she sleeps. Her legs sprawl beneath her, one bent slightly upward at her side. Her mouth is parted in what I can only imagine is a deep and peaceful sleep. I frown slightly, feeling a twinge of envy and trying to shove it back down. I wish I could sleep like that, instead of in fits and bursts, interrupted by violent nightmares and confusing visions.

There's a sour tang lingering in my mouth that brings back the troubling images of Nimai that visited me again during the night. I recall my eyes flying open and throwing the sheets off myself before lunging to the washroom, barely making it before I heaved the contents of my stomach, nausea churning through me from the jagged pain slicing every inch of my body.

Despite efforts to keep quiet and contain the interruption to myself, my convulsing body had betrayed me and woken Ash. She had run to my side with concern etched across her face, frantically trying to help in any way she could. But there was nothing she could do, it just took time for the pain to pass, for the visions to fade. I told Ash of the nightmares and the visions before, but I imagine actually seeing me in the throes of one was quite different than just hearing it. Ash stayed with me, stroking my hair, pulling it back from my face as sweat beaded across my forehead and fell in racing drops down my neck and back. She held me until the wracking sobs that came after had dwindled and I was ready for sleep once more.

Each night, the torment is worse than the last, the visions of Nimai more realistic. I try my hardest to focus on the images from last night, like Cato suggested. Nimai's too-thin body was thrown upon the floor, her legs curled under her, palms pressed into hard ground beneath.

Dirt. The ground had been packed dirt. Somewhere old, the smell damp and musty and laced with something awful. Something foul and old, something I'd never smelled before and never want to experience again. She was panting, her head down, a dark expanse of hair shielding her face.

There had been a noise as well. One that I'd concentrated on, but had been unable to discern. A scraping sound possibly? Or scratching? Whatever it was, my sister's head had lifted at the sound, her eyes widening to vast expanses of mossy green that clouded with fear and pain. Her screams still echo in my head, sharp and scouring the inside of my body like hundreds of blades.

I shudder at the memory so vivid and clear. But the ache has faded now and all I can do is wonder what on earth is happening to her. Are the images ones of the future or the present? Are they even real at all?

CHAPTER 24

Evander

After riding for a few hours, Quinn and I stop in a small grove to rest. The southwestern route we followed out of the mountains has been littered with signs of spring. Now, here in the grove, we are surrounded by giant trees beginning to bud with new leaves. Early flowers are bursting through the light layer of snow on the ground, forcing their way up to the crisp air to have the sun dance along their petals of light yellow and pale violet. A faint floral aroma wafts on the light breeze, and I pull in a long inhalation, breathing in the beautiful scent. It's a welcome change from the dry smell of winter and snow. The weather is more pleasant too and we've both stripped ourselves of the fur-lined cloaks needed back in the mountains.

The sun is high in the sky now, directly over the grove, indicating it's almost time for us to head back to the camp. It's been an uneventful trip which, while relieving, also means I've been lost to my own thoughts for much of it.

Now I sit, reclining against a fallen tree, the bark scratching against my back as I relax my body into the damp ground. Quinn mirrors me, setting his broad, muscular body beside mine. We haven't spoken much throughout the ride here, and what Quinn did say was only met by grunts and growls on my part. He gave me the space I needed to work through my emotions while we rode.

Though now that we rest, the spring breeze seems to whip the anger from my body and whisk it away. Something about being outdoors, being in the fresh air, has always agreed with me.

I thought about Bria the whole way, my mind constantly wandering back to her no matter how I fought to forget the shit Quinn told me. I'd wanted to find her, needed to find her, to ask her where she was last night and more importantly to ensure that boy keeps his hands off her. This physical reaction to jealousy is more than I was prepared to handle, the tightness it elicits in my chest only adding to the aching I already have for her.

Needing to rid myself of the thought, I focus on the sounds of the grove—small animals nestling or burrowing into their homes, or birds chattering and singing about. But I quickly find there are no such sounds. The grove is eerily quiet. Has it been this whole time? No, we would have noticed.

Something has shifted.

Quinn stiffens beside me, his hand quickly reaching for the hilt of the sword at his side. He notices the change as well. At nearly the same time, we launch ourselves from the ground, stances wide, shoulders broad. We stand back to back, watching the trees around us for threats. Something is out there.

As I scan the edge of the grove, a figure begins to emerge from the trees. It's far enough away that I hope it hasn't spied us yet. Because this beast? This is a creature of legends. Something I've only heard about in stories or read about in books. And I have no interest in coming face to face with it.

I push back on Quinn, grasping his arm, my fingers digging into his flesh. I feel as he rounds, coming up next to me.

"Oh *shit*," Quinn breathes, a whispered curse laced with genuine fear.

We back slowly and silently to the horses, one foot behind the other in a crouched shuffle. They've smelled it, their hooves lightly scraping the grass and stamping, discerning there's some threat out there, something they don't like. The beast is scanning the grove now and we have only a few more feet to go before we can gain access to the mounts and flee. As long as the damn horses don't take off without us. Though really, that fucking monster would be on us in a heartbeat if it wanted to. Horses or not, we wouldn't stand a chance.

From here, I can see the giant beak that curves into a vicious peak, capable of eviscerating both me and Quinn where we stand. The wings that splay out behind the beast are enormous—a monstrous display of tawny brown and saffron feathers that soar feet above its hulking form. It would be majestic were it not the most terrifying thing I've seen in all my years on this earth.

The animal turns its eagle head away, one massive, clawed foot poised midair. It hears something and thank the gods it isn't us. The wings above it twitch, flicks of muscle and feather as it tunes in to the noise, far too distant for either of us mere mortals to register. The talons on the enormous foot seem to grow, flexing forward with a menacing curl.

In an instant, the creature angles its robust back legs, covered in fur, and propels itself into the air. The beating of wings echoes off the trees surrounding us and sends a fresh breeze rippling through the grove. The beast disappears through the tops of the trees, quickly vanishing from sight. It takes off flying in the same direction we had been heading. Toward the Forsaken Woods.

Quinn breathes heavily beside me, gulping down air, and I become keenly aware I've been holding mine. As I heave air into my lungs, the smell from the breeze strikes me as familiar—with hints of rose and...lavender. Images of Bria come flooding back into my mind at the scent with such force I feel I may be knocked back.

"The Guardians." Quinn is stoic, his face rearranged to convey no emotion after the shock of seeing the beast. A soldier through and through.

I watch as he straightens, jamming his foot into a stirrup and swinging his body over the saddle. I'm still frozen, however. Still crouched and waiting to see if the monster will reappear.

"Ev?" Quinn is staring at me now, his hazel eyes serious, searching for clues as to why I'm not moving. "We need to go," he states firmly, turning his horse and forcing the heels of his boots into the stallion, urging it forward.

Willing my body to move, I follow suit, swinging up and over the horse. Kicking my heels down, the stallion takes off at a gallop, strong legs thrumming under me as the wind tears through my hear and stings my eyes. I turn at last to watch as the grove disappears from sight.

After maybe an hour of riding, Quinn decides we've put enough distance between the beast and us to slow our riding to a steady pace. He drags a hand down his face, rubbing his chin with a hard grip. The unease radiating off him is palpable.

I understand. We had all heard of the Guardians over the years, but no one had ever seen them. Or at least no one saw them and lived to tell the tale. Because not only were the Forsaken Woods forbidden due to the pretentious king and his rules against magic, none had set foot there since the Keeper fell. Honestly, the king and his priests *can't* step foot there, despite what they want people to believe. That magic should only be wielded by the worthy, those chosen by the mystical god they worship. The Guardians would devour them if they tried—better to let the people believe the place is outlawed than to think it's a place protected by ancient magic and the power of the old gods.

Better for Braddock if they don't know the truth.

Because those are the lies Braddock and his priests spread throughout Easthallow and to the far reaches of Azudora. He continues to allege that those selected by Vaohr are the only ones to possess power, but that the Keeper and his daughters had stolen what was rightfully his, as had the others—that they acquired the Forsaken Woods and its powers before hoarding it for themselves. Then they'd spread their stolen magic amongst the unworthy, a plague upon the people, having these powers that were not meant for them. They were tainted. And that now he's working to remove those with power from the kingdom to maintain safety among the people, to please Vaohr, and return that stolen power to the priests. Or so he claims.

Lies. Awful, degrading lies.

Most of the nobles believed these lies over the years. In fact, many throughout Azudora did, and were unaware of what happened in the depths of the castle. But the truth passed down through generations by those who had magic in their blood. Bloodlines like my own kept the stories alive, and those who aided in the rebellion knew the truth—that Braddock is a jaded and selfish man whose insolent family had been shamed by the Keeper. That he is greedy and manipulative. But his lies worked. So many turned against those with powers, my own father included. But now? Everything my mother told me as a child is coming true. And now I fear we won't be able to pass through to the Woods, that the Guardians won't let us in, just as they have not let anyone in for over a century.

"There are four Guardians, correct?" Quinn's rough voice splinters through my thoughts.

Quinn's family has no magic in their bloodline. His father and mother were normal people who befriended others with magic, stood up for them even when their lives were on the line. His older brother lives in the southern camp, became a rebel commander like Quinn but a year earlier, a year before the attack that drove us from our home. They aren't close, never were really. But the circumstances surrounding their childhood pushed them both into service, pushed them both to try and do something better with their lives.

His family was quite unlike my own, meaning he was not brought up hearing the stories every night before bed. He didn't go to sleep dreaming of the Keeper and the Guardians, of Lilith and Kiara and the magic that grew within the Woods. He didn't grow up hearing about the Current and the Incendiary and how beautiful the world was when magic and the gods thrived. Hearing faerie tales of magical places and legendary creatures.

But I had. From my mother. And he knows enough from me and his years in the rebel underground to understand what the beasts are.

"Yes," I respond, clearing my throat of the sudden lump that formed along with the image of my mother. "One to each direction of the compass. They prowl the areas surrounding the Woods to protect it. They have ever since the Keeper was killed and Lilith and Kiara fled." I'm recounting the stories, remembering pictures of the Guardians in the books my mother read to me, always when my father was preoccupied with his duties to the earl.

"Legend says they are gryphons—fierce predators that will kill to protect what they are bound to," I finish, rubbing my eyes with callused fingers. But the effort does nothing to remove the images of the creature, half lion and half eagle, with a wingspan wider than the length of my horse. "They have keen sight. We were lucky the beast heard something other than us."

Quinn grunts in response. "I remember the pictures from your books, even if it was years ago. But seeing it before us...prowling through that grove..." His words taper off and I catch the chill he shakes off, the one that crept up his spine at the thought of the animal.

We narrowly escaped the clutches of the beast —this time. What would happen if we came across it again, or one of its brethren who stalks the areas surrounding the Woods? From what the stories says of its location, we were still a day's ride or so from the mystical forest when we happened upon the grove. Though I suppose, with wings, the Guardians could survey a wide expanse of surrounding land. So, we should not be quite so shocked to have witnessed it out there. But still...something about it had seemed off.

My head bobs in understanding. "We should talk to the captain when we get back. Maybe she has some insight as to how we can pass, something her and Cato discussed."

There isn't much in this world that causes fear to crackle through my veins like ice and set me on edge like this. But the knowledge that this mythical creature has one job and one job only, is enough to strike fear into me now. That job is to protect the Forsaken Woods, to protect the magic that grows within the area, the home of the gods.

Will it let us pass when we arrive, or will it decide to gouge us all with those curved black talons? Will it rip our insides from us as it tears that blade-like beak through our bodies? I already know it will let Bria in, she's destined to go there, the home of her magic. But will it let me and Quinn? Will it let Silas? Neither Quinn nor I possess any magic, despite my mother's power. I was never blessed —or cursed, rather — with a gift. This may be a death sentence for us all.

CHAPTER 25

Bria

I can't recall when I was last so at peace. Not in a long time. Definitely not since I came of age, that's for damn sure. Not since I started hiding my gifts and then went into hiding myself. It's odd and freeing at the same time to feel this way, even though I know it can't last. It won't last.

Ash joined me for a hike up one of the nearby mountains this morning. She packed a light lunch filled with the usual foods: heavily salted meats, fresh cheeses from the goats we kept in the pastures, and some of the last apples that fell before the snow. Though to be fair, they are getting a bit nasty despite being kept in the cold ass cellar storeroom. As I lie back on the blanket Ash stowed away in the bag, I snuggle fully into the warm fleecy material.

From here, I can see the expanse of the sky. More blue than gray today. Spring is coming. I can smell the ripening of the earth as I breathe, trying to take it all in, to remember all the sights, and sounds, and smells—the billowing clouds that flow past and the tips of the black Kaanos Mountains, peaked with glimmering white snow.

The mountains look foreboding from the village below, but once you're in them, they transform. Become majestic. Though we traveled only partially up one of the smaller mountains, the view is breathtaking.

It would have taken the better part of the day for a hike to the summit, and I am positive Ash would not tolerate the required attire of leggings and a tunic for that long.

The mountain air has a chill to it, and I pull the thick cloak tighter around me, warding off the cool. The reaches of winter have not relinquished their tight grip on the mountains just yet, despite the early kiss of spring that touches the earth around us.

Ash flops her body to the ground in a heap next to me.

"Remind me once again why we must exert ourselves for your pleasure?" She speaks with feigned irritation but the heavy breathing she's exhibiting betrays her real and true exhaustion.

I'm used to hiking and running the trails in and around the mountains, so it causes me no distress to come up here. But Ash is not in quite the same shape. Not that any of the men ever mind. She is naturally perfect with envious curves that draw a man's eye to all the right places. I, on the other hand, am now swathed in lean muscle. My thighs and calves can easily carry me up the mountain and my arms can shove a dagger clean through a man's skull. But I'm not devoid of curves, I have plenty of them on my small frame —they're just never on display the way Ash likes hers to be.

Given my lot in life, I've attempted to attract little attention while here in the camp, hiding my body in tunics and leggings instead of putting it out there in the open.

"I just wanted to see the beauty of it once more," I say, a quiet confession regarding the thoughts swirling in my head.

"Masochist," teases Ash playfully.

A hearty laugh falls from my lips in response.

"What exactly do you think is going to happen when you and Nimai reunite?" Ash is stretched out beside me, hands folded behind her head, hair wild around her.

I sigh heavily, not sure I want to think of it right now. Not with this beauty all around me. But my fate impacts Ash as well, and if it's on her mind, I'll sate her curiosity.

"If Cato is right, then the Woods will recognize us as the descendants of Lilith and Kiara. It's supposed to strengthen us, allowing full access to our potential, our powers. And then the prophecy can be fulfilled." I swallow before continuing. "I'm not sure what will happen from there. I assume we will plan and start the journey to meet with the rebel forces outside of Castle Eccleston."

Ash sets her rouge-tinted lips in a firm line. "Right away?" she queries.

I nod. "I don't think Helara wants to wait. It's been long enough, and the king continues to...*collect* people like me."

"Do you think you'll be able to do it? To take him down for good?" I realize that though my own personal destiny may be unfortunate, if Nimai and I fail, the destiny of the rest of the Kingdom of Azudora— the rest of the world as we know it, would be just as bleak.

I bite my lip, chewing on the smooth skin inside. "I hope so," I answer, nervousness apparent in my tone.

Ashbel reaches a hand out to grasp mine. She holds tight, her fingers intertwining with mine, and squeezes. "Me too."

We stay like that for some time, silently watching the clouds overhead while we relax and pick at the food. I listen to the birds singing in the evergreen trees that thrive in the black mountains. It makes me blissfully happy to spend this time with Ash and I don't want to leave the quiet of the mountain landing when the sun starts to set.

"We should probably get going," I finally mutter, the words shattering the surrounding silence.

Ashbel rises to her feet, brushing away the pine needles that had gathered around the ankles of her leggings, sticking to the top of her worn leather boots. I stare at her, the way the fading sun sets her hair alight. My chest tightens and I once again feel the stinging in my eyes. I cannot fall apart, not yet. There's still too much for me to do. But I save that image of her, tucking it away in my mind, knowing it may be one of the last moments we spend together.

I leap to my feet, sniffing and trying to hold back tears. Instead, I busy myself, I shake out the blanket before folding it neatly and stuffing it back into the pack we brought, then turn to look at Ash, whose face is also beginning to fall. She feels it too.

"Drinks?" I ask with a raised brow, hoping to distract her before either of us becomes too emotional.

"Oh, gods, yes!" she exclaims.

Her face breaks out in a gleaming smile of white pearl and emerald. I truly hope she finds happiness in this life. So far, it hasn't been kind to her. An only child now, she lost her father and younger sister when we were teenagers to a terrible illness that struck our town of Elwyn. Her mother then perished in the attack on my father's estate, along with my father and quite a few others who resided there. Some were killed, others taken.

Though not of blood, Ash is my sister, and I love her fiercely. I know in this moment that I will do whatever it takes to make King Braddock fall. I will make it so that Ash and the others can lead normal lives. Lives where they aren't isolated in a remote mountain village, forced to live as unworthy outcasts. Somewhere Ash can wear her dresses and raise a family of her own, where Quinn can fight in a real army. Where Evander can find a love that he deserves.

CHAPTER 26

Evander

Upon returning to the camp, we stable the horses and quickly make our way to find Helara. She's overseeing the training of a few promising villagers. Standing beside Garrith, her back is straight in her leather armor, charcoal hair piled atop her head. She is striking in all black against the stark white of the snow surrounding her. The fearless rebel queen.

I let Quinn approach first, bowing his head in acknowledgment of our captain. He stands to the side, one hand on the hilt of his sword, the other tucked behind his back, feet wide as he inspects the training. I take up a spot next to him and wait.

The captain breaks her gaze away from the new recruits. "You should release them, Garrith. It has been a long day and they have plenty of those ahead of them."

Garrith grunts in approval before stalking toward the villagers. His back is hunched as he moves away from the group. Helara turns toward us then, once Garrith is out of earshot.

"Commanders?" she says, her voice lilting up at the question. She is decked out in her midnight black leathers, a sword on either hip. Her bandolier stretches tight across her chest and is crowded with newly polished and sharpened blades. She's ready for the upcoming battle. Ready to face the king again.

Quinn takes a hushed and hurried tone, visibly worried that someone will overhear what he has to say, though no one is close enough for eavesdropping.

"We saw a Guardian," he tells her, his face remaining blank while he stares out at the villagers.

Something sparks in her dark eyes—fear, perhaps. Not once has this woman shown fear, not that I know of. Even at the capital they spoke of her ferocity. Though it was often followed quickly by how she fled. Fled to save her people, fled to rise again, fled from the death and destruction the king wrought upon this world.

She looks around as she speaks and even with no one nearby, she appears wary. This close to the end, this close to getting everything she wants, she should be wary. Letting down your guard is too easy when victory seems in your reach.

"Let's speak of this in private," she remarks before setting off for the library. It's probable there will be few people still out and about as dinner is nearing. We stride through the doors and follow our captain to a back corner of the main room. She stands away from the flickering fire that pushes forth a wall of heat throughout the room. Instead, she tucks herself amidst the shadows cast from the sconces on the wall, her dark features barely readable.

There doesn't appear to be anyone in the library as far as I can tell. And if there is, we won't be seen or overheard in this location. There's a musty scent wafting off the books that mingles with the smoky ash of the fire as we stand huddled together, a mass of black and brown leather decorated with blades amidst an armory of tomes.

She waits a few beats before speaking. I can tell, despite the shadows, that she's listening—tuning her ears in to the sounds of the old building around us. Though we didn't witness anyone as we entered, she is checking to be sure. I stop to listen as well, holding my breath.

The fire crackles, the logs within hissing and making short snapping sounds. But there is no whisper of flipping pages, no creaking of old wooden chairs, no footsteps. We are truly alone.

When she is satisfied of that fact, she straightens her back, pulling herself up to that full regal height. She is a tall woman, and broad through her shoulders. *Definitely built to be a fighter*, I think as I look at my captain—or where my captain should be. I can barely see her over here in the dark corner.

"You saw a Guardian?" she presses, her voice sharp.

I decide to take the lead and answer, well aware I know more about this topic than my friend. "Yes. We happened upon it in a small grove about a day's travel from the Woods."

"And...you're both here." She's quiet, pondering how this is possible. "You're alive."

A chuckle escapes my throat despite my attempt to remain professional. "It appears that way, yes."

"Strange," she responds, shifting in her stance. The unease is clear in the way she stands, the way she begins to fidget with the hilt of her sword, absentmindedly picking at the worn leather bound around it. I can hear her nails scratching the surface and know the reaction is odd for her. She's always composed, consistently hiding her emotions without wavering.

Quinn crosses his arms over his chest, narrowing his eyes at the captain in the dark, noticing the reaction as well.

But I'm too curious to let her statement go. "Strange that it let us live?" I clarify. "I'm fairly certain it didn't see us before it was led away by a noise in the distance."

I can feel her dark stare poring over me, feel it without seeing her eyes. "Yes, but stranger so that it was out so far from the Woods." I hear her boots shift on the floor before she continues. "It shouldn't be so far. And it saw you, absolutely it did. But there was a reason it was there, and a reason it left you two alone."

Quinn speaks then, his voice low and gruff. "Will it let us pass?"

Her nails are tapping rapidly along the hilt now. All her fidgeting is beginning to make me nervous. She doesn't have the answers. Not this time. And it's pushing her out of her comfort zone.

"It should. Or rather, it *will* let Bria pass and it might allow Silas. There's a chance the two of you will be let in, or a chance you will have to stay back. But it won't attack you. You present no threat to the

Guardians. And delivering Bria back to the Woods should alleviate any instinct it has to protect the area," she explains.

At least that satiates my concern. For now. But not my curiosity about other things.

"If the Guardians are real, what about the other legends?" I ask, well aware that Helara knows a great deal about the days of old, when magic reigned over the world.

"It's hard to say," she replies, and when she speaks, stories of the Ancients, nymphs, and dragons, all swirl in my head.

"But it's possible," I add hopefully, desperately wanting to know how much truly exists in the magical home of the gods.

"Yes, it's possible," she responds softly before turning on her heel and striding to the door.

We follow quietly behind as she leaves the library, but when the captain points herself toward the inn, I peel off and head away.

"Do you plan on telling me about the other legends you and the captain were talking about?" Quinn asks as he steps beside me, the snow crunching loudly as he speeds up to match my brisk pace.

"At some point. But right now, I need a drink."

"I believe I offered that as an option last night and you refused. Glad to see you've come to your senses." I know Quinn is just giving me shit for brooding all night—and this morning, for that matter. But I don't care. I need to get my mind off everything—the Guardians, whatever else lurks in the Woods, Bria...*Silas*.

CHAPTER 27

Evander

When we enter the pub that night, the damp warm air within greets me. It's a nice change of pace from the cold, though the air is thick from all the people. The pub is thrumming tonight. It appears many of the new arrivals are drinkers and enjoy a bit of a party. A few of them have even come prepared with instruments and are playing music in the back corner by the bar.

Relief washes over me as I observe that Silas does not appear to be among the group of villagers. There are a few young women that seem to catch sight of us as we enter, and I vaguely recognize them as girls from the village we rescued. Quinn tends to draw attention when he walks into a room. He's only a few inches taller than me, but that puts him around six foot three and he is all muscle. Bulging biceps stick out from the tunic that clings tight to his body. His shoulder-length ebony hair is pulled partially into a knot, thin pieces framing his face and others falling about his shoulders. His eyes gleam a rich honey color in the middle, rimmed with bright green. *Apparently, all that masculine energy is attractive to some women*, I think.

Though, honestly, I hope one of them approaches Quinn and that maybe tonight he'll take up the offer. At times he gets so encompassed in his work, so stuck on the missions and his purpose, that he forgets to enjoy himself. He can be quite...rigid. It's not like he's celibate or anything, but he stays quiet about it. He never talks to me much about any of them. Maybe if he finds someone tonight, spends some quality time with a woman, it will get him off my back.

I start toward the bar to grab drinks as Quinn filters through the others to find us a space to sit. Taking the mugs from the barmaid, I weave my way toward the front of the pub, to a table by the windows, frowning as I notice it's the same table —the one we had the last time we were all here, and my mind immediately shifts to Bria. Pushing a frothing mug of ale toward Quinn, I drop heavily into the seat across from him.

The group of women from the village are still turned toward us, I notice. One of them appears to be eyeing me from across the room so I lock eyes with her and tilt my head cordially, raising the glass to my lips in greeting. The cool foam hits them, and I watch a giggle spread between the young ladies. They must be only nineteen or twenty and all three are pretty, though there's nothing special about them. Nothing noticeable or memorable. No flames of sapphire and cobalt raging in their eyes, no flowing locks of precious metal or glint of otherworldly energy hiding beneath their skin.

Would approaching one of them help to get my mind off Bria? To move on from the brooding and find someone to heal the pain I feel every time I think of her? Even the idea of it brings a scowl to my face. I don't want anyone but her. I don't care about the pain it causes, either. I'll suffer every day if it means being with her.

Quinn catches sight of the scowl and raises a brow. "Are you upset that a group of women are ogling you? Doesn't seem like something to be concerned about, in my opinion."

I let out a short laugh. "I'm not sure it's me they are eyeing."

At that, Quinn relaxes back in the chair and kicks his legs out. He pulls the strands of his hair back from his face before crossing his arms comfortably over his chest.

"Might the almighty warrior be looking for a companion tonight?" I tease, the corner of my lip pulling up into a smirk.

But a fierce glare meets me, narrowed eyes that glint with humor. Just barely.

"We have a day and a half travel to the Forsaken Woods, then gods know how long we will spend there and on the travel to Castle Eccleston. I think we should *both* be looking for a companion before what lies ahead of us." He pauses. "Might be the last time, Ev."

I shrug. I can't deny that he has a point, and when I look up, two of the women have pulled away from their group and are sauntering toward us. They both sport mousy brown hair, one with long curls, the other with an elaborate twist along the back of her neck. They wear common dresses, tight bodices tipped with lace, breasts swelling above them and skirts billowing below.

Taking another swig of the drink, I glance toward Quinn. "Here comes your companion now. Take your pick. Or better yet, take them both and leave me the hell out of it," I say, trailing off as the women sidle up to the table.

The curly-haired one is all over Quinn. She giggles like a young schoolgirl and eats up all of his stories of patrols as she sits next to him, perched on the edge of her chair, ready to climb on top of him at a moment's notice. The other decides it's a good idea to take the seat next to me, to my dismay. I don't know if she's there because she finds me attractive or if she's there because her friend wanted to approach Quinn, but either way, her presence is irritating.

Twisty-hair coos and touches her face while Quinn speaks, and she flicks her eyes to me often, but I pay her no mind. I'm not trying to be rude to the girl, but she has nothing of interest to say. Mostly, she nods in agreement with her friend. I'm positive the curly-haired girl is named Rosalind, but I stop paying much attention to the one next to me. Delilah maybe? It doesn't matter what her name is. I don't intend to remember it anyway.

My thoughts drift from the conversation of the group, not that there's much of note being said. Mostly I'm watching Rosalind throw herself on the stoic Quinn, who is pleasant to her, though I can see a glint in those hazel eyes. He'll be leaving with her tonight, and I catch myself smiling at the thought of it. At least he will be tolerable tomorrow if he spends his night with dear, sweet Rosalind.

A hand on my knee snaps me out of the thought. I look down to see twisty-hair's hand, the dimwitted Delilah or whatever the fuck her name is. *Her* hand is on my knee and creeping upward. She gazes at me from beneath lowered lashes, batting them in a flirtatious gesture. *This girl has some gall*, I think.

I level my stare on her. Her eyes are a light brown, the color of creamed coffee. She isn't terrible to look at. No, this girl is pretty enough even if she has the conversation skills of a brick fucking wall. But she doesn't interest me in the least. I want fire and flames. I want pain and agony. I want Bria.

Eyes locked, the girl begins to creep her fingers up my thigh, sliding her hand gracefully along the inner seam of my trousers. I'm in utter shock, fairly positive I've done nothing to indicate any interest in her, but she's proving now that she is quite interested in me. I'm about to say so to the girl, to try and let her down easy, when I feel a prickling along the back of my neck. Pins and needles creep up my spine and my eyes shoot to the door.

Just inside the threshold is Bria. And I can tell from where she stands, she is getting an eyeful of my situation. And the hand along the inside of my thigh.

I snag her gaze and the blue fire smoldering inside. She purses her lips and shoves her way toward the bar. Ash is behind her, smirking at me. *Fuck*. I jump up out of the seat, shaking the girl's hand from my leg. She lets out a cry in protest at the harshness of it, but I pay her no mind. The girl can go find someone else's leg to fondle, some other idiot to spend her night with.

Bria had seen the girl and likely assumed what was happening. I can't blame her for that, but I want to explain that it wasn't what she thinks. As I round a group of people, they come into view —Bria and Ash—huddled in the corner together, drinks in hand.

She's leaning against the wall behind her, and Ash is stuck to her side. Her hair is down, not in the normal braid that she wears regularly around the camp. It falls in luxurious waves over her shoulders, glittering strands of gold. It always has those waves to it when she takes it out of her braid, just another detail about this girl I shouldn't be so aware of. She flicks her cobalt eyes in my direction and instantly my stomach tightens at her beauty. My body ignites more in one angry glance from her than anything that twit of a girl at the table could do—including sliding her hand up my thigh.

Her lips straighten as she watches me, holding my stare. There's something there, something in her face that she's trying to hide with the flat look she throws my way. I can't quite place it, but it feels a lot like sadness. And that's the last thing I want to be responsible for when it comes to her.

"Bria, I—" I start, but Ash cuts me off before I can get the words past my lips. Just my luck to fall for a girl with a bulldog for a best friend.

"Oh, Ev, you looked busy over there. I hope you didn't leave that girl hanging just because we waltzed in," she croons, but the look on her face is sinister and her green eyes glint with menace. "She looked like she had her hands full," she finishes, her words biting.

Heat rises into my face, burning with her remarks. I'm embarrassed and ashamed that Bria saw what that girl was doing, that had she walked in a moment later, she would have seen a very different picture.

"I have no interest in that girl," I throw back at Ash, noticing the entire time that Bria's eyes have not left me.

Bria responds, quiet but firm. "Ev, you have nothing to explain to either of us. Just go enjoy yourself." She smiles at me, but it doesn't meet her eyes.

I know I should listen to her and leave, to allow the women to have a night of peace. But I can't tear my gaze away from hers. I want to pull her outside, away from the reaches of Ash's anger, and explain everything to her. To wipe the sadness from her and get back that look of desire that was all-consuming when I kissed her.

But as I open my mouth to speak, her gaze finally leaves mine. She glimpses something behind me, and her eyes brighten, her face softening. She somehow becomes more beautiful and radiant than she already is.

I turn to see what could have caused the shift in her and my breath stalls in my chest.

CHAPTER 28

Bria

Wanting Evander to be happy and having to witness it are two very different things. I'll be gone soon though, and will no longer have to sit on the sidelines and watch as some silly, indiscreet girl shoves her breasts at him and caresses the inside of his thigh. I grip my lips together to keep from showing my true feelings and attempt to brush it off instead.

Ev saw my reaction to the girl and was attempting to explain. But there's nothing to explain to me. He isn't *mine*. He owes me nothing. One kiss doesn't mean he's tied to me in any way. I'm contemplating how to make that more clear to him because his gaze is heavy, weighing on me, when a pulse strikes low in my belly.

That energy center within me coils then unfurls, like a cat waking up from a long slumber. I search and scan the area behind Evander to see what could be doing this, what could be around that would pull and tug at me like this. And then I see him.

Silas. He's standing behind Evander, his eyes glued to me. That icy blue stare makes me shudder, but not in fear. No. It's because he sees me, sees into my soul, and I can feel it in the way he looks at me.

I can do nothing but stare, enthralled as he brushes past Evander without a sideways glance and comes to stand in front of me, effectively stepping between Ev and me. He grabs my hand, pressing his fingers into mine, concern gripping his features.

"Are you hurt? What happened?" he asks, lifting a hand to brush my cheek, ensuring I'm alright. His fingers are warm, unnaturally warm, heated like my own get when my magic is flowing.

I'm still not sure how any of this works. Cato had explained little about this to either of us before he left. I knew those with magic would be drawn to my sister and me. That they would be connected to us through their gifts. That there would be a loyalty there, and a link, almost binding us together. Those with powers can become bound to the descendants of Lilith and Kiara because we have the blood of the gods. And they would go to their graves defending us. But he had said the connection between Silas and I was strong, something he noticed when I pulled energy from him. He sensed my emotions yesterday and now, when I'm fighting overwhelming anger and jealousy, he registered something was wrong and came to me.

"I-I'm fine," I lie, looking at him while he holds my hand in his own. My eyes flick to Evander without thinking, then quickly back to Silas. Though the glance is fleeting, I see the rage blooming in Evander's eyes, the seething look he sets on Silas.

Silas also notices the shift in my attention and turns to look at Ev, as if he were just noticing him, despite passing the man when he entered the room. His eyes narrow on Ev and his jaw hardens, clearly discerning where my emotional storm is coming from. But the last thing I need is for Silas to open those feelings up to Evander, for Ev to understand what I feel for him. No, that is better left unsaid after tonight.

Thinking fast, I pull Silas by the hand, breaking his hardened gaze on Evander. I tug him toward Ash, whose eyes are wide, brows raised in wonder at the odd interaction she just beheld. I imagine it's quite intriguing for Ash to witness the magical link between us, especially when I struggled so hard to convey it.

The glance I spare back to Evander proves to tighten my chest further, twisting my heart as he stares at my hand—the hand that is still wrapped around Silas's, his fingers now intertwined with mine. I register the heat rising into his face once again, but not from embarrassment this time. This time it's fury that fills him, given away by the tight line of his jaw, the flexing muscles that twitch in his neck. When he lifts those eyes from our hands to me, I want to drop Silas's hand and run to him, begging for forgiveness. But I hold my ground. *I've done nothing wrong,* I remind myself.

He grits his teeth and begins to speak. "Quinn mentioned you two were...connected," he seethes, the words lashing out at me like a slap.

I take a steadying breath and release Silas's hand as I turn my body to fully face Evander.

"Yes, it's complicated," I start, prepared to explain it to him, but not here with so many eyes on us. So many ears that might be listening. The others in the camp don't know of my gifts or connection to the prophecy. And having Silas and Evander make a scene right now is not going to help with keeping that secret for long.

The harsh scoff that escapes his lips wounds me, digging that hurt deeper.

"It doesn't look too complicated from here." His lips raise in a sneer as he watches us, a cold look he's never cast at me before this moment.

Silas moves behind me, placing a hand on my lower back, and Evander's eyes track the movement. His hand is warm as his fingers press into the light fabric of the tunic. I feel my energy pulsing from his magic, from his touch. Not only could I strengthen him, but he can strengthen me, just with his presence. Cato said as much, and even without pulling the magical energy from him, I can feel it.

I half expect Ev to throw a dagger from his bandolier at Silas when he touches my back. His eyes bulge, and his nostrils flare with the too-familiar gesture he initiates. Despite my need to explain, to make him understand, I'm wary of the crowd and remain silent.

"Ev." Quinn is standing a few feet away now, having made his way across the crowded room to us. He's been watching the entire interaction and must have had a similar thought to my own. None of us needs to attract any unwanted attention. Not when we are so close to fulfilling the prophecy.

Evander's shoulders tense as he hears his friend speak from behind him, his whole body visibly straining against the fury building in his blood. And when Quinn reaches out to touch his shoulder, Evander shakes him off, shoving through the warrior toward the door.

Quinn focuses back on me from where he stands. He takes in my stance and Silas's behind me, then blows out a loud breath and shakes his head. I make a move to step forward, to follow Ev, but Quinn steps in front of me, blocking my path to the door.

"Don't," he warns, looking down at me from his immense height. "You need to let him cool off."

Quinn leaves me then, stalking back to the table with the girls and sitting down next to the curly-haired one. The one who was all over him when we entered the pub. The other sets a glare on me and I stare back, feeling the heat of flames sparking in my eyes. Silas's hand presses into my back as he slides closer. My eyes stay fixed on the girl, heat churning, flooding my senses and threatening to pour out of me. She shudders, a visible shockwave running through her body before she casts her eyes quickly down, averting her gaze from the intensity of mine.

"You need to calm down before someone notices. What's wrong now?" Silas questions with concern.

"Nothing." The lie is obvious, but I don't care. Silas will recognize it's a lie no matter what I do or say right now. He can feel the anger swirling through me.

Quinn turns to narrows his eyes at me, his lips forming a tight, straight line, silently telling me to back off when he sees the reaction of the girl across the table from him. The curly-haired one resumes her groping of him, running her hands down his chest and staring at him while she giggles. Even as he turns back to his date, I can tell he's displeased with my reaction, and clearly bothered by Silas.

But not the way Ev had been. There was hurt behind that rage. And I am all too aware that I was the source of that hurt—the exact pain I'd tried to avoid this whole time with anyone, but especially with him. It was why I'd avoided him for days when I'd sensed my feelings for him were growing. And now, he hadn't taken the time to understand. He had just judged what he saw.

Though, to be fair to him, I know what Silas and I look like to the unknowing. More like lovers than friends. Something in my body is drawn to him as he is to me. I feel as though he is a part of me, and perhaps he is now that we are connected. The link that formed when he allowed me to take his energy was powerful. And that conversation is not one I am willing to have in the pub, with all these ears and eyes tuned in to us.

Silas is close to me still, the warmth from his hand spreading along my back and easing the tension that has coiled within my muscles.

"When you're in pain, or angry like this...something happens," he says behind me, his breath warm across my neck. He's confirming the assumptions I already have as to why he showed up in the pub in the first place. "I get—" He stops without finishing the sentence. But I already know what he was about to say.

"Visions," I whisper, turning to face him. His hand slowly falls from my back when I spin toward him, so close I can feel his breath on my face now as he sighs heavily. He feels so familiar to me, and his presence is comforting, reassuring. By the look on his face, I know he feels the same. He smiles at me, his pale blue eyes glowing. He has the faintest dimples on each side of his face. They make him look even more hand-some, more genuine and beautiful.

"Yes," he agrees. "I can feel your anger, your pain. And I can see where you are if I focus hard enough."

For years I had been alone with my magic, a powerful being hiding among a sea of normal people, trying to fit in and remain unnoticed. Having someone to connect with now feels unbelievable, as if I'm home when I'm near him, and it makes me wonder how it will feel to be around Nimai, my mother, and others with magic. Will it be like this with everyone?

Even though I know what it must look like to Ev, this is not a romantic attraction. This is a physical response to his magic. It's not that he isn't extremely handsome, but this is different. We are linked by our gifts, and he is devoted to me. It's strange, I can admit that to myself. But somehow, it also feels right. Something in us calls to one another, an ancient fire rumbling inside.

Though it does appear Silas is more in tune with the visions than I am, more in tune with all of it—and is accepting the changes better than

I am. I'm still seeking more information from those visions, more clues as to what's happening with Nimai.

If Silas is able to feel my anger and pain, if that creates visions for him when I'm feeling it, then Nimai...I suck in a sharp breath at the realization. The pain I've been feeling *is* Nimai's pain. They aren't just dreams or visions of some possible reality. If Silas felt the connection to me in that very moment as it happened, then something is happening in the here and now with my sister.

But as far as I know, Nimai is tucked away in the southern camp awaiting her birthday in a few days. So what could her pain even be from? The next vision that comes, I will concentrate all my effort on finding out what it is. I have to.

I try to shake off the thought, visibly shaking my head as I do so. When I glance up, I'm met with emerald eyes darting between me and Silas. Ash is grinning ear to ear as she stands to the side, behind him.

"What?" I snap.

Silas stiffens at the coldness of my tone. His hand reaches back out for me, curling around my waist protectively as I stand facing him. It causes a twinge of guilt to pull at me. The lack of control over my emotions tonight is causing chaos for him. It isn't fair and I need to get a handle on myself.

But Ash is unphased by the sharp response. No surprise there.

"That was...intense. That's all," she offers, her tone cool and even. Silas turns toward her finally, his hand still resting on my waist.

I tilt my head to watch Silas fully take in Ashbel. He had been so intent on protecting me when he arrived that he was unaware of her presence, just as he was unaware of Evander. *That's a first*, I think, for any man to *not* notice Ash the second they walk into a room.

But there it is. He looks almost awestruck and I have to hold back a laugh at the enchanted look on his face.

"Ash, *this* is Silas," I say, introducing the two.

Ash makes an amused sound. "I gathered that." She waves a hand between the two of us, her eyes focusing on his hand as it lies gently on my waist. Gentle but possessive, I note.

Silas tips his head in recognition of the introduction. His eyes are roaming over her, taking in every inch of Ash, every curve—from her flaming curls, to the bright green of her eyes, the smattering of gorgeous freckles across her nose and cheeks, to her naturally plush and rouge-tinted lips. I feel his hand drop from where it sits along my hip, and I try to contain my smile but am unsuccessful. A smirk brims on my lips, turning the corners of my mouth up at the sight. Ash notices his roving gaze as well and pops her hip out, showing off the glorious curves. She obviously finds him attractive, who wouldn't?

For a moment, I entertain the reservation niggling at the back of my head. I wonder if it may not be the best plan to leave Ash and Silas here together, given the way they are looking at one another. But it also seems that no matter the hold Ash has on him physically, he will follow me into battle. And that's the part that matters for me. That he remains loyal to me in that sense.

So let them have their fun, I think, coming to terms with what is undeniable attraction between the two. Instead, I check in on Quinn, turning to see what he's up to across the room. He has pulled the curly-haired girl into his lap and his head appears to be buried somewhere in her thick hair. I cringe inwardly, hoping they leave soon to finish *that* in private. It's unlike Quinn to be so bold in public. Maybe the events of the last week have gotten to him more than I thought.

At least the other girl is gone. And it does mean that Quinn is preoccupied, leaving me a window of opportunity to go see Ev. I just hope that wretch of a girl hasn't thought to go find him as well.

"Hey," I say, looking between Silas and Ash, but they barely register my existence. "I'm going to head back to my room. I'm getting tired."

At that, Silas jerks his head back to me. *Shit*. Has he sensed something else from me?

"Let me know if you need anything. Anything at all, Bria," he responds quietly, icy eyes focused on me once more.

Relief hits me when he shows no indication of any more problems. So far, it seems anger and pain are what he senses from me, and I hope to keep it that way. I have no need for all my emotions to play out in his mind.

Ash turns to face me, her eyes gentle now, understanding. She knows I'm not headed back to my room. But she also isn't about to say anything, either. Or stop me, for that matter.

So, I slip out the door of the pub and wrap my cloak around myself at the harsh bite of the night air. The fur lining fights the cold trying to creep into my skin, though heat still radiates through me from Silas's touch. Quinn is nestled into the woman at the table by the window, but I yank the hood up, hiding my face, just in case he decides to look up toward the dark night.

Evander

I stomp through the crisp snow, icy now in the night chill, and the snapping sound rings in my ears. Blinded by my rage, I stormed out of the inn, shoving through Quinn in the process and not even knowing where I was headed. I still don't really know.

Maybe I should go to the stables. Take out a stallion and ride off into the night. I could be gone before anyone was the wiser. Be rid of this place, of the prophecy and of her. There are plenty of small towns aligned with the rebels who would take me in. But even the thought of leaving her, of never seeing her again, causes me anguish. It's foolish. I'm a commander in the rebel army, and I have a job to do. Leaving would be abandoning that job. And tomorrow my role will require me to spend a day and a half with her. And with Silas.

My stomach flips and then knots when I recall Silas and Bria—his hand on her back, how close he stood to her. And her face. Her face had shown with a brilliance I've never seen when Silas touched her. She had vibrated with energy, it had pulsed from her, and I couldn't have been the only one to notice. So much magic flowed between them.

I grimace at the images and set my sights on the inn. No matter what I feel right now, the right decision is to go to bed. Even if I have to drink myself into oblivion to make that happen. I can sleep it off and deal with whatever comes in the morning.

My mind has other plans, and I can't stop the racing thoughts. Did the other night mean nothing to her? I understand we shared only a few kisses, but it felt like so much more. It had felt like things were building between us—a connection that I've never experienced with anyone else. I had stayed with her that night, happy to just be in her presence, to smell her and touch her and taste her.

A snarl escapes me as I reach the door to the inn, thinking about how foolish I was and how I should have heeded Quinn's warnings. My fist slams into the hard wood, splintering it with the impact. Knuckles bursting open, a fine spray of blood mists the night air and falls to the snow beneath me. I lean my head against the door, feeling the cool surface beneath my skin, and breathe. Better the door than Silas's face. I can't bear the thought of how she would look at me if I pummel the boy. If she only knew how many noses I had crushed, how many cheekbones I had broken over the years for her.

I'm not sure how long I stand there, just waiting until my breathing evens out. It's long enough that the blood on my hand is beginning to clot, the rivulets running down my arm drying in the frigid breeze.

Eventually, I force myself into the cozy atmosphere of the inn, quiet and still. I make my way up to my room, determined to wash away the memory of tonight.

By any means necessary.

CHAPTER 30

Bria

))))○((((

Staying hidden within the warm hood of the cloak, I crunch my way back to the inn through the ice and snow, thinking of what to say, what to do when I find him. I have no idea if Evander went back there or not. For all I know, he could have met back up with that girl. She mysteriously disappeared shortly after him. Some severe form of jealously rears its ugly head inside me at the memory of her possessive hand creeping up on him, acting as if she *owned* him.

I close my eyes, willing the image to leave and never return. Because even though I had seen hurt in Evander's eyes tonight, even though I caused it, I also experienced it myself. Despite trying so hard not to, I am falling for him. And no part of me knows what to do about it. Nothing is making sense anymore.

By the time I make it back to the inn though, my mind is made up. I will go to him, explain what is happening with Silas, with the magic. I can't bear to travel a day and a half with him like this, to witness that coldness in his eyes, to have Quinn look at me the way he did tonight. Whether it's the right choice or not, I don't care. I will be truthful. Because at this point, I have nothing left to lose.

Nearing his room, I notice the uneasy twisting in my stomach resume. I push forward toward the end of the hall and stop at his door.

The sconce at the back wall is out, and I lay my hands on the old wood, palms flat, inhaling before I lift my hand to knock lightly.

The door swings open before me, far faster than I anticipate. He is swathed in shadows from the dim light of the room. His hair is in disarray, and it looks as if he has been running his hands through it, tugging it out of place. The tunic is gone, and the tanned skin of his chest is magnificent in the low light. I can see the thick pink scar running down his arm and I remember how soft that skin had been beneath my fingers the other night.

Shit. Stop thinking like that and concentrate, I tell myself, forcing my gaze to lift from his chiseled body to search his face. His jaw is tight, and a long line of tense muscles run down his neck to his shoulders. He stands in the doorway, blocking my sight of the rest of the room.

"Are-are you alone?" I ask warily, trying to keep my tone neutral. I know that the hesitation in my voice is betraying my concern that he might not be alone—that he met back up with *her.*

His lip curls and he backs up, allowing me to view the full expanse of the bed. It's empty. The sight comforts the anxiety welling up inside of me and I stifle the sigh that threatens to push past my lips.

"I told you," he starts, his voice so low it's almost a growl. "That girl meant nothing."

I take in the anger in his tone, the indignation, and I chew on the inside of my cheek so hard I taste copper.

"Can I come in?" I question, holding my breath for his response.

He backs up further, stretching out his arm in an animated flourish to let me into the room before closing the door softly behind me. I walk a few feet in before turning toward him. He stands, crossing his arms over his bare chest, his upper arms flexing.

But I am undeterred by his attitude, and I unclasp the front of my fur-lined cloak. His room is warm and the energy that began to build inside of me at the pub is causing me to overheat. I slip the cloak from my shoulders and reach behind me to toss it onto his bed. When I look back, he's watching at me, his nostrils flared, jaw set.

Unsure of what to do with my hands, I straighten the fabric of my tunic. Nervous under the intensity of his stare, I shift on my feet. No one else in my life has made me this unsteady just by looking at me. It's unfamiliar, to be uncomfortable like this, to feel the need to explain. The need to wipe the anger and the sadness and the hurt from him.

"What do you want, Bria?" he asks, his words clipped short.

"I want to talk to you...to explain—" I start, but he cuts me off, irritation growing in his voice.

"Couldn't it wait until morning?" he questions, sadness flittering behind his eyes. "We have a long journey ahead of us. You will have plenty of time to talk...to whomever you choose." He adds the last part not to inflict pain upon me, I realize, but because he's giving up.

He's giving up on me. It's defeat in his eyes that I see now.

It throws me off guard—his tone, his eyes, and the lump that forms in my throat along with those words. But I shake my head, letting hair fall around me, hoping it will hide the grief I'm sure he can see spreading across my features. Hoping it will hide the anguish.

"No, Ev. It can't."

He moves away from the door toward the edge of the bed. I turn, following him as he moves silently through the room, noticing his feet are bare and his trousers are unbuttoned. He wasn't expecting me when I knocked on the door and was probably getting ready to sleep. As he sits, he drags a hand through his tangled hair and lets loose a long breath.

"Get on with it then," he says quietly, looking up at me, his eyes glimmering in the low light of the room. His hands are clasped together, falling between his legs as he leans forward. There are specks of dried blood on his hand and his knuckles are bruised and busted open, but I think better of asking him about it. I know he has a tendency to become aggressive when upset. Fist fights and punching walls were not unknown activities to Evander.

I could leave. Just go now, cross the hall to my room and be done with it, let him think what he wants of Silas and me. It won't matter in a few days or a few weeks anyway. So why do I stay? Why do I need him to understand? Because every fiber in my being wants him. It's a different kind of pull than what I feel with Silas. Something in me is still drawn to Evander no matter the circumstances, no matter the pain or the fate I hover closer to. He is under my skin, in my bones and my blood. And I'm not giving up on him this easily.

"Whether you want to be around me or not, you're stuck with me for at least another few days," I begin, tentatively at first but as his eyes lock on me I know I have to keep going.

"I know you don't understand what's going on, but I need you to try," I continue, taking a steady breath as the words pour out. "There's some sort of link, some bond that lies beneath the surface of all those with power. It connects Nimai to me, and Silas. Or that's what Cato told us."

I pace the short distance between where I had been standing and the small dresser a few feet away. I feel his eyes follow me with each step, the skin on the back of my neck prickling.

"He wasn't sure at first. But the other day, when we trained, it became clear." I stop at the dresser and spin toward him, instantly lowering my eyes from the vehemence in his gaze and tugging up the sleeves of my tunic. I shove the fabric as far up my arms as I can manage. I yank at the neck, pulling it away from my body. It feels like I'm burning up. The swell of energy from when Silas came to protect and strengthen me is still bubbling up in my body, threatening to erupt at any moment.

He remains silent, staring. And fuck if that quiet isn't jarring, but he's merely waiting for me to finish my rant. I roll my shoulders, trying to move the heat around in my body. If I could just get the energy out, if I could cast shadows or go for a run or douse myself in a cold bath... Anything to snuff out the flames.

"I know-I know Ash told you about the dead. And no matter how much I practiced I could only raise and control one warrior. I just didn't have the energy in my body to do more than that." My hands are wringing together as I breathe through the flash of heat, hoping he can understand. Hoping he cares enough to try.

"It was draining me. I was exhausted each night and I could barely get up in the mornings. Every muscle in my body was sore and throbbing from the effort. And then, I showed up for training the other day and Cato had Silas with him."

I slide my eyes to him as I say the name and watch his jaw tighten reflexively. His hands curl into fists and I can just make out the white of his knuckles where he grasps them together.

I don't know why he has such a strong reaction to Silas, why he bothers Ev so much. Some of it might stem from his job and his want to protect me, but I can't let myself believe this is all about me. Perhaps something happened at the village or during the travel back that set this dislike in motion. A part of me, a very dark and slightly disturbing part, wants this reaction to be wholly because of my connection to Silas. Because that means he truly does care about me, enough to be jealous and enough to fight for this.

What we share means more to me than he will ever know. Evander is the only person aside from Ash who has made me feel like a normal person in the last five years. Made me feel like something other than the Prophecy. I want to hold on to that feeling, to be consumed by it—to be consumed by him, even if I already know of the girls back at the capital and that I may mean little more to him than any of them did. None of that lessens my want, my need for him. So if he feels even a sliver of the jealousy I had coursing through my veins tonight, I'll take it.

"Cato had me work on pulling energy from him." I try to think of the right words to convey what happened between us. "Pulling" seems right. After all, that's what it feels like. It had also felt like satiating a hunger, a deep hunger that made my bones ache, but I don't think *that* is something I should admit right now.

Evander skims his hands over his face, scraping them along the rough hairs of the short beard he is now growing.

"You *fed* off his energy. That's what Quinn said." The displeasure in his voice is apparent, as is the lingering sadness. It's hard to think he's disappointed in me. As per usual, I did what was expected of me as the prophecy.

"Yes and no." I roll my lip as I work out what to say. "It's not as if I did anything wrong, Ev!" His heavy stare is making me increasingly more upset and defensive.

I feel guilty and I have to remind myself there's no reason for that. I am strong. I am skilled. I am powerful and gifted. And Silas is helping make me more powerful. *There is nothing wrong with that.*

"Yes, I *fed* on his energy. I pulled it from him and when it flowed into me, I felt invincible." My breathing comes heavy, remembering what it felt like to have that rush of power. Heat keeps pulsing through me, making my hands itch and my palms flame. "It was as if my body came alive with his energy. I pulled and my core filled with heat, with magic. I was able to raise ten dead just from the energy he gave me. *Ten*, Ev! Do you understand what that means?"

He probably thinks I'm insane, but I keep talking. There's no damming the flood of emotions and words pouring out of me now. The fire in my body is building, burning stronger with each word I speak. "But I also wanted more. I could have killed him, and it scares the shit out of me to do it again. I know I have to but—"

"Bria," he interrupts, cutting me off, his eyes wide. He's searching me, looking all around my body as if he is noticing something.

Glancing down, I notice them too. My hands are balled into fists and the tips are dark, my fingertips dripping with shadows. Tendrils of darkness swirl around my fingers, hands, and wrists, and continue to creep up my arms. The light breeze from them lifts my hair as they coil around me.

I must have summoned them with my emotions, with the fear and anger. But with no purpose, nowhere to go, no one to be, the shadows linger. Engulfing me in black flames.

"Shit!" The curse bursts from my mouth as I recognize how little control I have right now.

Marching quickly to the window, I fling the sides open into the frigid air. The cold stings my face, but my body is boiling now, the tunic suffocating me. I yank again at the collar, and it tears, leaving a giant gape below my collarbone. But I can breathe, and I greedily gulp down a deep breath, the chill cooling the fire welling up inside.

Focus. I need to focus. Closing my eyes, I seek the shadows, reaching out with my mind. I shove all of that energy, all of those emotions and anxieties and fears, into the shadows. They bend and twist and warp into nightmares.

I mold them, stretching fangs to points, sharpening elongated talons that then click on the ground next to me, moving from my mind into reality. I hear them dragging down the dark wood of the floor, gouging it with a sinister scraping noise. The dark forms circle me, wings springing from their backs, stretching high above their mangled bodies. I thrust my arms out into the chill air of the night, ripping my eyes open as the heat rushes out of me, radiating through my veins and bursting from my fingertips.

Breaking their circling, the creatures follow the push of energy I project outward. They leap from the window, their claws clutching the old wood, splintering it as they project themselves into the night. Wings flare to life, picking up the breeze and allowing the nightmares to coast further into the dark. I watch them for a few minutes as they fade and dissipate into the night air, arms falling slack at my sides. It's enough of a release that I can inhale deeply now, filling my lungs as I catch my breath.

I half expect him to have left during that display, to have fled when I called the creatures forth—when the shadows twisted and curled around my body and he saw the girl he knew cast terrors out into the dark night. Not that he isn't brave, I already know that he is. He is the bravest man I have ever met, given what he escaped in the king's court. Given what he did to survive and create a life for himself. But seeing the darkness that resides within me could elicit a different level of fear.

But he's still standing there when I turn around.

In fact, he's moved closer. Evander had risen from his seat on the bed and moved around toward the window. And now, he's standing before me, close enough to touch, beautiful brown eyes wide with brows lifted in perfect arcs. His lips are slightly parted, astonishment plastered across his face.

I wonder when he decided to move to me. And why.

The cold breeze rushes in through the open window, and I revel in it. My skin hasn't cooled down despite the release of power. Silas's magic strengthened me without either of us intending that and losing control of my emotions had caused a surge. I had lost the ability to keep my gifts locked in. Something like that hasn't happened to me since I first began training with Cato. And even then...it wasn't like this.

Wind whips golden tendrils of hair around me, and I tip my head back, closing my eyes at the feel of the frost in the air, the chill dancing along my skin. The darkness engrossing me from the midnight sky is heavenly and I relish the way the cold lessens the flames coursing through my veins. The roiling energy inside is subsiding, now just a quiet simmer below the surface.

When I steady the panting and come back into my body, into the present, I open my eyes. I immediately sense a familiar flutter in my stomach, though it's not from the power this time. Instead, I feel it deep in my core, threatening to break me in an entirely different way.

The way he's looking at me.

This. This is the hunger Ash had spoken of. The hunger I denied was there, that I refused to see for fear of what it would mean.

His eyes have waned from the shocked expression of before and are darker now, fixated on me. Wind continues to rip into the room, tossing hair into his eyes but he doesn't break his gaze. I meet it, that fluttering inside me intensifying.

A torrent of uncertainty hits me. I don't know what to do, what to say. What *can* I say after that display of power? Cato and Silas are the only ones to have observed my gifts in that capacity before. Having magic themselves, there is less of a surprise factor but I'm aware of how intimidating my power was to both men. Cato had been fascinated by it. Silas had been drawn to it.

But what I see on Ev's face isn't intimidation, nor is it apprehension. He didn't run. No. He had come closer to me, had witnessed while I summoned shadows and spiraled them into nightmares in this very room. And still, he came closer.

I open my mouth to speak and before I can breathe out the words, he's on me.

A rough, calloused hand slides behind my head, grabbing my neck and tangling in my hair. The other clutches at my back, gripping his fingers into flesh. His mouth slams into mine and I welcome the fierceness of the kiss. It's not soft like the last time, it's brutal and aggressive and needy.

His tongue sweeps out and I open to him. I had forgotten the indescribable sweetness of his kiss even if it was only days before that he'd kissed me for the first time. It feels like a lifetime ago now. It feels like that whenever I am not with him.

When my tongue meets his, the connection sends heat down my middle, tightening every inch of my body. Grasping his hair with both of my hands, I yank him harder into me, deepening the kiss. It's unhinged. I lose control of my body from the rush of power followed by this wave of desire.

I crush my body against his, and his hands grasp my waist tightly. Sweeping me up against him and pulling my feet off the floor, Ev turns and takes the few steps to the bed, never breaking the contact of our bodies. He dips down, laying me out beneath him. His arms move to each side of me, his palms pressing into the mattress below.

When he breaks from the kiss, his mouth moves to my ear, nipping at the edge. His teeth cause a sharp bite of pain followed by a spike of pleasure. Evander's face nestles into my hair, his breath caressing my neck and sending a shiver down my spine when he speaks.

"Fuck, Bria. You're incredible," he whispers, and I clench my legs together, the gruffness of his voice making me pulse with want.

He says it with such genuine awe that I am struck again by his presence. How he's still here. I want to say as much to him, but he chooses that moment to drag his tongue down the column of my throat, leaving a slick of wet that makes me forget the words on the tip of my tongue. Stopping at my collarbone, he kisses the hollow there. I'm unable to move, frozen beneath him as he trails kisses down my chest, straight down the smooth skin that lies between my breasts.

He glances up then as he grabs the edges of the torn tunic and wrenches it down. There's a sharp sound of ripping fabric, leaving my torso exposed to the frigid air. My nipples harden, pebbling from the breeze and the eagerness of his stare. The second the cold breeze hits them, Evander's mouth tips up, a grin gleaming on his face. When that dimple pulls into his left cheek, my chest tightens. He's gorgeous. Made all the more beautiful because he's seen *me*. He's seen me and he is still here.

With one arm propping him above me, he moves to cup one of my breasts that feel full and heavy under his watchful gaze, almost painfully waiting for his touch. And when his finger drags across the center of it, my body pulls back into the mattress at the jolt that runs through me. His grin widens, watching me as he flicks his thumb over the sensitive area again before dragging it in lazy circles, teasing. The need for him pulses between my legs and I ache for more.

He tips his head down and I suddenly feel the warm wet of his tongue slide over my breast, following the same circles as his thumb. Pressure increases in my body, and I grasp at the crimson sheets below, twisting my fingers into the soft material as my body writhes under him. Evander grazes his teeth along my skin and fastens his mouth over my nipple, flicking his tongue. I gasp, relishing the deep tingling sensation that comes along with the motion.

Releasing me, Evander slides his body up mine. He's heavy on top of me and the hardness of his cock presses against me. His trousers are low—low enough that I could easily slip my hands in, already knowing his body is just as ready for me as mine is for him. He stares into my eyes, and I can see the tiny flecks of gold sparkling along the deep brown backdrop. Reaching up, I smooth away a strand of chestnut hair from his beautiful face, needing to see more of those otherworldly eyes.

Ev smiles again and brushes his lips against mine, a whisper of a touch. Velvety smooth. I push back, eager for more. I circle my arms around his neck and pull him into me, thrusting my tongue back toward him, devouring him. Evander lets out a low laugh into me and I still, pulling my head back to assess him.

"There's no need to rush, Bria," he drawls, his gaze sweeping over me. "I've wanted this for so long, I'm taking my time. I'm not going anywhere." The words send a wave of heat rushing into my cheeks and he bends to kiss my forehead. A tender kiss that pains me as reality comes crashing back into me, knocking the breath from my chest and replacing it with real, raw fear.

He notices the shift in my features. I pull an arm from his neck to stroke his cheek and my eyes sting, tears fighting their way to the surface.

"But I am." The words stick, clogging in my throat as I try to swallow over the thickness building there. "You know that."

He flinches. "The prophecy."

I nod. "It's the only way we win this. *The moon shall die, and the sun shall give birth to a new day,*" I quote the line that tells of my demise, the words that have echoed through my mind for years, have forced me to bear the weight of my fate. Because I am the moon, the descendant of Lilith, the darkness.

"I *have* to die. For all of you to live." My voice cracks and a tear escapes, running down the side of my face.

He reaches up and gently wipes away the tear before kissing the area where it had been. He brushes his lips back to my ear, letting them coast along my skin, the softness of his breath tickling when he speaks.

"But not now," he breathes.

My brows furrow with confusion as he lifts his head back to look at me. There's the beginning of a grin again, a devilish look that tells me all I need to know about his intentions.

"For now, we live," he says, his eyes searching me for understanding. "Do you want to live, Bria?"

I want to live. I *need* to live. To be with him, even if only for a few hours, a few days. And he feels the same, I realize. No matter the agony it causes in the future, we will live. For now.

"Yes. Yes, I want to live." I have not spoken truer words in my life than in this moment.

He gently sweeps his tongue across my lips once again and I know I want this. To live. With him. So I push back, deepening into him. Our tongues slick against one another as he angles his mouth over mine, kissing me as if it's the last time. And it genuinely could be.

The hem of my torn tunic is pulled away and his fingers trail along my exposed stomach, tracing the edge of my leggings. The pulsing between my legs picks up speed, needing him to move his hands, to touch more than the flat expanse of skin. Just as I notice it, he dips that hand below my waistband. He creeps lower, a gentle caress against my hip bone, fingers dragging across my thigh, then moving between them. Rough fingertips press to the very center of me, and I suck in a sharp breath. He moves in slow circles at first, his touch makes me writhe and I close my eyes, taking in the feeling. The intensity.

He quickens his fingers, and that pressure starts building again. I let out a low moan into his mouth and reach out to grab his shoulders, letting my fingers grip his tight muscles. But before I know it, his hand is gone, and he pulls out of the kiss. The ache inside me seems to cry out. But it isn't the ache, it's me. A small cry escaped my lips when he stole his hand away, shocked at the sudden coolness I was left with.

I open my eyes to see the smirk on his face as he slowly grabs the fabric on either side of my knees and begins to slide down the leggings. His fingers scrape along my skin, sending pulses of pleasure through me.

He's staring at me as he pulls the pants to my ankles then tugs off each boot before sliding them fully off my legs. Slowly. Torturously. Teasingly.

Evander kisses the inside of my ankle then works his way up, laying gentle kisses along my skin, causing my body to become more wet, more ready with anticipation. When he reaches my inner thigh, his tongue traces a line along the sensitive skin, sending a shudder down my spine. And then he pulls that tongue right across to my center, where his fingers had been only moments before.

It feels glorious and unlike anything I've felt before. Not something Cedric had ever done.

Dear gods, how could I ever be angry about his time in the capital if he learned how to do *this* there? I grasp the sheets, tangling them around my fingers, holding on to anything to keep me grounded as he moves.

He hums, a distinct sound of pleasure forcing its way past his lips when he makes contact. That small sound vibrates through me, eliciting another moan from my needy body.

"You taste even better than I imagined." My body reacts to his words almost as much as his touch. There is no hiding how my body is responding, he can taste the arousal building. And when his fingers drift back to me, moving one inside and then two, I see his eyes flare.

"Fuck, you're so wet. Just for me?" he asks, a grin creeping into his face as he curls those fingers inside me, causing a whimper to escape my lips.

The ache deepens between my thighs as he moves his tongue, alternating between swirling and flicking and sucking. All the while, those fingers proceed deftly—curling and pushing, causing the burning to build, becoming unbearable and delicious at the same time. I dig my hands into his hair, groaning as I move my hips into him, unabashedly grinding myself on his face.

"Ev," I breathe, ready to beg him to let me come, to give me the release I'm chasing.

He pauses, but only briefly to speak. "Just for me?" he repeats, "Say it Bria," he commands before sending his tongue straight up the center of me.

"Just for you."

Taking that as the confirmation it is, I feel his mouth latch onto me, increasing the pressure and the pace while he drives his fingers into me again and again. I cry out as waves of pleasure crash over me, arching my back and tensing my legs with the contractions deep in my core as his fingers fuck me into oblivion.

CHAPTER 31

Evander

I fight a smile as I watch her face and the pure ecstasy etched upon it when I push her over the edge. And I want to do more. I want to have every inch of me inside of her, not just my hands and tongue. Forcing myself to show restraint is harder in this moment than it has ever been before. But I know how the magic can drain her and how it's only a matter of minutes before exhaustion starts to take over. She needs to have some strength, some energy left for traveling tomorrow.

I can wait because I want to see her reactions, to have her fully present when I take her for the first time. I want to watch her writhing beneath me for hours while I make her come again and again. Because there will be more. That, I will make sure of. I'm going to taste everything, touch everything. I'm going to make sure we live, just as I promised her tonight.

There is no giving up on her, no turning back now.

Climbing into the bed, I wrap my arms around her. I hold her tight and drag her body flush against me despite the fact that my cock presses into her, still rigid with want. She curls back into my body, and I bury my head in her hair, breathing in the lavender that remains on her. Bria's body is relaxed now, and I feel her settle even more as she leans into me. Realizing her lower half is still exposed to the cold, I yank the blankets up over her. That tunic is doing her no good at this point either. It is torn nearly in half and I smile, remembering that I contributed to most of that. And that she hadn't minded in the least.

She likely doesn't need protection from the chill. Heat is still running through her, making her skin warm to the touch. I, however, am beginning to get cold. Goosebumps are breaking out across my bare arms, so I bend down to kiss her cheek before rising to cross the room and close the open windows beside her.

Pushing the doors shut, I lock the latches in place across the wooden frames and turn. My heart stops beating. I'm sure of it. She is so striking, her hair a radiant cascade along my pillows. Her eyes are closed and there is a gentle smile pressed into her lips. Thinking that what we just did—that I have anything to do with that smile—makes me happier than I ever thought possible.

I stay there for a moment, taking in the image of her lying in my bed. How long I'd waited for this, hoping against all odds that it might happen and here she is. I lean back against the frame of the window, crossing my arms over my chest as I watch her. I never want this to end. I want to spend the rest of my nights this same way.

Glancing down, I notice the amulet hanging around my neck. The symbol of her fate. The symbol of her demise. It strikes fear into my heart, and I reach up to undo the clasp, gathering it in the palm of my hand and shoving it deep in my pocket. I can't bear to look at it any longer.

She opens her eyes a fraction, just enough to see me standing across from where she's lying. Her cobalt eyes are now soft and warm as she gazes up at me, almost glowing. And right then, I know for sure what this is.

I love her.

I have always loved her. I loved her then, and now, and all of the time in between. I had let the boundaries of our stations keep me from her when we were younger, and the threat of her fate keep me from her as we grew older. But not anymore. Not ever again.

She stretches out her arm, extending long fingers and wiggling them toward me. I push off the ledge and reach my hand back to her, intertwining my fingers with hers.

"Ev," she says, her voice breathy and sexy as hell. When I look down, she closes her eyes again. "Come back," she whispers, pulling me back toward her.

"Happy to oblige," I reply, my lips pulling into a smirk as I crawl over her, lingering above her and taking in the sight for a moment before slipping back behind her.

My body curls back around her petite frame, letting my fingers find the hem of her tunic and settling my hand on the soft skin of her stomach. I kiss her neck before laying my head on the pillow beside her. She makes a small noise and wriggles into me, pushing herself right up against me with the movement and making my cock twitch in response. I have to fight to steady myself and not allow the urge to pull me under. She needs to rest. We both do.

I fall fast asleep, my body wrapped around her as we breathe in unison.

I'm not sure how long I've been asleep when Bria is ripped from beside me. She lurches from the bed and falls to the ground in a heap. Startled, I clamber over the mattress and land on the floor next to her, my knees slamming into the hard wood.

"Shit!" A stream of curses flies from my mouth when I realize what's happening to her.

She's having a vision again, there is no doubt in my mind. Her head is thrown back and I watch as her eyes roll until I can see only white. Her body is still, and I'm not sure if I should pick her up or not. Helpless, I stare as it takes over her body, unable to make it stop. Useless.

I grasp her face in my hands, urging her to look at me. Within moments, her eyes slam back and she gasps, trying to catch her breath before screaming out for her sister, the noise tearing from her throat. I slap a hand over her mouth, stifling her cries from the rest of the inn, not wanting anyone running in here when she's in this state.

"Shhh, I'm so sorry," I tell her, over and over, trying to calm her down. I pull her to my body, ensconcing her in my arms as she shudders and an aching sob breaks free. Bria clings to me, clenching my arms as her hot tears streak down my chest.

We stay that way for some time, allowing the sobs to quiet, allowing her body time to settle and come down from the magnitude of the vision. I whisper to her as we sit on the cold, floor, running my hands up and down her back, soothing her. I urge her to breathe, to stay with me, to come back to her body. Back to me.

When she pulls her head away from me and looks up, there are blue flames dancing in her eyes, red rimming her lids, and drops of tears decorating her fine lashes. I press a kiss to her forehead, holding her tightly. I don't want to let go but that look has me questioning whether she's slipping away. Something isn't right.

"I have to go."

The words are spoken so softly I barely hear them. But there is a firmness behind them. It isn't a question.

"What? Go where?"

She reaches a hand to my face, smoothing her fingers over the stubble to cup my cheek. She looks sad, broken, and I swear I would do anything to wipe that look from her face, to put those broken pieces back together.

"Bria. You're not going anywhere. We leave for the Woods tomorrow," I remind her.

She keeps her hand on my face, her voice quiet even now that the sobbing has subsided. "Something is wrong," she begins. "I'm not going to the Woods yet, I'm going to get Nimai."

Dread floods my senses. We've had no word from the southern camp that anything is wrong with Nimai. I knew the visions had been of her sister, but assumed it was just another magical connection like we spoke of earlier, that it's been increasing because Nimai's birthday draws near. I say as much to her, but she's insistent.

"No. This is different. She is in pain, horrible, all-consuming pain. Coming into your magic is not like that, it doesn't hurt. And she's scared. I can feel it when I see her," she explains, her gaze and hand never leaving my face. "She's not safe."

I shake my head, not willing to believe it even if I can tell she thinks there's truly something wrong. She believes what she saw and felt in that vision. "That's impossible, Bria. She's in the southern camp. She *must* be fine. Reinhardt or your mother would have told us if something happened, if she was hurt at all."

"She's not in the southern camp, Ev." My heart clenches as she says my name. "She's in the capital, the dungeons."

My eyes widen. Nimai cannot be in the dungeons.

"No." I take a deep breath in. "No, she can't be. How-how can you be sure?"

"I saw the dirt floors, saw the barred door...and I saw *him*." She swallows. She's holding back telling me, but I already know the *him* she's talking about.

"No," I repeat. There is no possible way Nimai has been captured and we are unaware. Not by them. Not by him. I refuse to entertain the thought, physically shaking my head over and over again.

"Your father has her. She's with the king and Aamon in the capital." Bria drops her hand from my face and moves herself away. I grasp her hand as she stands, clinging to her fingers. "And I'm going to get her back." Her voice is fierce, a determination in it I've never heard from her.

"You can't!" I'm moving now, jumping to my feet to stop her.

I seize her other arm, holding her, gripping my fingers too tightly. My eyes plead for her to understand. I try to calm my voice before speaking again. "Bria, they are evil men. Barbaric. What they do to people with magic, it's—you cannot go there." I watch her face, trying to see if she is registering the gravity of my words.

"We can tell Helara and Quinn and I can go. We can go tell her right now, and she can send soldiers to back us up. I can go, Bria. I can get her back."

Bria's head drops to her chest. "You can't. None of you can." She won't look at me and it's killing me inside. "Helara can't defeat him, she can't infiltrate the castle. It has to be me."

I tug her toward me before grabbing her face in my hands and tipping her head back. "Bria, look at me!" I demand and she caves, tears streaming down her cheeks and trickling onto my fingers. "You will die.

They will do horrific things to you. They will use you and kill you. I can't let you go to Easthallow." My voice is cracking as I beg her.

She reaches to grasp my wrists with her fingers, holding my hands in her own. "I know, Ev."

My heart aches as she brings her face to mine, rising on to the tops of her toes to kiss me gently. I have the slightest sense of relief before she drags her mouth to my ear but everything stops when she whispers, "I'm so sorry."

She quickly wrenches her body from me, taking a step away as disbelief spreads across my face. Shadows swirl and undulate around her, a fine black mist thickening and turning menacing.

"Bria!" I cry out, reaching for her again. Tears sluice past her lids and down her face as she backs further away. "Bria, no!" I try to move toward her, but the shadows circle me, pushing me back toward the bed. Caging me in.

They sweep in, coiling around my legs and arms. Tight binds form around my ankles and wrists. I fight against them, but the shadows latch around the posts of the bed.

Shackled. She's fucking chaining me. I yank my arms to no avail, the shadows continuing to swirl like sinister vines along my body, curling further up to my shoulders and locking me in place.

Her eyes are red and raw from the tears, and I can barely see her through the ominous mist.

"I'm sorry, Ev," she whispers again as she grabs her boots and the cloak that had fallen to the ground, turns on her heel, and rushes out of the room.

Thrashing at the chains binding me, I scream her name, but the black vines sweep up, covering my mouth and muffling the sound before it can leave my throat. The tight grip of the shadows bites into my skin, leaving a warm trickle of blood seeping from my wrists.

She's gone.

CHAPTER 32

Bria

I sprint to my room across the hall, ripping the shredded tunic from my body and dressing hurriedly in warm clothing. I yank on a fresh tunic and clean leggings before tugging on my leather armor and strapping it into place. My hands are shaking uncontrollably as I hear Evander start to scream my name again. Then nothing. I close my eyes tight, blocking out the sudden silence.

I desperately hope no one heard him before he was gagged.

The shadows are hurting him. *I'm* hurting him. And it eats at me. But I need to find Nimai. What I felt from that vision was worse than the ones before. It's what I imagine it would feel like if someone was pulling your soul out of your body, pulling strands of your very being from every inch of you. All at once.

Shoving my feet into the leather boots, I stand and strap on the bandolier, jamming daggers in quickly. As I hurry out of the room, I slide a sword into its sheath at my side. Swinging my cloak around me, I pull up the fur-lined hood and slip out of the inn and into the night.

Running through the dark, the snow crunches beneath my boots and I cringe, hoping no one can hear and cursing the cold weather. I aim toward the stables. The shadows won't contain Evander for long. There is no way for me to maintain them once I leave the camp. My magic will only extend so far, and I can feel the effort from his fight draining me already.

The barn door slams open, and the warm, earthy air hits me like a thick wall. I hasten to saddle a horse and lead it outside. The only way I can do this is if I drop the shadowy bindings once I get to the guards so I can cloak myself. I can't split my magic between keeping Evander contained and covering my escape, and I need as much energy and strength as I can muster if I'm headed to the capital.

Tears sting my eyes and leave an icy chill on my cheeks as I mount the horse and steer the reins toward the road that leads southeast, out of the mountains. To my sister. And into the home of my enemies.

CHAPTER 33

Evander

Screaming against the binds does nothing but make my throat burn. My voice is muted, and the shadows seem to stretch further over my face and body the more I fight them. It doesn't stop me from trying though, and I yank and thrash, attempting to free myself even just a little, straining every muscle in my body to do so.

When the vines ensnaring my arms and legs finally begin to crawl backward and the darkness withdraws from my mouth, I swiftly break myself away. I watch as the magic fades into the shadows of the room, gone as abruptly as it appeared.

My arms and legs are covered in bloodied scratches, purple bruising already blossoming across my skin. But I straighten my body against the pain, fumbling as I button my trousers and throw a tunic over my head.

Bria must be outside the camp by now. Otherwise, I would still be caged in shadows. I know enough about that gift to understand it has a range at which she can control it, which only serves to make me more frantic, knowing she is already ahead of me as I fumble with my armor and weapons. Grabbing my cloak and crossbow, I stalk to the door before stopping short, my hand resting on the knob. Something calls me back toward the dresser.

My mother's ring sits on top, a gold band of intertwining vines that blooms with black obsidian flowers. Before she was ripped away from me when we first arrived in the capital, she had pressed it into my hand, whispering that it would protect me. I had no idea what kind of old-world magic she spoke of when doing so, but I trusted her. And we need all the protection we can get. I shove it deep into my pocket and take off at a jog down the hall, careful not to disrupt the sleeping commanders. My fist hits the last door in a rough knock, and I listen for a moment. Hearing nothing within, I swing the door wide. I have no time to wait.

Quinn jolts up in bed at the sound, his sword already in hand. My lip curls up at the sight. Always a warrior. This is why I need him and no one else tonight.

He registers quickly that there's no threat, realizing it's only me in his doorway, and rubs a hand down his face. He takes in my face, my stance, my body armed to the teeth and his eyes dart to the form beside him. A mess of brown curls peeks out from behind Quinn. The girl from the pub is tucked beneath the quilts of his bed.

Quinn stealthily creeps out of the bed and over to me, yanking pants on as he walks, remaining quiet to not wake the sleeping girl. I'm at his room in the middle of the night, dressed like I'm ready for battle. He knows something is going down. And we don't need anyone else in the camp getting word of it.

"She's gone, Quinn," I whisper, distraught and grabbing a fistful of my own hair. Agony rips through me when the words finally leave my mouth, reality setting in like a fucking brick to the face.

Quinn's eyes flash open, and his mouth sets in a hard line. We need her to defeat Braddock and restore the whole of Azudora, to restore balance to the world. She's supposed to save us all. And not only that, but she's also one of his closest friends. Hearing those words hurts him nearly as much as it hurts me to utter them.

"Where?" he forces the word out but he's already moving, silently gathering his clothing that lay in a heap on the floor and dressing. Quinn checks the girl once more to ensure she's still sleeping and snags his weapons.

"To the capital. She said Nimai is there," I push the words past the lump in my throat, working to swallow over it, my eyes searing.

The questions start the second we make it far enough away from the inn that he's sure he won't wake anyone. I welcome the interrogation though, it gives me a point to focus on, instead of worrying what my father will do when he gets ahold of Bria. They have searched for her. For years. They won't kill her right away. It will be far worse. And she is heading straight for them.

"How long?" he asks.

"She's probably a half hour or so ahead of us now," I respond, and Quinn's face betrays his worry that we won't catch her in time.

"What the fuck, Ev!" he exclaims. "How is she that far ahead of you?"

"She-she shackled me with her fucking shadows!" I throw up my hands.

How else can I explain what she did? Without experiencing it, I never would have believed a thing like that was possible. From what I knew, she could form them into nightmare creatures, I saw as much last night. But apparently, she can also make them into whatever the hell she desires, if tonight was any indication. Pride swells inside at the notion that she's grown so powerful, but I stamp it out. I can't be too proud since her actions have made it that much harder for me to protect her.

We reach the stables and Quinn starts tacking his horse but halts, taking in what I said.

"She what?"

I let out a long exhalation, fighting the urge to punch him as I tighten my saddle. We need to leave, and he clearly thinks I did nothing to try and stop her.

"You know she has gifts, Quinn. You know she can manipulate the shadows. We've just never witnessed her really do it. What we've seen pales in comparison to what I saw her do tonight," I continue. "She trapped my arms and legs in these vines, these shackles made of darkness. I tried but I couldn't free myself. It wasn't until she dropped the magic that I was able to come to you." I pull the reins of the horse to lead it out into the night.

Chill air hits my skin and I turn to Quinn, sliding up the arms of the tunic to reveal the torn skin drying with blood and bands of purple and blue. Quinn silently takes in the marks.

"She's so much stronger than we realized, Quinn." My voice breaks. "She has no idea what they are going to do to her."

We race on our mounts toward the same road I'm sure Bria took. The hair on the back of my neck prickles and I scan the area as we leave. That odd sensation that someone is watching us keeps niggling at the back of my brain, but I see no one.

The camp is still asleep and the guards on duty pay us no mind, only nodding as we ride past and out of the camp. The two of us have ridden out together at all kinds of hours. No one will balk at us leaving in the dead of night. Nor will they dare question two commanders.

But Bria got past them, and I can't help but wonder how. The guards know she is high up in the rebel forces and close to Helara. But they remain unaware of who she really is, and even without that knowledge they would have stopped her. *Should* have stopped her. If for no other reason than to inquire as to where she was going. Unless she used her magic.

We speed up as we exit the foothills after descending from the mountain camp. The road opens down here, allowing the two of us to ride side by side once we are free of the mountain range. The sky yields as well, a swell of sparkling stars strewn about a mass of midnight black, peppered between the giant trees. The moon issues forth a glow that seems to light the way toward her, nearly full but not quite yet. Quinn brings his mount closer to mine and I hear his voice rise over the thunder of hooves and the wind whipping against my face.

"Why does she think Nimai is in Easthallow?"

"It's her visions. She had another tonight and she saw Nimai with my father. She saw the dungeons, Quinn. She said Nimai isn't safe."

I had told Quinn of the dungeons when I escaped the capital and my father, had recounted the evil I saw there and what they did to those with magic in the depths of Castle Eccleston—*what I did* to those people in the damp dark underbelly of that castle. Quinn and Helara are the only two who know the full extent of my time there, though Bria and Ash know most of it.

Quinn's eyes dart to me for a moment then back to the road ahead, focusing as we race through the forest of evergreens. I can hear the tightness in his jaw as my words register and he pieces together the evening.

"How did you know, though? You left the pub. You left her there with Silas."

The boy's name still makes my stomach knot, despite my understanding of their connection and what happened tonight between Bria and me. I debate on lying to my friend, for a moment. But even in the dead of night, I know Quinn will detect it. The man has an eerie knack for picking up on lies. Probably one of the reasons he's so terrifying.

"I did leave, but she came to see me. We were together when it happened, she was in my room." I spare Quinn any details of our encounter, not ready to face his rage just yet.

Tension from Quinn's body ripples across the empty space between us.

"And why in the fuck was Bria *still* in your room in the middle of the fucking night?" he yells.

"It's none of your fucking business, Quinn," I spear back, my tone sharp and cutting off any further conversation about what transpired between us. Or so I think.

Quinn scoffs. "Like hell it isn't! When you left the pub, she tried to go after you, and I told her to stop. I thought she listened." He's shaking his head now, the moonlight glinting off his ebony hair, unbound and whipping around his face in the wind. "Why don't either of you ever listen?" he exclaims, frustration flowing through his words.

My blood is boiling now. Why does everyone presume they can tell her what to do? She never asked for this and yet everyone feels the need, the *right*, to control her.

"Because she doesn't *have* to listen to you, or Helara for that matter. She's a gods damned person, not just your fucking prophecy. She feels immensely, she has wants and needs and dreams..." My words cut off when the reality of them sinks into my chest and settles with a heavy weight.

Tonight had proven it to me—that she doesn't want this but was born into it and is doing everything in her power to see it through. But it torments her. She'd said she wanted to live, and I know she means more than just that one moment with me.

"No. You're not pulling that card, not now. This has more to do with *your* needs than hers."

The harshness of his comment sends me reeling. "If you have such a problem with it, why did you let me come here? You've known that I care for her. You've known since we were children." I'm trying my best not to scream as I fume, not wanting to attract any unwanted attention as we ride through territory that does not belong to us.

"I thought the horrors you witnessed, that you *took part* in, would have made you understand her worth. That she is untouchable."

My teeth clench. How dare he insinuate I don't know her worth. I know more than anyone how precious she is, how fucking incredible. And I know better than anyone that she is untouchable. I'll kill any man who tries.

"You have no idea her worth," I seethe, staring across the mass of black at Quinn. "Or how untouchable she truly is." I urge the horse forward, done with the conversation.

CHAPTER 34

Bria

I curl into my cloak and slow the horse when I reach the outer limits of the forest where the earth opens up before me, seeming to soak up moonlight across the grassy expanse. It glints off boulders and rocks that stipple across the land, leaving a trail from the mountains through the foothills and forest, and down into this scrubland. The chill of winter is still present, though the snowy ground ended in the foothills of the Kaanos.

Many of the remote villages in the Gravenear Territory had been wiped out by King Braddock over the years. Too small to hold their own, their loved ones were either killed or ripped from them and taken back to Easthallow. And those who remain are said to be ruthless nomads. Many work for the Crown as bounty hunters, even. Seeking out people like me. Meaning this might not be the safest area, but so far it appears quiet.

As much as I want to push the horse to get through these open areas quickly, I have enough knowledge to slow. The stallion needs to carry me for three days and we rode hard through the forest to get to this place. I can't wear him down in the first few hours of the trip or we'll never make it there. My body already aches from the riding but going hard in the beginning had its purpose. I was putting space between

Evander and me. If he follows, he will need to take the same breaks as me, need to rest himself and his own horse. He's a far better rider and has spent more time in the area outside of the northern camp. I need to be careful, smart, and fast if I expect to keep my distance or he's bound to catch up.

And I am not about to let that happen.

I may not have all the details of his time in the capital, but I have enough. Quinn told me how his father broke his mother down, forcing him to watch as he tortured her until she eventually caved to serve in the Crown. Because like me, Olaphina was gifted. I don't know what happened to her. Evander rarely speaks of her and never said if she still lives. He never said what his father made her do to serve Vaohr. But I think she must have perished, given the way his face falls whenever he mentions her.

And Evander. What Aamon did to him was debatably worse—assigning him to travel Azudora with the high priestess, seeking out those with magic so she could use them back at the capital. Ev oversaw returning them to the castle and settling them in the dungeons. Quinn spoke of interrogations once, and I gather he was also the one who questioned them, who coaxed information out of them in whatever way he needed to. To find more people with gifts for the priests to use.

Given how the king and Aamon treat those with magic and the people harboring them, I would assume Evander has a great deal of blood on his hands. He's alluded to it without saying just how many people he tortured and killed. But it's for those reasons I don't want him to go back there, to relive the suffering of witnessing his mother tortured, the terror of what would happen to her if he did not obey his father. Having to kill innocent people and do who knows what else to them. Quinn told me of the dungeons but never the specifics of what happened when those with magic were brought there. Neither had Evander. They never wanted me to know, never wanted to fuel the nightmares further.

That puts me at a disadvantage now, I think, given that's where I'm headed. The shadows are my only option right now, my only way in. They're how I slipped past the guards at the outskirts of the northern camp, curling the shadows around me until I was nothing more than a whisper in the darkness, quietly riding out of the confines and into the night.

Cloaking like that took a good deal of energy and without Silas to pull from, I need to conserve during this trip. Only use magic when necessary. Because to rescue Nimai, I might need to cloak for an extended period—through the capital and into the castle with no idea how long it will take me to find her and get her out.

I have time though. I have time to figure it out. I will get my sister, even if it means I die trying.

Breathing in the crisp feel of the breeze, I try to soak in the freedom of being out of the camp. I let my hood fall, leaving my unbound hair streaming in the moonlight. This newfound feeling of being alive is consuming me. I may have bucked the rules as a child, but not nearly as much since finding out I was part of the prophecy. And now, letting Evander in, letting my walls come down and truly being with him, has set something free inside me. My only regret is that I didn't do it sooner so that I could have had more time with him.

Those thoughts are sweet while they last.

In an instant, my world flips upside down. All thoughts of Evander and Nimai and freedom rush away as the cold, hard ground rises to meet me. My feet slide from the stirrups when the arrow hits me, piercing straight through the worn leather armor across my shoulder with tremendous force and sending pain radiating through me.

Foolish. It was foolish of me to not be paying more attention to my surroundings, I realize as my body is thrown from the horse, the arrow firmly lodged in my shoulder.

There's no way whoever shot me knows who I am, knows what I can do. I used no magic when I entered the scrubland, so these people are out for blood. Or worse. My body crashes to the ground, knocking the wind from my lungs, my head snapping back and slamming on something hard.

CHAPTER 35

Bria

The world around me is sideways, an open expanse of bushes and shrubs stippling the patchy grass. Sideways, because I'm in a heap on the ground. A stinging sensation fills my shoulder and back, sending pain rippling down my arm. I gently move my other hand toward that stinging and feel a sharp wooden shaft and a warm, sticky liquid that is most certainly blood. I quickly flick my eyes open to confirm. *Fuck*. Sure enough, there's an arrow lodged in my left shoulder.

Voices filter through the dark and I try to focus on them, closing my eyes to ensure they think I'm still knocked out. The pounding in my head makes it difficult to discern what I'm hearing. Two different voices —no *three* I realize, as they trickle through the roaring in my ears.

Three. I swallow hard. Being skilled with a sword and dagger in training is one thing but fending off three men is another. The fear that my skills won't be enough is paralyzing. On top of that, my energy is low. A small fire still burns within, but the arrow is draining me of other things. Like blood and life.

Keeping my eyes clamped shut, I breathe deeply. The voices are close but not right next to me, meaning they are unaware of the threat I pose to them. *What are they doing?* I listen to the sounds, the clinking metal, the whinnying of my horse.

Rifling through the saddle bags, that's what they are doing. Looking to see if I carried any money or anything that might tell them who I am. I had unwittingly made myself an easy target. *Idiot*, I think. I had let my mind wander from the task at hand, let my guard down and revealed myself as a young woman riding alone at night, for all to see. And they saw. Now, they're going to leave me here, alone and injured and far from any help. The fuckers will probably take my gods damned horse too.

They won't find a lot in those bags though. I don't have much on me aside from a small pouch of gold, and they can take it if they want. I can make do without it if I need to. If I survive this. I didn't stop to think, let alone gather water and food or anything else of value before I took off, meaning their rummaging through my things won't take them long. And when they finish... My stomach roils when I think of what they might do to me, my thoughts receding to a dark place in my mind where I know just what a group of nefarious men are capable of.

Bile creeps its way up my throat, stinging and causing me to gag. Concentrating on my magic is the best I can do right now, so I focus inward. That tiny fire deep inside begins to grow just a little as I tune myself in to it. The moon is nearly full and over the years I've found my gifts come easiest when there's abundant moonlight, during the brightest stages of the moon. Lilith was said to be the dark, the moon, the goddess of death. And I was born in the dead of night when the sky was pitch black aside from the bright light of the moon.

Hearing footsteps approaching, I falter, my confidence wavering and concentration dropping as I overhear their conversation. The stinging sensation from my shoulder filters back in when I lose my focus and I have to stifle a gasp at the sharp pain.

"Even if she does have a bounty, doesn't mean we can't have a little fun first, right?" The voice is deep and grating. It scrapes against my skin like the sharpening of metal, sending a chill down my spine.

Murmuring agreement from the others sets off every alarm in my body. I have to fight. Not just for myself, but for Nimai. I can't save my sister if I die out here in this field.

Blocking out the sounds of the approaching men, I let my thoughts drift back to Nimai, the way I remember her, at least: young and happy, without a care in the world. We were naïve about what was happening in the world around us, unaware of what our parents hid from us about our future. Even as we got older, she remained that naïve girl and I took on the role of hiding my power from her, keeping secrets so she could retain that innocence as long as possible. I remember how she would climb into my bed each night and ask me to read to her. She had an insatiable thirst for knowledge and wanted to learn everything she could. A little bookworm who kept to herself. Nimai had been able to read from a young age but still begged me to do it up until the attack in Elwyn. I think about the way she would curl into me, laying her mass of blue-black hair in the crook of my arm.

I feel her now, the warmth and the weight from her body, pressing into me, the smell of her favorite soap, the scent of rose filling my nostrils. I let the warmth fill my veins and turn my attention from Nimai to the shadows around me.

Finally opening my eyes, I see one of the men standing close by. A towering man with a sneer that reveals a mouth of horrid yellow teeth, half of them broken to nubs. The smell wafting from him is acrid and makes bile rise to the back of my throat again.

Fuck. I swallow it back down, determined not to vomit right now. Two other men come into view, one to either side of the giant sneering monster in front of me. Both are huge, one with a menacing scar running down his face from the top of his head straight to his neck, the other with a gut that makes his width rival his height. Three massive men cornering me in a field by myself.

"You're awake. Good," Yellow Teeth says, walking closer so that he stands over me with a wide stance, his feet on either side of my legs, trapping me. "I prefer my cunt conscious."

An almost feral snarl escapes me, and I hear him call me a "feisty one" as I pull the shadows together in my mind, forming the darkness into one large, taloned beast twisting into place behind where the men stand. Fangs take shape, lengthening to pointed tips that drip an inky black. I look directly into the man's eyes, noting they are a grotesque yellow-brown.

When I rear back, the pain from the arrow stabs so hard I worry I may go unconscious again. But I push through, lifting my knee to my chest and slamming my heel between his legs. Before he can grab me, I roll to the side, snap the shaft of the arrow, and snatch a dagger from beneath my cloak.

"Bitch!" Before the curse hit my ears, I'm on my feet, Yellow Teeth doubled over in front of me. A dagger in one hand, I thrust out the other arm and the shadow beast lunges, taking the scarred man off guard. It slices through his abdomen with one sweep of the razor talons, locking its jaw around his neck.

Cracking bones and ripping flesh echo in my ears. The other two hear the sickening crunching and the wet tear of flesh, turning to see what's happening. That's when I seize my chance, leaping toward Yellow Teeth's back, my feet leaving the ground as I latch on to him, clinging to his body even as he thrashes backward in an attempt to shake me off. My fingers grip tight but slide in his sweat, clawing at the dirt and grime caked on his clothes as I grapple for purchase. The stench of him makes my stomach flip over.

By the cries that ring out... I'm certain the shadow beast made contact with the other man as I intended, envisioning it ripping him to shreds. My energy is wavering though, the fire flickering and sputtering, threatening my ability to keep the shadows woven together.

I slash with the dagger, all of my training lost to the fear I feel in this moment. Terror takes the reins, steering my body to fumble and become careless, turning my movements from precise and calculated to reckless and inefficient. His constant movements make it hard for me to hold on and each time he thrashes, my shoulder wrenches, blood pooling around the shaft of the arrow, leaving the fabric of my tunic warm and wet.

Yellow Teeth bucks and I fly off his back, slamming into the ground. The impact rocks my shoulder and sends my breath out in a whoosh, my dagger bouncing from my hand and skittering away into the grass. It lands too far out of reach and before I can grab another from the bandolier, his foot meets my right wrist. His boot pinches, pinning my arm and biting into the sensitive skin. He's covered in slashes, blood seeping from where some of my dagger swipes made contact and marred his dirty flesh. But most bounced off his leathers, leaving the giant monster standing over me, dripping blood. Yellow Teeth stares down at me as he grinds that boot into the fine bones of my wrist and a sickening crunch vibrates through me.

The fire inside me sputters and an otherworldly scream tears from my lips.

This is how I die.

Not in the capital saving my sister, or in the battle that will save the world. Not as the prophecy, but as a foolish girl who thought she knew better than the people who protected her. Thought she knew better than those she loved.

Agony floods my senses, making it impossible to focus on anything else but blinding, searing, all-consuming pain.

His pock-marked face glares down at me, that menacing sneer pulling on one of his lips to show those nubby yellow teeth and making those gruesome brown eyes narrow into slits. I thrash as much as I can, but his boot just presses further into my wrist, making each and every bone shatter beneath it. Fighting back feels hopeless when I see the blade in his hand, and it's apparent the plans he has for me have turned more sinister after my assault. He's going to kill me.

That boot moves further down my hand, twisting and turning, grinding down as I scream. More bones crack beneath his enormous weight. My vision falters, blurring on the edges and darkening. My body is shutting down to ward off the torturous pain overtaking it.

There's noise around me and his mouth is moving. Speaking or yelling, I can't tell. I can't hear any of it or make out the words flowing from him. Stars twinkle in and out of my peripherals, the darkness creeping further in until it takes over completely. At least I won't be awake for whatever he has planned. I blink, then let my eyes remain closed, feeling more than hearing the loud thump on the ground beside me before I black out completely.

CHAPTER 36

Evander

The edge of the forest breaks before us and Quinn slows his pace. I follow suit, keeping my eyes peeled and my hand on the hilt of my sword. We are too exposed out here at night, crossing through an area we both know is prone to threats of all kinds. The patchy spots of high grasses and thick shrubbery that stud the fields allow for predators to lie in wait—both animals and humans alike. I focus on the sounds, trying to detect anything that might reveal someone hidden. Or something hidden. Soft rustling and chattering of small animals are the only noises my ears identify, until sharp cries ring out from the open field.

Darting my eyes toward Quinn, we both pause, pulling back on the reins. The horses stall as we listen.

Men. The cries are from men. I take a shaky breath, realizing that those screams are not from Bria.

But whatever is making them scream like that cannot be good news. That animal or creature, or whatever it is, is not something I want to come across tonight. The horses stamp in place, clearly uncomfortable with the sounds, what they scent on the wind that whips toward us.

Pushing them forward, we continue slowly, treading carefully through the shrubbery. I keep my ears tuned into the surroundings for any clue as to what may be occurring up ahead, not wanting to fall prey to an ambush. But another scream comes quick on the heels of the last and this scream makes my stomach drop nearly out of my body and my blood run cold as ice.

My eyes flare open as I look at Quinn. And I know he sees the wide-eyed fury, the rage within me, when I hear that noise.

"Bria!" I shout her name and slam my heels into the horse, taking off without a glance back to see if Quinn is following.

Even though I wish I didn't, I know that scream. I've heard it tear from her lips when she had the visions of Nimai. Only this time, it sounds so much worse. This is her pain, not her sister's, and the grip she has on my heart twists, nearly sucking the breath right out of me with the thought.

My earlier comment to Quinn echoes in my ears. *You have no idea how truly untouchable she is.* I'll kill them. Whoever this is—whoever dared lay a hand on her—they won't live to see the sun rise.

I jam my heels again, forcing the horse to thunder across the field. Clumps of grass come up to meet my shins as I scan the area for any sign of her. The thick shrubbery conceals much of the ground, but I spot a hulking figure a little way off the path. The man stands in a small open area, his head cast down toward the ground.

Bria.

Yanking on the reins, I point myself toward him, closing in. His face looms closer with every hoofbeat. The sword in his grasp is raised and when I near, I launch myself from the horse, rolling into the grass toward the man. The sharp impact barely stuns me, rage keeping my body moving. Landing the roll in a crouch, I pull myself up to full height and draw the swords on either side of my hips.

He spins, shock rippling across his haggard face. He clearly was not expecting a trained soldier to come up on him in the middle of the night. Bria's crumpled form is beneath him, his boot still resting on her hand. An arrow is lodged in her shoulder, mere inches from her heart, and I thank the gods she has on her armor, or it would be even deeper. My own heart wrenches so hard in my chest at the sight, I worry I may fall to the ground beside her.

Blinding rage engulfs my body. Teeth and jaw clenched so tight they might crack, my hands grip the swords with such effort the leather is bruising. A guttural growl, more animal than man, erupts from my lungs before I slam the swords into him, piercing either side of his neck. He wears no armor that high up and blood pours from his mouth almost instantly. I wrench the swords, digging them in further and watch as his mouth goes slack, gasps turning to gurgling as blood floods his mouth and lungs. I kick a booted foot into him, yanking both my swords free with a repulsive and satisfying rip of flesh, shoving his body away so it lands with a loud thud on the ground.

My knees hit the grass beside her, hands trembling, searching her body for a pulse. Grasping her neck, I work to regulate my heavy breathing so I can feel her skin. Her body is warm, and after a moment, the steady beating of her pulse registers strong beneath the pads of my fingers where they lay on her neck. I breathe out a long and ragged exhalation, moving my hands to touch her blood-spattered face. She's alive.

Scrambling myself behind her, I tug Bria's body into my own, cradling her small form in my lap. I make sure to move her gently, careful of the injured shoulder and wrist. Her wrist looks horrid, and her fingers are mangled. The bones must be shattered from the way it hangs limply from her body.

I press my mouth into her forehead, kissing her hair.

Quinn moves in front of me then, hand on the hilt of his sword. He's looking down at me, staring at Bria's lax body resting in my lap. His mouth sets in a hard line and muscles flick along his tensed jaw, his eyes narrowing on her.

"Is she—?"

"She's alive," I choke out. "She passed out. I'm going to guess it's from the pain. She's been shot with an arrow and her wrist is broken, maybe her fingers too. He had his fucking boot on her, crushing her."

Quinn curses and kneels beside me to gingerly examine her wrist and fingers.

"We need to bind it for now, until we can find a healer to set her bones and make sure she can actually use the thing. There's no way she'll wield a weapon right now. Not like this." He's shaking his head as he uses a dagger to tear away the hem of his tunic.

Quinn begins wrapping it around her lifeless hand, through the space between her thumb and fingers and up her forearm before tying it off. He works quickly, stealing glances at her, fearing she may wake up while he jostles her injuries.

"It's going to have to do for now," he says when he finishes, and I nod in agreement. Bria's eyes flutter but she remains unconscious.

"Did you see the others?" Quinn asks, his face shrouded in shadow. Something like fear lurks behind those hazel eyes.

I shake my head. "No. What others?"

Quinn slides his hand down his face, leaning back on his heels. "The other men, the ones we heard screaming. She tore them to pieces before this happened. Shit, Ev. You weren't kidding." He finally saw her power, and I know how eye-opening and frightening it must be for him.

But I peer down at her and there's no fear in me. I've witnessed the shadows she possesses, the dark magic that lies within her blood and bones. And all it did was strengthen the admiration I have for her, strengthen the love I feel, the connection to her. She's brave and strong and fierce as all hell, something to admire, not something to fear.

Her face is peaceful. For now. It's funny what shock does to your body. She will hurt when she wakes, but I will be here for her. I'm not leaving her side again.

"Ev." I've been sitting here, staring at her in the moonlight, unable to break my gaze away when I hear Quinn's voice. "We need to get the arrow out before she wakes. It will be easier on her."

My body tenses, knowing the suffering it will cause her already wrecked body.

"I know," I acquiesce before pressing another kiss into her hair. I don't care anymore what Quinn says about it, or anyone else for that matter. I will kiss her if I damn well please.

Gripping Bria tightly against my chest, I lean back to allow Quinn access to the arrow, watching as my friend places one hand on her armored chest and grasps the remainder of the arrow with the other. Our eyes lock for a fleeting second before he yanks his hand back, ripping the arrow and the tip out with it.

Bria's eyes fly open, and another scream tears from her lungs. I hold her closer against me, her head on my shoulder and press my hand firmly into her wound to staunch the blood. Resting my cheek against hers, I whisper to her, trying my best to calm her rapidly beating heart and her gasping breath.

"It's okay, Bria, you're okay. I'm here," I repeat the words, letting it sink in that she's not alone, that she's safe and alive, hoping I can wash away her fears as the shock fades and she comes back to the present. I stay there, pressed against her for a few minutes as her body tenses and the pain floods her system. The warm wet of her tears pool against my cheek and I bring my lips to kiss them away, each and every one, letting the salt seep into my lips and tongue and wishing I could kiss the agony away.

Bria tilts her head back, looking up at me with gleaming eyes. No fire now, just her beautiful cobalt blue eyes sparkling with moonlight.

"Ev." Her breathing is ragged, and sobs are catching in her throat.

She goes to move her hand, to reach up to me, but a hiss escapes her lips instead. Pain is likely lancing through the shoulder where she was shot. My heart sinks when I notice she doesn't even try to move the other hand, still wrapped in the hem of Quinn's tunic. She was awake for that torture then, knows exactly how broken and battered that hand is.

Moving her gently to the side, I cradle her back in my arm so I can see her face. I wipe the remaining tears from her dirt-stained face with my thumb.

"My hand?" she questions, not looking down at the lifeless limb.

I swallow before speaking. "We'll find you a healer."

When I stroke my thumb over her cheek again, she smiles, though it doesn't fully reach her eyes. Instead, it twists her beautiful face into more of a grimace, misery radiating through her features.

"I got two of them. Two out of three," she says wistfully, her eyes brightening just a bit.

The corner of my mouth tugs up. "I got the third," I respond, lowering my face to hers and placing a gentle kiss across her lips. Despite her suffering, she kisses me back, letting her lips linger softly on mine.

"I hate to interrupt," Quinn's voice breaks the moment of peace between us. Bria pulls back when she hears him. Her eyes leave me for the first time since she's woken, and I think she's just now realizing he's also here.

"But we need to get the hell out of here before there are more. I can't imagine all the screaming hasn't attracted attention." He rises to his feet, moving to gather the horses.

Quinn returns a moment later with our two, Bria's nowhere to be found. It must have taken off when she summoned the shadows. I say as much to Quinn, who agrees. Though, there's not much we can do about it now.

I adjust Bria in my grip, holding her tight and keeping her cradled in my arms when I stand before depositing her gently on the ground in front of me to adjust the saddle and bags. As much as I want to hold her all night, she has no injuries to her legs or feet and is perfectly capable of standing. I just don't want to let her.

There's no horse for her to ride and I am unwilling to be separated from her for even a moment. She's riding with me. Before she can stretch her wounded arms up to the horse and try to mount it herself, I wrap my arms around her once more and lift her from the ground effortlessly. When I hold her in my arms it makes it seem impossible that such a dainty little thing could usher forth such menacing and gruesome magic.

"Thank you," she says quietly, before grabbing the pommel with her left hand and cradling her shattered wrist in the crook of her arm.

I glance at Quinn before I hop up into the saddle behind her, impressed that he didn't argue for Bria to ride with him instead. I know Quinn witnessed each one of the kisses I laid upon her, and he was keeping silent about it. For now, at least.

My arm slides gently around her waist and I hold her close, backing her body up into mine. The lavender smell is faint on her hair, mixed with the earthy scent of the dirt she had been lying in and the copper tang of her blood. I breathe deeply, letting her smell ease the fear inside I had when I thought I lost her. She was here. She *is* here. And when she lays her head back on my chest, I rest my cheek to hers again before kicking the horse to get moving.

"You killed him." A soft affirmation of my actions as the horse begins to trot away.

I move to kiss the side of her neck.

"As I will anyone who lays a hand on you," I promise, and we set off into the night.

CHAPTER 37

Bria

We ride through the next day, making our way out of that dreaded scrubland, the wretched Gravenear Territory where I was attacked. We only pause for a few short breaks to stretch weary limbs and allow the horses to graze and drink. None of us packed food, all fleeing the camp in a rush the prior night. But Quinn scavenged through the belongings of the downed men, finding enough dried meat to suffice and some money to aid in buying more should we need it.

As we travel further southeast, the weather markedly improves. The beginnings of spring are apparent in every grove we pass. Hues of moss and mint speckle the soft, muddy ground, rose and apricot-colored buds dotting the trees. And the breeze. I inhale the warm air, infused with a fresh floral scent. It reminds me of the gardens where we grew up and makes me yearn to go back there. Whatever is left of it, that is.

Quinn had mentioned a large town we would cross into soon. Fallholt, I think he called it. He said we should be there by dark, and the plan is to find lodging for a few hours so we can rest and allow the horses some time to recover. There, we can stock up on more food to last the remainder of the trip. The town rests on the edge of the Gilded Forest which will take us another day to fully pass through. But then...then we will be on the outskirts of the capital. Easthallow and Castle Eccleston will be within my grip.

Evander and Quinn had been deep in discussion all day and I struggled to keep my attention on them, my body dropping in and out of sleep. Weariness had taken over, along with the pain of my injuries, and I was having a hard time keeping awake at all. Not to mention I was trying to sleep while atop a horse. It's not the easiest thing to do, and it's been making any sleep at all happen in short bursts.

Their talks are of strategy, formulating plans for how to approach the town and how to infiltrate the castle. I need to keep my gifts under control this close to the capital. And traveling through a town with no clear reason will rouse suspicion if we aren't careful. I've gathered that much from the bits of their chatter I've actually managed to listen to.

Listening to their conversation, I realize that any town this big that happens to still be standing will be sworn to the king. And therefore, be full of people who will capture me without thinking twice about it. They settle on a story where the two of them are escorting me from the small southern town of Dunnwurth to stay with family in Easthallow. We all happen to be familiar with Dunnwurth, having grown up only a few towns over from there and are hoping it will serve as enough of an excuse. If anyone asks questions, we know at least enough about the area to answer with some detail, though the idea is to be out of there before too many questions can be asked anyway.

Despite my drifting in and out of consciousness, I'm awake now. Dusk is settling around us and the horizon is striped in crisp orange and deep pinks. I figure we must be getting close to Fallholt by now. The pain in my wrist and fingers is a constant, dull ache, but if I move it at all, sharp jabs radiate through my bones and make my stomach twist and turn with nausea.

Once we find a healer, setting the bones will be unpleasant, to say the least. I see how limp my wrist hangs and how my ring finger bends at an awkward angle. The wrist is completely shattered, and I worry there may be no way for a healer to completely fix the damage that's been done. They can try, and I can at least get something for the pain. I press my back against Ev, leaving my body flush with his chest, letting the warmth of him encompass me along with his arms that encircle my waist. One hand rests on my hip, and I nestle further into him.

"You're awake," he says against my ear when I move. The feeling of his breath sends a shiver down my spine. There's the lingering scent of lemongrass in his hair, but it is quickly being replaced with a more damp, musky aroma from sweat and fighting the night before.

"Mmmm," I hum, tipping my head back to his shoulder.

We are positioned slightly behind Quinn, the road narrower here, not allowing the ease of riding side by side. His outline is faint as the sky darkens and he is wholly focused on getting to the town ahead of us. Small pinpricks of glinting lights are emerging in the distance indicating how close we are.

Evander moves my hair to the side and trails his nose up the edge of my neck, pressing a kiss into the hollow below my ear. The tickling sensation sends me wriggling against him, and he stiffens, tightening his hand on my waist, fingers gripping into me.

His breath is hot against the skin of my neck, and he latches his teeth around the lobe of my ear, nipping quickly before releasing the skin. I stifle a cry at the unexpectedly sharp sensation that's quickly followed by a throbbing throughout my body. We should both be focused on getting to the town, but the distraction from the uncertainty ahead and the agony of the here and now is welcome. So instead, I press against him again, pushing my hips back and grinding. Warmth floods through me, dulling the aching I feel in my shoulder and wrist, effectively giving me the distraction I crave.

He groans in my ear, fingers pressing deeper into my hip, and my skin flushes in response.

"What do you think you're doing?"

The action is far bolder than how I've normally been around men, or around him, even. Maybe it's the impending future, the unknown. Maybe it's the fact that I nearly died and now knowing that I still have time. But I want more of what we shared. Want to experience everything I can with him while there's still time to do so.

"Thinking about how to thank you for last night," I respond, my voice only a fraction above a whisper, trying not to attract Quinn's attention.

It happens to be the truth. That's exactly what I'm thinking about. He gave me a night of pleasure and I repaid him by trapping him in my shadows, getting shot, having my wrist and hand destroyed, and dragging him into this mess of a situation.

His voice remains low, his tone turning firm. "Bria, you never have to thank me for protecting you," he insists. "Not only is it my job to do so, but I want to."

I shake my head, feeling his face pressing against mine as I do.

"I wasn't talking about that." I move my hips again and his hand dips inward on my leg, letting me know he now understands what I mean. His fingers leave my hip and trail along my thigh, sending a pulsing between them.

Evander's lips graze over my neck, his fingers creeping slowly across to my inner thigh and coasting steadily upward. He pushes his thumb directly to my center, pressing the seam of my pants against the swollen and needy area. I suck in a sharp breath, stilling and waiting for him to continue.

"Not here," he says firmly, quickly removing his hand and laying it back on my hip. I sigh heavily, disappointed in the annoying reality that he's right. A quick glance to Quinn shows no indication he noticed the interaction, but it shows in my body's response to him, burning and slick with desire.

But then the town of Fallholt comes into view, the beauty of it striking and it puts a damper on the urgency I feel for Ev. Lanterns hang from posts lining the cobblestone road into the heart of the town. Stately homes are woven in with shops and businesses. People are roaming the streets, going about their normal lives. Some turn their heads to look at the newcomers, probably because we look a bit worse for wear right now. But most mind their own business and we fall into the bustle easily.

I had forgotten what being in a real town was like. The sounds, the smells, everything is hitting me at once. It's overwhelming and exciting at the same time. This place makes me think of Nimai and how we would walk through the streets of Elwyn together, perusing shops, buying treats, and spending the day with one another. It only takes a few moments with those memories before I remember my purpose here. Nimai.

A chill runs through my veins. The mark of Vaohr—an icy blue circle inlaid with a crystal-tipped spear—is everywhere, the emberstone that is said to have ended the Keeper. The true story, of course, is that he cleaved his magic in two to create his daughters and that without that happening, Edwin's men would never have killed the god. But that's not how the Eccleston family likes it portrayed. The priests took the symbol as their emblem to prove how they retrieved the magic for the rightful god. Their god.

My parents privately worshipped to the gods of the Woods—the Keeper, Uldnoir, the god of life and death; the Current, Rhezenar, the god of water and wind; and the Incendiary, Caarae, the goddess of earth and fire. The true deities in this world. But they had done so in the quiet of their own homes, never exposing us as heathens.

Many others did the same, the magical bloodlines remaining true to the gods of the Woods in secret. I know Evander's mother was one of them, that she prayed to the rightful gods until her husband took them to Easthallow. I sometimes catch myself speaking to Lilith when I'm alone. Not a prayer per say, but more of a one-sided conversation. I was never much for prayers.

But this symbol makes my blood boil, knowing the men who destroyed my family bore the emblem of Vaohr and the king. An obvious contrast to the emblem of the prophecy so often worn in secret by the gifted, the symbol I know Evander still wears after all these years.

Just as I think of him, he stiffens behind me, also catching sight of the symbol etched into nearly every surface. We need to remain vigilant, no matter how passive the town seems right now. We aren't safe here.

CHAPTER 38

Evander

We approach an inn just after Quinn and I lift Bria from the horse, carefully avoiding her injuries. We hand the horses over to a stable hand for the night, hoping this will be enough rest for them. Inside, the establishment is small and cozy, insanely similar to our home back in the northern camp. No side parlors or meeting rooms here though, just an open dining area where a few people from the town sit eying us when we walk in.

Despite the warmer temperatures, I asked that Bria remain cloaked in an effort to hide her fractured hand from view. The material is blood-stained and dirty, but I stamped out as much of it as I could before putting it back on her. And now, the dim lighting of the inn should keep it from being too visible. Attracting the least amount of attention possible is our plan here.

Quinn approaches the innkeeper, asking for two rooms, one for the two of us and one for Bria. I listen as he politely converses with the woman and he requests the rooms be next to each other, likely so we can be close in case anything happens to her. But I'm not leaving her side. Quinn can have the other room to himself whether he likes it or not.

She sends a maid ahead of us with heated water for the baths and we follow the innkeeper up the stairs shortly after. She's kind and has no questions for us when Quinn inquires about a healer she could send up to the room. The woman informs us dinner has already been served but she will have the maid bring food up to the rooms and will request the healer as soon as possible. No issues there, it seems.

I stop at the first door and swing it open, ushering Bria inside with a hand on her lower back. Quinn stares at me wide-eyed as I step in behind her, but I shut the door before he has the chance to utter his complaints. I'll hear it at some point tonight, but it doesn't need to be right this second. Right now, Bria needs rest, food, and a bath while she waits for the healer.

Once in the room, I ensure the door is locked before helping Bria with her cloak and boots, asking her to get some rest while we wait. She falls fast asleep within minutes, and I slip into the adjoining washroom, strip down, and drop my body into the bath, only using one of the buckets to clean myself and happy for a quiet moment to wipe the reminder of last night from my skin.

When I finish scrubbing myself raw, cleansing my skin of the sweat and crusted blood, it's reddened and smells faintly of sage. The worn towels of the inn are soft and warm, despite their age. As I dry off, I catch sight of my reflection in the mirror and realize I desperately need to shave, or I'll be sporting a full beard by the time we get to the capital. I make a mental note to ask the innkeeper for a razor in the morning before we set off.

Once the bath is drained from my blood and dirt, I refill the basin, pouring in the buckets of hot water, their steam rising into lazy curls around me. I pull my trousers back on and maneuver softly back into the bedroom, sitting down on the bed next to Bria and attempting to gently rouse her from her exhausted slumber. I stroke her hair, trying my best not to startle her awake, lest she injure herself further before the healer arrives.

"Bria, wake up. You need to bathe," I whisper as she stirs beneath my hands. We weren't able to sufficiently clean the wound in her shoulder while in that scrubland. Quinn only managed to pour some water on it during the first stop we made while I held her still. Infection remains a real concern if she doesn't have it cleaned out soon. By the looks of those men last night, I can only imagine the state of their weapons and the arrow they shot at her.

"Is there water?" she asks, her voice thick with sleep.

"Yes, it's waiting for you," I assure her, helping her to her feet.

Having little faith she can do all of this herself given the injuries she's sustained, I plan to stand outside the washroom while she bathes. There's no chance she can use her right hand in its current condition and her shoulder is bothering her more than she's likely to admit, making her range of motion limited.

"I'll be out here if you need me," I tell her, stepping out and going to close the door behind me to give her privacy. But her quiet voice carries to me before I can go.

"Ev." I spin back around to face her. Her hair is a tangle of gold and bronze, streaked with the deep crimson of her blood. She looks better than she did last night, the color returning to her pink cheeks, but she's still drained. I can tell by how drawn her face is and how her shoulders slump when she moves. I suppose that's probably from the agony she's experiencing.

"I can't get this tunic off," she admits, her face contorting in a frown.

"Right, I should have realized that." Heat creeps up my neck and face and there's no hiding the blush. I still haven't put a shirt on, so the flushed skin of my embarrassment is on full display.

Bria raises her left arm above her head, hissing with the movement. My stomach clenches at that noise, wanting to tell her to just go back to bed and rest, but I know better. She needs to clean up and the hot water will relax her aching muscles until the healer arrives and can give her something to ease the pain.

I grasp the hem of her tunic and lift it gingerly, holding the excess in my hands as I slowly move it up her body. My knuckles drag along her sides as I expose the skin of her stomach, then the swell of her breasts. I pause so she can slide her left arm down, releasing it from the tunic before I gently pull it the rest of the way over her head. I move carefully to release her right arm, ensuring I don't disrupt the wrapping Quinn managed the night before.

My gaze lifts to hers and she meets me with a coquettish grin. The fire is back in her deep cobalt eyes as she gazes at me, the flicker of flames warm and inviting. The tunic falls from my grasp and I slide my hands to the waistband of her pants, hooking my fingers into each side. Dropping to the ground, I kneel before her and tug them free of her hips. When I graze a kiss across her hipbone, I hear her suck in a sharp breath before I yank them the rest of the way down and over her feet.

Gripping her calves in each hand, I run my palms up the smooth lines of her legs, resting them just below her ass. Her perfect, supple ass. When I grasp it in both hands and squeeze tight, she shudders beneath my touch. I know I should let her rest, let her clean up, but I'm dying for another taste of her. To lick her until she comes in ragged gasps all over my face like she did last night. My eyes meet hers again and it occurs to me that I've never seen her fully naked before now. She's glorious and perfect and fucking made for me. She's exhausted and covered in dirt and grime and blood. And my sadistic ass has never been more turned on or wanted someone more.

A loud knock breaks our locked gaze from one another as we both turn our heads toward the bedroom. The interruption sets my jaw in a tense line and I stand, picking her up gently and lifting her into the awaiting tub. When her body lowers into the steaming water, she closes her eyes, wincing as her shoulder dips under. I press my lips to her forehead and head toward the bedroom.

"I'll be right back," I say as I walk away, closing the door to the washroom to keep her warm and adjusting my trousers to hide the raging erection that lies within. *Gods.* Damn whoever is knocking at the door right now because I'm tempted to leave them out there and squeeze my body into that tiny bath with her.

When I fling the door open to find Quinn, I almost slam it right back in his face. But he has a tray of food in his hands and folded clothing tucked under his arm. His ebony hair is still damp, pulled back into his usual knot.

"They just brought this up and the innkeeper, Rayna, said that the healer should be here shortly. She'll bring her to us as soon as she arrives." Quinn moves to come inside the room, and I step aside, allowing him entrance even though I don't want to. "I figured we could all eat and discuss the plan for when we get to Easthallow.

When I turn from the door, Quinn has made his way to the corner of the room, laying the tray of food on the small table. He stands beside it, staring at me with heavy eyes. We are all bone-weary and drained from the travel and lack of sleep over the last day.

"Where's Bria?" he questions.

"In the bath," I respond, crossing my arms.

Quinn nods. "Good, she needs to get that wound cleaned out." He moves to open the tray of food and a mix of mouthwatering scents waft from beneath it. Fresh bread and a pot of hearty stew with beef and vegetables are set upon the tray, along with a variety of dessert pastries. The way my stomach growls just from the smell makes me realize just how little we have eaten today—a few sticks of salted meat, stale and sour with the beginnings of rot.

"I'll go check on her, she needs to eat before the healer gets here," I reply, making my way back toward the washroom. To my surprise, Quinn doesn't make a comment or try to stop me. Instead, he casts his eyes down toward the table and proceeds to ladle stew into the bowls.

CHAPTER 39

Bria

The warm water soothes my aching body once I let myself relax in the small tub. I make sure to keep my fractured wrist propped on the edge. It hangs lifeless and I look away, unable to stand the sight of my shattered bones, even when wrapped and shielded from view. I know how broken it is and every time I look at it, I can hear my bones crunching under that boot. Quinn's deep voice travels through the closed door. Knowing it isn't the healer yet, I decide to stay and soak away as much of the pain as I can.

I chance one look at the gaping wound in my shoulder before deciding it isn't worth the nausea it causes. The water around me is swirling with pink and red tendrils from the seeping blood. It stings, but it's nothing compared to my wrist and fingers. My concern over whether the bones can be set and healed is increasing by the minute.

If there's no healing it, I'll be going into the capital—into the castle —with only magic to protect me. Magic I have to hide. If my wrist and hand are beyond repair... I push away the thought, shoving it deep down inside, not willing to even think of failing my sister.

Closing my eyes, I sink deeper, my knees still exposed to the air. I was an idiot for leaving that way, I acted like a child, and now I can only wish I would have paused for just a second to think about what I was doing instead of reacting so brashly in the moment. I could have asked Silas to come with me. Then maybe the attack would not have ended the way it did. Maybe I would have more energy to save Nimai.

Silas. *Shit*. I hadn't even thought about him until now. Is he going to come after me? There's no way he didn't feel something when I had that vision and even more so when I was attacked.

Evander comes back into the room quietly, interrupting my thoughts and pulling me back from the spiral of shame I'm losing myself to. There is no sense in dwelling on it. We're here now, and I need to deal with it. He kneels beside the bathtub, his hand caressing my hair, still matted with blood.

"The water is getting cold and you need to eat," he says, taking in the fact that I've been sitting here, wallowing in my own idiocy and filth, and have yet to actually bathe.

I purse my lips and grab for the wash rag, grimacing when a stabbing sensation ricochets through my shoulder. Evander watches me closely and takes the rag from my hand, lathering it in soap. He stays kneeling beside the tub, his molten eyes watching me.

"Can you lean forward?" he asks, his voice low and husky.

My body tenses when it occurs to me that he means to wash me. Heat floods through my body at the thought but I nod and move my torso for him. Ev gently works the soap into my back and neck before moving to my arms and shoulders. The wash rag is soft, his touch tender, and the smell of sage wafts up to meet me. He squeezes the cooling water out of the rag and into my nasty hair before slowly detangling it, taking his time.

It's relaxing, to my surprise. Evander finishes my hair, rinsing out the soap and lathers around the front of my shoulders, treading carefully around the wound so as to not cause any harm. I notice his eyes roam across my body as he bathes me, taking in every inch of exposed skin and sending a pulsing between my legs. The thought of what else we could be doing right now causes me to clamp my thighs together and bite down on my lip. It's embarrassing and a bit twisted that he's taking care of me and all I can think about is dragging him into the bath on top of me.

He hands the rag over with a seductive grin as if he's been reading each emotion as it plays across my face and knows exactly what I've been thinking. *Chivalrous of him*, I think as I take the cloth and begin scrubbing the front of my body. I'll admit, I wanted him to continue and wash the front of me as well, but Quinn is outside of the room. The intensity of Evander's gaze as his eyes remain fixed on me tells me enough to guess he doesn't care about Quinn, so I pick up my pace.

When the dirt and blood is freed from under my nails, I sit up in the tub, exposing myself to the chill of the air in the room. But before my body has a chance to register the temperature change, Ev is there pulling my body from the bath and wrapping me in a soft towel. I thank him quietly when he places me gently on the ground and holds the towel tight as he reaches for clean clothing.

"The innkeeper," he responds, answering the question in my arched brows.

"Nice of her."

"Your clothes are a mess. I think they may just burn the other tunic," he remarks, wrinkling his nose, and I snort. It's disgusting, covered in blood, torn from the arrow and my fight the night before.

This new tunic is black with a snug fit and the sleeves are shorter than those of the usual tunics I wear. The temperature is much warmer here, so it makes sense. The fabric is soft as Ev drops it over my head and it brushes against my skin. He helps me slide my arms through the holes, which takes more effort than I'd like to admit, and tugs it down.

The pants fit nicely, a thinner pair of leggings that will be easier for me to maneuver in. As he shimmies the leggings up my calves, I steady myself on his shoulders, fighting the urge to run my hands down his still-bare chest. He's not wearing the symbol of the prophecy any longer and part of me longs to ask him about it. Did he take it off because of me?

Gods, what is wrong with me? He's helping me because I cannot do this myself. That's all this is, and I try to focus on that, feeling slightly perturbed by the muscles that bulge in his abs as he moves to stand. How *dare* he look like that.

But then he leaves his hands in my waistband and meets my gaze and I can't help myself. I raise to the tops of my toes to graze my lips along his. He pulls me closer, yanking me by the pants, and kisses me back, the force slamming my body flush against him as his tongue swipes across mine. I groan into him, wanting more.

Quinn slams his hand on the door forcefully. "You two realize I'm still out here, right?"

Ev pulls his head back and smirks. "How could we forget?" he drawls before planting a gentle kiss on my lips. Heat rises into my cheeks. I had, in fact, forgotten he was in the other room, completely consumed in Ev and the moment.

He slides his hands out of my waistband and holds my hand in his before turning toward the door. I allow Ev to lead me out of the room and come face to face with Quinn, who does not look amused. His face is set in a perturbed grimace as he watches the two of us and our interlocked fingers. His eyes dart to Evander, and he rolls his eyes.

"Put on a gods damned shirt," he snarls. "The healer is here."

Evander drops my hand and goes to gather his shirt while Quinn strides to the door, opening it for the healer. She's an older woman, likely older than my mother. Her long brown hair falls in cinnamon waves around her shoulders and her eyes are a shade of rich brown sparkling with gold. They remind me slightly of Evander's eyes and it makes me warm to the woman instantly.

"Sit on the bed, love, and let me have a look at your wounds," she commands quietly when she enters.

I oblige the woman and go to the edge of the bed. Quinn brings a wooden chair from the corner table over to the woman. Now that I'm awake and clean, I survey the room and the small table by Quinn. Then I see the food. I can smell the stew and my stomach grumbles audibly.

The woman chuckles at the sound and sits her plump form directly in front of me.

"It will only take a few minutes, love. Then you should get some food and rest." She gives me something to drink and tells me to relax before pulling aside the tunic to reveal the wound in my shoulder. The drink smells herbal and is not something I would choose to drink again if given the option, but I assume it's a tea meant to ease the pain. And that, I will gladly take. Any reprieve from the suffering is welcome.

I wonder if Quinn told the woman of my injuries beforehand when she hones in on the wound. She begins plucking splinters from around the hole, likely from when I snapped the arrow shaft. I wince, realizing I probably did more damage to the area with that move than I thought.

I shoot a look at Quinn in the corner of the room. His hazel eyes are wide and set on the woman. He meets my stare, knitting his brows together and shifting his head side to side, slightly. So, he didn't tell her about my shoulder. I glance to Evander next, who leans against the dresser, his focus is set on the woman as well. *Peculiar.*

The healer follows up by rubbing an ointment into my skin and directly on the wound. I brace myself for the shock of it, but nothing comes. Whatever painkiller this woman gave me must be strong, some tea with nearly immediate effects.

"There," she says, tugging the tunic back over my shoulder with care. "No infection will grow now that it's cleaned up. Now let's see the wrist."

She moves to grasp my limp wrist and unwinds the binds, gingerly taking off the shredded bit of tunic.

"Where are you from?" I ask.

Whatever this woman is, she's not just a healer and I feel an urgency to know more about her. She's strange—she knew of my wounds without anyone telling her. Sure, the wrist is bound and she can see that easily, but I was dressed to cover the shoulder. And there's also this feeling when she touches me... She feels warm and inviting and familiar.

The woman continues to unwrap my wrist, holding my arm gently as her fingers move.

"Oh, far west, my dear. Not anywhere you would have been, I'm afraid," she answers dryly as she begins to touch my skin. Her fingers are soft against the fragile bones of my wrist, and she gently dances them across my skin.

She makes a "tsk" noise in her throat and closes her eyes as she considers the damage, then moves her fingers deftly around. The warmth emanating from the healer's skin increases and seeps into my pores. She shifts the bones and still there is no pain, only heat trailing behind her fingers. The embers within me spark with her touch and flare to life.

I recognize this feeling.

"Magic," I breathe, watching the woman before me. Both men's eyes are on me, the skin on my neck pebbling beneath their stares.

A wry smile creeps across her face but she doesn't look up from my hand and instead proceeds to wind a new bandage around my wrist to stabilize the bones.

"I have no idea what you speak of," she remarks, rising from her chair and gathering her basket of supplies from the floor. "You should be better shortly, and you will regain use of the hand. It will be back to normal before you know it." She strides to the door and plants her hand on the knob, turning to me before she leaves. Her brown eyes glow with the same inner flame I feel.

"Oh, and Prophecy?" she says softly, the name slicing through the silence of the room. "Good luck and may the gods be with you." And with that, the mysterious woman slips out the door.

I sit there staring at the door for a few beats, not daring to take a breath. *What the fuck just happened?* I hear Quinn moving before I see him, his boots scuffing against the wooden floors.

"Shit!" he continues spitting expletives as he paces to the door and locks it behind the healer. "How did she know?" He spins on his heel, eyes flaring at me.

Remembering to breathe, I take a long inhalation and lift my good shoulder. "I'm not sure, but—" I stop, concentrating on that feeling I had. "I could feel her energy."

Evander shifts on his feet by the dresser, arms crossed over his chest.

"Like with Silas?" He's watching me, and I can see understanding dawning on his face. He gives me a faint smile and my heart warms over.

"Yes," I confirm, nodding.

Quinn leans back against the closed door and shoves his hands into his pockets. "It doesn't make sense," he says, looking between the two of us, trying to piece together the puzzle of the bizarre woman who just left. "For someone with magic to be *here*. In this town. Did you see the mark of Vaohr? It's everywhere."

He has a point. How has she survived here for so long?

"Perhaps because she could hide it through her work as a healer," Evander offers, pushing off from the side of the dresser and walking to the small table in the corner of the room. He scoops up the remaining bowls of stew and comes to sit next to me, resting a bowl on the bedside table for me.

I thank him, moving closer to the food and starting to eat. The stew is still hot, and the savory broth is exquisite compared to the salted meat as it hits my taste buds. I'm so hungry I would shovel it down my throat if given the option, but using my non-dominant hand is more challenging than I expected and I struggle not to spill it all over myself.

"My mother told me of them. The healers of old would travel to different towns and villages aiding those in need. They've been around for ages," Evander pauses, swirling the stew with his spoon. "But they came from the Forsaken Woods. Some of the first blessed by the gods and the land."

He stares at his bowl, and I gather thinking of his mother must be very painful for him. I reach my bandaged hand across the space between us and place it on his thigh, letting him know I'm here and I understand.

His lips turn up slightly at the gesture and he continues. "She told me as a child that they still walk the lands even with the king and his...laws. I saw some of them in the dungeons, I thought he had found them all. Their power is great and could be of such use if they could openly practice, but Braddock doesn't discriminate what someone's powers are, just the magnitude of them. Though now, it appears my mother was right. There's no telling how old that woman is and how long she's been here."

Quinn's shoulders slump, relief settling into his bones when Evander is done speaking. Someone with magic would not be out to get us, meaning the healer is not a threat to us, no more than she is to herself in this town.

Evander has begun eating, scarfing his stew comically fast. I clamp my lips together, fighting the smile that strains against it as I watch him. Quinn notices as well and shakes his head. "Did you tell her the plan for the capital?"

Evander chokes on his stew, coughing, and covers his mouth. "No," he sputters.

I finish my own meal and sit up straight, throwing a pointed look toward Evander.

"What plan?"

"Well, what I was saying—" Quinn starts, but Evander cuts him off.

"It's. Too. Risky," he says, punching out each word to make sure his point is heard.

I scoot my body back closer to him, sitting with my legs crossed under me, and lay my injured arm across his leg. "Ev, just let him tell me what it is." My voice is soft and his tension lessens, though only slightly, as he places the empty bowl beside him on the mattress.

Ev drags a hand through his hair, still damp in spots from washing up before waking me. Then he looks at Quinn, whose hands are shoved deep in his pockets. He appears slightly more relaxed here, taking in the lack of armor and weapons. I'm confident his body still houses weapons I cannot see, but there's no show of it. He's also fresh from bathing, his dark hair pulled back from his face revealing the beauty of his jawline and eyes. He looks far less menacing like this.

"We were discussing strategy on the way here. I think the only way we can get you into Castle Eccleston safely is for Ev to bring you." Those endearing hazel eyes are steady on me as he speaks, gauging my reaction.

My plan had been to cloak myself in shadow and I say as much to him, but Quinn frowns and shakes his head. Evander slips his hand behind my back, hugging me tight to his side. Quinn's jaw goes stiff at the all-too-familiar gesture, but he keeps talking.

"You got past two guards that way, Bria. This is different. There are sets of guards placed throughout the castle. And from what Ev has said, the dungeons are more heavily guarded, not from the outside, but once you get into them. Soldiers walk the hallways at all hours, shifts of them move through constantly." He shrugs before continuing. "There's no way you would have the energy to cloak yourself for that long and then cloak both you and Nimai to escape. It's unlikely you would even make it to her. Not to mention, you've never been in the castle and have no idea where you're going," he finishes, his lips set in a firm line.

Well then.

I run my tongue over my lips and purse them, thinking. I know from years of being his friend that I won't win this argument with him. The castle is not my territory, these are not people I know, and I am not a soldier, despite the training I've received. This is an area he excels in and though it frustrates me to admit it, he's right.

"Fine," I concede after mere moments of contemplation, my eyes locked on Quinn's. The corner of his mouth turns up in a winning grin, hinting at the gorgeous set of dimples I know he possesses. But a full smile out of Quinn is rare.

"Fine?" Evander is incredulous, jolting his head back to look at me, his nostrils flaring. "Are you out of your mind? Do you have any idea what you're agreeing to right now?" His head snaps to Quinn, who is still grinning.

The prick always has been a sore winner.

"There has to be a way we can help her cloak better. We can tell her where all the guards are. I know where she needs to go." His voice hardens at the last part.

Quinn shrugs again. "Wasn't it just you and Ash who said she has no choice in her life? Who said she should be allowed to live as she pleases?" Quinn queries, one brow quirked at his friend.

Evander goes silent. Quinn always wins these types of conversations. I'm certain he only argues when he already knows he's right. Which is, irritatingly, all the time. *Cocky bastard.*

Wanting more information about how he thinks this could possibly work, I press him. "So what? He's going to turn me in?" I ask.

"Such a smart girl you are, Bria." I catch a flash of the full smile, the deep dimples, and his glistening eyes. No wonder that curly-haired girl was all over him. "That was my first thought as well."

One glance at Evander and the confusion I feel is mirrored on his face. At least it isn't just me who feels out of the loop with all of this. Quinn keeps going.

"But realistically that won't work in your favor. In that case, you would be alone, locked in another dungeon until they could figure out what to do with you." He sighs heavily. "It would give you no access to Nimai and Ev can't help you. There's no way they would let him near you."

Evander stiffens at that. "I could figure out a way to get to her. If we *must* do it your way." His hand tightens around my waist.

Quinn shakes his head, a tendril of ebony escaping to frame his face.

"I believe you think that Ev, and I believe you would do whatever you could to get to her. Including getting yourself killed or outing yourself to your father."

There he goes. Right again.

Ev's shoulders fall a little and I move my hand against his leg, trying to reassure him. Quinn is a master of tactic, he's been a soldier all his life. We just need to hear him out. Quinn ignores our interaction and brings his gaze back to me.

"No, he's not going to turn you in, Bria. He's going to waltz right in there with you on his arm." His eyes darken and the look on his face is deadly. This is the soldier at work.

"As his betrothed."

B ria tenses beside me, and it takes me a minute to register what my friend just said.

"What the fuck are you talking about?" I snap once I can form words again in my suddenly dry mouth.

The bastard still has a smile on his face. This fact that this is his plan is a bit shocking. He's a gods damned commander and had been trained long before he came to the rebel camp. Quinn is the most strategic person I know, unbelievably skilled when it comes to all things battle related.

"If she is your betrothed, you will be allowed to stay together," Quinn says, proudly fleshing out his plan as we sit, bystanders to his performance. "At least in the beginning, to keep up pretenses, that is. You can get her into the castle, and you can get her out."

"But why would Aamon accept me as Ev's betrothed? He's the one who betrayed my family. He wants me dead," Bria says, her voice hard.

But Quinn has a point. I know what he's getting at and as much as it hurts to tell her the truth, she deserves it.

"He doesn't want you dead, Bria," I explain, as her brows furrow with puzzlement. "He wants to use you for your magic, wants to deliver you to the priests." The pieces of Quinn's plan are becoming clearer.

"But you said they would kill me, you've all told me that for years."

I sigh, "And they will, eventually."

Bria doesn't know enough about what happens in the dungeons. We had decided to spare her when I came to the northern camp, chose to keep the details hidden with the thought that she would never have to face the reality of what occurs at Castle Eccleston. But now she does. I pull back the loose strands of hair in my eyes, and turn to face her, unable to move my hand from the small of her back—needing that connection, that touch.

"Bria, what they do to people in the dungeons, it's..." I struggle to find words to describe the horrors.

"People like you are kept captive for as long as they can stand it. They are beaten, burned, whipped, and tortured. They're drugged into complacency. Then the high priestess drains their energy, drains the magic from them, leaving them just enough to sustain life. Eventually, the person is drained completely, and they're left to rot down there." The shock and disgust her expression stings, but I continue, knowing she needs to hear it.

"The priestess channels all of this energy into these...orbs—these blue glass spheres that the priests wield to show the world, to show all of Azudora, that they are the rightful magic users. The priests use the energy sparingly because they know that the ruse is up if their supply runs out. I'm genuinely not sure where most of it goes, because they pull far more energy than they use. But with your power, they won't want you dead right away—they'll want to use you for as long as possible."

Bria sucks in a sharp breath at the new information. She was aware they were using people with magic, but we had never told her what they do once they have them, how truly awful it is.

"So why wouldn't Aamon just drug me, or beat me, or do whatever it takes to drag me down into a dungeon with my sister the second I arrive?" she asks, her voice wavering.

Quinn pushes off from the door and comes to sit in the chair beside the bed directly in front of Bria. He looks at her and grabs her uninjured hand, holding it in his own as he talks to her.

"Because you are unbelievably powerful, Bria." He breathes out, staring at her. I watch the interaction, listening to Quinn rationalize the plan.

"He knows you're the prophecy, along with your sister. He's known for years. It's why he turned you in, it's why he's hunted you. Nimai has yet to come into her gifts, but you...you've shown what you're capable of, at least some of it. Aamon is aware you've shown some of Lilith's gifts already. They aren't prepared to subdue you."

Quinn hangs his head, still holding her hand. She doesn't move her eyes from him.

"If they don't see me as a threat, there's no reason to subdue me. Not yet."

Quinn glances up at her, a hint of a smile returning to his face. "Smart girl," he replies, squeezing her hand.

"If you are there willingly, believing that the king and the priests are right and that they will protect you—that Vaohr will protect you—then there is no reason for you to fight them, and no reason for them to control you," he continues. "At least not at first."

I clear my throat that feels so dry and scratchy now. "We would need to be in and out within a few days. Once they figure out how much sedative to give you or get any inkling that you may not agree with what they are saying, things will change drastically."

Concern weighs heavily on my chest. This may be our best bet, but it's still extremely risky for Bria and risking her is something I have no interest in. But she nods, coming to full understanding of what's being asked of her.

"So, I need to pretend that I think I'm unworthy of my gifts, that I want the protection of Vaohr and that Ev has convinced me the capital is where I need to be to make that happen?"

"Precisely," Quinn agrees. "And Ev gets to play the bad guy." He smirks at me then, and I give him a disgusted scowl in return. I played that role for four years and never planned on returning to it.

"You need to be convincing, Ev. Make your dad think this was all a game of seducing the girl and bringing her back to the castle on your arm." His eyes are a dark shade of green and gold when they narrow on me. He knows what it means to ask me to do this. He knows more than anyone how that place broke me, how long it had taken me to heal.

"There needs to be a reason you left. And a reason you've returned. You know that."

My jaw tenses, the muscles in my neck stiff as I look at Bria. The warmth of her eyes makes my chest ache. I will do this. But I know in my heart I'm not doing it for the sake of the world and the prophecy, or even for her sister. I'm doing it for her. And only her.

"I understand."

Quinn sits back, releasing Bria's hand, and stuffs his hands back down in his pockets. He surveys the two of us for a minute. His gaze moves from Bria's arm hanging over my leg to my hand pressed along her lower back. We remain close, her seeming to need the touch just as much as I do. Quinn throws his head toward us.

"At least you won't have to pretend that you're fucking."

CHAPTER 41

Bria

Evander lets a low sound escape his lips, a growl in response to Quinn's remark. But I sit still as his hand presses into me, trying to soak in all the information I just received. The horrors of the castle were something I knew of only distantly, not expecting to ever need to come face to face with them. And knowing my sister is down there, and what could be happening to her, makes my stomach twist up in knots, the stew threatening to make a second appearance.

Those who went willingly to the priests were said to be blessed, allowed to live a full life in commitment to Vaohr because they recognized their unworthiness. They were sacrificing themselves to right the unbalance of the world. But that was a lie and always had been. Those who turned themselves in saw no different fates than those who were captured. All were brought to the dungeons. All were used and abused in the name of the one true god.

"Okay," I say finally.

"That's my girl," Quinn coos, shooting me that beaming, two-dimple smile.

Evander is scowling. He hates the idea of going back. Even before tonight, I was aware his time there was horrendous, and I wanted to avoid him having to return at all costs. But now, hearing more of what actually occurs there, I want even less for him to go. But Quinn is right, it's the best shot we have at saving Nimai and getting out alive.

"So where will you be? You can't come with us," I ask softly, realizing we'll need to part from our dear friend during this journey.

"Right. Aamon would recognize me the moment I step foot in Castle Eccleston." He crosses his arms over his chest, leaning further back into the chair. "And unlike you, lucky Bria, he has no use for me. We'll take the path of the Gilded Forest. I'll stay there and wait for you both."

He continues speaking and I wonder how I ever could have missed the warrior in training when we were younger. I'd been too consumed with my own life, my new powers, and my family to see it, I suppose. His family was intertwined with the rebels, as was mine. But I was unaware. Quinn had not received that luxury. He was bound with a secret from a young age and the lines marring his handsome face show the years of worry, of having to grow up too fast. Though, maybe we all had experienced a little of that.

"You will arrive on foot," he continues. "Cite the attack and your horse taking off during the incident, if anyone asks. Though they will probably be too absorbed in your return, Ev."

"Not entirely untrue," Evander chimes in, the grit still in his voice. I lean into him more, seeking his warmth and comfort. His body relaxes slightly under my weight.

"Why wouldn't we just take the horse?" I question.

His teeth flash and my stomach does a somersault, having a mind of its own when it sees that smile. *Good luck to anyone who tries to snag him*, I think. The man's smile could set you on fire. And apparently talking tactics makes him a very happy man indeed. It's the most I've seen him smile since we were children.

"Because if you do, that horse is staying there. If you manage to rescue Nimai and get all three of you out of the castle, you'll still need to get to the stables. And from there, steal two horses and, what? Ride off into the sunset?" He lets out a chuckle. "Ev would be killed, and you and Nimai would be drugged and dragged back to the castle before you even made it out of Easthallow."

Right again. Insufferable. Cloaking the three of us in shadow would be easier for me if there were not massive horses to also cloak. Again, he's making sense.

Quinn stands staring at the two of us, his gaze lingering on all the places our bodies meet, likely realizing that his push to keep us apart has been futile. He grimaces, his expression pained.

"Get some rest, you both need it. I'll come get you in the morning. We can figure out the details on our ride tomorrow."

He moves toward the door, and a fresh wave of panic takes over—the injuries I experienced in the scrubland, the fear when I almost died, the emotions I'm sure to battle the entire time we are in the capital... Whether Nimai receives visions of me like I do of her, I don't know. But there is another person I have a connection to. And I'm positive he knows exactly what's happening and both Quinn and Evander need to be aware of that as well.

"Quinn."

He turns back, eyeing me warily when he notes my expression, one hand still positioned on the doorknob.

"What about Silas?"

He keeps his expression neutral. "What about him?"

"He knows. He *has* to know," I explain, holding up my damaged wrist. "He's going to come for me." Evander's grip on me tightens, but Quinn just sets his mouth in a flat line.

Maybe they finally understand. Or at least they are accepting the magic that keeps Silas and I tethered to one another. It's odd, but since I left the camp, there has been an ache I can't quite pinpoint, something that's missing. My body—my magic—wants him back.

"I'll find him."

And with that, he leaves, closing the door gently behind him. Despite the fear I have about going to the castle, I also feel confident that Quinn knows what he's doing. Confident that he will indeed find Silas and keep him safe until I return. But when I let my gaze find Evander, the same surety is not registering on his sorrowful face.

"You're sure about this?" he asks, his face softening as concern blossoms in his chocolate eyes.

I snort, somehow finding the morbid amusement in the situation. "I'm not really sure what other choice we have."

"But seeing my father again, being forced to lie about who you are and what you believe... I just want to make sure you're okay with it. As much as you can be, that is."

He's too wonderful, thinking about me throughout all of this instead of himself. I angle my body to fully face him, his hand slipping from my back as I move. Looking into his eyes, I can't help but focus on the warmth within.

"It's going to be far harder for you to face your father. So really, Ev, I should be asking you if it's okay. Not the other way around. You're risking your life to save my sister."

"She's not just your sister, Bria. She's also the future of Azudora." He reaches out to hold my hand, stroking his thumb along the back of it. "As are you. And I will do everything in my power to keep you both alive."

I swallow hard, nodding my head. He means it and he will try, but it doesn't push away the feeling that we might both meet our end in the walls of that castle, that neither of us may make it back to Quinn and Silas. And where would that leave the rebel forces? Without a prophecy to end the years of hiding, protecting their own, and trying to right the wrongs of the king and his priests.

Even thinking of Helara and the other rebels makes grief and guilt surge through me. If I survive this, the rebel captain might just kill me for leaving in the dead of night. The woman has become a second mother to me over the years and this betrayal of her trust will cut deep. Not to mention she happens to be a very close friend of my parents and had sworn to keep me safe.

"Ev?" I ask quietly, my eyes cast down at our intertwined hands, his tanned skin so dark against the pure white of my own. "Do you think my mother is alive?"

The thought has been racing through my head since the moment I found out where Nimai was. He stiffens beside me, and his hand squeezes mine.

"I truly hope so Bria," he whispers softly.

There had been no word from the southern camp before the visions started. But somehow, Nimai was taken. My mother could be in the dungeons with her. Or she could be dead. There's no way she would have fled without Nimai, I feel sure of that. But her magic would not have aided the rebels in an attack. My mother could bless. She could bestow a brief gift upon another, be that a boost in strength for a limited time or an increase in fortitude. It was a useful power, one that could provide immense support in battle, but not something that would have saved her or Nimai.

Evander releases my hand to take the dishes back to the tray. He places it outside of the door, the gentle clinking ringing through the quiet room, and locks it behind him. He strips off his tunic, the muscles of his abs gleaming, and strides to the other side of the bed. He takes his trousers off and remains only in his undershorts. My stomach clenches as he climbs in beside me and I throw him what I hope is a coquettish grin.

A low chuckle escapes him before he opens his arms for me. I happily oblige, scooting my body into the curve of his, my back to his chest. He winds his top arm around me and interlaces his fingers with mine. I feel him nestle his head into my damp, unbound hair and brush a kiss across the back of my neck. My heart wells up inside me, the gesture feeling so intimate and welcoming, feeling so right.

We stay like that for some time, not speaking but just soaking in the touch of one another—the closeness, the silence, just being here together. At some point, fitted snugly into the man at my back, I drift off to sleep.

CHAPTER 42

Bria

There are no dreams that night. No visions, either. And upon waking, I grow more concerned. I'm worried the connection has been severed, that something awful has happened to Nimai. But I stuff the worry and grief as deep down inside myself as I can. I will not allow any of those feelings to surface until I know for sure.

When I roll over, I take in the sight of Evander still sleeping beside me. His arm is hanging over my torso. I had been sleeping curled into him all night. His bare chest rises and falls steadily, his breathing easy. His jaw traces a firm angle along his face beneath the stubble and his nose is a long, straight line, surprisingly free from any knots or bumps given how many fistfights I know he had been in as a boy. It's amazing really, because it's impossible he never broke it.

I want to spend every day staring at him, taking in the soft hair that falls onto his forehead no matter how he tries to style it back, and the golden flecks that make his eyes gleam. I don't want to get up and move on with the day, to face whatever lies ahead of us.

The urge to touch him overpowers me and I reach out a hand to pull back one of the strands that trails along his forehead, twirling it around my finger as I push it into place. The hair on top is longer than the sides and he tends to keep it back, but I love when the pieces break free. I gently trace my fingers along the side of his cheek, rough from days of not shaving. I smile, thinking of how handsome he looks and how I never want to leave.

But getting up right now makes more sense. Quinn is not one to sleep in, especially not in a town like this, when we are surrounded by potential enemies and need to get moving again. So I drag my nose along the bridge of his before planting a kiss on his forehead. But when I move to roll away, Evander tightens his grip around my waist, pulling me back toward him.

I erupt in a girlish squeal, thinking he was fast asleep.

"Where do you think you're going?" His voice is a low growl, thick with sleep.

I can't help giggling slightly and he opens his eyes, raising a brow in response. I'm not one to giggle. Ever. And he noticed. But I feel lighter when I'm with him. My worries fade for a time when it's just the two of us.

"I was going to get up and get ready," I say, pretending as if the giggle never occurred.

But Ev rolls me quickly onto my back, his arm still locked around my waist. He arrives flat on top of me and stares down, his eyes molten once again.

"Mmmm." He drags his lips up the side of my neck to whisper in my ear. "I thought there was a discussion of repayment."

The way my body reacts to him, both to his touch and his words, is unlike anything I've felt before. An instant surge of pleasure pulses between my thighs.

"I'm not sure we have time for all I had planned," I breathe back, hoping I come off as more seductive than I feel.

Ev leans his head back to look at me, his eyebrows raised again, and I lock my gaze on him, flashing him a full smile before I roll my hips beneath him.

His jaw clenches. "You're killing me," he murmurs, dipping his head to run his tongue up the front of my neck before flicking it across my lips.

He pulls his arm from around my waist to trail his fingers along the waistband of the leggings I still wear, slowly sliding his hand underneath. I suck in a breath as my core heats under his touch, my body already becoming slick with want.

Watching me intently, Evander moves his hand to cup me before dragging a finger lazily across my center. My body arches back in response, and I reach for the front of his shorts. The corner of his mouth turns up slightly and he begins to move his fingers again, quicker this time. I let out a moan as the pulsing between my legs heightens and yank the band of his shorts, dropping my hand in to grasp him, hard and ready. His eyes close when my hand slides over him and back down again and he lets out a groan of pleasure.

Gods. Feeling just how big he is in my hands makes my mouth go dry.

The loud knock at the door jars both of us, forcing me to drop my hands from his body.

Evander snarls. "I'm *actually* going to kill him," he fumes, slipping his hands from my pants and rising to go to the door.

But I slide off the bed quickly and move in front of him before he makes it across the room, placing my hands on his chest to stop him. Evander looks down at me with a confused expression.

"Maybe I should get the door," I suggest with a glance down at his shorts, straining from the aftermath of our morning encounter. The sight is damning and causes another surge of heated desire to wash over me.

He groans again and grabs me by the neck, sliding his tongue into my mouth quickly before dropping the kiss. But it's enough to bring the flush back into my cheeks, a pleasant burning rising inside me. As he strides to the washroom, I watch the muscles of his back ripple and the curve of his ass in the tight shorts. *Breathe, Bria.* I let out a long exhale to steady myself and open the door.

Quinn is standing with one shoulder against the door jamb, already dressed in his leather armor, weapons strapped on. The dark and ominous warrior is back. He gives me a small smile as I run my hands through my hair, trying to straighten it.

"Don't bother," he says, pushing off from where he is leaning and walking past me into the room.

He flops himself onto the edge of the bed, the half-smile still lurking, and sets a bag down next to him. "I heard you through the door."

My face flames, heat rising up my neck and into my ears, embarrassment surging through me. My hand flies to my mouth, covering it when realization of what he said hits me. He heard *me* through the door.

Quinn waves it off. "It's fine, Bria. I don't care anymore." His gaze softens on me. "He's been in love with you since we were kids. Clearly there's no keeping you two apart."

In love with me? Surely Quinn is mistaken in that. I stand completely still, staring back at Quinn without speaking, and he cocks his head to the side in observation.

"You mean to tell me you never knew?" I shake my head in disbelief and Quinn shrugs. "I guess I did a better job controlling him back then than I have now."

A million memories swirl in my head when he speaks. All the times Evander found an excuse to touch me, to hold my hand, to pick me up and physically carry me back to my room when we all drank too much. All the little moments we shared together over the years, all the times I took for granted, assuming he was just a friend. Assuming that, though I cared for him and thought he was the most beautiful man I'd ever laid eyes on, he thought of me as a friend and only a friend. That even though we were allowed to be *that*, we would never be more.

"I figured the fistfights had clued you in a little," he says, a low laugh erupting with the words.

My eyes narrow on him. "What do you mean?"

"Most of them were about you. He defended your honor to a fault, getting himself knocked out on quite a few occasions. Though, it was different with Cedric." A smirk spreads across his face, and I remember the two of them rolling around on the ground. I remember when Evander landed a punch that nearly broke Cedric's jaw. Neither had ever told me what it was about, but I suppose now I know. "That one was a bit more personal. Jealousy at its finest."

"I never knew," I reply, still struggling to take in the new information.

"Cedric stood a real chance with you, and Ev knew it. But gods be damned if he didn't try to stop it anyway. He knew you were too far above him, knew it would never work. But it didn't stop him. I thought when he left, he finally got over you, but I was wrong. The second he came back to the camp with me, I saw it, the agony on his face when you wouldn't so much as look at him."

Quinn watches me for a moment before continuing. "You want to know why I tried to keep you two apart? It was for both your sakes. I knew you felt the same for him. Deny it as much as you want, you've always been drawn to him. And I knew losing you would crush him more than anything else in this world could."

My mouth opens to ask him more questions. I want to know everything. But before I get the chance, Ev is in the doorway of the washroom, dressed, clean-shaven, and ready to go.

I mutter an "excuse me," ducking my head past Ev and grabbing my armor off the dresser before walking into the washroom.

Pushing the door shut behind me, I lean against it, breathing heavily. *In love with me?* My stomach flutters at the thought, warmth coiling through me. I want to stand here and soak in the thought of it, the thought of truly being loved by someone. By him. But he didn't say those words to me. Quinn did.

I fight to shift my focus to today. I need to think about Nimai. By the end of the day, we will be through the Gilded Forest, and I'll be presented to Aamon and the king as Evander's betrothed.

If circumstances were different, being betrothed to him and going to meet his father would be a wonderful occasion, one to make me giddy, even. But these are not normal circumstances. The betrothal is not real. His father is a fucking a monster. The capital is cruel and wicked. My sister is their prisoner.

There's no telling the horrors of the castle and what evil fate awaits us there. They may not know I'm coming, but it still somehow feels like I'm inching closer to something deadly, something that I fear I may not come back from.

The door to the washroom closes behind Bria. She whisked by me on her way in, something off in the way she kept her head ducked and avoided contact with me. I move to the chair in the corner of the room and tug on one of my black leather boots.

"What did you say to her?" I ask, my eyes narrowing at Quinn sitting comfortably on the edge of the bed, hands resting between his legs.

"Only that I've given up trying to keep you two apart," he says, his lips tilting up.

"Good," I respond, bending to lace up the boot.

"Oh, and that I could hear her through the door."

Asshole. I grasp the other boot in my hand and fling it across the room at Quinn, eyes flaring. He quickly ducks his head to the side, snatching the boot before it can hit him in square in the face. I knew he said something to bother her, I just didn't expect him to have said *that.* Quinn doubles over, bursting out in a genuine laugh. I try to remain angry, but a responding smile breaks across my face as he tosses the boot back to me.

"You're a prick, you know that?"

"I've been called much worse," Quinn replies.

He has. And mostly by me. I toss my head, gesturing toward the bed. "What's in the bag?"

"Turns out the healer is Rayna's sister, which makes me wonder what other secrets that woman is keeping. But it means this inn is not too keen on the priests nor the Crown. Rayna caught me this morning and handed me the bag. Said she knew who Bria was and she wanted to help."

He reaches into the sack as he's talking and pulls out two necklaces holding the mark of Vaohr. The crystals of the emberstone spear reflect the light in the room, bouncing rainbows off every surface. The sight of those necklaces makes my whole body go rigid. The first thing I did when I fled the capital was rip the seal of Vaohr from the armor on my chest. I had sworn to never wear it again. Yet here it was. Mocking me.

"Nice touch," Bria's voice carries from the doorway and floats across my skin.

Her armor is strapped on, the bandolier fitted into place. Her hair is woven in a cascading braid that trails over her shoulder. She stands straight, shoulders back and arms linked across her chest. The sight of her dressed fully throws me off.

"You got your armor on by yourself?" I question, not realizing the healer's magic was that potent, that powerful, to have her moving so well today.

She gives me a knowing smile and taps her shoulder where the arrow had pierced her skin.

"It's just about healed. The pain is there but it's lessened," she begins, holding out her still-bandaged wrist. "The wrist still hurts, but I can move it today."

I can't help the beaming smile that contorts my face, the overwhelming joy I feel at seeing her own face free from pain. I feared that if it came to combat while in the castle, she would be unable to hold a weapon. Not that she's going to need one. I'll keep her safe at all costs and she still has her magic. But it will be better if she has the option, and by the looks of it, she'll be wielding at least a dagger by the time we get there.

Quinn stands from the bed, holding the necklaces in his hand.

"That's wonderful, Bria," he says, and I notice the tone of relief in his voice when he tosses one of the necklaces to her.

She catches it easily, her body moving like it should, not jerky and aching like the night before. Bria latches it behind her neck, careful to ensure the crest sits on the outside of her armor. I wince, watching her bear the symbol of the people who hate her. The people who will gladly use and kill her.

Quinn snatches the bag from the bed and strides over to me next. Grasping my shoulder with his hand, his fingers dig in and he stares at me, his gaze piercing. He holds out an open palm with the matching necklace sitting in the center. The glinting crystals make my stomach curl and a familiar scent of burning flesh sears through my memory. There's no need for him to speak, to say anything to me about what this means. Quinn understands how awful this is for me but I understand the gravity of our situation, and that I have no choice.

I cringe in disgust when I clasp the chain around my neck, leaving the crest on full display. Anyone who passes us will assume we are devoted to Vaohr. That's the plan.

"Let's get a move on then," Quinn orders, moving toward the door. "We can eat on the way," he says, tapping the bag in his hand.

Bria moves from the doorway of the washroom toward me, and I stretch out a hand for her. She clasps it and immediately intertwines her fingers with mine, squeezing my hand tightly in her grasp. We walk out the door together and slip through the back of the inn to the stable behind the building, careful to avoid the main area and any prying eyes that might try to glean who we are or where we are heading. Bria climbs onto the horse in front of me and I hold her tight as we set off for the Gilded Forest.

CHAPTER 44

Bria

The forest is breathtaking. From the moment we set foot inside, I understand why it was graced with the name. The trees drip with gold as if they had been carved from the precious metal and laid there, tree after tree, to form a sea of beautifully crafted statues. When we first enter, I raise a hand to brush my fingers over one of the glinting leaves, needing to touch it to see if it's real, to see if it's hard like the stone it resembles. But the leaf feels as any other would—soft, with slender grooves where the veins splinter it and ridges curving along the edges.

Legends say that Kiara died in this forest. That she attempted peace with the old king despite Lilith's insistence that she not. Kiara was light and love and wanted to see Azudora righted, wanted to see the world at peace—for those with magic and those without to live side by side in equilibrium, just as the rebels do now. She had traveled to the castle to speak with the king, leaving her family behind. And after her visit where he assured her things would change, she fell ill in the forest. Knowing he couldn't outright kill her without bringing down the wrath of Lilith, the king had poisoned her. Kiara was made by a god, but that didn't mean she was immortal, and she never made it out of the forest and back to her family. It's said that the trees wept gold for the sun that was lost that day.

Though the forest is thoroughly exquisite, the expanse of trees is dense, and that makes trekking through on horseback a bit tedious. The tightly packed trees are the reason it will take us a full day to get to the other side—we have to move at a slow pace to allow the horses ample time to maneuver around the roots. There are no paths, no roads through. So, we pick our way across the forest floor, bit by bit.

Wildlife is present in abundance. There are so many places for animals to live and survive, to thrive here with no sign of human life having etched its way into the forest. Evander explained to me that few pass through for fear of the king's wrath. He has promised to punish those who try to obtain the magic of Kiara that so clearly still possesses these woods. The wildlife is different too. I'm used to seeing rabbits and squirrels everywhere, as well as the occasional mountain lion, or wolf, in the mountainside town where we dwell. But here, there are tawny and cream deer, flocks of multicolored birds that nest in the golden trees, foxes with glimmering red coats, and striped wild cats. All beautiful in their own right.

"What is that?" I ask when we happen upon a majestic bird whose feathers look as if they are carved from the most precious gemstones. Sapphire and emerald glisten along the golden backdrop. It's large, and feathers fan out behind it as it strides over knotted roots.

"Oh, that's a peacock," Evander answers, as if the bird were a common occurrence everywhere. But I've never seen such an arresting creature and I stare, wanting desperately to stop and touch it.

Evander leans in to whisper in my ear.

"They were Kiara's favorite bird. Supposedly, she had dozens of them at her southern home, including ones that shone white like they were encrusted with diamonds. The forest changed when she died. Not only did the trees turn to gold, but the peacocks arrived. Pretty good reason, if you ask me, for why the king wants his subjects to steer clear of the place."

Pretty good reason indeed. This forest screams of magic.

I lean in, pressing my cheek against his as he speaks and breathing in the lingering sage that scents his skin. He shaved this morning, leaving his face smooth against mine. He was likely trying to look presentable before we made our way to the capital. Though I have to admit, he was dashing with the beginnings of a beard. It had been a rugged change that made him all the more endearing.

"How do you know so much about her?" I query.

He always seems to have the answers when it comes to the old ways, old magic. I feel him swallow before speaking, his jaw clenching against me.

"My mother," he responds, his voice low.

Of course. His mother had shared so much of the history with him. His father knew of her bloodline, knew Olaphina's veins ran hot with magic. But he insisted she keep her magic and beliefs to herself. She obliged, keeping some semblance of a normal life and leaving her history behind her, at least when her husband was around. I knew that much from what Evander had told us since his return.

His love for his mother was apparent. And watching her be tortured at the hands of his father had broken him. Quinn helped to pick of the pieces when Ev fled the capital, as had Ash. And it caused me grief to know that my own hatred of his father, of the people he spent those four years with, had kept me from being at his side during that time, had kept me from being a friend to him, and maybe more.

But going back there now, I'm overly concerned what memories might be stirred for him. Whatever happened to her must have been horrific, given his refusal to speak of it.

I turn my face to him and brush a soft kiss along the smooth skin of his cheek, wanting him to know I see the torment he feels, the mental suffering he endures when he talks about her. It makes me think of my own mother and how much I hope she still lives. It's a hard spot I find myself in—wishing she made it out alive and also wishing she were in the dungeons with Nimai so neither is alone.

The day wears on and we never leave the horses, with Quinn insisting that we eat while on horseback to keep moving. Anxiety increases in my bones as we travel, and I fidget constantly with the edges of my tunic. I notice when the sun moves from its perch high in the sky and dips back behind us, sensing the impending night.

As the daylight wanes, though, the forest comes alive. When I notice it, I suck in a breath and lean forward, eyes wide to take in as much of it as I can. The glittering gold that emanates from the trees when the evening sun is barely peeking through is breathtaking. Ev tightens his grip around my waist, pulling me back into his warmth.

"Enchanting, isn't it?" he remarks as though reading my thoughts.

"Yes, it truly is."

"I used to ride out here whenever I could," he whispers, his mouth close to me. "I would sit here and think...think about all of you."

I reach my hand back to touch his face and feel the curve of his smile. Ev had tried for years to find out where we were. It made my heart ache to think of him out here, in this forest of gold, by himself. He'd risked coming here, knowing it could get him killed, just for some solace from the capital and the monsters who reside there.

"I'm sorry." The apology leaves my lips before I fully register why I say it.

I was sorry for his time alone, sorry for the horrors he faced, sorry that I had not been there for him when he needed me most, and sorry that I was dragging him into all of this. Dragging him down with me when we both know the fate that awaits me. And as if he understands all the apologies that lie within that one, he presses his face to kiss my palm.

Evander moves our horse toward Quinn, getting closer to his friend who has been riding in front of us.

"We're close now," he tells Quinn, who nods in response.

"Right, let's find a place for me to make camp." Quinn trots off, searching for an acceptable area to hunker down for a few days.

After a bit of searching, he finds a cluster of golden trees whose branches are almost woven together, providing some shelter and privacy from anyone who may be risking the king's orders and passing through. Dismounting the horses, Quinn ties them together to let them graze.

The webbing of interlocking branches is a masterpiece of nature, or possibly of magic, given the history of the forest. I run my hand along it and when I pull it back, I half expect to see a glimmering of gold dust from the bark, but my fingers remain clean. The gold emanates from within the trees, pure sunlight radiating out of them, not just a mere coating of gold.

The roots below my boots bulge in swells and peaks, crowding the ground. Quinn will have a hard time finding a comfortable position for sleeping. The thought makes me feel a bit guilty, knowing I'll be staying in a lush room, likely with a huge bed, covered in silky pillows and luxurious sheets. Though surrounded by people who want to kill me and suck the life out of me, still—I'm the reason he'll be stuck out here. Had I not gone off gallivanting into the night on my own, he wouldn't be camping in a forest alone. I can only hope we make it out in a few days, and he's not left to suffer too long.

We help Quinn settle in, moving some downed branches in a few areas nearby to make it less likely for anyone who braves the woods to happen upon him. Not that they would survive if they did. There's no chance Quinn would let someone find him and live to tell the king.

Beads of sweat form along my hairline and I brush them away with the back of my bandaged hand. It took quite a bit of exertion back at the camp for me to sweat, but here, the air is warmer, and there's more than a hint of moisture to it. Even with the sun dipping below the horizon, the temperature has not cooled. Both Quinn and Evander have rolled up the sleeves of their tunics, revealing the sun-kissed skin of warriors. I dropped my cloak during the ride and am grateful for the short sleeves Rayna brought me back at the inn.

Once Quinn feels the area is safe enough for him to make camp, we sit and eat. I perch myself on a large root with Evander beside me and Quinn across from us, leaning his back against the gilded bark of a tree. Rayna packed plenty of foods fit for travel: jars of salted nuts and dried meats, some hard cheeses, and crusted bread. But she had also given Quinn containers of ripe spring berries that burst with sweetness.

Quinn reaches into the bag and brings out a small package wrapped in paper. He hands the package over to me and I respond with raised brows. What could he possibly have grabbed before we left the inn?

"Just open it," he mutters, irritation in his voice.

Carefully, I unfold the paper, my fingers aching a bit with the motion. My fingers and wrist are healing quickly but some pain lingers.

The smell hits me first. Vanilla and butter mixed with the tart scent of blueberries. *Scones.*

I let loose a small laugh and meet Quinn's eyes. The side of his lip turns up. He remembered they're my favorite. In our years at the camp, Ash tried to make them as best she could for me, tried to mimic her mother's recipe. But we rarely had all the necessary ingredients, and enough to spare for a more indulgent item like this.

"Thank you," I say, picking up one of the small pastries and taking a bite. I let out an embarrassing moan when I taste how buttery and flakey it is, delicious with the sweet and slightly sour burst of the blueberries. They taste so much like the ones Ash's mother made for me when we were younger, though hers were filled with chocolate. She knew I had always preferred chocolate to fruit.

Quinn waves his hand as if to suggest it was nothing. But it wasn't nothing. I'm lucky to have the foreboding warrior as my friend.

"I just figured you should have something you love in case it's your last meal."

Evander shoots him a glare, but I choke out a rough laugh. A full laugh that makes my body shake and my heart warm over. The morbid fact is it could be my last meal. I very well could find myself in a damp, dark dungeon within the next hour and not in a luxurious bed. We are betting on Aamon having a use for me. And we are placing our lives on the line for this bet.

When we finish eating, Quinn shifts the conversation back to strategy.

"You can't linger when you are in there. You need to find out where Nimai is as soon as possible. And once you find her, you need to get her out." His face is all hard lines, his hazel eyes serious.

We both nod in agreement. He had gone over the details of what we needed to do numerous times with us during the ride here. I needed to save my energy, not use magic at all while I was within the walls of the castle. I would need to cloak the three of us on the way out and Quinn didn't want anyone to see my gifts. If they found out more about my abilities, they would find a way to control me.

Quinn looks at Evander and his gaze softens on his best friend, his brother by choice.

"You need to prepare yourself for him. This is not the time for vengeance."

"I'm aware," Evander replies, but I can see the tension in his shoulders and the set of his jaw.

Quinn keeps on, a note of urgency in his voice. "Take his orders, do as he says, and make yourself the picture-perfect son. You've returned to him to serve his righteous god and you've brought him the one person he's hunted for years."

Evander drags a hand through his hair and sighs heavily. "I get it. I'll be fine."

Quinn scoffs. "I highly doubt that." His eyes slice to me. "Bria, you need to keep an eye on him. Rein him in if you see him breaking." His gaze burns with the same fury I feel when I think of Aamon. There is no love lost between Quinn and Evander's father.

"Whatever you feel for Aamon, know that Ev feels it worse. And the bloodlust you both have for him, for any of them, can wait for battle." He uses a hand to push off the base of the tree, pulling himself up to his full height. "Keep the necklaces visible, keep your heads down, and stay the fuck out of trouble. Please."

The pleading in his voice makes my throat tight, and he stretches his hand out toward me. I take it and let him gently tug me to stand. Still holding my hand, he grasps it tightly, and gazes at me. His hand is rough, like Ev's, like my own, and the callouses scratch at my skin.

"Bria," he starts, and the heartache in his eyes makes me want to sob. He's saying goodbye. And not just a normal goodbye that he would offer if we were to see each other in a few days. He too fears something may happen inside the walls of the castle, and that we may never speak again.

Unable to meet the sorrowful gaze he sets on me, I pull him into an embrace, wrapping my arms as far as they will go around his thick chest. He folds me into his arms, and I feel the soft kiss he plants on the top of my head. He whispers into my hair as I hold tight to his body, not wanting to let him go.

"I'll see you soon," he says, and he pulls back from the embrace.

Tears sting the back of my eyes, knowing he hopes those words will turn out true as much as I do. When he moves toward Evander, they clasp hands and pull into one another roughly. I cast my eyes away, wanting both to give them privacy and keep myself from crying. I stare at the trees instead, taking in the magnificent gold, now turning to a sea of sparkling stars with the glittering moonlight.

The men exchange a few muffled words and Evander moves behind me shortly after, placing his hand on the small of my back. And when I turn back to Quinn, he's already by the horses. Knowing Quinn as well as I do, I see the gesture for what it is. He said his goodbyes. He won't linger now. And neither will we. So, I allow Evander to steer me toward the edge of the forest. He grasps my hand and leads me through the thick trees.

We only walk for a short time before the gilded trees thin to reveal the massive stone walls that rise up around Easthallow. The walls are enormous but not as sturdy as I imagine they once were, with bits crumbling, leaving the structure jagged and foreboding. Evander stops at the tree line, tugging my hand back to stop me before I step out of cover.

He shoves his other hand deep in his pocket, fishing around for something. I arch a brow in response, waiting patiently for whatever he's doing. The smile that he throws back at me melts my heart, that left dimple pulling at his cheek. And when he drags his hand out of his pocket, I see a glint of crystals in the moonlight.

"Bria," he whispers, taking a step closer and moving into my space.

My breathing stalls in my throat when I see what it is he's holding. It's a ring. Delicate golden vines twist into an elaborate band that blooms with flowers of black crystal. He holds my left hand gently and I let him slide the ring into place, admiring the dark flowers embedded within it.

"It was my mother's ring," he explains while I stare at my hand, still resting in his. "The black tourmaline is said to protect. She gave it to me before..." He trails off, either not able or not willing to finish that sentence.

I lift my eyes from the ring to meet his gaze.

"It's gorgeous," I say, and I mean it. It may be the most stunning ring I've ever seen. Handcrafted perfection.

He smiles again and pulls my hands around his waist before placing his own on the back of my head. I have to lift my chin to keep my eyes on his. The gold within them warms me and I hold tight, content to have this brief moment to ourselves.

"I'd hoped to give it to you one day," he admits, a bit sheepishly.

My heart hammers in my chest in response to his words. My mind is spinning. Quinn said he had loved me since we were children and now here he is giving me his mother's ring and admitting his feelings, right as we are possibly about to go to our deaths.

"I just didn't imagine it would happen like this. His eyes darken before he leans down and places a soft kiss across my lips.

"Are you ready?" he asks, the whisper floating across my mouth, his face still hovering a breath above mine.

"Yes," I reply, pressing my lips back into him.

The ring is part of the role we need to play, and I understand that. But what he said means much more to me right now. He *planned* to give me this ring, his mother's ring. And that knowledge makes me ache inside. I want to live, to get the chance to make a life with him. He *planned* it, knowing that I would die. And not die old in my bed but young, long before I could love him properly or give him children. But now, I'm determined not to die within the walls of this castle. I will not die here, not now. I will get more time with him, even if it ends shortly thereafter.

He pulls back from the kiss and holds my wrists gently in his hands. Evander presses a kiss to each of my palms before he grasps my left hand in his, locking our fingers together. I feel the weight of the ring where it rests on my finger and a smile flits across my lips.

We push through the last few feet of the Gilded Forest and Castle Eccleston rises, an ominous sight blinding my view. It rips the happiness from my body like it is tearing my own heart from my chest.

We're here.

CHAPTER 45

Evander

Moments before pushing through the glistening trees of the Gilded Forest, I had felt utter bliss. Bria took my mother's ring, and though I gave it to her as a piece of the scheme for infiltrating the castle, I managed to tell her my true feelings about it, my intentions of one day giving this ring to her for real. She doesn't need to know I've thought about marrying her since we were young or that I had knocked Cedric out and nearly broken his jaw when he'd scoffed at the thought of her being his wife. But one day, one day I plan to tell her all of it.

Standing in front of the walls of Easthallow right now though, my heart sinks. I spent years here. The four longest years of my life, trying to figure out how to escape the reaches of my father, the reaches of the priests and the king. And now I'm back. Images of the dungeons, of people dying, and my mother...they all come flooding back.

And the smell. I can smell the crisp salt air from the sea already. Once, I had loved that smell. When I was living at home, I found Saturnine Bay a wonderful place. I remember sneaking off with Ash and Quinn and Bria and swimming there in the moonlight. But after my time in Easthallow, the smell makes my stomach surge. Because here, it isn't just the salt of the sea. No, this smell is tainted, tinged with burning flesh, the damp dirt of the dungeons, and the metallic tang of blood.

Clasping Bria's hand tighter within my own, I stride forward, following the edge of the wall until we come upon the main road. As we approach the main entrance to the city, I observe two guards standing to either side. One steps forward to stop us, hand on the hilt of his sword, his chest blazing with the emblem of Vaohr.

"Please state your bu—" The guard begins, but he's cut off by the other, rushing from his station toward us.

"Evander?" the guard cries out, disbelief rippling across his features.

He moves to clasp me around the shoulder, and my mouth breaks into a joyous smile. Theo. I drop Bria's hand and step forward to embrace my old friend.

Bria stiffens beside me, probably confused as to why I'm hugging a guard at the capital. But I did make a few friends during my time here, and Theo had been one of the closest. I'd left in the middle of the night, unexpectedly, and now I was returning after a year gone. None of them knew where I had been, though I assume rumors swirled in my absence about my betrayal.

"Where...where have you been?" Theo asks, pulling back to look deep into my eyes. His searching gaze leaves me wracked with guilt. I'd needed to leave, I did the right thing, but that doesn't mean I didn't hurt others in the process. The second guard stays still, not moving his hand from his sword, carefully watching the interaction between us.

"It's a long story, but I'm back now," I say, shrugging and reaching out a hand to pull Bria toward me.

"This is Bria," I begin, and she stretches out her hand toward the guard. "My betrothed."

Theo's eyes go wide at that statement, but I continue despite his surprise. I had not come off as the type to settle down during my time here. Not because I wanted to sleep around for the rest of my life, but because I held out hope that I would find her again. And I did.

"Bria, this is Theo."

Theo takes Bria's hand and kisses it lightly.

"It's a pleasure," she says softly, and he nods toward her in acknowledgement.

"Congratulations are in order, it appears," Theo responds kindly, looking between us. His eyes linger on Bria for longer than I like before he drags his gaze back to me.

"We must get a drink and catch up. But I assume right now, you would like to see your father?" he queries, his face turning dark.

Every muscle in my body tightens at the mention of my wretched father, but I force a small smile onto my lips.

"Yes Theo, can you let him know we're here?"

Theo gives a curt bob of his head and turns to the guard next to him.

"I'm going to escort them to Castle Eccleston." The guard gives Theo a confused expression, clearly not understanding who we are. "Send word ahead of us. Tell Captain Lansing his son has returned."

There it is. His eyes go wide and shift to mine. So, he *has* heard of me. I can't help the smug-as-shit grin that curls my lips. Who knows what the man has heard about me? What lies, or even truths, does he know? It's no matter, I'm going to set them all straight, make them understand I left for the cause.

As we follow Theo under the archway, I venture a glance up. There are large stone structures on either side that end in a giant metal curve. Right in the middle is an enormous symbol of the temple: a glowing blue circle with the crystal spear through the middle. The sight sends a shudder down my spine when we walk through.

We make our way toward the castle, and I keep a firm hold on Bria's hand. Tension is leaking out of her body and her hand is so hot against my own that it makes both our palms slick with sweat. The anger and fear she must be feeling right now are probably overwhelming. These are the people who killed her father, captured and have likely been torturing her sister, and would use Bria until there is nothing left if they had the chance. But they won't ever get that chance.

Theo attempts small talk, telling me what happened in my absence, how some guards had been promoted or moved on to other jobs, a few leaving to live quieter lives outside the city. We pass various shops and businesses as we wind our way through the city. It looks magnificent at night. I had forgotten how the city glowed with light. Townhomes stretch in rows to either side, nestled beyond the shops that line the central road, leading straight toward Castle Eccleston. Mostly the wealthy—the nobles—live in the glorious homes that pepper the street, leaving those less fortunate to make their own way further from the center.

I know these streets. I patrolled every inch of them when I lived here. But I also know all of the ways in and out of the city. I have an intimate knowledge of their weaknesses and strengths in terms of how the city is protected. There were numerous areas where the walls had crumbled, places one could pass through without fear of the guards. The king was so focused on his mission, on the magic and his control of the people, that he had no time for silly repairs of the wall. And from the look of it, that hasn't changed while I've been gone. When given the chance, I'll check to ensure the gap in the wall I used when I was here to escape to the Gilded Forest still remains. It's close enough to the castle that it could be our way out when the time comes.

I watch Bria as she takes in the city, her head swiveling around as we walk down the main road. She's never traveled here, and Easthallow is a great deal larger than Elwyn or Fallholt. I imagine that if things were different, she might actually like this city. The sights and sounds are so different from where we live now, and even from where we grew up. It's so much more...alive. And the people are genuine and wonderful...most of them. I've always felt a bit bad for them, having to live under such a cruel ruler and being forced to turn on their own. Though those in the capital have it better, there are no people with magic left here to turn on. Those bloodlines have been wiped out entirely after years of purging anyone with a drop of it. There's no one left here to conceive a child with gifts.

"Oh, and Luthais," Theo is still speaking about the other guards, and I cringe as I hear the name escape his lips. I was only half listening to my old friend drone on about people I don't care about. Thankfully, Theo is walking ahead of me and doesn't see the reaction.

"He's your father's second in command now. A recent promotion, but one he's flaunting around the city any chance he gets."

I grit my teeth and stretch out the tension that clenches in my neck. Bria presses closer in response, moving her body to tuck into me. She squeezes my hand, and I feel the warm metal of my mother's ring on her finger.

Theo swings his head around to grin at me just then.

"And yes, if you're wondering, he's just as much of a prick now as he was when you left," he says, and I bark out a laugh at the comment.

I've missed Theo. I'd pushed aside the thoughts of my friend while I was in the camp, knowing he would never understand the betrayal. He's loyal to a fault. But that loyalty to the Crown and the priests ran deep, far deeper than our friendship ever had.

"Not surprising that my father chose to promote him. The man is lethal," I say, looking to Bria so she understands. I want to be sure she knows to stay away from Luthais. At all costs.

"Who did he have to kill to get that position?" I question, prying my old friend for as much information as I can gather before seeing my father.

Theo laughs and it's a deep and genuine sound that pulls at my chest. I feel awful using Theo for my own purposes. Realistically, the man had done nothing wrong except for choosing the losing side in this war. But I can deal with the guilt later. The road is curving up ahead and the castle is in full view. We will be at the doors in a matter of minutes now.

"Not kill, but capture," he replies, his voice filled with glee as he glances back at me.

"Word around the city is he captured someone big. Someone who could take down the king with magic, someone working for the rebels." His voice lowers and he drops back next to me as he speaks. "I heard it was one of the sisters. The ones from the prophecy."

My stomach twists and I glance at Bria. Her face is pale, losing color and hardening, her mouth a straight line. From here, I can see the blue flames surging in her eyes. I trace my thumb along the back of her hand, urging her to calm before we enter the castle.

I flash a smile at Theo. "Well, good for Luthais then, sounds like he earned that promotion."

The words almost hurt as they leave my mouth, knowing I would prefer to cut Luthais from head to toe with my sword and instead I'm left here complimenting the bastard. When I look back at Bria, her eyes are set forward on the castle.

"Looks like you can congratulate him yourself," Theo remarks wryly, tossing his head in the direction of the doors.

The ornate double doors to the castle have opened ahead of us and I stiffen as we approach the granite steps. My father stands tall above me in crafted metal armor emblazoned with the mark of Vaohr, his hand on the hilt of his sword. From here, the light glints off his hair. Once a darker shade of black, it's now peppered with silver and white. His face is drawn, lips pursed, and his eyes widen as he takes in the sight of me, as if he expected the guards had lied when they said his son had returned. But the look he sets on Bria is far worse. A mix of awe and satisfaction whirls through his features.

He remembers her. How could he forget? She was breathtaking to anyone who saw her, with radiating cobalt eyes, long lashes, round cheeks, and that golden cascade of hair. Even now, her ivory skin gleams as the light reflects off it, a faint blush making those cheeks a rosy hue and brightening her face. My father watched her grow up, and not only that, but he hunted her. For five years. I imagine he saw Bria in his dreams each night, he thought of her that often.

Beside him is Luthais. He dons matching armor but without the ornate touches on the edges. His lip is curled into a sneer as he watches us at the base of the stairs. His cool gray eyes lock on Bria, and I want to pull her closer, but force myself to continue moving.

I tug Bria's hand, urging her to follow me as we ascend the large slabs of granite one torturous step at a time, bringing me back to the place I had hoped to leave and never return.

CHAPTER 46

Bria

My legs turn to lead as I follow Evander up the stairs to the castle. I want to run, and I have to stifle the urge to take off and drag Ev with me. But my sister is in there, so I steady myself, noting the two sets of eyes boring into me.

Aamon's gaze is heated, and I swear it's burning a hole straight through to my soul. He hates me for escaping, for making him look like a fool to the king. But he seems to be doing fine here even with that little tarnish on his name. And no matter the hatred he has for me, the feelings brewing in my core are far worse.

The shadows threaten to rip from my hands. I want to send my midnight vines out to strangle him, to steal his breath while I gut him where he stands. I had taken lives when warranted, but only a few over the course of my years, like those when we fled Elwyn and the men in the scrubland. But the moment I see Aamon, I know I'm prepared to do so again. And would not bat an eye at the aftermath.

The flames within me ignite at the thought and I try to concentrate on breathing. I need to control the energy, to control the magic inside. I have to save it for Nimai. *This is not the time for vengeance*. I can hear Quinn's words echoing in my mind and I straighten my spine to meet Aamon's searing gaze.

The other man's eyes are on me. I notice the odd slate gray as we ascend the steps. Perhaps they would be bluer if he were not wearing the metal armor, but here and now they are pure gray. *Luthais.* Ev had called him lethal, and I can see it. He emanates a wicked sense of power, and I have the feeling if I were to turn my back on this man, I wouldn't live to regret it.

Aamon's mouth curves into a conniving smile as we approach and stop in front of him.

"My son," he remarks. The words feel like oil against my skin. Slippery and slimy.

He breaks my gaze to set his sights on his son. And now I watch as Evander gives a curt nod to his father, that hardness still etched in his jaw.

"Captain Lansing," Evander says, sending a clear jolt of irritation through the normally stoic man.

"Please," he croons, a fake sweetness in his tone. "Let's not be so formal, Son." Aamon moves to embrace Evander and he lets my hand drop abruptly.

I'm not prepared for the sudden exposure without him next to me and my eyes dart to Luthais. He hasn't broken his stare, a sneer still plastered across his face. The light from inside the castle shines on his light blond hair, cropped close to his head on the sides and sweeping back in a roguishly tousled style, a little shorter than Ev's. His stare makes me shift on my feet, uncomfortable under the scrutiny of his gaze. His lips widen into a grin as he takes in the discomfort he causes.

Pulling back from the embrace, Aamon lets his eyes fall to me once more.

"Lady Bria Saldhene." His voice ghosts across my skin, causing a shiver to crawl like a spider down my spine and making all the tiny hairs on my neck stand at attention.

"To what do we owe the pleasure?" he purrs, his eyebrows raised.

The smile I force out toward the man who killed my father is thin lipped and I fear he will see right through it. Anger seethes inside, making heat surge through my veins. But before I can respond, Evander slides his body back to me, wrapping an arm around my waist and raising my hand in his. The light from inside the castle hits the crystals of the ring and sends sparkles falling all around us onto the granite steps.

"We've returned," he replies, his gaze shifting from his father to me. Evander's lip tilts in a genuine smile, and that gorgeous dimple crops up again, making me forget for a second that we are in front of our enemies. "We've come home to marry."

Evander glances back at his father whose face is rigid with shock at the unexpected news. He tries to hide it, regal captain that he is, but for a brief second, his walls come down and I catch it. There's a glimmer of hope that sparks to life inside me when those walls drop. Hope that this might actually work.

"To dedicate our lives in service to the king and Vaohr," Evander finishes, placing a whisper of a kiss along my hand.

When those lips brush my hand, I suck in a breath at the familiar gesture and the feeling of pleasure that comes along for the ride. Clearly being surrounded by these monsters is doing nothing to dampen my desire for him. Not to mention, he's doing far better than me at hiding his true emotions. Plastering a beaming smile on my face, I look at Evander, not at the villains before me. Happiness wells up inside as I gaze at him, helping me hold back the tingling of magic licking at my fingertips.

Aamon regains his composure quickly, setting his face in a gentle smile and reaching his arms out wide.

"What a truly unexpected and lovely surprise."

He steps forward to fold the both of us into another embrace and my body instantly begins to recoil. But Ev's hand is curled around my waist still and he presses me forward along with him, his fingers gripping into my side with bruising force.

Aamon touches my arm and I swallow, stifling the nausea that's creeping up my throat. Over his shoulder, I catch sight of Luthais with his eyes still fixed on me. Watching me.

Not wanting to give him any reason to think poorly of me, I play the part and wrap my hand around Aamon's waist, imagining my hands wrapping around his neck instead. So, when a small, wicked smile creeps across my face, it's authentic and Luthais notices.

His eyes narrow on me, and I smile wider, giving him a flash of teeth. A nefarious grin, had he known me at all, as I stand there imagining my shadows crushing both their windpipes and watching the life drain from their wretched faces. But he doesn't know me, none of them do. Aamon steps back, hands still clasped upon each of our shoulders.

"Let us get you both settled then," he declares, face beaming with joy. I wonder how true that joy is. Though I suppose he has no reason to doubt his son right now. And having me by his side is proof that Evander has not betrayed his father.

Aamon glances at me. "My dear Lady Bria, you must be exhausted from the trip. Perhaps you should retire for the night. Evander can fill me in on how this wonderful revelation came about."

Though I hate the idea of leaving Evander with these men, I nod my affirmation. Aamon holds out his arm to usher us forward and we stride into the castle. I may have grown up on an estate, my father being an earl and all, but this is grander than anything I have ever seen. I'm no stranger to the noble side of life, but this is not just nobility. This is royalty.

It's spectacular.

The entryway is brightly lit by an elaborate chandelier that drips with crystals, making it feel as though they are raining down upon me. Dropping my gaze to the floor, I see an exquisite mosaic of a deadly battle. I watch the story play out as we walk across the grand foyer, heading to the right of the main doors.

Realization hits me as we get to the end of the mosaic. There's a large man, depicted with long fangs and razor-sharp talons, not unlike the nightmarish creatures I call forth from the shadows. Darkness swirls around him, and through his heart is an emberstone-tipped spear. The gory depiction of the Keeper's death, or their version of it, sends a shudder rippling through me.

When I tear my focus from the god who created me, the powerful being I descended from, I notice Luthais watching me intently. The man is relentless. He smiles at me, the corner of his mouth turning up, and gestures to the floor beneath us.

"Gorgeous work of art isn't it, Lady Bria?" he probes. His voice is deeper than I expected. It's dark and soothing, a lulling sound that I imagine would come off very seductive to someone who was unaware of his cruelty. It sends my skin prickling.

"It is exquisite," I concede. Then, thinking of my role and trying to act the part of a demure woman, I add, "And please, call me Bria."

Luthais nods and extends his arm toward the staircase. "As you wish, my lady. King Braddock had it made to show all who enter Castle Eccleston who the real demons are in this war."

Evander tugs me in closer with the comment, making it apparent he does not want me to converse for longer than necessary with this peculiar man. Though, I have to admit, something about him intrigues me.

The ornate set of stairs in front of us curves up to a second floor. A carved wooden banister swirls alongside it, encrusted with gold leaf. As we begin ascending the wide stairs, Aamon stays in the front and Luthais behind. Intriguing or not, I still hate the idea of him behind me, worried what the man might do. But I remind myself of what Evander told me at the inn. These people want me alive, at least for now.

A beautiful rug sweeps over the stairs, a waterfall of sapphire that lines each step with a soft cushion, making our footsteps imperceptible. The walls around us are covered in priceless artwork and windows that run the height of the great room, stretching from the ground up to the second floor and framed with enormous velvet curtains of deep blue and gold.

Guards stood outside the doors when we arrived, but I had yet to see more until we hit the second floor landing. Here, I notice another guard, hand on his sword, patrolling the long corridor that stretches to our right. I imagine there are others, completing the same patrol around other parts of the castle. Braddock is not known for being a very trusting ruler.

The ceiling rises higher still above us, a domed cap soaring past the chandelier. The carved banister curves inward to create a balcony overlooking the grand entryway. Another mirrors it on the other side with a second set of ornate stairs. I assume that's the side of the castle where the royal family is housed. It is truly magnificent.

The deep blue carpet flows down the large hallway in front of me. The walls meet in a peak above where smaller versions of the crystal chandelier I saw before hang from the ceiling, sending more sparkles shimmering ahead of us.

"We had two rooms made up for you once we heard of your arrival," Aamon says from ahead of us, sending a glance back.

Evander has not moved his hand from around my waist and for that I'm immensely grateful. I don't know if I would have made it down this hallway, into the heart of the people who hate me, without his guiding, steady touch.

Doors line the hall, most of which are likely bedrooms, I think. Though every few hundred feet, the walls part on either side to shorter passages filled with more rooms—common areas, meeting rooms, and other gathering spots.

They are tucking us into the back of the castle, the last rooms in this unbelievably long hallway. My throat tightens as we near the end. It's so far away from any external doors. Probably far away from wherever the entry to the dungeons is. So far from Nimai, and from my freedom.

"Ahhh, here we are," Aamon croons, spinning on his heel and gesturing to the rooms across from one another. "I imagine you will find this room a bit nicer than your previous lodging in the guards' quarters, Evander," he says, attempting a dry bit of humor.

Evander lets out a short laugh. "I imagine I will."

He stretches out his hand to clasp his father's tightly, finally releasing his grip on my waist. I feel as if I might fall when he lets go, not realizing how much of my weight had been resting on his arm. I falter on my feet for a moment before a strong hand clasps around my arm, holding me steady before my body loses balance completely. I catch my footing and turn quickly, coming face to face with Luthais.

He smirks at me, his face uncomfortably close to mine. His hand is warm on my arm, and it makes my skin pebble with goosebumps.

"Careful, my lady." His voice caresses my skin, sending a shiver through me. I feel as though someone has poured cool water over my spine.

"Thank you," I manage between clenched teeth. I want to tear my arm from his firm grasp but hold myself back.

"It was my pleasure," he purrs back at me, releasing me. My skin sears where he touched me, and I would not be surprised to see burn marks where his fingers had been mere moments before. I worry my gifts are boiling over if I feel so much with just a touch.

When I turn back around, both Evander and his father are staring back at us, watching the interaction. Evander's eyes are narrowed, his gaze fixed on Luthais while Aamon's flick between us, confusion plaguing his features.

"I lost my balance," I explain. "I must be more tired than I thought." I force out a small laugh and place my hands at my waist.

Aamon's gaze softens. "Of course you are. I've had the servants draw you a bath and lay out some clean clothing for you."

He walks over to me. *Don't run, don't run.* I keep repeating that in my head as he picks up my hand, the one with the ring, and looks at it closely. *Does he recognize it?* I wonder. He blinks a few times and looks back up at me.

"I'm so very happy you've come, Bria." Bending down, he plants a chaste kiss on my cheek before stepping back.

"Oh, and I almost forgot." The smile leaves his eyes, and I can see the man who betrayed my father. The killer who lurks beneath his skin. "Your sister arrived the other day. Such a happy coincidence." He watches my face carefully as he speaks, inspecting me for any hint of knowledge about Nimai.

I bite down on my tongue so hard that it stings and copper floods my mouth. I will kill him.

"Nimai?" I question, flaring my eyes wide in feigned shock. "She's here? Can I see her?" I let the words pour out, tipping them with excitement at the thought of seeing my sister.

He smiles once again, and it meets his eyes now. Maybe I'm not such a bad actress after all.

"I'm sure she's already asleep by now, Bria. You and my son arrived very late this evening and most of the castle is in bed. But we can ensure you see her tomorrow. I give you my word."

Aamon angles away from me and looks at his son.

"Shall we?" he asks, clasping his hands behind him.

Evander nods. "Of course. Allow me to say goodnight first, if I may," he requests, holding his hand out in a gesture toward me.

Aamon chuckles. "Ahhh yes, say goodnight to your betrothed, Evander. Commander Keating and I will wait here for you."

With that, Evander moves to place his hand on the small of my back again and opens the door to the room ahead of us. I let him push me into the space and spin as he shuts the door behind him. He presses a finger to his lips as I open my mouth to speak. Evander closes the gap between us in a stride and wraps his arms around me, his mouth touching my ear.

"Quiet, Bria," he warns, his voice a whisper.

I lay my hands on his chest and breathe. They are just outside the door. I need to remain calm. But panic is setting in now that I'm in the room. Fear is surging through my body, my heartrate increasing, my palms becoming sweaty and itching.

"You're going to leave me in here?" I question, not daring to raise my voice. "And go with them? Are you sure that's a good idea?" I know the rising concern is conveyed in my words.

His heavy sigh brushes across the side of my neck, sending heat through me.

"What other choice is there? I must explain to him. He needs to believe this is real if we have any chance of it working," he whispers, his hands tracing circles along my back as he speaks.

He's right. I know that, but I still worry for him, going off with his father and Luthais. Knowing what they are capable of. So I nod, my cheek pressing against his.

"Please, be careful, Ev," I say softly, my grip on his shirt tightening.

Evander pulls his face back to look at me, his lip tilting upward. He gives me only a hint of a smile as he draws a hand up to cup my cheek. The gesture makes my heart ache.

"You're worried about me," he teases, curling a lock of my hair in his fingers before tucking it back behind my ear.

I smack my hands into his chest, and he laughs, pulling me tighter into his body.

"You're an ass."

He chuckles. "I'll be fine, Bria. I'll be back to check on you later." He brushes his lips across mine and I lean into it, deepening the kiss, taking in as much of him as I can. My fingers curl into his shirt and hold him close.

He breaks away and grabs my face in his hands before planting another soft kiss on my lips. But before I can pull him back for more, he turns and strides out the door. It clicks softly shut behind him and I rush to lock it.

I'm suddenly very aware of my surroundings.

I'm in the castle that belongs to the people who hate me. My only friend just walked out the door with two murderers. And my sister is somewhere far below me. In a dungeon.

Fuck.

CHAPTER 47

Evander

The fear in her eyes when I leave the room is agonizing. I long to stay with her, to keep her in my sights, worried what might happen if I leave her alone. But the words I spoke just moments before are true. Meeting with my father and Luthais right now is crucial in our story being accepted, a critical piece of my father believing me and my reasoning for returning. And luckily, the two people most capable of harming Bria are right here with me.

Luthais stays by my father's side the entire excruciating walk down the hallway. I was never keen on Luthais. I remember hearing he was orphaned as a teenager and ended up in the capital, though I never heard what fate befell his parents. Aamon made a habit of gathering any children of age who were abandoned to the temples each year and training them for the king's army. Luthais was one of the children taken in by the priests who worshipped Vaohr in his later years. Brought up inside the tainted religion.

He joined the army my last year in the capital, making him about twenty, I think. So young to have risen the ranks as quickly as he had. But there was something about Luthais. He was a merciless killer, naturally gifted with the agility and strength befitting a warrior. The only other natural-born warrior I'd met like that was Quinn. And despite my loyalty to Quinn, the rumors of Luthais made me wonder if even Quinn could best him.

Luthais had never spoken of his life before he came to live here. And no one in Easthallow seemed to know his history. He kept his personal life secret and the lack of information surrounding him made me uncomfortable. He was an enigma here and I had no trust nor use for the man.

Aamon turns down one of the side hallways and strides into a large meeting room. There is a fireplace in the center of the back wall, though it remains unlit. Most of the fireplaces in the castle and throughout the city are never lit. They're merely decorative pieces added to rooms to make them feel more comfortable, to make the palace rooms cozier for guests. The temperature rarely gets cold enough here to require use of them.

When my father takes one of the high-backed, crushed velvet seats, Luthais settles into the one directly to his left. I wince at the slight despite myself and move into a chair across from them. A servant comes to deliver a tray with a crystal decanter of whiskey and three glasses on the low table nestled between the chairs before taking her leave. No one speaks until she's out of earshot.

Reaching forward, Luthais moves to pour two glasses, handing one to my father before sitting back in his seat with the other. Another slight, but I let it go. His gray eyes are firmly set on me. Aamon takes a sip of the amber liquid and clears his throat, resting it on his crossed legs as he throws me a glance.

"So, Evander," he drawls, eyes piercing as they watch me. "Tell me *exactly* what you have been up to over the last year."

I'm ready for this question, having practiced my lines with Quinn for hours today while we picked our way across the Gilded Forest. Both Quinn and Bria helped to craft a perfect response that should hopefully keep us from being found out. I was not prepared to have Luthais staring me down while I deliver the well-thought-out lines, but I choose to ignore the man.

He's trying to get under my skin, though I can't quite figure out why. And he was watching Bria closely, to a degree that makes worry creep through me. I could try to glean more information about him while we're here, but I know the attempt may be futile given how guarded he is about his life. So, I steel my eyes on my father and let the half-truths and lies flow.

"As I'm sure you are aware, I spent the last year with the rebels. I found one of their camps, the one in the north," I begin, settling my back against the chair to assume a more relaxed position.

"Yes." Aamon's eyes darken and he speaks through clenched teeth. "I heard my only son ran off with the rebels. You'll need to let us in on that location, my boy."

Luthais cuts in before I have a chance to respond. "The whole of Easthallow heard about it Evander." His lip curls into a sneer once more, anger radiating from him. "Heard how you sold out your own to that rebel bitch Helara."

"Careful, Keating." Aamon cuts the man a sharp glare before setting his eyes back on me. "Your feelings aside, you are still speaking to my son."

This comment should have made me feel as though my father loves me. It would have made any other child feel protected, swell with confidence that their parent cares enough to stand up for them. But I know better. I'm aware that my father's love only extends so far, and this has more to do with my usefulness right now than any feelings he harbors toward me. Aamon wouldn't want to ruffle any feathers, knowing I have who he wants so badly—knowing I hold her in the palm of my hand.

"Of course I'll give you the location. Perhaps you could find me a map tomorrow and we can discuss where they are hidden. But he's right, Father," I acknowledge, sitting forward to pour myself a generous glass of the whiskey.

I keep an eye on Luthais to gauge his reaction while I agree with his scathing comments meant to wound.

"I did sell you out, I left in the middle of the night, and I rode straight until I found that camp. I gave that rebel bitch you speak of anything and everything she wanted." The retort hits hard, and I sit back in my chair with the whiskey.

Luthais's eyes are vast orbs of slate gray now, and the sneer is gone. The last thing he expected from me was this type of confession. He was looking to cut me down until I broke from rage. But this is what I had practiced.

I look back toward my father. "For years, since we arrived at the capital, I was searching for the location of the rebels."

Aamon nods, taking a sip of the drink clasped tightly in his hand.

That was something I never tried to hide from my father or anyone else, my inquiries regarding the rebels. I took part in countless tortures of innocent people. It was a prominent part of my job while here. It was expected of me. To burn, beat, carve, and worse. I steal a glance down at my hands. These hands had done those things. The torture I was forced to participate in was for the Crown to gain information on the rebels, but I'd used it to gain any information about where my friends were. Where Bria was.

Often those being tortured had no inkling of where the rebel forces were or what they were doing. Some were rebels themselves and never yielded any information, even when tortured. Others were just attempting to keep a family member or loved one safe and had no information to give. More still were turned in by angry neighbors, betrayed by friends, and they were innocent. Though, I suppose they were all innocent, no matter which side they were on.

One day, we found a boy. I can see him now, his lanky form and young face with striking, forest green eyes. He must have been maybe sixteen or seventeen when we caught him sneaking children out of a nearby village. I was on patrol that day, returning to the capital, when we crossed paths with the boy. He put up a fight but was untrained and the three people he was leading to safety were unarmed. Those three people were children, children with magic in their blood, being transported for safekeeping before they came of age and revealed any gifts they might have. I wanted to let them flee, to let them all go and live their lives, but I was not alone that day.

Theo had been there, along with another soldier, Matheus. We bound the children's hands and carried them back to the castle on horseback. I was the one who subdued the boy after he nearly lodged a dagger in my throat. I recall knocking him out and tossing his limp body across my horse before chaining him in the dungeons below Castle Eccleston.

When the boy came to, I was the one standing in front of him, Matheus by my side. That night, I interrogated him while Matheus dissected him with daggers, careful to avoid any vital organs or arteries. And when the change of guards came, allowing us reprieve of our roles for the day, Matheus left. But I stayed. I stayed and rubbed salve on the boy's wounds. We always allowed some healing to occur before we inflicted more torment, keeping prisoners on the brink of death but not letting them tip over the edge before we were ready.

The boy begged for death, pleaded with me to put him out of his misery. His body had been slack with blood loss when I'd hauled him to his feet, drawing my own face close to his ear so only he could hear. I spoke to him of the old gods, of Lilith and Kiara, and revealed the amulet I wore, hidden deep under my armor—the circular pendant, filled with sunstone and moonstone. The sun and moon united as one. The prophecy.

Something in the boy's eyes had shifted, realization spreading across his tired face. He understood what I was asking and that I was no threat to the rebels. He'd told me then of the location, where the northern camp was hidden among the Kaanos Mountain range. And then I complied with the boy's request for a swift death, plunging my dagger deep into the boy's heart and stopping it quickly. I stayed there, holding him, and watched the light fade from those forest green eyes. I had taken away as much of his pain as was possible, but I still saw those green eyes in my dreams, in my nightmares of this place.

That night. That was when I fled. Out into the night, before anyone could stumble across the boy's dead body.

Kicking a heel over my other knee, I mirror my father's stance. I rest the cool glass on my leg before carrying on with the carefully crafted narrative, the boy's face still haunting my thoughts.

"The night I left the capital, Matheus and I tortured a boy, looking for information regarding the rebel camp's location." I drag a hand along my face, rubbing my chin that's already beginning to sprout a fine layer of stubble.

"We found him with a hole in his heart the next morning," Aamon responds, quirking a brow at me.

I tilt my head. "Yes. Once Matheus left, I got the boy to talk. He told me enough about their whereabouts that I knew I would find them, and I had no more use for him." Keeping my expression neutral, to act as if the boy meant nothing to me, is a fight. That's what they expect of me. A cool and calculated killer. One of them. Most of the time I was, but that boy was one of the only souls that still weighs on my conscience.

"Then why did you flee into the night like some sort of criminal? Like a coward?" Luthais is trying to bait me again, and I grip the glass tighter, taking a swig of the liquid. I allow the burn to run down my throat and relax my body. I want to punch him in the face for the comment, knowing that the followers of the Crown are the true cowards, refusing to stand up for the innocents in this world, refusing to acknowledge their own failings.

"Keating," Aamon warns. His voice is sharp, cutting across the silence of the room like a blade.

"Again. You're not wrong," I offer. "I thought I knew better. I thought that I could infiltrate the camp on my own. Could gain access to Helara and Bria." I throw a pointed glance at Luthais and keep on. "And I was right." *This* is the cocky bastard they expect me to be. *This* is the son of the captain of the guard who has no morals, no soul left to worry about.

"It may have been a foolish move in the moment, but I knew that night that I could do it. I knew Bria as a child, we had a friendship, there was a...connection between us, even at a young age." I weave the truths and lies together seamlessly as I speak, wondering in reality if my truths are the same as hers and shoving down the curiosity as to whether she feels that same connection to me—if she's felt it all this time, even if she's never shown it. "Seducing her would be easy. I could turn her over to the Crown and we would win not only the war against the rebels, but we could defeat the prophecy. Had I told my father and the king, they would have stormed the camp and killed them all. Bria would have died, killed herself before she allowed you to take her. You both know that. And how would her death help us serve justice to Vaohr?"

Luthais scowls back at me. "And what information did you give regarding the Crown in your yearlong escapade with the rebels?" His voice is steady as he leverages the accusation at me. "How much did you reveal about us while you got your cock sucked by some unworthy cunt?"

I steady my breathing. I will not take the bait. I will not allow this asshole to gain the upper hand and see how deep his words cut. Instead, I smile, curling the side of my lip up and tilting my head. I will remember those words, tucking away the insults for another day. Luthais will pay for what he's said about Bria tonight.

"You sound a tad jealous, Luthais," I remark, keeping my voice low, even while he bares his teeth at me. I learned to play the bad guy during my years here and though it pains me to be back, the mask falls into place like I never left.

"I understand it may not make as much sense to you as kidnapping a child, but I assure you, the outcome was well worth it." I let a deadly smile creep across my face when the slight stuns him. "And Commander Keating," I drawl, "I would advise you to watch how you speak of my betrothed."

The comment hangs in the air and I worry for a moment that he sees the threat for what it is. A threat to steer clear of Bria.

"You're not really going to marry the girl!" Luthais snaps, incredulous.

I let out a low chuckle. "Of course not. Don't be a fool." My gaze shifts back to my father, and the wheels are turning behind his cold eyes.

"I brought her here for you, Father," I admit. "To serve Vaohr, as I said when I arrived."

Aamon clears his throat and drains the rest of his glass, setting it down on the table in front of him. He steeples his fingers together and presses them to his mouth, his lips pulling into a firm line. A few moments pass before a terrifying grin spreads across his face. It sends a chill up my spine and I stiffen.

"She trusts you," he remarks coolly, finally breaking the silence.

"With her life," I reply. *Truth.* "She believes she is unworthy. She is ready to serve Vaohr and the Crown. To do whatever necessary to prove herself." *Lie.* The weaving gets easier and easier as I go.

Luthais scoffs derisively but I pay him no mind. My father is hooked. I've just handed him Bria on a silver platter, and he is eating it up.

"This is…unexpected. Unexpected but quite appealing nonetheless." Aamon is beaming at me. "The king will be thrilled to hear of this tomorrow."

"And what of the sister?" Luthais chimes in.

Aamon's eyes darken instantly, and I keep my composure at the mention of Nimai.

"Right, how exactly did you manage that?" I query calmly.

"Keating made nice, clean work of it," Aamon answers, glancing at the man.

Luthais dips his head, appreciating the show of pride from his captain.

"We set fire to the southern camp after we got her out. I'm sure some of them survived but I honestly don't care." His teeth flash as he smiles at me. "Though I'm sure taking her did far more damage than the fires."

I swallow the curses that threaten to spew forth. "You're probably right. The southern camp was not as well developed as the northern camp from what I understand. Burning it was likely a deep hit. And who knows how many rebels you killed in the process."

"It's perfect timing that you and Lady Bria left when you did," Luthais continues. "If word had made its way to your camp, I'm sure this whole ruse would have been undone." He gestures toward me as he speaks, and I let my gaze go slack, not making eye contact with either of the men, fearing any emotion that may be perceived.

Burned. How many of the rebels made it out alive? How many were dead? Was Bria's mother among them? Quinn's brother?

"I can only imagine the rebel empire is crumbling now with both of their saviors missing," I manage, knowing the comment doesn't come off quite as cocky as I'd hoped.

Aamon's eyes gleam with delight at the prospect. I casually flick an invisible spec of lint from my trousers, carefully selecting my next words.

"You placed her in the dungeons I'm assuming? Her birthday is quickly approaching." I'm hoping my tone is as relaxed as I want it to be. Acting like I know better than him will piss him off further and keep him from examining me.

"We know," Luthais grinds out between clenched teeth, seemingly perturbed by my presumption. My tone is working after all. "Of course she's down there."

"But you told Bria she was here," I reply bluntly.

"Yes, I debated heavily on whether to tell her or not. But Nimai's presence is not unknown, many of the guards have flapped their lips. Word that we have part of the prophecy has leaked." He shoots a seething glance at Luthais, who recoils ever so slightly. "She will undoubtedly want to see her sister. Keating will have her brought to a room tonight and warn her. We cannot have Bria finding out she was in the dungeons. Not yet."

He presses his fingers to his lips again, deep in thought. "We will have to act swiftly to subdue Bria. It's only a matter of time before Nimai lets something slip about what we have done. And then we risk losing them both." He glances over his fingers at me. "Tell me, Son, is she as powerful as we thought?"

Even with the dire circumstances and regardless of the monsters who sit before me, I can't help but feel pride swell in my chest when I speak of her, when I think of just how powerful she is.

"Even more so," I respond, the truth in my words shining through. The maniacal sparkle in Aamon's eyes tells me how captivated he is by the prospect of her power.

"The sedative?" he questions.

That shit. I remember the nasty concoction they use to keep those with magic in line, dosing the prisoners we captured and those who came to the temple willingly to give themselves over. It was used to keep them restrained, not allowing them to wield any magic against the high priestess once they learned what she would do. Once their minds and bodies were shattered, tortured and mind-fucked beyond repair, they typically didn't need the sedative any longer.

I shake my head. "No. I don't think it will work on her. At least not in the usual dosage," I clarify. *Truth.*

Bria is too powerful for their sedative, crafted from belladonna berries found in the Gilded Forest. The priests experimented for years until they found the right dosage for the typical magic wielder. I know many died during their experiments, had heard the stories from Father Mallory. But that was years and years ago. Now it was a well-groomed and manicured process. But the priests had never come across someone like Bria and even with her petite frame, she would likely need more to dampen the fire inside. If she were a normal girl, the usual dosage would be lethal. But she is anything but normal.

Luthais still glares across the space between us, his eyes narrowed, nostrils flared while Aamon contemplates the new information, deciding on the best course of action.

"Very well. I will speak with the priests tonight. Perhaps we can give her a higher dose and test the effects. Though I'm hesitant to go too high. I don't want her dead at our hands, not when she could be so much more."

Aamon looks up at me. It feels as if both men are trying to peer into my soul, waiting to see my reaction to the orders. The ones I know Aamon is about to impart.

"You'll need to dose her, Evander." His voice is deep and dark, his eyes scanning my face for any hint of reservation. "You are the only one who can get that close to her."

"Understood," I agree, nodding to my father before letting a sly grin slide across my face. "I wouldn't have it any other way."

The scowl returns to Luthais's face. I'm starting to think he lacks the ability to express anything other than a sneer or a scowl. Miserable prick.

"We should place a guard outside her door. Be sure the girl doesn't try to flee or rescue her sister," he suggests. A fine idea in any other circumstance, but he's not trying to be helpful. He's trying to suggest a lack of competence on my part. And I need my father on my side right now.

Aamon glances from Luthais to me, his brows raised in question.

"Something to consider, for sure. What do you think, Evander? Will she try to leave?" he queries.

Testing me, both of them. All of this is a test to my devotion and willingness to comply. Draining the liquid from my cup, I stand. Placing it on the table, I look down my nose at the men seated in front of me.

"She will not leave, and she will not go searching for Nimai. I'll see that she is kept...occupied," I respond, the corner of my lip turning up at the flare of anger in Luthais's eyes.

He wants me to show weakness. He wants to prove I'm unable to pull off this ruse. The last thing he expected was for me to suggest fucking the girl to keep her complacent. Another mix of truth and lies—I'll happily do it—but not to keep her contained.

"Good boy," Aamon's words break with a slight chuckle.

Straightening my tunic and armor, I make a gesture to the clock. "I should retire though, before she has time to worry or have second thoughts."

"Indeed," Aamon concurs, rising to grasp my hand across the small table. His hand is rough, his skin cold and clammy against mine, and my body wants to revolt against his touch. He was never an affectionate father and ever since the attack on Bria's home, my disgust has grown. How Bria managed to keep herself from killing him when he touched her is beyond me.

"I'm proud of you, my son." The words would have meant a great deal to me as a child, but I know who he is now. And though warmth spreads into his normally cold eyes, I remind myself of that.

"We can talk more in the morning," he finishes, dropping the grip on my hand.

Resisting the urge to bury a dagger deep in my father's chest, I dip my head to break eye contact. "Happy to be of service, Father."

I give a cursory nod to Luthais, who merely bares his teeth at me in a predatory grimace. Turning to leave, I stop at the threshold, nearly forgetting where I am.

"To Vaohr," I say without turning back to the men behind me. But then I hear the responding calls.

"To Vaohr," they reply in unison.

I leave, striding down the hallway, keeping my head up and my back straight. Knocking softly on her door, I wait, hoping Bria is still awake. I pause for a few moments, willing her to come to the door, feeling the sear of Luthais's gaze tracking me down the hallway, ensuring I'm making good on my promise to keep her distracted. My body sags in relief as the door before me swings open and I slip inside the elegant bedchamber.

CHAPTER 48

Bria

After locking the door, I clamber to the bed, hugging my arms around my knees. My body shakes from the shock of the night and my palms itch from my magic simmering so close to the surface. I close my eyes and breathe, taking long inhalations and extending the exhalations, calming my body as Cato had taught me over the years.

After a bit, I scoot to the edge of the bed. It's enormous. A large ornate headboard carved of a rich black walnut with a sea of royal blue silk sheets and matching bedspread sprawl behind me. There is an absurd number of pillows, various hues of blue and gold decorating the top of the bed and spilling into the center. No one needs so many pillows.

Standing, I take in the expanse of the room. The entirety is decorated in similar fashion to the bed—cream wallpaper with whorls of gold and silver. A large armoire sits to one side, the handles glistening with gold leaf inlay, and a table and chairs all made of the same black walnut sit nearby. A clear crystal pitcher of water rests in the center of the table with a decanter of red wine and several glasses. A beautiful crystal bowl filled to the brim with bright fruit and a smaller matching bowl with assorted nuts and chocolate sit on either side.

When I make my way across to the bathing chamber, I can see the steam rising from the giant clawfoot tub. The sparkling white porcelain is capped with gold feet, so much larger than the bathing chambers back in the camp.

As I unbuckle the armor, there's a gentle ache in my hand when I grasp the leather straps. I strip off my clothes, letting them fall to the ground in a heap by the bath. Bending down, I snatch a dagger from the bandolier and place it on the small table that rests next to the tub, refusing to be unarmed or caught off guard here. There's a fluffy off-white towel with gold threading along the edges and a luxurious robe folded alongside it. A cream-colored sleeping gown rests there as well and I run my hand over the fine silken fabric.

My body slips into the oversized tub, and I soak in the water, letting it scald my skin. Small glass bottles litter the edge of the bath, filled with soaps and oils. I lift one to my nose and notes of jasmine and vanilla waft from the bottle. My stomach clenches when the vanilla hits my brain and thoughts of Ash come pouring in. She's likely going out of her mind with worry. Yet another person I've hurt with my foolish, selfish actions. I can only hope Silas was still with her when he found me in his mind. There's a chance that would have kept her calm, knowing where I was and what I was doing. I hope Quinn found him. The thought of anything happening to Silas is unbearable, like a piece of my soul would be removed if he were to die. This magical bond between us is no small thing, I realize.

I pour some of the oil into the tub, breathing in the intoxicating fragrance. Unwinding the gauze fabric from my wrist, I flex my fingers and rotate the joint in circles. It feels good, only a slight tenderness left, but my bones have healed. Holding a dagger—and possibly a sword if needed—will be feasible when we flee with Nimai. I bring my fingers to the opposite shoulder, feeling the soft pink scar tissue that has formed over the wound. Just like when Evander was healed.

I duck my head under the water and think of how he's doing with his father and Luthais. He's been gone a while now. If I don't hear from him by the time I'm done bathing, I'll go looking for him with the excuse of feigning hunger or thirst. But then I recall the food and drink laid out for me on the table in the bedchamber. They had made sure I have everything, so leaving the room will prove more challenging than I originally thought.

I come up for air and scrub my body in the jasmine and vanilla, the soap gliding across my skin and leaving it soft and supple. I dunk my head below the water again, rinsing the soap from my hair as I dig around for a reasonable excuse to leave the room. A soft knock comes from the bedchamber and I startle, staring toward the door.

My body stiffens and I scrabble for the dagger on the side table. I slip out of the bath, stepping onto a soft and fluffy rug meant to soak up the water dripping off my body. Wrapping the robe around myself, I tie it loosely at my waist and pad across the room and into the bedchamber, leaving wet footprints behind me on the floor. The dagger remains tight in my hand as I approach the door and I hesitate, unsure of who stands beyond. It needs to be Ev.

The breath that I inhale is deep as I step to the side and open the door, keeping my body tucked slightly behind it, assuming if it is someone sent to kill me, they will charge once the door is opened. Instead, I let loose a ragged sigh of relief and press the dagger to my chest when Evander slides through the opening I made.

His eyes shoot to the dagger in my hand, and he arches a brow, a smirk pulling at the corner of his mouth.

"Now, Bria, I may be playing the part of the bad guy, but please tell me you don't intend to use that on me," he teases.

The scowl I shoot him is well-deserved and I move to place the dagger on the bedside table, dripping water as I go.

"You're soaked," he states with disapproval, taking in my still-saturated hair and the glistening footprints I leave behind on the cool marble floor.

"I was bathing when you knocked," I explain, folding my arms across my chest.

Evander walks to the edge of the bed and sits, unlacing his boots and kicking them off.

"Please, don't let me disturb you," he replies, the teasing tone still apparent in his voice as he strips off his armor and bandolier, tossing them to the floor by the bed. He unsheathes one of his swords and lays it on the bedside table before unhooking the scabbard. "I'll just wait here until you're ready to talk business."

My eyes narrow on him. "I'm ready now," I insist through clenched teeth. I want to know everything he learned from his father tonight. And when we will get to see Nimai.

Evander grabs the neck of his tunic and pulls it over his head, letting it fall to the floor by his armor, then maneuvers his body up the bed and leans back. He places his hands behind his head and crosses his legs over one another. His tanned skin is beautiful against the blue hues of the bed, and I can see each ridge of his chest and abs. I have a strong urge to run my hands and tongue along every edge but shove it back down. Not the time. He glances over at me where I have unknowingly moved to stand beside the bed, like I've been drawn in just by his presence.

"As much as I love the robe, Bria, you should really get dressed. It's distracting," he drawls, letting his eyes close as he relaxes into the enormous bed.

No matter how gorgeous he may look laid out on my bed, and how much I long to know just how distracted he is by my outfit, he's still pissing me off. I roll my eyes as I stalk to the bathing chamber, pulling the door shut loudly behind me. The resounding chuckle from beyond the door does nothing to lessen my irritation with him and I yank the soft robe off, hanging it on one of the golden hooks by the door. The fluffy white towel is luxurious on my skin when I dry my hair and body before sliding on the silken sleeping gown. It feels somehow even softer once it falls against my skin. The thin straps delicately grace my shoulders and the short length grazes my upper thighs. I debate pulling the robe back over myself to cover some of the barely-there gown but it's soaked now, and I think better of it. It's also just too warm here to want to sleep in a robe.

When I exit the room, I move swiftly back across the cool marble of the floor. Evander is still lying there with his eyes closed, comfortably sinking into the lush mattress. It's annoying as all hell that he's so relaxed while my body vibrates with anxious energy. The breathing and the bath helped calm my magic, but I still pulse with nervousness to hear what he's learned. I go to the other side of the bed and climb up, sitting across from him. I go to cross my legs in front of me but recall the short length of the gown and pull them under my body instead.

Evander pries open an eye and catches me glaring at him, arms folded across my chest once more. He pushes out a long sigh and rolls onto his side to face me. His eyes widen as he takes in the sleeping gown, and he grimaces.

"What?" I demand, my irritation growing with every second.

"I was wrong," he groans, his voice deepening. "You should have stayed in the robe."

The familiar burning I feel when we are together kicks back in. A feeling low in my core spurs to life with the tone of his voice. His eyes rake over me, lingering on the high rise of the skirt, sending heat rushing into my face and chest.

I'm not sure what it says about me that part of me just wants to give in to that burning right now and move toward him, but I can't. I need to hear about their conversation and Nimai.

"Talk," I order, looking at him pointedly, ignoring the comment about the gown and the blush blossoming across my exposed chest and neck, rising into my cheeks. My body's reaction to him betrays any words I try to say.

He drags his gaze back to mine. The blue and gold around him bring out the flecks of gold in his own eyes and my heart warms, letting go of a bit of the annoyance I currently feel toward him and the situation.

"They bought it," he says, propping his head in his hand and tucking his elbow beneath him.

I shoot my brows to my hairline in surprise. *They bought it?* Could we be so lucky?

"Well, at least Aamon did. I'm not quite sure about Luthais, but I imagine we will be gone before he can be much of a problem for us," he continues.

"Did they say anything more about Nimai?" The eagerness in my voice is apparent, desperate to learn more about my sister.

He shakes his head. "No, not much." Evander combs his hair out of his face with his fingers. "She's in the dungeons, but now that you know she's here, they plan to move her. Luthais is to bring her to a room tonight. I assume she will end up in this wing along with us, though Aamon mentioned being wary of how much she would say to you. So, they may keep distance between you two. They intend to act quickly, Bria, to bring you under control as soon as possible. Before you can be turned by Nimai or understand what is actually happening here."

A terrifying prospect. Things will unravel fast now that we're here, especially once they allow me to see Nimai. They cannot risk too much time with us together.

"How?" I ask, curious as to what action Aamon has decided to take.

"Oh, I'm to drug you," Evander replies nonchalantly, his dimple shining through as my nostrils flare.

A small laugh at my reaction escapes him and he quickly reaches out to rest a hand on my leg, tracing his thumb along the hem of my gown. The fury rising in me at the thought of Aamon ordering Ev to drug me washes quickly away with his touch, replaced by an ache to hold him and wrap my body around his.

"I'm not going to do it, Bria," he states softly.

"I should hope not."

He lets his hand drop and rolls to his back once more, closing his eyes.

"Well, you're going to have to act a bit out of it if we have any hope of fooling them into thinking you are actually drugged," he explains. "My father intends to speak with the priests tonight to determine a correct dosage. I told him you were far too powerful for their typical amount. I figured that would give you one night free from having to feign impairment."

"What is it? The drug?" He's mentioned it before, but I never had the chance to ask many questions and now I'm curious as to how they subdue all these powerful people.

"It's made from belladonna. The priests have worked for a very, very long time to determine how much is necessary based on a person's body composition." He stretches his arm out to me, laying it across the sea of pillows behind him.

"But they've met their match with you. We can talk more of it tomorrow, once my father has spoken with the priests. You need to get some rest."

The lush blankets call to me, and I push them back, sliding my body in beside his. I lay my head, hair still damp, in the crook of his shoulder, my face pressing against his chest. I trail my hand along his collarbone and rest it above his heart, feeling the steady beat below. Evander wraps his arm around my back, coasting his fingers down the exposed skin. The roughness of his calluses scrapes against me, and I wonder how rough my own hands feel on his skin. And whether or not he minds that I don't have the smooth hands a lady should have anymore. I tilt my face up to kiss the edge of his jaw before nestling my head back into him.

"We'll find her tomorrow, Bria."

His whispered promise squeezes into my heart, planting roots, causing a bud of hope to blossom. I clamp my eyes against the stinging tears rising behind them and let Evander's caresses on my back lull me into sleep.

CHAPTER 49

Bria

Moss green eyes with an unwavering intensity stare back at me. Nimai is dressed in a gown of emerald, her black hair flowing in waves around her shoulders. Gone is the dungeon. Instead, she is seated on a bed that looks strikingly similar to the one I had fallen asleep in. She smiles at me, though the smile doesn't meet her fierce eyes. Instead, I see the faint flicker of green flames within. It's barely perceptible, an inkling of the power she holds. Nimai speaks, but her words are barely audible over the roaring in my ears.

"It isn't safe here. Run."

I wake with a start, opening my eyes to find my face still pressed to Evander's chest. His arm is wound around my back, fingers hooked under one of the thin straps of the gown. And my leg, I notice, is tossed over his waist. I had pressed myself tight against him during sleep and it had felt warm and comfortable. Safe.

The safety seems a bit ironic given where we are and the nightmare. A part of me doesn't want to rise and face my enemies in the light of day, but today, I'll get to see her. And no matter how jarring the dream or vision of Nimai had been, it'd left me with a glimmer of hope because it had been proof the connection between us is still there. She is alive and she is well enough to reach out to me. And just as Ev told me, she is no longer in the dungeons. But there was a warning nonetheless and I will now be even more guarded, given her words.

The morning light bleeds through the small gaps in the heavy curtains, indicating it's probably time for us to rise. I slip out of Evander's grasp, moving quietly to allow him the chance to rest. I make my way to the side of the bed and stand, creeping silently toward the washroom. When I return to the bedchamber, my hair brushed, my face and teeth cleaned, I see Ev is sitting up.

Dragging his hands over his face, he pulls back the blankets and swings his legs over the bed, meeting my gaze. He smiles and it makes my heart skip.

"Morning," he says, his voice thick with sleep.

"Morning," I reply, watching as his eyes rake lower over the gown.

Gods. One look from him and I'm ready to jump back into the bed, something stirring between my legs when his gaze lingers, bringing along with it the harsh realization that I should get dressed. The barely-there nightgown is doing neither of us any favors if he needs to meet with his father soon. After all, they have the matter of drugging me to discuss. And I'm eager to see my sister.

I gesture toward the bathing chamber, toward my clothing. "I'll grab my things and you can use it."

"Bria." I stop at the sound of his voice and turn, my hands bracing along the frame of the door.

"The armoire." He tosses his head behind him, toward the giant wooden structure.

My mind had been on the pants and tunic lying on the floor by the bathtub, forgetting that I was in the castle. I would be expected to wear a gown, not the common clothing of the rebel camp. Had he not stopped me, I would have emerged with my armor and bandolier strapped in place too.

"Right," I respond, a bit embarrassed, walking past him and the bed to the closet and swinging the doors wide.

In my time at the rebel camp, I had longed to wear a dress again. Now, with numerous fine gowns hanging before me, I find myself at a loss. It has been years since I sucked myself into a tight-fitting bodice, and I don't know how to move like a warrior in one. But then again, I'm not supposed to, not here. Here, I am meant to blend in, to act like the noble-born I am. Well, *was.*

Evander's footsteps are soft as he comes up behind me, wrapping his arms around my waist. He kisses the side of my neck before resting his head on my shoulder, looking over me at the gorgeous gowns. The weight of his head grounds me, helps me focus.

"I-I don't know what to wear," I admit, my hands still gripping the doors, white-knuckled.

"Go with the blue," he offers, nodding toward a deep cornflower dress.

The gowns are full of silk and tulle, gossamer, and lace, unbelievably crafted with painstakingly delicate threading and detail. I imagine they have an entire army of seamstresses creating the most elegant and fashionable gowns here in the capital, and possibly even more just working for the king and his court.

He bends his head back down and leaves a soft trail of kisses up my neck to my ear. I lean back into him, relishing the warmth of his embrace, the closeness of him.

"It brings out your eyes," he whispers as he reaches my ear, sending a delightful shiver down my spine, still mostly bared to the air.

"Plus," he adds, reaching his hand from around me to push aside the gowns. "Some of these are a bit scandalous. And though I definitely want to see you in some of the skimpier ones, no one else needs to. You should come off as wholesome if you're planning to tell the priests how unworthy you are."

He makes a good point, but I twist in his arms to throw him a scathing look, though the heat of his words sends torturous waves of desire through my body. He stifles a laugh at my expression, leaning down to drag his nose over the bridge of mine. When he hovers his lips above mine, I hold my breath, waiting for the feel of him when he kisses me.

"You should get dressed," he whispers against my mouth before turning and striding toward the bathing chamber.

I glare as I watch him retreat behind the door before turning back to the dresses. Gathering the cornflower one between my fingers, I gently remove it from the armoire, ecstatic to see that these gowns are more modern, bearing no corsets. Some have sculpted bodices and others are lined with fine boning. They would be far more comfortable and easier to move in. All boast long flowing skirts that will hug tight to my body, not the fluffier skirts that make it difficult to maneuver through a doorway. These will do.

CHAPTER 50

Evander

The cornflower blue gown clings to her, coasting down the edge of her body, hugging her gorgeous curves before splaying out wide below her waist. The bodice is delicately embroidered with an intricate pattern, threads of a deeper blue and silver intertwining throughout. Sheer sleeves trail to her elbows. When I emerge from the washroom, she is seated on the edge of the bed, weaving her golden hair into a long braid.

Though some of the other gowns in the armoire boasted plunging necklines, this one is more modest, skimming the top of her breasts and showcasing the crest of Vaohr that hangs from her throat. It's the right choice if she is to see the king or the priests today. The color is perfect, bringing out the cobalt in her eyes and making her hair shine an even deeper shade of gold. She is striking. Striking and mine.

She glances up at me and smiles, the gleam in her eyes making my heart ache. I don't want to bring her in front of these monsters. Every instinct in my body tells me to run with her, but she will never leave without her sister.

"You should leave your hair down," I suggest as I move to gather my tunic off the floor in front of her.

Her hands fall from where she's braiding it.

"More wholesome?" she questions with a teasing tone.

"No," I reply, tossing her a flirtatious smile as I tug the shirt down over my head. "I just want it down so I can run my hands through it."

She rolls her eyes at me, but I know the comment will keep her mind at ease. And I really do love how she looks with her hair down.

"You're a tease," she jabs.

"Only for you," I croon. "I'm going to see if my father placed clothes across the hall for me. I can't show up like this if you look like that," I say, gesturing to her in the gown.

I gather my things before leaving her room and walk the short distance across the hall. To my dismay, I catch sight of Luthais down the hall, leaning against the wall, watching me. Does this man ever let up? I nod to him, letting a smirk curl on my lips before I push open the door to my own bedchamber. It's not a bad thing that Luthais just saw me leaving Bria's room so early in the morning, solidifying that I kept her placated all night. Even if it wasn't the way he thought or the way I wished.

My room is laid out the same as Bria's, and I imagine most of the rooms set up for guests are of a similar fashion. Aamon was correct that the lodging is a far stretch from the quarters for the king's guard in the lower half of the castle.

In the armoire, I find a black dress tunic and matching pants, golden thread woven throughout. I glance at the brown leather armor I had thrown on the bed when I'd first entered and decide to leave it there. If we are to make this work, I need to appear as though I trust them. So, I strap one sword around my waist and tuck one of the daggers deep into my boot, pulling the chain from Rayna out of the tunic so that the crest of the temple is visible across my chest to match Bria's.

Though when I emerge from the room, Luthais is walking away from me, a few doors down. And he has Bria with him.

I assumed the soldier was watching me, but it seems he waited for my absence before approaching Bria's room. My jaw hardens as I see Luthais place a hand on the small of her back, ushering her down the hall. She is willingly walking with him, but him touching her sends a searing hot rage through my bloodstream.

There is no doubt in my mind that we do not want to learn what

Luthais will do or say to Bria if he has her alone. I pick up my pace, half jogging up the hallway to meet them, grasping Bria's hand as I slide in beside her. She immediately locks her fingers with mine and I feel the brush of the ring against my palm.

"Where are you two rushing off to?" I ask, keeping my tone even, not a hint of the irritation waging war inside.

Bria's eyes flick to me, and relief is apparent in her face. Her hand is hot to the touch, and that look in her eyes tells me her magic is flaring. I stroke my thumb along the back of her hand and lean in to plant a light kiss on her head as we walk. Keeping her calm is crucial. I've witnessed firsthand what happens when her magic needs release.

Luthais reluctantly removes his hand from her back since he was unsuccessful in steering her away quickly enough.

"I was escorting Lady Bria to the dining hall. Captain Lansing is waiting," he clarifies, shooting a seething glance at me over Bria's head.

"Thank you so much, Commander Keating, but I assure you, I can take it from here." I maneuver Bria closer to me and pick up my pace, watching in delight as Luthais falls back behind us.

"Thank you," Bria whispers. She too fears what might happen if she remains alone with Luthais.

We walk hand in hand until we come to the grand staircase. I wait for her to gather her train before winding my arm behind to steady her. It's been a very long time since she's worn a dress, let alone a gown like this, or real shoes instead of boots. I bite the inside of my lip to keep from laughing and my nostrils flare as she hesitates before descending. But Bria catches it.

"Is something funny?" she hisses, keeping her voice low with Luthais only a few steps behind us.

"Absolutely not." I duck my head toward her, hiding the grin spreading across my face. "You look ravishing," I add, and a responding flush blooms across her chest.

She quirks her lip up at me. "As do you."

Jasmine and vanilla tickle my nose as I breathe in the scent wafting from her hair, tightening my grip on her waist. She left her hair unbound like I asked, so it pours like liquid gold down the back of the dress. Even after all her time in the rebel camp, she looks at ease in the gown, regal. This is the noble girl I fell for so long ago and knew I could never have. Yet here we are.

Bria is powerful enough to take down Easthallow, especially with the aid of the rebel forces and her sister at her side. And I could see her ruling an entire kingdom if she chose to do so, but the sharp reality is she will never get that chance, the chance to be the fearless leader that is seemingly bred into her. The fact that she has to die for any change to happen is something I am unwilling to accept. No matter how ignorant and naïve it makes me.

As we make it to the end of the stairs, I watch as Bria stares at the mosaic floor once again, entranced by the depiction. The bloody battle commissioned by the king was something I had forgotten before yesterday. Yet another way for Braddock to display his power and get those who trust him to believe in the false story.

I pause, allowing Bria to release her dress, but keep my hand locked tightly around her. Unsure of which dining hall we are going to, I allow Luthais to walk ahead. The servants' halls, the guards' quarters, and the dungeons were where I spent most of my time when in the castle, seeing little of the formal areas in my years here.

Following him down another hallway, we come to a large dining area. Far larger and more formal than what I'm used to. The table is an expanse of black with an ornate gold runner that cuts through the center of it. A large swath of freshly picked spring flowers rests in the center, flooding the room with the pleasant scent of hyacinth. A tray of tea and coffee is poised in front of my father and the high priest seated next to him.

To my relief, the high priestess is nowhere in sight. Nor is the king. I am all too aware that I will need to face them eventually, though I dread the prospect. Any delay to that is welcome.

Aamon rises as we enter, as does Father Mallory. They stand on the opposite side of the table. I'm glad to have the space between Bria and the supposed holy man. Father Mallory has been in Easthallow for ages and although I don't know his exact age, he has to be in his late seventies at this point.

Bria bows her head as we enter, a polite gesture to the evil men standing before her. She is a lady after all and holds a rank above my father, whether he wants to admit it or not. Being forced from her home and joining the rebels did not change her status and she holds her posture straight, exuding the stature she once had, further driving home the thought that I am not worthy of this woman who stands at my side. But I have to remind myself I'm not worthy of her in *their* world. In our world, Bria and I are equals. Made for one another.

"Lady Bria, may I introduce you to the Reverend Father Mallory, the high priest here in Easthallow," my father says, gesturing to the man beside him.

The decrepit old man reaches across the table and grasps Bria's hand in his own, his wrinkled eyes darting to the crystal-inlaid ring upon her finger. He smashes his thin lips onto the top of her hand, and I move my own hand from her waist to the small of her back, steadying her to accept the disgusting gesture.

"A pleasure, Father Mallory," Bria replies, a fake sweetness smothering her voice.

I have to stifle a grimace as the old man licks his lips after releasing his grasp on her hand. It's as if he can taste the magic emanating from her body. His eyes are secured on her and only her, looking as if he wants to devour her, not managing so much as an acknowledging glance at me since we entered the room.

The high-backed chair in front of me makes a grating noise when I pull it out for Bria to sit. I place her across from Aamon and sit to her left, putting myself face to face with the creep of a priest. The large table could have fit a dozen more people and seems a bit grand for such a small breakfast. However, I suppose Aamon and Father Mallory want to impress Bria. They will go to great lengths, as will the king, to ensure she is instantly hooked. It will make their job easier, after all.

Luthais moves to take the seat to Bria's right and my teeth clench. He's complicating things by being so watchful and I'm becoming increasingly concerned that getting Nimai may prove more challenging with him around.

Aamon and Father Mallory discuss the upcoming day as servants shuffle about with several trays filled with savory and sweet arrays—another attempt to woo Bria into submission. Anger courses through my veins at how they underestimate her. Sitting across from them is the most powerful woman alive, the most powerful to have existed since Lilith and Kiara. And these pricks think she can be swayed with flakey croissants and poached quail eggs.

My anger fizzles though when I see the overflowing tray and notice the scones. I can't help the smirk that tugs at the corner of my mouth. Perhaps I was wrong. My girl does have a weakness for the sweet breakfast pastry, as silly as it is. She's listening to Father Mallory droll on about the temple and how he wants her to go there after we finish breakfast. So, I reach forward, selecting one that appears studded with chocolate and place it on the plate in front of her.

Bria's eyes flick down, breaking her gaze with the priest, and a genuine smile graces her lips. She stretches her hand out toward me beneath the table and brushes her fingers along mine. The touch sends a jolt through my body, and I glance quickly over at Luthais, whose brows are furrowed.

He observed the touch from Bria. *Good*, I think. Let him see all the authentic hidden touches and stolen kisses between us. They will only serve to prove the lies of seduction. And if I'm being honest with myself, I can't keep from touching her. No matter the dire circumstances. I crave her whenever she is out of reach and her touch soothes me, just as I know mine does the same for her.

"You shall meet the other priests today. I know they will be just as taken with you as I am," he croons as he stabs his fork into the poached egg, the runny yolk overtaking his plate.

"It would be an honor to visit the temple of Vaohr and meet your fellow reverend fathers," Bria replies.

That voice is different from her normal tone. She's forcing her voice to be quieter and meeker while she's here. She is softening herself, making it appear as though she is an easier target than she really is— twirling them around her fingers only to break them when she steals away in the middle of the night with her sister. Oh, what I wouldn't give to see their faces when both halves of the prophecy slip through their blood-soaked hands.

I scoop a heap of fried potatoes onto my own plate along with some sausage and fresh strawberries. The quality of the food shocks my taste buds. Only a year away from this place and I've forgotten how rich it is.

Everything is fried or slathered in butter and heavily spiced. It's a delicious change for my palate, having become so accustomed to the blander food in the camp.

And when my eyes slide to Bria, I note the small smile that lingers on her face as she bites into the chocolate scone. Even now, she can find pleasure in the simple things. But really, she's always been that way deep down—a lady who befriended the children of servants and guards and refused to bend in her ways, never fully accepting her lot in life.

"You should come too, my boy," Father Mallory is saying to me. I had been lost in myself, consumed by my thoughts while I watched Bria. Too consumed, I realize, that I stopped listening to the old man. My fork is poised above my plate, waiting for him to continue, to give any clue as to what nonsense he's spewing now.

"Your father tells me you are here to pledge yourself to the Crown and Vaohr once more. You will need to partake in the rite again, Evander."

The rite. Fuck.

I forgot about the sacrament of Vaohr. It was not much of a ceremony, but I would be required to stand before the statue of the god and receive him. This meant allowing the priests to use their power on you however they deemed fit. The rite is not the same for everyone. The priests claim that Vaohr speaks to them and determines the punishment or blessing that will be bestowed depending on the purity of their soul.

"Yes, Father. I will join you and Lady Bria at the temple this afternoon to take the rite." I give a slight bow of my head and continue eating, the rich food turning to ash in my mouth as the man's thin lips spread into a smile.

"Good man," the priest says. "Vaohr will be pleased with you for returning."

I swallow the bite of food and lift my eyes to Father Mallory's. The smile has widened, and his lips curl back from his gleaming teeth. I can't shake the sinking feeling that my soul will be found tainted today.

Meaning I will be receiving one hell of a punishment.

CHAPTER 51

Bria

It's excruciating—physically painful to be sitting at a table with the man responsible for my father's death and sitting next to the man who captured my sister. The other...well, the high priest is debatably the worst of the three. He has so much blood on his hands, blood of the innocents he has drugged and left in the dungeons for the capital's use. I am doing everything in my control to just get through breakfast without raining a storm of beastly shadows down on the men to tear them to shreds.

By the way Father Mallory looks at me, I can tell he feels my energy thrumming inside. He's been around enough people with power to recognize it for what it is. Whereas others seem to disregard the heat, the jolt of electricity that pours out of me at times, the flicker of magical flames in my eyes—he's eating it up. I loathe the man and feel a sense of relief when he says Ev must take the rite. At least I won't have to travel to the temple on my own today or be alone with him. I worry how long I can keep my gifts in check around more men like him.

Evander appears at ease throughout the meal, but I'm not foolish enough to believe the facade he wears. There's a reason he survived here for four years. He's learned to erect a wall around his emotions and drop a mask into place, one that shows the king's court and the priests what they want to see. Because of that, he is well trusted. *He* is the reason this is working, not me.

I force myself to eat as the priest drones about Vaohr and how much it means when the unworthy give themselves over like I am. The food is fantastic but even the scone lands like lead in my stomach. I catch myself wondering why Aamon doesn't just drug the food. It would be easier than getting close to me.

The deadly berries of the nightshade have a seductively sweet taste, or so I've heard. But Ev had said something about dosing last night. Could the priests not determine the correct dosage in food? Or was the ask of Evander a test of his faithfulness to the Crown? Maybe it was both.

"Commander Keating, perhaps you could bring our dear Lady Bria for a stroll around the grounds whilst I speak with my son?" Aamon looks toward Luthais as he speaks, and the man nods in acknowledgement.

This request doesn't appear to come as a surprise to him, but it does to me. And to Evander. Tension ripples off him with his father's words. He doesn't want me alone with Luthais and has made that abundantly clear to me.

Aamon stands, pushing his chair back, Father Mallory remaining seated beside him. "I hope you enjoy the weather, and your trip to the temple, my lady." Aamon partially bows toward me, effectively kicking me out of the room. "I shall see you tonight, when we have dinner with the king."

I've kept my mouth shut all breakfast regarding Nimai, but now I can no longer contain myself. How had he not said a word about her? Especially while the old man talked for what seemed like hours about their ridiculous god, the temple, and the fucking rite.

"Thank you, Captain Lansing. It will be an honor," I purr, forcing my face into a polite smile. I rise from my chair as well, followed by the men seated to either side of me.

"And will my sister be joining us? I am so very desperate to see her." The sweet and unassuming voice that comes out of me is not my own and it makes me sick to hear it.

Aamon's jaw twitches. He must have expected me to ask about

Nimai. But it bothers him, nonetheless. Luthais talks before the captain can fix his face back to the normal cool composure he wears.

"Lady Nimai has also been invited to dinner with the king." That honeyed voice drips over my skin, and I turn to face Luthais.

"I accompanied your sister here," he continues, though by "accompanied" I know he means he kidnapped her and dragged her here unwillingly. "Come, let's walk and I can fill you in on how she's been doing here at the capital." He extends his arm toward me, his elbow crooked for me to take.

Holding my breath, I move to hook my arm in his, but feel Evander close his hand around my elbow, his grip tight. Spinning me toward him, he pulls me close, wrapping his free arm around the back of my head, his fingers digging into my hair. The rough movement sends a flutter through my stomach as he brushes a soft kiss across my lips before placing his mouth next to my ear.

"Breathe," he reminds me. "Keep it in." He plants another kiss on my cheek and pulls back, releasing my hair, but it feels like his eyes remain intently on me while I turn toward Luthais.

"What a happy couple," Father Mallory croons from behind us.

All eyes are on me as I stride toward Luthais. Waiting for any misstep, any suggestion that I am not who I claim to be. I slide my arm into his and walk out the door, arm in arm with my sister's captor.

CHAPTER 52

Bria

The air outside the castle is warm and wet. The salt from the sea fills my lungs as I suck in a deep breath. The Feral Sea lies beyond Castle Eccleston, and I'm eager to see the water. We grew up only a short walk from Saturnine Bay and the smell of the ocean brings back so many pleasant memories. I've heard of the tumultuous seas beyond the castle. No ships have dared to brave the treacherous waters in hundreds of years, making it the perfect spot for an impenetrable fortress.

We leave through a side entrance, and I notice now that he's leading me toward the King's Garden. It's probably a lovely location for a stroll in the morning air, but I want to be by the sea.

"Commander Keating," I begin, glancing at him to gauge his reaction to my request. "I can smell the ocean, and it reminds me of home. Would it be alright if we walked by the water?"

He's taken aback by the honesty in my words. He doesn't trust me, that's clear in the wary way he watches me. But I need him to at least not view me as a threat. Otherwise, he will only get in my way. And as much as I would love to toss him into the Feral Sea, I understand that would attract some unwanted attention.

He sucks his teeth, the curve of his mouth hinting at a smile. "Of course, my lady," he purrs.

Luthais switches directions, following the paved path that curls around the back side of the castle. I keep my arm locked in his, though the closeness makes me antsy.

We walk in silence for a few moments, passing by other nobles out for a stroll. No one here knows who I am. For all they know, I'm a visiting lady from some wealthy town they've never heard of and don't care about. After some time, I break the silence, completely convinced that this man could stay quiet for a millennium if not provoked.

"You spoke of my sister, said you accompanied her here." I keep my eyes straight ahead as we pass row after row of windows along the castle walls. Decorative shrubs with thin, spiked leaves line the stone path and vibrant clusters of hyacinths sprout up throughout the manicured lawns.

Luthais clears his throat. "I did, my lady. It seems as if the two of you have come to similar conclusions about your future." His voice is even, cool, and collected. This man is a skilled liar.

"We had word from the southern camp that your sister wanted to commit her life to Vaohr. Knowing of your gifts, she assumed she would also have them. And she wished to give them back, to pay back the god whom they were ripped from."

Anger is welling up inside me, flames licking at my core with every lie he spews. *Keep it in*, Ev's words echo in my mind.

"Nimai has always been one to do what's expected of her. Even as a child, she never strayed from the right path," I say, letting the truth of my words shine.

"But you strayed, did you not?" Luthais is questioning my time with the rebels, shifting the focus from my sister back to me. I may not have expected to be alone with him, but I was prepared for some line of questioning surrounding this topic.

"I did indeed," I agree as we round the back of the castle.

The vast sea surfaces, stretching as far as the horizon. It's an exceptional view. The path opens before me and leads to a giant ledge overlooking the jagged cliffs. I can see the white caps of the rolling waves in the distance. I choose to continue talking, hoping that I can make myself more of a person to him and less a symbol of all he hates.

"But I didn't think of it as straying. Not at the time at least," I explain.

We near the edge, and I observe the beautifully crafted railing that keeps people from the raging sea below. It's made of delicate knots of iron, rolling like the waves. Not much of a barrier, but enough to keep a drunken nobleman from accidentally falling to his death, I suppose. And the sea below has a fervor to it. The water crashes fiercely against the edges of the cliffs, frothing and swirling as though it were a trapped animal trying to escape.

"Is that so?" he asks softly, and I feel again as if someone is pouring honey over my skin. It makes the hair on my neck stand up, goosebumps pebbling my arms. "Were you not brought up in the house of an earl? Did you not know the word of the Lord?"

Unwinding my arm from his, I reach out to touch the iron railing, biting back a scowl. I can't possibly throw him over. He has to be the same size as Quinn and solid muscle. Plus, there are other people milling about who might notice the captain of the guard's second in command going over the cliffs. I purse my lips. I'm stuck with him for now.

Looking out over the sharp and uneven edges of the cliffs to the roiling water below, I see now why ships stopped trying to come in and out through the Feral Sea. It's impassible here.

"To an extent," I reply, running my hand along the smooth edge of the metal, cool beneath my heated fingers. His line of questioning is beginning to get to me, stoking the flames within. The chill of the iron on my hands helps to quell the energy, if just for a moment.

"My family was not very religious. We did not openly worship any gods," I offer, turning to place my back against the cool iron. Keeping my words closer to the truth is easier for me, decreasing the chance I can be caught lying. It has never quite been my strong suit.

Luthais comes up next to me, propping his hip along the railing and crossing his arms to look at me.

"Well, I would think not." His gray eyes are fixed on me. "An earl openly worshipping the old gods like the Keeper and his bastard daughters would not be a good look."

His words are biting but he winks at me, a gesture so at odds with the man before me. He is a devout follower, and I am everything he hates. Luthais is testing my reactions because he doesn't trust me. And the fact of the matter is, his instincts are spot on.

Keeping my expression neutral, I agree. "No, it would not. But as I said, I did not perceive my actions as straying from the righteous god." I gaze up at the castle in front of me. It towers high, giant gray and sand-colored stones clustered together to create a magnificent palace.

"Being born with a gift, knowing there is something different about you..." I pause before letting more truth flow from my lips. "It can be a bit terrifying at times. Especially in a world where those around you wish to cause you harm." My voice is softer now and I hope he's listening to me, that he will take the truth I'm using to manipulate him and let it ease his fears and distrust.

"I assure you, Lady Bria, I do not intend you any harm." His stare sears through me, making the skin on my neck prickle.

I turn my head back to him, the wind off the sea whipping my long hair around my face.

"I understand that now, but can you blame me for following the rebels when I was younger? They promised a world of peace, where I could be myself and not be hunted for a gift I did not ask to receive." I lower my lashes but keep my eyes on Luthais. "But Evander showed me the truth of it. They only protected me so they could use me against Vaohr. They had no intentions of letting me live the life I wanted."

His features ease. Those deep gray eyes become a bit lighter, and I realize now how strikingly handsome he is. Some sort of otherworldly beauty lies beneath the cold exterior that I cannot quite put my finger on.

"So, you left the rebels to pledge yourself to Vaohr because you would be serving a purpose?" he asks, his voice a bit softer now as well, the biting harshness of his tone disappearing.

"In a sense, I suppose I did." I am a bit surprised at how easily those lies spill out of my mouth. And how this monster of a man seems to lap them up, like a dog from a bowl.

"Why would I choose to serve those who would use me for blood-shed when I could turn over my gifts to their rightful owner? When I could be blessed by Vaohr for admitting my mistakes?"

He quirks a brow at me. "You believe yourself unworthy of the gifts you've received even after years of honing them and making use of them in the rebel camp?"

Interesting. He knows I've been training. Though perhaps he's making assumptions considering I arrived in armor, or Evander may have relayed that information to them last night. Either way, he's pushing me, making sure my story has no holes. Meaning I have to tread carefully around the lies, sprinkling in truth and weaving a web that will end in their destruction and not ours.

"Yes," I reply, drumming my fingers along the iron railing. "I learned to use my gifts before I understood the consequences of using magic when it was not mine to use. When it was stolen."

He swallows and I brace myself, waiting for whatever question he plans to ask next.

"And what of your connection to this...prophecy? That tells how all of Azudora will fall at your feet and those of your sister? That she is to rule the new world?"

I cast my eyes down toward my hands and spin the ring on my finger, watching as the light bounces off the black crystals and sends sparkles raining down upon the stone walkway.

"I'm sure you are aware, Commander Keating, that the prophecy you speak of also tells of my death." I gaze up at him again through lowered lashes.

"I do not wish to die, selfish as that may seem. And if I'm in the hands of Vaohr, no one will hurt me. No one will kill me if I'm turned over to help the righteous god. Will they?" I ask, letting a note of pleading seep into my voice.

Luthais reaches his hand out to me, pushing a strand of hair out of my face. He grasps my chin between his thumb and pointer finger, tipping my face up to look at him fully.

"No one shall harm you, my lady," he says quietly, leaving his hand resting on my chin. His grip is firm but not painful. "You and your sister are too precious for that."

The lies sweep over his lips as easily as they do mine. But the slight spark in his eyes makes it seem as if he's not lying. He cannot be that foolish to believe no harm will come to me and that no harm will come to Nimai. More likely, he is just heartless enough to not care. I don't have time to consider which possibility may be correct. I gave him the responses he desired, and now I want more information on my sister. So, I smile at him, though I want to sink my teeth into the fingers that hold me.

"Will I have a chance to speak with her at the temple this afternoon?" I attempt to keep the question light, tamping my eagerness.

Luthais drops his hand, the stoic mask sliding back into place across his face, and replacing that kindness—that softness—with cool, hard granite.

"I believe Lady Nimai has already met with the priests, as well as the high priestess." He shifts on his feet, a rare show of his discomfort. "They will want to see you alone, but you will reunite with your sister at dinner tonight."

Fuck this. All that honey that pours out of his mouth is tainted. The fire inside me ignites, heat rushing into my face and chest.

"I understand," I respond through clenched teeth, attempting to stifle the flames. *Not here. Not now.*

Luthais catches the shift in my tone and tilts his head, scanning my face.

"Are you alright?" he asks, and what sounds like genuine concern comes through. His hand reaches back up to cup the side of my face.

Breathe. Keep it in. I can hear Evander's whisper in my ear. I close my eyes and deeply inhale the crisp salty air, then extend my exhale. My hands prickle with heat, my veins boiling. The smell...the smell makes me think of home and I try to relax, to let happy memories flood through me and take away the heat. But home. Home is where I had my father, and his face flashes into my memory—my father being stripped away from me. My life being stripped away from me.

And here I am, with the people responsible for his death. The people responsible for so many deaths.

Breathing is not working. My attempts to calm myself are not working. The magic courses through my veins, and I clamp my eyes tighter against it, gripping my fingers into the iron behind me—steadying myself, willing myself to keep it in. *Inhale*, I tell myself. *Just keep breathing*.

"Shit!" My eyes snap open as I hear Luthais curse, and he rips away from me. He's holding his hand and staring at me, his eyes wide with shock.

Flames are coating the inside of my hands, igniting the iron beneath them. Dark shadows flick at the edges of my fingertips, tipping them in black. I quickly remove my hands and tuck them behind me, unsure of what to do but desperate for him not to see the dark emanating from them. I didn't intentionally release any power, but the heat... The heat of my magic raging against the cage of my body had warmed the iron enough to burn him.

"Bria, my love," Ev's voice splinters through the roaring in my head, and I spin to look at him, knowing my eyes are wide and out of control. His gaze locks on me, and I know he sees it. He sees the war waging inside my body, the flames in my eyes, the terror running through me that I could mess this all up.

"There you are," he says softly, coming to stand beside me. "One of the seamstresses would like to see you, to ensure your gown fits for dinner tonight."

Evander slides his arm around my waist and nestles his head into my hair to plant a soft kiss. I melt my body to his side, placing my arm gently around him as well. My body responds to him, the feel of him dampening the flames, stifling the heat that threatens to encompass my whole being.

"Are you hurt?" Luthais cries out, still holding his hand. From where I now stand, I can see that his palm is red and blistering the slightest bit. I bite my lip tightly and shake my head, casting my eyes down to avoid him.

"She appears to be fine, Commander Keating," Evander informs him as he pulls me in closer.

"The iron was on fire," he states, staring at the place where my hands had just been. "I went...I went to touch her, and the iron burned me," Luthais continues, holding his hand out to us.

Evander lets his lip curl into a snarl, flashing his teeth at Luthais.

"Sounds as if you angered Vaohr. Maybe next time, you should keep your hands off my betrothed if you wish to keep them." The iciness in his tone is so unlike the man I am used to that I flinch.

It pains me to know that he has to act this way for us to live but the look stretching across Luthais's face makes it almost worth it.

"I assure you, I'm fine," I say before glancing at Evander. "Can we go find the seamstress then?"

Evander nods and moves his hand to hold mine, squeezing the palm tightly. I squeeze back, feeling the flames recede a little more with each touch he gives, with each glance, each kiss.

"Thank you for the walk, Commander Keating." My eyes dart back to him, still holding Ev's hand while he gawks at us. His jaw twitches and he sets his lips in a straight line, rearranging his face to the stoic mask he wears.

"A pleasure, my lady. I'll see you at dinner." Luthais spins on his heel and storms away without a glance back at us. I take in a deep breath and look up at Evander.

"Thank you," I murmur.

"For what?" He chuckles as he pulls me to start walking. "I didn't make that up, Bria, there really is a seamstress waiting for you. It was just good timing that I got to you when I did."

"Still," I remark, worried about the burn that Luthais sustained. "I'm having trouble keeping myself in check right now." I look back to the iron railing and the raging sea below.

"Not for much longer," Evander replies.

I stop moving and he halts with me. "There's something that happens with you," I start before pausing, concerned about how he might react. His brows raise to his hairline as he waits for me to continue. "With your touch, I mean." My face flushes and I hurry to finish explaining. "Something about you just calms me. So truly, Ev, thank you."

Evander smiles deeply, the beautiful one where the dimple sinks into his left cheek and his eyes crinkle with the effort. He places a kiss on my hand and pulls me close as we set back off to the castle.

My shoulder aches from leaning against the wall outside of Bria's bedchamber. The seamstress found it appalling when I waltzed into the room behind her, fully intending to stay. Perhaps I should act a bit more formal around her, though it's difficult changing our relationship to fit the castle rules.

It must have been at least an hour now. I could easily have walked across the hall and lounged in my own room during this time, but who knows when Luthais will decide to show back up and come knocking on her door? I'm not willing to take the chance.

Maybe that comment I made about him angering Vaohr had stirred something in him. He is, after all, a man of god. A devout royal guard. And there is no reason for him to be touching Bria. Ever. I meant what I said about losing a hand the next time. Or both.

After what feels like ages, the heavy wooden door opens and the plump woman shuffles out, shooting me a dirty look. I throw her a wink and slip through the doorway behind her, pushing it tightly shut and locking it before slumping against the frame. I heave a sigh.

Bria looks up at me and cringes. "I'm sorry," she offers, pity and guilt straining across her face.

The look makes me laugh and I drag a hand through my hair,

pulling the loose strands from my eyes. My back is sore from standing so I push off the door and stride to the bed, flopping dramatically on my back onto the lush mattress.

"Would it help if I say the gown is worth it?" she inquires, and I note the teasing tone of her voice. I've missed that tone.

Before all of this, Bria had always taken that flirty and teasing tone with me. It had driven me crazy.

Pressing myself up to my elbows, I watch her lift the glass decanter off the table to pour a small glass of red wine. Not her favorite, not by a long shot. But I assume she's drinking it because it's the only thing in here. She's probably exhausted from dealing with the seamstress and the flare of her magic earlier. Keeping it contained cannot be easy. She swirls the deep current-colored liquid before taking a sip. Her lips tighten. Definitely not her favorite.

Her hair is coiled into a bun atop her head so the seamstress could work around her shoulders without any snags, the long line of her neck now visible.

"Yes, I would say that helps a great deal," I respond, reciprocating the teasing tone and trying to force out the image of running my tongue along that line of her neck. I genuinely cannot wait to see her in the gown.

"We don't have much time before we need to leave for the temple," I add, tracking her hands as she tugs out the pins keeping her hair in place. Each one she removes pours more gold down her back and I get the familiar urge to plunge my hands into the soft tendrils, knowing she'll smell of vanilla and jasmine just as she did earlier.

"Then talk," she says, shaking out the rest of her hair.

She pulls up the skirts of her gown to sit at the table, crossing one leg over the other. A flash of ivory skin contrasting with the deep corn-flower blue of the dress fixes my gaze. She makes no move to cover the exposed flesh of her legs and I eventually drag my eyes up to meet hers. The flames of cobalt still dance in her eyes. She's holding it in, but just barely. I hope she can contain it throughout the trip to the temple and the dinner.

She meets my stare. She feels the heat in it, sees the desire I have for her. Bria tilts her head to the side, golden locks falling gracefully over her shoulder, and she smiles. The full smile that makes my heart ache and sends blood rushing to my groin.

I love her. Fiercely. I want desperately to tell her, to show her with my hands, my lips, my tongue, and teeth. Her confession that my touch calms her, that it smothers the magical fire that builds inside of her, did nothing to stifle the hunger. Instead, it fed it, making me yearn for her more.

Knowing now—when we are so close to getting Nimai—is not the time, doesn't make it any easier.

Sitting up a little further, I shove my hand deep in my pocket and my fingers close over the tiny vial inside. I pull out a small golden bottle—thin, no wider than my index finger, and tightly corked to keep the lethal contents inside. I give it a little shake and toss it across the room to her. Bria easily snags it out of the air and holds it up to the light.

"Belladonna?" she asks, though she already knows the answer. Her eyes glint from the light reflecting off the vial.

"With a few other herbs sure to keep you docile. Though they don't know you at all if they think that possible for even a moment." She glances back at me, a smirk pulling at the corner of her lip.

I recline back on my elbows, letting my body sink into the soft fabric of the bed.

"I'm to place it in your drink before dinner. Aamon expects me to come to your room and escort you but share a drink beforehand." I roll my lips tightly, not wanting to do any of this. "They want to watch, Bria. To see what kind of effect it has on you. So, you'll have to be convincing."

"And how am I to do that?" Her tone is exasperated.

I think about it for a second. She *has* to be believable. "Watch Nimai, I suppose. She will actually be sedated. They won't risk bringing her around you when she's not. It's another reason Aamon wants you drugged tonight, so you don't notice the full effects of what is happening to your sister."

Bria bares her teeth at the remark, and I realize the error in what I just said. *Idiot.*

"Why don't I just drink the concoction and see what happens, then?

I wouldn't want to be *unconvincing*." I hadn't meant to antagonize her, and her irritation is clear as she toys with the cork topping the vial.

I grind my teeth together at the thought. "Absolutely not, Bria."

Quickly pushing myself to my feet, I walk swiftly over to her and snatch the vial from her hand. Before she knows what I'm doing, I stride directly into the washroom. She can see me clearly from where she's sitting, and I make a show of staring back at here while I uncork the vial and dump the contents down the bath. I toss the vial in the bin and Bria sits back in her chair, arms folded, glaring at me.

She doesn't get it. "They have no idea what they are doing, Bria. They could just as easily kill you by dosing you too high and I'm not willing to risk it."

"But they are dosing Nimai," she counters quickly.

"Yes. And she hasn't come into her powers yet, has she? They are drugging a teenage girl, Bria. It's much different for you." Does she really not understand how astounding she is?

Bria takes another sip of her wine and looks over the glass at me. Taking a beat before she speaks again, she quirks her lips.

"Maybe we need something a little stronger before dinner then," she says playfully, the sparkle back in her eyes.

I laugh at the quick change in her mood. The wine sparked an idea, and she has a point. Drinking a little before dinner could give her the edge she needs.

"I'll ask for some whisky to be brought up. But you don't need to be drunk. We just need them to think you aren't a threat, let them think they can pull power from you."

I walk to her then, holding out my hand, and hoping she will take it. She does and I pull her to her feet and directly into my body. I caress her face with my hand, moving to cup her cheek, the skin soft and smooth beneath my fingers. It's crucial she grasp how important this is, how if they think they have her figured out it will make things so much easier for us all.

"If they think they've done enough tonight to keep you calm, then we won't need to do this charade again."

She nods, her skin warm against my hand.

"I'll try my best," she confirms, and I know that she will, that she will do whatever it takes to free her sister.

"Wonderful. And then we can get the fuck out of this place before they can do anything else. To either of you," I say, looking deep into her eyes and hoping she can see the sincerity there.

I want to put as much distance as possible between us and this place and wish the world stretched further west than the Forsaken Woods or further north than the Kaanos Mountains so we could never be found. I wish I could take her far, far away and live the life we both desperately want. The life she deserves.

She raises herself onto her toes and leans into me, the scents of jasmine and vanilla wafting from her. Her lips press to mine, and I stifle the urge to drag her to the bed or better yet, just take her against the wall. I have to keep reminding myself there is no time. I move my hand to trail through her hair before pulling her head closer, letting my tongue reach out to touch hers. The kiss is gentle, a reminder of who we are and that we are in this together. She needs that right now, and she seems to know that I need it too.

CHAPTER 54

Bria

Two horses are saddled and ready for us when we leave Castle Eccleston. Evander and I mount the horses for the ride to the temple. It was constructed in the furthest corner of Easthallow and though we could have walked, it would have taken much longer, and the high priest has requested us to be there now. I'm fairly used to riding, but being on a horse in such a long gown is not the easiest feat, and I find myself longing for my leggings and boots. Relief flows over me when I see that Luthais is not joining us, and neither is Aamon. Apparently, the sacred rite is not something to be shared, not a public ceremony.

As we ride, I watch Evander. I'm not sure how I can go back to how our lives were before this. As a betrothed couple, we have spent nearly every second together and it feels right. I feel at ease around him. He steadies me, he calms me, and I feel...loved.

Although I know I might be reading into things, I can't help but recall the conversation with Quinn. I feel something from Ev, something more than the friendship we've shared for years. The attraction between us has been evolving for a long time, but it's shifted, morphed into something more. I had hoped Evander was smarter than this. That he wouldn't let himself fall for a dead woman. But that night in the Gilded Forest, he'd said he wanted to give me the ring one day. And not just because of the parts we were playing.

That statement made me realize I was lost. I was his entirely and there was no going back after this. Not for me.

But I don't want Evander to feel the pain I'm experiencing right now—the deep ache in my chest, the tearing that rips through me when I think about losing him, about losing everyone I hold so dear. But they won't be lost here, not in this city nor in the castle, because I am going to make sure we all get out.

For now, the best I can do to make that happen is play the part as we ride to the temple. The city has a whole different kind of beauty during the daytime. It's alive with people crowded around taverns for lunch, gathering their groceries from the market, and purchasing goods. Just living. Going about their lives normally. I miss having a real life like that. A life that isn't controlled by a prophecy and being hunted.

The bitter tang of jealousy hits and my throat tightens as I watch a group of women browsing shops and chasing after their small children, another thing I want but will never get to have. Another aspect of life I will be deprived of. It hurts, but as we ride past the children, I smile, thinking that if we are successful with all of this, then my friends and families will be able to live these lives. Maybe I can't, but they can. They will. Nimai will meet someone and fall in love, Ash will have a family, and Evander and Quinn will become fathers. They will both be wonderful fathers.

"Are you alright, Bria?" I hear his voice, breaking me out of my thoughts.

Grabbing the reins, I steady myself on the horse. We've been silent during the ride so far, not wanting to bring any attention to ourselves. But now we near the edge of the city and I expect Ev noticed my expression.

"I'm fine." It's a blatant lie.

A lie because I don't want to make things any more difficult between us. He doesn't need to know how desperately I crave children and the experience of being a mother. Because though the children I just saw brought those feelings up, it was brief—a fleeting sense of jealousy and sadness. I had come to the realization when I first met Cato, first began my training, that my path was changed forever. I accepted my fate already, long before this day. I'm not meant for that life.

"Liar." He scowls, turning his face back to the road ahead. "Are you nervous about the temple? About the priests?" he asks, prying for the reason my mood shifted.

The temple appears now as we come out of the city, no buildings to block the view any longer. The thought of going into the wretched building is absolutely weighing on me, but it's not nervousness I'm experiencing. It's anger, seething anger in fact, at the prospect of spending any time with those horrific men.

"Not nervous, no," I admit, knowing he's not going to let up. He knows me too well, can read my emotions even when I think them to be well hidden. And right now, I have not hidden them well at all.

"Ahh, you're thinking of sinking a dagger into each of their hearts? Debating on how many of the priests you can hold down with your shadowy vines?" He shoots a glance my way, one eyebrow raised, and the corner of his mouth turns up. That dimple. It makes my own mouth break into a smile despite myself. He has firsthand experience of how powerful my vines can be.

"Maybe. But I have no dagger right now," I remind him, shifting the reins into my left hand and gesturing to the long gown I wear. The stupid dress forces me to ride sidesaddle, and it's unbelievably uncomfortable and slow. But it's an effort in keeping some semblance of purity and innocence, lest the priests see my bare legs as I hike the dress up to ride normally. I wish I had a dagger or any other weapon on me going into the temple. If problems do arise, I can use my gifts if absolutely necessary, but that will open up a whole host of issues for us. I still miss the weight of a blade at my side and strapped across my chest.

"Well, we will just have to find someplace to hide one going forward," Ev says, his eyes sliding up the length of the gown. My stomach knots with anticipation, following the line of his thoughts.

"We should probably keep talk of daggers in hearts to ourselves though." He nods forward and I notice we are directly in front of the temple.

The giant smooth slabs of gray stone stretch upward toward a massive golden dome. There are no windows along the sides, just large, scalloped archways. One singular stained-glass window stands high in the center of the front-facing wall. It's an enormous circle formed of various shades of blues and whites, with shards of gray slicing through the center. It ends in a sharp, pointed pane of glass, glistening a deep burnt orange. The building is old, clearly built shortly after the fall of the Keeper. But it has been kept in good condition. The stones are intact, the window clean and well cared for. No surprise there, given this is the foundation for their kingdom of lies.

As we approach, the tall doors open, and Father Mallory stands on the steep stone stairs to receive us. Evander heaves himself from his horse, hitching the stallion to one of the wooden posts before walking over to me. He holds out his hand and I gracefully give over my own to him, dropping the reins in the process. I slide down the saddle toward him and feel his arm wrap tightly around my waist. My feet don't hit the ground. He catches my body before, easing me down.

The gesture has me pressed flush against him, the thin fabric of my gown not feeling like much of a barrier. I bite my lower lip, resisting the urge to sink my hands into his hair and wind my body around his. But before I can act on any of those feelings and make myself look like a fool in front of the priest, Ev lowers me fully to the ground. He bends forward in a gentlemanly act and kisses the top of my head.

"If you don't stop, I'm going to grab that lip with my own teeth," he whispers into my hair, all pretenses of being a gentleman gone in that one sentence. I immediately release the grip on my lip, my mouth falling open. "And I'm not sure the high priest will approve of what I do after."

My stomach flips. *Dear gods.* He pulls back then, a devilish grin on his devastatingly handsome face, and grasps my hand.

"Shall we?"

I nod, not able to process a response after his words, a flush creeping across my chest and neck. We walk up the short path to meet Father Mallory and he turns, opening the large, heavy wooden door behind him.

"Welcome, Lady Bria. And welcome back, Evander. Vaohr will be most pleased that you have both arrived." He holds the massive door, ushering us inside.

The temple is much as I expected. A grand room with a soaring ceiling, the dome I observed from outside. Sunlight shines through the huge stained-glass window, cascading light into the space. The floor is pure white marble, slick and polished, reflecting the light and letting it bounce around the room.

Small benches sit in a circle, spaces for people to sit and worship in the presence of their god. And in the back of the room, where the light spreads out in a wide bath of pure white, stands the statue of Vaohr. I stare at the fake god, a slab of pure white marble carved into a robust man. Depicted as being taller than a typical man, he towers above, rippling with muscles. He has long hair that comes to his shoulders and a perfectly square jawline. His arms are outstretched as if he were giving something to the people and receiving them at the same time. I want to laugh at the absurdity but think better of it given my current situation.

Evander kneels before the statue, and I feel a tug on my hand as he goes to the floor. I look down at him and hesitate for a moment, not sure of what he's doing, my face contorting in confusion. *Am I meant to kneel as well?* Probably.

I gather the flowing train in my free hand and gently lower myself, tucking my feet and knees under. Watching Ev out of the corner of my eye, I mimic his movements. His head is bowed in a reverent prayer, so I do the same, staying like that for some time in our false prayer. His fingers are still interlocked with mine and he trails his thumb along his mother's ring on my hand.

Our time on the floor feels like hours but I'm aware only minutes have passed. I have no patience for this level of worship. *How much longer are we supposed to stay like this?* I wonder. The hard marble is cold through the gown and not to mention, painful. If you are expected to kneel and pray, the least the bastards could do was put out a cushion or a rug.

After a few more moments though, Ev lifts his head before raising from the half-kneeling position. He pulls me up to my feet as well and we turn back to face Father Mallory together. He's staring at us as I flatten the skirt of the gown, and I notice that disturbed glint in his eye. He makes my skin feel dirty, filthy even. And I want to rush back to the castle and scrub it as hard as I can to get his stare off me.

"What a truly lovely couple you are," he croons, his eyes glued on me.

He continues to say things like that, about how happy and lovely we are, and it strikes me as odd. We are convincing as a couple, and why should we not be? We care for one another deeply, having shared years of friendship and clear sexual chemistry. And Evander has done a wonderful job convincing his father, at least, that he seduced me for the cause. So, I cannot tell if he is trying to put me at ease with these comments, to make me more pliable to his will if I think the priests approves of our union, or if it's something else entirely. I can't be sure, but something about his words just makes my skin crawl.

"Lady Bria, if you would join me." He gestures toward the closest bench, and my body tenses, every muscle going rigid at the thought of sitting with him. "Evander must take the rite and I would like you to watch, to meet the priests and witness what Vaohr has to offer."

Shit. My eyes dart to Ev, who remains beside me. With a slight nod from him, I begin to move, forcing my body into motion even though it fights me the entire way. My mind screams that this man wishes to cause me harm and in the worst ways imaginable. The bench is barely big enough for the two of us and I have no desire to be that close to this bag of bones. But I walk past him anyway, quickening my pace as I see his outstretched arm. His fingers brush my elbow and I shudder. When I sit, he settles in next to me, comfortably fanning out his flowing robes. Expensive fabrics swathe the man, and he reeks of herbs and some sort of metallic tang. He's too close for comfort. His knees touch mine and I will them to stay in place and not to retreat as they so want to. I purposely rest my hands in my lap, appearing more ladylike, and immediately feel his fingers tracing mine.

"What a lovely ring," he remarks, clasping my hand, encasing it in his spindly fingers.

The flames crackle within my core, building, and I try to hold them off. My hands feel hot—too hot, and heat rises into my face. He can feel it. I know he can even before he leans in to whisper in my ear.

"You don't have to hide around me, my pet." His voice is slick as oil. It shoots a chill straight up my spine. But I breathe. *Remember to just keep breathing, to keep the flames caged. For now.*

"I'm not hiding anything, I assure you, Father," I reply, turning my voice into the sickly-sweet tone they have come to expect from me. From the corner of my vision, I see more priests pouring out from the doors behind the statue, filling in the benches and coming to surround the statue of Vaohr. And Evander.

He chuckles and I feel Ev's eyes on us. Watching Father Mallory.

"Ahh, but you stifle your gift. I understand. You think it stolen and you wish to give it back. But that is not what Vaohr has planned for you, my dear." His breath is hot against my face, damp and acrid.

What is he talking about? What he has planned for me is to take the magic that is rightfully mine and use it for the Crown's own fucked up purposes.

"It is stolen, Father. I wish to be of service in whatever capacity Vaohr deems appropriate." Lies flow, but the mask of the docile damsel remains in place.

"Shhh, my pet," he says as he pats my hand but does not release his grasp on it. "Let us listen."

Fighting the impulse to rip my hand away, I let him hold them and imagine slamming my fist into his sniveling face instead. I wish to yank out his tongue and slice it off so he can never call me *pet* again.

"The almighty Vaohr created all life, good and evil. He hung the moon and stars in the sky and poured light into the sun. Vaohr bestowed upon this land the creatures that now roam, the people who now breathe, the plants that now grow."

The priest standing before Evander has begun speaking and Ev sinks to his knees once more. His head is down, hands splayed in front of him at the feet of the priest. I hate it more than I can stomach. He should not kneel to anyone. Especially not these charlatans.

One day, though. One day, I will bring these men to *their* knees. And I will do it for Ev, for Nimai, and all the innocent lives these people have stolen.

The priest is retrieving something from the folds of his cloak and Father Mallory begins to speak again, his tone hushed.

"As I am sure you are aware, dear girl, Vaohr revealed himself as the true god to King Edwin over a hundred years ago now."

I nod. I know how their faerie tale goes.

"The Keeper had refused to give a gift to the king. The king was furious that he would be slighted, thinking the Keeper was a god and not the demon he truly was. But Vaohr saw that the king had good in his heart and revealed himself. He brought the priests to the king, granting them the ability to wield his power in the name of Vaohr. It is the one reason the Keeper was felled. He was no match for the king once he had the power of Vaohr at his side. No match for the one true and righteous god."

I want to strangle him until all the air leaves his lungs and no more nonsense can spew forth. When he squeezes my hand, flames lick at my fingertips, fighting back at my attempts to lock them down.

Father Mallory smiles, a twisted curve of his thin lip. "You know the power I speak of, pet. You likely feel strengthened just being in the presence of all the priests, by being in this sacred place."

I feel no such thing. What I feel is rage and a longing for vengeance when I force a small grin to seep into my face.

The priest standing in front of Evander is chanting a prayer to Vaohr while holding one of the blue orbs they use. Ev hasn't fully explained the orbs to me, but I gather that this is how they channel power. How they contain it for their own use. The others have them on the top of staffs, but this one he holds in his bare hands.

Father Mallory leans back in, and his breath is like a hot knife slicing across my cheek.

"Evander must allow the power of Vaohr to course through him, to feel what the god wants him to feel. It will allow him to understand his purpose and fully commit himself to the temple."

I arch my brow. "He will be struck with Vaohr's power? But how?"

"You will see, my pet. Be patient and watch your betrothed commit himself to the cause." His voice is like gravel being ground into my skull. Irritating and painful to listen to.

The priest stops chanting and looks down at Evander, who finally raises his head. I hate this. I hate not knowing what is going to happen and having to sit idly by.

The priest grasps the blue orb, light bouncing off it as he observes Evander kneeling before him. Then he thrusts his arms out, the orb still poised tightly between them, and a flash of blinding white light erupts from the orb and strikes Ev. He goes down on the marble floor, his forehead making a loud cracking noise as it hits.

Gasping, I quickly raise my hand to my mouth in an attempt to stifle it. I hear Father Mallory let out a soft snicker beside me.

"Impressive, is it not, my dear?"

Not nearly as impressive as what I can do. Or what Silas can do, for that matter. This is a watered-down version of his ball of light. Something less than. But Father Mallory mistakes my concern for Evander as shock regarding what the priest did. Ev is alive. I can see him breathing and keep myself seated. No magic they contain in that orb holds a candle to what I am capable of.

"He will be fine," Father Mallory continues, clearly realizing my silence means I'm concerned for my betrothed and nothing more.

He is absolutely knocked out, but the priests just keep on with their business. Some come over to be introduced to me, walking around Evander passed out on the ground. As much as I want to go to him, I know I cannot, and Father Mallory keeps my hand held tight, introducing me to the miserable lot of men.

I smile and nod, feigning interest in them while keeping my eye on Ev.

When the last of them has filtered out, Father Mallory turns his gaze back to me.

"Vaohr is so pleased with you, my dear girl." As if he has spoken to the fraudulent god himself. Fucking maniac.

"I am happy to be of service, Father. Will I also partake in the rite as Evander did?" I'm digging, trying to get more information as to what this man might be up to.

He grins, patting my hand again. "No, my pet. You have a far bigger role in this than you know." His eyes narrow on me, revealing the pure evil behind them, so dark they seem to bleed to black. Deep caverns of nothing. "You and your sister are not the same as the others with power. Your gifts are recognized by Vaohr. It is why you are so much more powerful than the rest. Together, you will usher in a new generation of priests and priestesses, brought up by the temple and chosen by the god himself."

My breath catches in my chest. They don't intend to just bleed us dry, soak up all of our energy, and leave us for dead as they did all the others?

He must see the confusion playing out in my expression, because he continues his explanation.

"Your marriage to Evander should be fruitful. He comes from a long line of those believed to be gifted, as we found out with his mother. So, though he is not chosen by Vaohr, he will do. We just need to find an equal match for your sister, which is proving a bit...challenging."

What in the fuck does that mean? He expects Ev and me to get married? Expects Nimai to as well?

"I am so sorry, Father, I don't quite understand what you mean," I choke out, trying to keep my face neutral while I wait for a response.

"Your children, my pet." My jaw drops to the floor before I can control it. "Your children will be those of Vaohr. The chosen ones who will guide the temple going forward. The most powerful people, returning to Vaohr and aiding in the cause."

Evander stirs in the corner of my vision and I turn to stare at him, barely hearing the words that Father Mallory is saying anymore.

"The king and I have discussed this matter at length, and had intended to tell you about it tonight at dinner. But you have a very curious mind. Your sister already knows of her fortuitous future."

Children. They want me to have children so that they can enslave them. Make them work for the king and promote their fake god to the entire world. To bring all of Azudora under their control. And they want to use my sister as well. To breed us like we are nothing more than livestock. I don't dare speak, watching as Ev sits up, holding his head. There will be a bruise for sure, but he seems alright. Though he won't be after I tell him this lovely new revelation.

"I'm sure this is quite shocking for you, to hear that you have such a bright future ahead of you when you came here ready to deem yourself unworthy. But child, Vaohr has found you worthy. Oh, so worthy." My fingers itch to smack him. To drag my nails down his wrinkled cheeks and draw blood, to rip the flesh from his bones.

I steady my breathing once more, worried that the flames will engulf my body and the shadows will rip forth if I cannot get a handle on myself. I will myself to speak past my clenched teeth and tight jaw.

"Yes, quite shocking. But also, such lovely news." I swallow, having trouble getting the words out over the lump that is building up in my throat. "I cannot wait to speak with my sister tonight."

"Oh yes, she was also quite taken aback by the news. I am sure she will be most pleased to speak with you regarding it as well." I see him glance at the pocket watch he has stashed in the folds of his robes.

"You really must be off, my pet. Dinner with the king requires much preparation for you and your sister. Evander can meet you there. He appears as if he needs a few moments to collect himself after receiving his blessing."

That was no blessing. There's a large red gash stretching across his forehead, blood seeping from the wound. He's risen and moved himself to the bench across from me. I catch his gaze now as he stares at me, and there is a deep sadness in his eyes. No part of him wanted to partake in that, and it drained him physically and mentally.

I finally wrench my grasp from Father Mallory and stand, getting my footing before I stride across the smooth floor to Ev. His eyes never leave mine and I feel as if I'm drowning in them, drowning in the madness of this insufferable fucking place. Unable to speak of what I just learned or hold him to ensure he's alright. He grabs my hand as I stop in front of him and laces his fingers with mine. The gesture instantly soothes me.

"Are you alright?" I ask, my voice low.

Ev cocks his head to the side. "I am blessed by Vaohr. I am better than alright."

Right. They are listening to us. His mask is in place and mine needs to be as well.

"Father Mallory would like me to return to Castle Eccleston to ready for the dinner." I want him to say he's going to come with me, but by the look of him, he's not ready to ride just yet. He probably has a concussion from that hit to the solid marble.

His lips brush against my hand and my stomach tightens. He lifts those molten chocolate eyes to me and his look turns feral.

"I can't wait to see the gown." He breathes across my hand.

The Keeper save me. This man.

I purse my lips to keep from smiling too wide. "I will see you at dinner then," I say, and he lets my hand fall, a smirk gracing his face as I saunter away to the door.

CHAPTER 55

Evander

The throbbing in my head is miserable. Fucking pricks knew exactly what they were doing. Father Mallory will have told Bria the usual lie, that Vaohr spoke to them and determined the blessing each individual receiving the rite would obtain. But that prayer Father Newcomb spoke over me was no prayer at all. It was a fucking incantation.

The priests learned how to use spells to make the magic work for them. They were not as precise as natural magic wielders but they managed just fine. Long ago, when the gods graced the world with their presence, Edwin rounded up witches to help them. The priests learned to harness it and found the right words to make it effective with their assistance.

In this instance, the rite was both a punishment and a warning shot. My punishment was for leaving the capital and forsaking Vaohr. It was no matter that I returned with their hunted. I see it in Mallory's eyes as he watches me. He believes her to be his. *Theirs.* That they own her now. It sickens me to think of what they plan to do.

"Your betrothed appeared quite concerned for you, Evander," the priest drawls.

When I raise a hand to my head, my fingers return stained crimson, dripping with my own blood.

"I will assure her it was nothing. I feel energized already from his blessing." Unfortunately, I already know how to lie to these people, how to float their egos and feed into their web of false beliefs.

"We need her, Evander. Her and the sister." He drums his fingers along the marble bench, staring at the statue of Vaohr. "More than you understand."

"I know exactly what you need her for. It's why I have delivered her here to you, to Vaohr." Does he think me a fool? I was part of the inner circle here that witnessed and took part in all of this.

Father Mallory stands, the crooked bones of his old hands smoothing down the folds of his robes. He clasps his hands together in front of him.

"Plans have changed, my dear boy. You have done so well. And because of that, Vaohr is asking more from you."

The priest turns to leave. What does he mean by that? I delivered Bria to them, that's what they wanted. That's all they have ever wanted, to own the two halves of the prophecy, to keep magic to themselves, and make the rest of the world worship at their feet.

"Asking what exactly?" I query, realizing the question may seem too forward, but also needing to understand what he means. What we might be walking into.

The priest throws up a casual hand to wave it off, not turning back to look at me. "We will discuss with the king tonight. You should go clean up before dinner."

My teeth clench at the dismissal. Rising to my feet, I blink, trying to clear away the blur in my vision. The blast they hit me with was excessive and I imagine that's what being struck by lightning feels like—a powerful surge that burns every inch of your body. A show of power for Bria and myself. I really should rest before dinner and try to sleep off the fogginess in my head.

Being in the temple now brings back memories of the first rite I took. Father Mallory himself presided over it and I was actually blessed with a boost of strength and speed before going out for a scouting trip to find people of power. But that was before I learned the truth, before I saw the dungeons and watched the high priestess in action. Now they granted me a show of power to prove they can keep me in check.

The sooner we leave, the better.

Maybe we could take Nimai tonight. Bria's power has been surging. Anytime I'm near her I can feel the well of heat oozing from her. If she stays around these people too long, she is going to explode.

But first we need to see how guarded Nimai is. To determine what their plans are before deciding when we can flee. Bria and I will figure it out tonight. I genuinely wish we had Quinn here to help. His mind for strategy would come in handy within the walls of Castle Eccleston.

I stand on shaky legs and move slowly across the shiny, polished marble floor, careful to keep from slipping and injuring myself even worse. Once outside, the glaring sunlight sends a fresh stabbing sensation through my head as I mount the horse and ride through the city, back to the castle. I take a short detour and check to ensure the gaps in the wall are still there, that Braddock has been too engrossed in his own endeavors to fix them. And thankfully, they are. We have a way out when the time comes.

To my surprise, and relief, no one is waiting for me when I return. I manage a solitary walk through the gilded halls, up the winding staircase, and down toward our wing. I make a point to check each guard I pass to see if anyone I know is currently assigned to the castle. Or to Nimai. That would help for sure.

Turning down the hallway toward our rooms, I see a familiar face leaning against a doorframe. The one next to Bria's. And there is no stopping the tension that radiates along my jaw, the way my hands clench and unclench with each step I take toward him. Luthais.

He can't be waiting for Bria again, can he? His eyes shift to me then before scanning quickly to my forehead and back. He grins and I shoot him a seething glare in return. The gash inflicted during my collision with the hard marble floor tells him everything. As I near, he pushes himself from the wall. His body moves smoothly to completely barricade the doorway to my approach.

He's not barricading Bria's door, but the one next to hers. Nimai. She has to be behind that door.

I fight all of my instincts, my fingers flicking along the hilt of my sword, itching to grasp the warm leather and sink the blade into him. I could gut him where he stands. But I wouldn't be able to get Nimai and Bria out without attracting attention. Not right now while they are attended to by servants, readying for the dinner.

Of course he was assigned to guard her. He was the one who captured the girl, and he's the favored guard of the king and Aamon.

"How was the rite?" Luthais taunts, his voice rife with contempt.

My hands clench again, the one on my sword gripping down into the hilt. I open my mouth, forcing my jaw to relax before speaking.

"It was an honor," I remark, continuing straight past him.

His derisive laughter reverberates through the hallway as I push open the door to my bedchamber. No matter how much I would rather go into Bria's room, there is no chance the servants would let me beyond the threshold.

When it comes to the battle with the king and his forces, Luthais will be there. And now I wonder if I'll get a chance to kill him, or if Bria will beat me to it. The thought makes me smile. The ferocity of that girl is something else. She is a force to be reckoned with. No damsel in distress, that's for certain.

Dinner is not for another two hours, so there's time for me to rest and wash up before escorting Bria. I cannot forget that I am expected to be seen entering her bedchamber before we descend to the royal dining room. Especially if Luthais is stationed next door. Part of his job will be to report back to my father if I drift from the plan at all.

Dropping myself to the bed, I lie back, sprawling along the wide mattress. I have yet to sleep in this bed and right now will be no different. Despite the headache, there is a buzz rippling through me. Anticipation and anxiety simmer below the surface as the time ticks down to dinner. Nimai will be there, and Bria is going to have a difficult time controlling herself. Not only does Aamon put her on edge, but she also nearly lost it earlier today with Luthais. Maybe letting her drink the whiskey before going down isn't such a bad idea. It might not only help her play the part of a docile lady, but also calm her nerves a bit.

It is worrisome, though, to bring her in front of them without the drugs in her system. Nimai will be drugged. Aamon revealed as much to me last night. Getting her out in that state may prove tricky. She may not understand what we are telling her, what we are trying to do. And she will likely not be able to run or fight. If she even understands, it will be pointless if she's incapacitated...unless Bria can cloak us well enough that I can carry the girl and get her out of this horrid place. Get all of us out.

She cannot have been here more than a few days now. Aamon and Luthais never mentioned exactly when she was captured. We would have heard from the southern camp if it had occurred much before we left, though who knows how many of them survived the fires. And it would take them some time to recoup and travel after that. But I know too well that it only takes a few days to break someone in the dungeons. Especially once they are drugged and the high priestess gets ahold of them.

To my dismay, my mind goes there even though I try to keep the thoughts at bay. I can't help but wonder if she was beaten in the last few days, and if Luthais or Aamon were the ones to do it. My jaw clenches at the thought of either of those men hurting her. Luthais is an imposing man and plenty of men get off on smacking around young girls.

Not all of the guards are privy to what occurs below the castle, but Luthais absolutely knows and is involved in it. And if he's guarding her, it makes it more likely that he's been expected to inflict pain upon her. The only semblance of assurance I have is knowing I can inflict the same pain upon him come battle.

She was moved today though, and at least that gives me some comfort. She is no longer facing any torture in the dungeons, nor will she ever again. Likely, Aamon took the opportunity when we were out of the castle to get her up here, not wanting to risk Bria noticing. Instead, he will wave it off that they moved her room to allow her to be close to her sister, if Bria were to ask. Which she won't. All their moves are planned out, approaching Bria in a tactical way. It's smart of them, showing that they at least have some inkling of what she's capable of.

Rolling off the mattress, I make my way to the adjoining washroom, quickly realizing that rest is evading me. The washroom is a mirror image to the one in Bria's bedchamber. Thankfully, there are buckets waiting for me and I proceed to dump them one by one into the giant tub. One of the pleasant perks of being in the castle is having chamber maids who attend to the room in the morning. I strip off my clothing, dropping my sword to the ground.

The mirror catches my reflection, and I can't help but examine the gash along my head. It's only about an inch wide, dried blood crusting along the edges, but the skin is already bruising and the pulsating pain in my head tells me I hit it harder than the wound shows.

The vanity has a multitude of drawers and I rifle through them, looking for anything I can clean it with but there is nothing. It must not be often that someone staying in the guest chambers of the castle needs to tend their wounds.

Turning to the tub, I slide into the hot water, letting it soothe my skin. Soaking one of the fluffy washrags and pressing it to my head, I let out a hiss at the stinging sensation. When I glance over at the table by the side of the tub, I notice the clothing folded neatly on the surface. Another detail that tells me someone was in my room while we were out for the day. All the more reason for Bria and me to remain together as much as possible with servants and others in and out of our rooms all day.

Steam ripples in waves off my arm and water runs in rivulets over the edge of the tub when I reach out a hand to touch the fabric. Running a finger along the long black dress tunic, I notice it glistens with silver threading and accents down the front panels, the collar raised high. Below it sit black dress slacks and black shoes that have been shined and sparkle with more silver. The outfit is far more regal than any I have worn in the past. Black is fine for a typical dinner, but the king tends to be a fan of bright hues and glimmering gold, as could be noted in the way he had the entire castle decorated.

They were getting at something with this outfit. It resembles the darkness of the night, the moon, and the stars. It reminds me of Bria.

CHAPTER 56

Bria

Readying for a ball back home had taken time, but not like this. This is far more extensive. I had been bathed and scrubbed, familiar scents of vanilla and jasmine wafting from my now-pink skin. Afterward, I was forced to sit for an uncomfortable amount of time and have now been standing for an equally excruciating period. My back aches.

My hair took the longest. Curling it at the long length I've let it grow to is no small feat. The women attending me said it was no trouble at all, but I could tell they wished I kept it a shorter, more acceptable length. When I leave it down it typically brushes the middle of my back. Now curled, I can feel it tickling the skin past my shoulders. No one back at the camp cared about the length of my hair since I was no longer a lady. But here, here it's different. I'm expected to act as I would back in Elwyn and changing my appearance and habits after five years where I've had no societal rules is proving difficult.

The last ball I attended was the last time my hair was curled and a small smile creeps across my lips as I think back to those times. To all the balls and parties. To Cedric. He'd commented on it curled once, told me I looked beautiful when it was done. I still remember that night when he tugged on one of the curls and later when he dragged his hands through it. And from then on, I'd asked Elia to help me curl it before any of the balls or gatherings where I might see him, making sure he would notice each time, that he would notice *me*. He always did.

But the rush of lust I felt when I was with him was always fleeting. It didn't stay coiled around me, curling my stomach into knots each time I saw him. I'd wanted Cedric and I'd cared for him. I did love him, truly. And even now, I have that distant hope that he is happy and has found someone to settle down with in our old town. But those feelings, that love, was nothing compared to what I feel around Ev. And what I feel when he's gone.

When he's gone, I feel wildly out of control of my power. It wasn't like this at home, but it is here, where my enemies stand by my side and speak with me, touch me. I can't bear it and I know I'm losing my grip. But when he stays next to me, something shifts. His touch is soothing, calming. It's almost as if he is absorbing some of the fire, some of the magic. Like he's sucking it in and allowing my body to quiet. Different from how Silas strengthened it, made the fire burn with a vengeance, Ev seems to relax the flames, contain them.

The women helping me, Leniah and Jaleesa, are kind and make small talk with me, discussing which of the king's guards they find attractive and commenting on how lucky I am to be dining with the king. Both are beautiful young women who have no idea the horror of a dynasty they work for. They live in blissful ignorance, not unlike how Nimai and I were before I came of age. Though would they have a choice anyway? Born into a working class, I know they are lucky to have these jobs working for the king.

As they finish with the gown, I watch them straightening pieces and removing pins the seamstress left. My muscles are screaming from standing like this and the relief at knowing it's coming to an end and that they are finishing up is washing over me.

Jaleesa strides to the armoire, throwing the doors open to reveal the full-length mirror within.

"Take a look, my lady."

My breath catches in my throat. My deep blue eyes are rimmed in ebony and silver, lashes coated in a black shine, my lips a sharp crimson. And the gown. The gown is even more amazing now that it's complete. It seems far too much for a dinner somewhere I don't intend on staying. But no one aside from Evander has the knowledge that we are leaving, that we are here to save my sister and for nothing else. So really, there is no reason to not be draped in luxury.

Not when I am their future.

Stomach churning with the words Father Mallory spoke to me earlier, I can only imagine how Nimai felt when she was told. She doesn't deal with the dark side of the prophecy. She was never forced to come to terms with death before she had lived a full life. For me, even if I was stuck here and forced to live the life Mallory wants of me, I would only be trading one death for another. But once the prophecy is fulfilled, Nimai is to go on living, able to build a future she wants. So to be told she is instead to be used as a vessel, to breed a new line of powerful people for the same bastards who ripped apart our family... The hurt she felt would have been unbearable, burdened by the disgust and the despair that must have taken her over down in the dungeons. And she had been all by herself. Alone.

But she is no longer alone, and I will make sure that she gets that life.

When I glance back down at the gown, I can't help but wish I could keep it. The smooth fabric is a deep midnight black that clings around me at the bodice, flowing down in a lavish skirt once it hits the bottom of my waist. The front of the bodice dips low, cutting a deep sweetheart neckline that reveals my collarbone and an expanse of cleavage. The back comes down just as low, and the ivory skin of my upper arms and shoulders can be seen contrasting with the dark fabric.

There's a feeling of overexposure with this much skin showing, especially here. The sleeves begin a few inches down my arm. They are sheer ebony fabric, cut off before the inside of my elbow, while the back tapers down the length of my arms. A long slit runs the length of the front, from the base of the skirt up to my waist. It reveals my legs any time I take a step, only covered by the skirt underneath that rises well above my knees.

Back home, the gorgeous gown would be scandalous, though the fashion is more modern in Easthallow. With silver threading woven throughout the dress, it sparkles in the light, and I'm not entirely convinced it isn't made of pure silver or even moonlight. It has been spun into whorls along the bodice, the arms, and the skirt, making the entire dress glitter, looking like a trail of swirling starlight along my legs.

Had it not been crafted by the king and his court, I might see it as an honor to wear it, something that is so clearly made for me, to recognize my connection to the dark side of magic. They are not honoring Lilith with this dress, though, nor Uldnoir. This is an homage to Vaohr, only acknowledging that I hold the darker side of his power.

It is a bit amusing, this whole night and the conversation I'm about to have with the king. None of the people who will sit at that table know of my ability to raise the dead. They are asking me, the mistress of nightmares, to bring forth life. Ironic.

Evander still doesn't know about the conversation with Father Mallory, and likely won't until later tonight. I glance toward the clock on the mantle and see how close the time is. We have merely fifteen minutes before we are expected downstairs.

Leniah removes the amulet Quinn gave me and sets it aside for the dinner tonight. In its place she now drapes a silver choker dripping with sapphires and diamonds along my neck. The center stone is radiant—a circular diamond, bigger than anything I have ever seen, that reflects the blue of the sapphires encrusted around it. It's a glowing orb like that of the temple. Or the moon. I clutch at it, feeling the cool, smooth surface of the stones as Leniah steps back.

I thank the two women and as they walk together to the door, I move to shut the armoire, a bit shaken by the image staring back at me. When I turn, I catch Ev standing in the doorway. He slipped through as the women were leaving.

I must stop breathing when I see the striking figure he cuts in the fine, black dress clothes. A broad chest and shoulders ripple down into muscular arms and abs, all noticeable in the way the fabric clings to him. The dark onyx of his tunic and pants makes his hair appear a darker hue and his chocolate eyes deepen into wide pools, more inky than brown. The corner of his mouth turns up, revealing that sunken dimple on his left cheek, and my heart resumes beating, racing to catch back up. He drags his eyes down the front of my body in the formfitting gown.

Ev doesn't take his gaze from me as he reaches behind himself to lock the door and starts moving toward me—a slow prowl with a bottle of whiskey and a leather strap dangling from his hand.

As he nears me, I realize I need to breathe and gulp down air. His hand reaches around my back, his rough fingers moving along the fabric until they meet bare skin, and the smile widens. He brings his lips to graze along my jaw.

"Oh, the gown is worth it," he remarks, the words trailing along my skin, leaving goosebumps in their wake and an ache between my legs.

I lean into him, breathing in sandalwood. Such a difference from the usual lemongrass he smells of, but a delicious scent nonetheless. His lips remain by my ear in a featherlight kiss as his hand flattens against my back.

"You like it?"

He moves his head again, hovering his lips above mine and allowing me to stare into his gold-flecked irises.

"I love it. Though I would prefer it on the floor," he murmurs against my lips before pressing into me and sending a flood of desire into my body at the imagery.

I can taste the spice of the whiskey on his tongue as he moves it inside, licking along the edge of my lips as he goes. I want him to keep kissing me, to drown out the world around us. I push back into him, letting my own tongue graze along his, sending sparks shooting down my spine. His touch and words send arousal to the deepest parts of me.

We could easily stay like this, melting into one another, exploring with our mouths. But reality is knocking, and we have places to be. As if we both understand this at the same time, we part, and I let out a long sigh.

He smiles again, his lips slightly reddened by my lipstick, and I reach my thumb up to fade the stain from his skin. He presses his lips to my hand and I have the shocking realization that everything about him is perfect, as if he were made for me. His touch calms me, his voice steadies me, he makes me feel alive.

Evander holds out the bottle of whiskey. "Drink up, my lady," he says, a teasing lilt to his voice.

My body starts to thrum with energy the second my lips hit the top of the bottle. I'm going to see my sister. I take a long swig, letting the warmth of the liquid seep down my throat and letting my eyes flutter closed. It's good, something higher quality here in the capital than the whiskey back in the camp. I take another long drink when I notice my hands are starting to shake. I have never been this nervous in my life, not that I can remember.

Evander grasps the bottle and I open my eyes to see him watching me, his eyes fixed on mine. I lift it from his grasp and take one more sip, not breaking my gaze. He huffs out a laugh and snatches the bottle from my hand before I can take any more.

"I think that's enough if you want to be standing when you go downstairs. Did you even eat anything?" he asks accusingly, arching a brow.

I grimace. I haven't eaten since this morning. My stomach growls in response to his words and he shakes his head disapprovingly.

"That's what I thought." With that, he takes a long pull off the bottle and moves to set it by the bed. He strides back over to me and picks up my hand, placing the leather strap he holds into my palm.

"For your dagger," he offers, his eyes darkening.

I let out a laugh as I examine the thin strap, a small sheath attached to one side. I have always worn my daggers in a bandolier, just like the men.

"Where exactly is that supposed to go?" I query and he takes it back, holding out the loop of soft leather for me to see as he kneels before me. My stomach tenses at the sight and I involuntarily clench my thighs together.

"Let me show you," he purrs, and he lifts my right leg, sliding the band upward, past the hem of my skirt. His fingers brush against my inner thigh and I suck in a breath. Thoughts of the other night come slamming back to me.

Evander watches me closely, as if he fully comprehends all the dirty things that are coursing through my mind. He smirks as he tightens the strap before dropping my skirt back into place. His hand shoots into his boot and he straightens, pressing the hilt of a dagger into my palm. I take it graciously and lift the skirt to slide it into the sheath. With the long slit and short inner skirt, it's easier to access than I would have imagined. Ev holds out his hand and I reach for him, letting our fingers clasp together.

"Let's go see your sister," he says with a grin, and I squeeze his hand as we walk out the door.

CHAPTER 57

Bria

I hesitate outside of the royal dining hall. The double doors are closed, high expanses of cream painted wood ornately decorated in gold. A lone servant stands between them, his hand resting on one of the intricate golden handles, waiting for us to approach.

A surge of energy sends flames flickering inside me and my body tenses. I haven't used any power in too long for me to be entering this room. Steadying my breathing, I force my exhale to be longer than my inhale. I will my body to relax a bit more. The whiskey is helping. I feel lighter on my feet and have a nice buzzing sensation in my head, but it's not enough to dampen the realization of what's about to happen, what I'm about to see.

Ev slides his body closer to mine, sensing my tension. He releases my hand and instead curls his arm around me, keeping me close. His touch evens my breathing, and my nostrils fill with sandalwood again. I feel his mouth on my ear, but don't move to look at him, my eyes fixed on the doors ahead. The flames stir inside but lessen.

"Breathe," he reminds me, whispering against my skin.

They are anticipating a more docile version of me, not the outspoken, magic-wielding warrior in training I typically am. Though, they have no idea who the real me is anyway, I suppose. Aamon only remembers me as a young girl with a smart mouth who bent the rules but never broke them. But to play the part now, I snake my arm around Ev's waist, melting my body against him, and we move in tandem.

The alabaster skin of my legs peeks from the dress with each step forward. I concentrate on my feet and keep moving, allowing Ev to guide us toward the doors. The servant opens them, and warm amber light seeps out onto the rich carpet before us.

The room is enormous, far larger than the ballroom back on my father's estate. Those same grand chandeliers dripping with crystal hang around the room, light falling out of them like stars. The walls are high, draped in the royal blue and gold of the main room with giant paintings covering the surfaces. I dart my eyes around, trying to take it all in. Servants are stationed in each corner, and there is a large stone fireplace on the far wall. The dining table in the center of the room is another long black walnut piece with space for at least twenty, though there are only seven chairs tonight—one high-backed, ornate chair at the end and three on either side, facing one another.

Aamon is already here, seated to the right of the high-backed chair, the seat of honor beside the king. It makes sense for his captain of the guard to be there. Father Mallory is across from him. The other chairs remain empty, and my heart sinks a little, noticing Nimai is not in one of them. Will they not bring her? Did they change their minds about letting us see one another? If so, we will be storming the dungeons tonight to get her out.

As we enter, Father Mallory shifts his focus to us and stands. Aamon turns at the sound of the doors, following suit and rising to his feet. He strides over to us, his eyes dragging over the matching outfits we've donned for the occasion. I stare straight ahead, forcing my eyes to glaze over a bit, remembering my role tonight. I allow Ev to hold some of my weight to make it obvious that I am not fully in control of my own body. Aamon's jaw tenses and his lip curls upward as he approaches us, extending his hand to grasp mine.

"Lady Bria, you look exquisite," he croons, pressing his lips to my hand.

It hurts to watch him. Evander looks more like his mother, but I can see the same cut of his jaw, the same curve of his brows, when I look at Aamon.

Plastering on a smile, I force out a girlish giggle that makes me want to vomit all that whiskey onto his polished shoes.

"Thank you, Captain Lansing." Ev tighten his grip on me, his fingers digging into my hip. Aamon's lip twitches. *Good*, I think.

Aamon extends his arm, showing us to our seats. We are to sit facing the doors, meaning I'm required to sit between Father Mallory and Evander, likely so that Aamon can watch me all night. So he can observe how the elixir impairs me. I like the occasional drink now and then—I often drink with Ash, Ev, and Quinn—but I don't indulge. I don't like to be out of control, to lose track of what my body is doing. I did that enough when I first arrived in the rebel camp—lost myself in whiskey because of my family and my fate. So tonight, it's important that I pay attention to what I drink, not too much but enough to keep me looking affected from the belladonna.

Evander drags out the chair for me and keeps his hand along my waist as I sit, ensuring he has his hands on me to show my unsteady footing. I straighten myself in the chair as he pushes it in before settling next to me. I can feel the weight of Father Mallory and Aamon's eyes glued to me and heat rushes into my chest. Acting is not a strength of mine. I prefer bluntness and not giving a fuck what people think of me.

Glancing around the room, I search for more alcohol that I can consume to dull my senses just a bit more. There's wine in front of me and though I abhor the taste of it, I could down the glass if no one was looking. Evander brings his chair in close to mine, far closer than where Father Mallory sits to my right. He lays his hand on my thigh and grips his fingers in. The movement isn't painful, but tight enough that the message gets through. I need to pay attention to my surroundings. To the eyes on me.

My brain is panicking, scrambling for ways to look sedated. Heat is building in my core as well, striking my spine like a match and flaring to life within me. But then the doors in front of me open again and all eyes turn toward the ethereal figure haloed in the frame of the cream double doors.

My mouth drops open and Evander shoves his glass of wine at me before I can think. I tip my head back and let the vinegar-like liquid pour down my throat before slamming the glass back into his hand. I glance over to Father Mallory, but he is nearly drooling, his mouth slack as he too stares at the doors. He didn't notice me at all in my rush to drink, too consumed by her. Aamon has risen from his seat but remains next to it, waiting for her. I glance back toward the door and allow my eyes to adjust to the figure before me.

Nimai.

She is just as I imagined her. Or just how the visions had been, I suppose. Which makes more sense. Because the mere fact that she is actually standing here before me means they were indeed visions, not just nightmares. Which also tells me that I did indeed see and feel her pain and terror. And heads will fucking roll for that.

Her long black hair is down, thick waves of obsidian shining with deep blue and violet hues around her shoulders. A choker matching mine sits around her neck, but she is shrouded in a gown of pure white and gold—almost the opposite of the one I wear—with gold lace atop the bodice, gracefully brushing along her collarbone and sitting just below her shoulders. It's far more regal and modest than what they've dressed me in and I suppose that should be expected. I'm the whore and she's the pure virgin. We're both pawns they want to use, but they're clearly making a statement regarding my place compared to hers.

Standing in the doorway, she looks radiant. Her mossy green eyes are glassy. I can see that from where I sit. They lazily take in the room, as if slowed down from their normal movements. But when she sees me, there's a spark. Something flickers in her eyes. Her perfectly pink lips turn up in a small smile and she moves to walk forward, staggering a bit. Luthais stays next to her and steadies her with an arm around her waist, the same gesture Ev just used with me to make it seem as if I was suffering from the belladonna. But she is actually suffering.

I notice Luthais is not dressed to match Nimai. That part is good. At least there is no intention of pairing her off with him. He's just here to drug and guard my sister. He grips her tightly and they walk slowly toward the table. Her eyes reach out to me, and I can feel her.

She's still in pain and her gaze does not break from mine as she moves. Behind the glassiness of her eyes, I can see my sister straining against the sedation. She's in there. No matter the drugs they gave her, she knows what is happening. And she's terrified. That fear stretches out to me, grasping around my heart. Squeezing it tight.

Evander must notice the gaze and the bond strengthening between us because he grabs my leg tighter, digging his fingers into the flesh of my thigh to remind me where I am. *Who* I am right now.

The wine is rushing to my head, making the bond between us feel fuzzy. It's there and open, the connection between us, a link like I have with Silas, only stronger. I'm kicking myself for drinking the wine, but I needed to, needed to have slightly less control over myself, even though it frays the edges of this connection and makes it harder to grasp.

Luthais half carries her to the table, holding her lithe body easily with one of his massive arms as he pulls out a chair for her and sets her down gently. She is nestled between Aamon and Luthais, seated directly across from me. Her body slumps a bit as she sits but she remains upright, almost as if the bones in her body have softened.

Flames itch at my palms despite the warm wine flooding my veins, mingling with the whisky. I don't dare look down for fear the shadows will swirl if I acknowledge my magic. Better to force it to rest.

"Nimai," I try to speak but the words catch in my throat, only allowing her name to cross my lips. It feels as if my throat is seared, like the fire inside has risen up and singed it.

Her eyes. I can't fully discern how badly she's impacted from the drugs but the look in her eyes tells me she's in there—a field of green set alight, sparkling with hints of fire. Perhaps she's fighting the effects of the nightshade, but I'm not positive she is strong enough to do that. She has merely a day left before her birthday, and I remember how my gifts started in fits and bursts leading up to that day.

Evander's fingers loosen on my leg as he starts speaking, trailing them along the edge of the slit, finding the opening and moving to touch bare skin. My stomach tightens with the boldness of it, his hand skimming high up on my thigh. It will be noticeable to Father Mallory if he looks over, but Ev doesn't care. He's trying to quell the flames.

"I think Bria is just a bit shocked to see you after so long, Nimai. You've grown so much." His voice is tender as he talks to her. "Even I can't believe you're here."

He reaches across to the bottle of wine on the table in front of him, refilling his glass. I'm sure he will push it to me as soon as he can and though I want my wits about me, I also understand his urgency. The surge of magic pulsing through my body seems to be keeping the alcohol from having much of an impact.

Her voice is a spring breeze floating across my skin—light and soft, making me feel warm inside when she talks. She is no longer the child who was ripped away from me five years ago. This is the voice of a woman. One of purity and power. It's what I imagine Kiara sounded like.

"Neither can I." Her words come out slowly as she looks at Ev, sounding like someone who has just woken from a long slumber. But her gaze flicks quickly back to me, holding me hostage in those green depths. "Hello, B."

Hot tears sting the back of my eyes, fighting to spring free. No one has called me that since my father died. Only the two of them ever used the nickname and grief washes over me when I hear it, threatening to drown me with the lost years, the time we've been separated. I open my mouth, gulping down air to keep myself afloat.

There is so much I want to say to my sister, but we have eyes on us. Luthais is watching Nimai, and I can feel Aamon and Father Mallory's stares boring into me now. But they are broken with the booming voice that echoes off the massive walls.

"Please rise for His Majesty, King Braddock." The servants are announcing the king's arrival, readying to open the doors once more.

I have to tear my gaze from Nimai as Luthais pulls her to her feet. He holds tight to her, spinning her body around as if she's floating on air. The others stand and Ev's hand leaves my leg to wrap back around my waist, hauling me to my feet. He tugs my body flush against his side and shoves the glass of wine toward me. I gulp it down, hoping this is the last I will need. As I hand the glass back to him, the doors open before me and there he is. The king.

To be honest, he's different than what I expected, having thought the man who waged war against me—against people like me—would be a sniveling little thing. But he is tall and graceful as he strides into the room, the deep blue velvet cape he wears swinging behind him. The crown atop his head is solid gold, embedded all around with sapphires and diamonds. He reeks of authority, and I can immediately understand how he has commanded thousands to follow him and the foolish god his family conjured. He's a natural leader with a kind face and trusting features. Even though I know that the entire foundation upon which his kingdom rests to be untrue, I can still see it, see how they would listen to a man like him.

We remain standing while he makes himself comfortable at the head of the table, removing the cape to reveal a tunic that nearly matches Nimai—a fine cream fabric dripping in gold accents. Had it been done on purpose? Or was she just dressed in the preferred colors of the king? There is gold all over the castle, the man clearly loves it.

He makes a sweeping gesture and everyone begins to sit. Evander yanks me down nearly on top of him, keeping his chair close, touching mine. Nimai slumps a bit as Luthais lowers her and I flinch. I hadn't noticed it when she first came in, too distracted by her stunning beauty and the pure shock of her standing in front of me, but I can see it now. They've tried to cover it up with makeup. Below her right eye is a blossoming bruise, a tinge of blue across her pale skin, barely holding a tan from her life in the south.

They've hurt her. My eyes shoot to Luthais at her side. It must have been him. He has been assigned to guard her, and he's the one who captured her. Stole her away in the middle of the night from her own bed and set fire to the southern camp. And now she's forced to sit next to the man who beat her and did gods know what else to her.

The edges of my vision are swirling a bit. The wine is coursing through me but along with it is a river of fire. A flush begins in my chest and travels steadily up my neck. My hands begin to ache, and I clench and unclench them, trying to relieve the tension. The crescent moons of my fingernails dig into the skin of my palms. *Breathe*, I hear Evander's whispers in my head and try to listen.

Evander's hand seeks my leg once again, grazing his fingers along where the slit is open so they can rest against my skin. Then Aamon speaks.

"Your Majesty, may I present to you Lady Nimai and Lady Bria, both daughters of the late Lord Saldhene." The words pierce my skin like daggers. How dare he utter a single word about my father. Aamon may not have killed him with his own hands, but it was on his orders that the estate was attacked. And he was backed by the man sitting to my right, and the king himself.

I dip my head as I answer the introduction, "Your Majesty," and hear my sister do the same. Our voices collide across the space between us.

The curve of my nails sinks deeper, biting into my skin. I'm certain there will be jagged half-moons on my palms if I release them, but it's pulling my focus.

Ev's hand moves, tracing the inside of my thigh with his fingers and creeping up toward the hem. A different kind of fire creeps along with his fingers and settles between my legs. My core aches, wanting him to keep moving his hand upward and at the same time being extremely aware we are not in private. Not by a long shot. And where his hand is? That is *not* something you do in public. Especially not in the presence of the king and the high priest. But even with that knowledge, my body is still reacting, dampening beneath his touch.

My eyes dart to him, but his are on the king and he ignores my glance, skimming down the edge of the slit and back up again. I'm well aware of what he is doing. Providing a distraction, quieting the roaring fire inside. And he knows it. I leave his hand there, letting it roam around the edges of my gown, feeling it slide a bit further each time it passes the hem, sending a jolt through my body with every stroke. My hands unclench though, and the prickling in my fingertips recedes as I relax under his touch.

I move my attention back to the king, who is watching Nimai. His hazel eyes gleam at her, taking in the unbelievable perfection in front of him. She is gorgeous, radiant in the white gown that contrasts so perfectly with her dark hair and bright eyes.

"I'm so pleased the two of you are here, that you have chosen to serve both the Crown and Vaohr." His voice is rich and deep, gliding over us as smooth as the caress of a lover.

Father Mallory pipes in, breaking through the haze I feel my mind becoming enveloped in. "Both halves of the prophecy, the light and dark that were stolen from Vaohr. Returned at last to our god and kingdom."

So that's where they are going with this.

Turning the prophecy to meet their own needs. Not acknowledging that the whole point of the prophecy is to bring the world out of this reign, this centuries-long ruling of corrupt kings, and into a new world. To push forth change. But they believe if they have us in their grasp, then the world—their kingdom—will not be overthrown. That they can use us to forge their own path, to solidify their hold.

Father Mallory's gaze slices across the space from Nimai to me before they flick to my lap. To where Evander's hand is disappearing under the hem of my skirt. I almost snatch his hand away, to hide it from the priest's view. But I think better of it and choose not to move an inch. His touch is the only thing keeping me grounded.

Let him see. Let him think I allow such bold action because of the sedation. He quirks a brow, but quickly averts his eyes and I sink further into my chair, allowing Ev's fingers to drag down my skin. The priest tenses beside me and I notice his gaze roaming to us repeatedly, but I no longer care.

"From what I understand Father Mallory has informed you both of your duties, your expectations while you reside here in the capital. Is that so?" Braddock's voice is disturbingly calming.

I'm not quite sure what he's referring to, though. Is it that our magic will be pulled from us whether we agree to it or not? Or is he discussing their plan to impregnate myself and my sister like breeding dogs? Probably both.

"I am afraid I have not revealed our plans in their entirety, Your Majesty. You had mentioned wanting to tell Lady Bria and Commander Lansing tonight." Braddock steeples his fingers to a point in front of him, the blood draining from the tips as Father Mallory talks. He was not expecting that answer. And he is not pleased.

Braddock grinds his teeth together, a small back and forth motion of his jaw, and his tone shifts. "Thank you for reminding me. Get on with it, then." Here is the man who commands power. Who seeks to kill anyone who steps in his way.

Father Mallory sits up in his chair, straightening his spine and flattening his palms over his robes. "As you are all aware, these two women are said to be our undoing, the ending of our world as we know it, the ending of our kingdom and our god. They are what we have feared for centuries, thinking a curse had been fixed upon us by the Keeper and his daughters."

The King's hazel eyes slide to me as Father Mallory goes on and I notice something shift behind them.

Hatred.

His lip curls into a sneer as he narrows them on me. Nimai was their plan, but I fell into their lap overnight. He wants Nimai, I can see it in the way he stares at her. But me? I am not who he wants, not in the least. I am tainted fruit, and she is the purest of them all. But he needs me, nonetheless.

"Vaohr spoke to me, told me of the light that shines in Nimai, that she can usher forth a new era in our kingdom instead of with the rebels, that her stolen gift can be brought back to its rightful owner. Little did we know that her sister would also be forthcoming and willing to take on a role beside Nimai."

The king grunts, waving a ring-swathed hand in circles at Mallory, urging him to speed it up.

"Tomorrow, Bria, you shall meet with the high priestess and give over your power. Give back to the one who owns you." My skin prickles at the thought. No one fucking owns me and my nostrils flare when I fight the urge to say as much.

"She has other business to attend to in the morning but assures me she will be available at the temple later on," he continues, completely unaware of my plotting how to kill him in my mind. My stomach clenches as I nod toward the priest.

We need to get the fuck out of here. Being stuck with the priestess will not end well for any of us. I blow a tight breath from my lungs, one I had not realized I was holding in, as Ev's fingers move again.

"Your wedding shall be planned within the week," Braddock states firmly as dinner is being served. Servants seemingly pour out of the walls with trays of food, a mix of sweet and savory aromas filling the room. I hadn't even noticed them enter.

Ev's fingers still and his grip tightens on my leg.

"A week? I apologize, Your Majesty, but may I ask why it needs to be quite so soon? Should Bria not have more time to plan as she settles into this new role?" He could just go along with it. We aren't staying here anyway, so there is really no reason to balk at the proposal, but I assume he is just trying to get more information out of them.

The king's eyes narrow on me as if I'm the problem as he answers Evander.

"The quicker you are married, the quicker Lady Bria can bear a child to be raised in the temple. We'll have no bastards here Lansing." The sneer appears again, and my heart sinks. There had been no time to get into their plans before dinner, so this revelation is going to catch Ev off guard. His fingers dig into the flesh of my thighs, a bruising grip, and my body tightens in response. I reach my hand down to sit on top of his, his mother's ring glistening in the light.

"Has your betrothed not told you of her future here?" The man is evil incarnate, just trying to push his power on us. "She and her sister are to serve the temple, to give back their stolen power so that the priests may wield it in the name of Vaohr. And they are to bear a new line of children, those who will be brought up in the temple and hold the power of the one true god. Power that has been blessed unto them, not torn from the hands of our god."

Oh, he hates me alright.

Ev clears his throat, his eyes set on the king. I glance between them, trying to read Ev's emotions, but it's nearly impossible. He has cleared his face, dropping that mask of the capital back in place, playing the villain once again. His fingers release their tight grip and intertwine with mine, resting on my leg.

"We have not been given much time to speak today, but I assure you, I understand. May Vaohr bless us." To hear him speak, you would have thought him a true believer. Someone willing to give up his own children, his own flesh and blood, to serve this blasted deity.

When I chance a look across to Nimai, her face has gone a bit slack, her eyes glassier than they were just a few minutes before.

Shit. She was fighting the sedation, but it appears to have won her over at last. The slate gray eyes next to hers are on me, widened to deep pools, shock rippling across Luthais's features. He is stunned. Apparently neither he nor Aamon were deemed important enough to be privy to this information prior to this moment.

"And what of Lady Nimai?" Aamon says finally, breaking the silence that is weighing the room down.

Nimai doesn't even raise her head when they mention her. She looks...broken. And my heart breaks with her and for her.

Braddock is completely focused on her, soaking in her beauty and not caring that she is limp and sedated. Not bothering to hide the clear desire he has for her.

"We need to find her an appropriate suitor. She will come of age in another day and can be married soon after her sister." He flicks his tongue out, gliding it along his bottom lip as he watches her. And I'm not entirely certain he won't try to make her his, in one manner or another. She's noble born and must still be a virgin for them to have dressed her this way and for him to be so keen on her. The perfect fit for a queen.

I stare at her, willing her to look at me, to see in my eyes that this will not happen. That I will get her out. I close my eyes and reach out to her, trying to feel around for her. Trying to let my mind seek her out like it did when I slept. Suddenly, her eyes shoot up and lock on mine.

I will get you out.

I keep repeating the thought over and over in my head. I need her to understand, to see that I will never let them do any of this to her. Her lips turn up a bit at the corners but don't remain that way for long. Even the effort of that small smile is too much for her. *How much had they given her?*

Silence settles back over the table as the king begins eating. I glance down at my plate and find it filled. When had that happened? Roasted potatoes doused in butter, a slab of braised meat, and crispy vegetables look back at me, but bile is rising in the back of my throat from this conversation and the company surrounding me.

Evander squeezes my hand before releasing it and picking up his fork.

"You need to eat," he orders in a hushed tone.

He's right. If I want my mind to be straight, I require food to soak up some of this damn alcohol. The edges of my vision are still blurred from the glasses of wine, but not as much as I expected. It's as if the energy surging through my body is just burning it off.

Luthais nudges Nimai and she startles, coming somewhat out of the trance she was in. Enough that she is able to lift a few bites to her mouth. I hope they are not keeping her like this all the time. Not only will her already thin body waste away to nothing, but how in the name of the gods will we get her out?

CHAPTER 58

Evander

Anger is seething through my body, and I have the strongest urge to slam the knife I hold through Braddock's thick throat. My father didn't know of this new plan. That fact is abundantly clear in the bewilderment that spreads across his face when the king mentions Bria and I having children. And giving them to the priests to raise. Even he, as devout of a man as he is, did not expect that—to be told he is to have grandchildren but that they will never be his. And yet he does not say a word about it or balk at the prospect.

Fucking gutless piece of shit.

It just furthers the reason I left these monsters. To think that I would go along with this, to give up my children, to allow Bria and her sister to be drugged and beaten, have their energy drained out of them and then used as human incubators... It's sick. Twisted. Even worse than what I expected from them.

My hand tightens around the knife, gripping the handle as I slice into the meat on my plate, forcing myself to eat. *Chew and swallow. Just keep up appearances until we can leave.* Bria is barely eating, and I'm not sure Nimai has touched her food yet either. Though I suppose both sedation and debilitating fear will do that to a person.

I notice Luthais keeps gently nudging Nimai, urging her to take a bite. What is he up to? Perhaps he's trying to ensure the future of the kingdom doesn't die on his watch, because he doesn't care for her as a person. That much is apparent from the purple-blue tint under her eye. Someone struck her. Hard. She must have put up a fight when she first arrived. I assume the long sleeves of the gown are hiding more bruising and the like. She has far more flesh covered than the gown Bria is clad in.

My father and the king are speaking of the wedding. *My wedding.* But I pay them no mind. I hear Father Mallory telling Bria what to expect tomorrow when she returns to the temple and my stomach sinks to the floor. I really should talk to her about the priestess before we go to her tomorrow. She deserves to know the truth, and I feel like a coward for not telling her before now, though I have no doubt in my mind she will not react well to the truth. I'm not sure I can bear for her to look at me like she did when I first arrived at the northern camp. I won't live through her rejection again.

I glance down at her hand on the table, my mother's ring still adorning her long, slim finger. It fits her perfectly. This is where it belongs. It makes my heart swell just to look at it.

"Shit!" I hear Luthais curse under his breath and look up. Nimai has dropped from her seated position and he caught her. His eyes dart around to see who noticed. The drugs have fully kicked in now and she's passing out. Despite his quick action, everyone sees the girl slide into him.

"It appears Lady Nimai has had a bit too much to drink this evening," the king croons as Luthais stands to gather her in his arms. I push my chair back a bit, readying to help him, but Aamon shoots me a glance, warning me to stay put—to stay with Bria. Her speech is slower than normal, and she is barely eating, but otherwise she's acting normal. By the way he's watching her, he will expect me to give her more tomorrow, unhappy with the effects.

Luthais bends his legs and sweeps up the long train of her dress, cradling her in his arms. She folds into him, and I'm in awe of how affected she is by the dose. I'd forgotten how it works, how it could turn someone into an entirely different person, easily swayed and demure. She is curled in upon the man who took her from her family, who beat and drugged her. His shoulders flex under his tunic as he walks away, servants opening the doors for him as he strides out with Nimai in his arms.

My jaw and teeth are clenched so hard I think I may crack a tooth as my eyes follow them out the door. I turn to Bria, who is still listening to Father Mallory, her shoulders tensed up around her. Her left hand is still on the table and I see the fingers bend, clenching inward, the faintest bit of black starting to bleed out of the tips. I run a hand through my hair, tugging it out of my face. I need to bring her to her room before she gets another surge of energy. She's been fighting it all night and can only hold it in for so long.

"I think perhaps Lady Bria and I should retire as well. It has been quite a day for all of us." I'm hoping the king will let us go easily now that his precious Nimai is out of the room.

His eyes go to Bria, and he observes her for a moment, his lips pursing. He too noticed that she isn't quite as affected by the sedative, not nearly as much as her sister. I don't think any of them will assume betrayal on my part just because of her demeanor. They have no reason not to trust me right now. But they are registering this as her being even more powerful than they thought. And that could be a very bad thing for us. Right now, they want Bria alive, but if it comes down to it, they still have Nimai. And I cannot let it come to that before we escape.

"Of course," Braddock drawls. "She will need her rest before meeting with the high priestess tomorrow." My stomach threatens to bring my dinner back up when he mentions it.

Standing from my place at the table, I stretch my hand out for Bria. She grasps it and I pull her up. She stumbles slightly, falling into me, but I catch her. Looking down at her, I can see the cobalt fire surging. The stumble is a nice touch, but I fear it isn't enough to make them think she is the least bit subdued. I steady her and slide my arm around her back, gripping my fingers into her waist again, turning us both to face the king.

Her body is hot to the touch. Too hot. Not a natural heat but almost feverish, and I know the flames of her power are raging inside. I look at the king and his eyes linger on her, taking in her body in the tight and revealing gown. The tension in my jaw returns as he stares at her, his eyes dropping to the porcelain skin of her long legs exposed by that ridiculously high slit that goes halfway up her fucking thighs.

Warring with the desire to knock him out for even thinking he can look at her like that, I manage a small bow in an attempt to hide the fury that he is sure to read in my face. Spinning us both around, I keep my arm tight on her waist as we walk toward the double doors, not allowing him another glance at her body. Bria holds on to the hand I have around her, making a show of clinging to me. We stride out of the room, leaving the king with Aamon and Father Mallory.

Bria begins to straighten up, moving her weight off me when the doors close behind us and we are well into the hallway outside of the royal dining room. But I know better. The king's servants will report back to him, report anything we do that appears off. I bend down to brush a kiss across her brow.

"Not yet," I whisper. Relief flows through me as she relaxes back into my side, putting more of her weight on me to move her up the stairs and down the long hallway. Luthais is not there when we make our way past Nimai's room. Which seems surprising. She may be drugged but they wouldn't risk leaving her unattended.

Unless...my stomach flips as I think of him inside the room. I want to break the door down and drag him out by his hair. When the time comes, I'll kill him slowly, rip every finger off those hands, cut them from him one by one for ever laying a hand on her.

I steer us toward Bria's room and open the door, pushing her forward gently with my hand on the small of her back as I stare next door. I'm about to enter the room, my hand still holding the door open, but I'm heavily debating on knocking on Nimai's door, just to be safe. Though if it's only her in there she won't be answering after passing out downstairs. But then I see her door swing inward and a tall figure emerges. Luthais slips out of the room, dragging a hand along his face and rubbing it as if he's trying hard to scrub the exhaustion away. He catches my gaze and acknowledges my presence with a tight-lipped smile, and for once, he doesn't look smug. He looks tired, and possibly upset.

"Give me a minute," I say quietly into the room before letting Bria's door shut in front of me, turning toward him.

"Is she alright?" I ask, gesturing toward the door behind him. He slumps his body against it.

I've never seen him like this. He's normally so stoic and put together and typically, just a completely insufferable ass whose cocky attitude keeps everyone at bay. He sighs audibly and drives his hands deep into his pockets, his shoulders pressed into the door behind him.

"I think so. She's asleep now. Or passed out. I'm not really sure which." Worry lines his face.

"They are dosing her too much," I offer, hoping he remembers this was my role before leaving. That I was part of the drugging and the tortures, that if anyone knew about this, it was me. Not the current me, but the Evander they all knew here in the capital.

To my surprise, he nods. "I said the same thing, but Father Mallory insisted. He didn't want to risk her telling Bria anything about her time in the dungeons."

Tension ripples through my body and I roll my neck, trying not to think of what happened to her down there. "Understandable."

"Bria's dose wasn't high enough," he remarks, looking back at me. "She was too aware of everything tonight. You're going to have to give her more before she meets with the high priestess tomorrow."

I nod. "I know."

"She cannot remember what happens when she meets with her. Or none of this will work," he continues.

"I'm aware," I say, speaking through gritted teeth.

"Did you—" he begins and runs his hand back over his face, as if trying to wake himself from a dream. Or a nightmare.

"Did you know about their plans?" he finally manages, his voice rough.

This man was brought up in the temple for years—he is devout, a loyal follower. So, though his face shows signs that he is warring with that faith right now, I remain wary. I don't want to reveal too much to him. "No, I didn't know until tonight. But Bria and I will do what they ask of us."

His eyes flash to me, a darker gray than before. His jaw flexes, the muscles in his neck tightening as irritation creeps into his features. "They have no choice, do they?" he asks, his tone tinged with sadness.

"They are far more powerful than the men here, yet they have no fucking choice."

I turn away from him. I have no use for his anger or annoyance, or whatever this is. He isn't part of their plan, their decision, and that's likely what's causing this change in him, not genuine concern for any of us. And I need to check on Bria. We have to discuss our escape, sooner rather than later given the turn of events.

I walk the few feet to the door and place my hand on the cool metal handle. "No, they don't. None of us do," I say before pushing the door open and sliding inside the bedchamber.

CHAPTER 59

Bria

I swing around at the sound of the door. Evander was right behind me when we got back but had closed the door for a few minutes. I could hear voices outside but wasn't able to make out who he was speaking with. He glances down at me, concern spreading across his face at my appearance. I'm sure it doesn't look good. I'm pacing around the room, my hand pressed to my chest. I'm just trying to breathe, the overwhelming surge of energy swallowing me whole, making it difficult to fill my lungs. Making it difficult to function.

"She's fine, Bria. She's asleep."

I gasp, sucking air into my lungs, heat searing my chest.

"Are you sure?" I manage to rasp out.

"Yes, they dosed her too high. Luthais saw it too. But she's sleeping it off. She's safe for now." He tracks me as I move around the room, and I vaguely notice as he walks to the doors of the balcony and throws them open.

This is that same flash of heat that happened before with Silas. Only this time, it isn't a bump from his energy. This is my body experiencing too much emotion. Rage at what they did to my sister had been building already, but when I saw her and heard what they have planned, it only dug itself deeper into me. The pain and sorrow emanating from her was too much to bear. Those emotions, coupled with my unchecked magic, are causing the well inside to bubble over.

"Luthais?" The name hisses out of my mouth.

The thought of him makes my body burn more and I shift toward the open doors. I want to let the shadows curl around him until they squeeze the last of his breath from him, let the beasts sink their talons into him and rip him apart like they did to those men in the plains two nights ago.

I know I'm losing control. My skin is on fire. The magic is craving release and I have to do something to stop the thrum of energy pulsing at my fingertips.

"I know what you're thinking. But he's guarding her room, Bria, and he did seem pretty pissed off by the revelations he heard." I can feel his eyes on me as I stand in front of the doors, wishing the air were cooler than it is. "I don't think he's going to do anything to her. Not tonight, at least."

"You saw the bruises!" I gasp.

"I did," Ev assures me. "But no one is beating an unconscious girl Bria."

I feel the heat creeping higher up my neck and into my face. Clutching at the choker around my neck, I rip at it. The metal is heating from my body, scalding my skin. "Shit," I breathe, tugging at the clasp harder.

Evander moves behind me. I'm panting and grasping at the stones, pulling at them to no avail. My fingers won't work.

"Bria, stop," he orders firmly in my ear, but I can't stop.

I can't breathe so I just kept grabbing, trying to keep the metal from melting into my skin. He snatches my hands away from my neck, pinning them to my sides, and pulls me flush against his body. I feel his heart pounding against my back.

"Stop," he commands again, but it's quieter this time, pleading with me. "I'll get it off."

He must feel the heat. His hands have to be burning from where they hold mine. But if he does, he isn't letting on. He says nothing as he slowly releases my hands. I fight the urge to rip at my throat again, instead letting him move to unclasp the choker. His fingers touch the back of it, and I hear him hiss, the metal hot to the touch. Once he works it free, he lets it fall to the ground.

My hands fly back up to my neck, feeling the tender skin where it had been resting.

"Bria, you have to relax. You're burning up." His breath is hot against my neck, against the lingering stinging from the burns.

Evander wraps his body around me, holding me around the waist and pressing his lips to my bare shoulder. His body is warm, not helping with the overheating, but I know his touch will relax me. In some corner of my mind, I'm aware that I need this and can't fight it—that I need him.

I shudder as we stand in the open air and I try to breathe, letting the warm breeze fill my lungs and pressing my chest upward. But the gown is too much, too tight against my chest that I can't get a full breath in with how fitted the bodice is against me. I need to cool off and breathe.

"Ev," I plead, but my voice is hoarse, as if the flames inside are frying my vocal cords. "Get it off!" I choke out.

He squeezes me tighter, not understanding what I mean.

"I did, Bria. The necklace is gone. It's okay," he whispers against my skin, planting a kiss on my shoulder.

I start to move, prying myself from his grip. I need to feel the air on my skin. I begin fumbling with the clasps, trying to move my hands to my back.

"Bria." The tone of his voice is enough for me to turn around and drop my shaking hands.

His eyes are wide expanses of molten chocolate as he stares at me, watching my hands that now rest at my sides. My breaths are coming in heaves, and I look down to see more shadows swirling around my fingers again, darkness licking up the length of them and turning them black, creeping up my palms.

There is nowhere for it to go. I stoked the fire with my rage, built and built the storm of energy within me, and there is no release for it. My body isn't used to this. I've practiced and perfected my magic for years, always releasing it when I need to, even in small amounts. But I used it in the cold, where I could cool my body easily if needed by just tossing open a window and breathing in the frigid air. This heat, the pain, the fury, are all working against me.

I could throw the shadows, cast them outward from the doors to the balcony. Let the beasts tear through the capital. But what then? They would be seen. There is no way the king left me unwatched, unmonitored. I cannot release them without causing more problems for myself. And for Nimai. If they see what I'm capable of, they will take her, move her too far for me to ever rescue her.

My hands fly back to my chest at the thought. I can't let that happen. The shadows lick my skin, bands curling around my now black fingers and up my arms. I suck in, gulping down more air, heaving breaths in and out, and grab the side of the door to steady myself. Panic is coursing through me along with the magic. I feel trapped inside this dress. And inside my own body.

Evander moves quicker than I even realize. He's behind me again, and he tears at the back of the gown, yanking at the buttons and clasps until they spring free. He pulls it down over my arms until the dress falls in a pool of ebony and silver at my feet. I step out of it, gasping as the humid wind whips around me, dancing along my skin.

He stays close. His hands circle my waist again, meeting bare skin. Anywhere his skin touches mine, the burning seems to subside. His fingers pull the heat from my body, washing it away and replacing it with an entirely different kind of heat, a pleasant burn that radiates through me.

I spin myself around in his grasp and grab at his tunic, frantic. His eyes widen but he gathers what I'm trying to do and tugs it over his head, letting it fall to the floor beside my gown. His eyes darken and his gaze wanders over my exposed body, my lower half barely covered in the underwear the women gave me to wear with the gown. The dagger is still sheathed along my thigh and the bodice had been tight enough to not need any additional support, leaving me all too aware of how bare I am to him.

My entire body tenses from his gaze, and I want him. I want his hands all over me, to calm the blazing heat. I want to feel his touch not just to cool me, but to light me afire again.

He cocks his head to the side, trying to determine if it's the magic coursing through my veins that's causing the shift in my demeanor or my desire for him.

"Bria, are—" He starts to speak but I'm already on my toes, pressing my mouth into his.

His lips part instantly, and my tongue slides inside. He grasps the back of my neck with his hand, his fingers curling into my hair. I still feel wildly out of control of my magic. I still need an outlet, a release from it. But this need for release is different. This is about us.

It feels as if he's drinking my energy, one mouthful at a time. I flatten my body against his, my hardened nipples dragging along his chest, digging my fingers into his back and the bands of muscles stretching along him. He doesn't flinch, even with my heated touch. It never seems to affect him. His body absorbs the heat, draws it from me.

The kiss is forceful—powerful, even. His hands move to grasp my thighs, his fingers gripping into the flesh of my ass as he lifts me against him. I wrap my legs around his waist, my tongue still searching his mouth. My arms circle his neck, tangling in his hair and pulling him into me, needing more. I tug his lip gently with my teeth before diving my tongue back into him and he groans into my mouth.

Gripping me tighter, he walks toward the bed. For a second, I pause, thinking he's going to lower me down, but he turns instead, sitting us down on the edge. I land directly in his lap. I jerk my head back and am met with an intensity, a need in his eyes. That hunger again. He moves his hands to grab the sides of my hips and I sink into him, grinding my body against his. A soft moan slips past my lips when I feel him through the fabric, the length of his cock hard and ready against me. But against me isn't enough right now. I want to feel him inside of me, needing to rid myself of the fabric barrier of his pants, knowing my body is already slick with need for him.

"You're incredible." His voice is a caress down my spine.

They're the same words he said to me the first night he saw the terrifying nature of my magic. But this time, he's looking at me, at my eyes that meet his. Not at the magic, not at the shadows swirling around my entire body now. At me.

He drags his hands up my sides and comes to gently cup my full breasts in his hands. He glides his fingers over the sensitive skin of my nipples, and they tighten in response. It sends a jolt straight between my legs, desire pooling there. Sitting up further, he traces the same lines with his tongue, and I clamp my teeth over my lip, stifling the cry that's threatening to pour out of me.

"What did I tell you about that lip?" His voice is so low it comes out as a growl, an almost feral noise.

Those molten eyes make everything in my body melt with them. Evander rolls so quickly that I'm on my back in an instant, pinned beneath the weight of him. With his body pressed against me, I can feel the full thickness of him and I move my hips again, raising them up to meet his.

He groans. "Fuck, Bria."

His mouth meets mine again but instead of his luscious lips, I'm met with his teeth as he bites my lower lip between them. The sharp pain is brief before he pulls his head back and it's swept away by the warm wetness I feel between my thighs, his hands now dipping below the low waist of my underwear. Pulling them down to the floor, he grabs the leather looped around my thigh and slides it off, slowly and gracefully.

He watches me as his fingers creep down lower, until they meet their mark, rolling in circles over the most sensitive part of my body. I ache for more, my back arching with each flick of his fingers. I need more of his hands, his teeth, his tongue, him. Just him.

A smile tugs his lips upward, revealing that damn dimple. I reached up to touch his face and see the shadows are still there, swirling, dark whorls of black around my hand. My magic is filled to the brim and ready to erupt, but I ignore it. I let go of the burning feeling in my body and give in to the feel of his hands. I push my hips toward him, urging him to continue.

He moves his thumb over that spot once more before dipping his hand lower. He releases a strangled noise from his throat when he feels the readiness waiting for him there, and he slips his fingers inside of me, pumping one, then two. In and out in a steady rhythm.

"Mmm." He hums. "You're always so wet, so needy for me."

"Just for you," I breathe.

"Just for me." He brings his lips to hover above mine, his fingers curling inside of me, pulling me apart bit by bit. "What do you want, Bria?" he asks, a whisper across my lips.

I reach my hands down, slowly unbuckling the belt at his waist, pushing the material past his hips until the solid length of him springs free. My breath hitches in my throat at the sight, at the feel as I drag my fingers over the smooth, velvety skin of his cock. He shudders with a sigh at my touch.

"You," I say, letting my words breeze across his mouth.

"You've always had me, Bria," he responds, his eyes darkening. "I'm yours and always have been."

His words crush me. The sense that he has been there all this time and it took me this long to find him... The feeling that this was meant to be, yet I'm going to lose him. Does he understand that? Has he truly ever understood that we can never be together the way he wants, that I cannot give him what he needs? His fingers curl again and I gasp, the sensation bringing me back to the present, pushing aside any thoughts of the future.

Removing his fingers, he angles his body fully above me now, making me release my grasp on him. His thick cock slides against the slickness below, teasing me with every motion. I fully open myself to him and he pushes inside, a cry escaping my lips as he fills up every inch of me. He keeps going and when I think I can't take any more, his eyes are on me. I suck in air at the feel of him, of my body closing around him, accommodating his size.

He begins to move slowly, pulling nearly all the way out before he settles deep again, letting out a rough groan. "Fuck, Bria."

Everything is alight again, with fire, desire, and want. My mouth finds his and I sweep my tongue in just as he thrusts deeper, seating himself fully within me. Each slow movement of his rolling hips sends pleasure pulsing through my body, a different kind of flame racing through my veins and making my heart pound.

I grasp his smooth, silky hair in my hands and pull it, forcing his head back so I can look into his eyes. They are so dark. Everything around us is dark. Shadows drift throughout the room, caressing our skin and curling around our intertwined bodies—a rich swath of darkness that blocks out the world around us, that allows us to just be here, together.

He sees it too. I can tell by the way his eyes widen and he stops moving. Looking around, he's mesmerized by the shocking cocoon of darkness enveloping us. I cup his cheek in my hand, aligning his focus back on me, trying to read the expression on his face, worried that the sudden release of power will be too much for him. That the hovering shadows will scare him off at last, scare him off when I finally have him. His molten eyes fix back on me, so inky in the black around us.

"What do you want?" I ask, worry flitting through me that he will leave.

His lips brush over mine again, grazing my jaw and settling next to my ear. "Everything," he whispers. "Give me your shadows, your darkness, your everything, Bria. Give me you."

I slam my mouth to his, bruising my lips against him as he starts back up, undoing me with his words and his body again and again. He saw my darkness and he stayed. Again, he stayed with me.

So I give him my shadows, my darkness. My everything.

Running my hands along the taught muscles of his back, I move with him, letting my hips rise to meet his, seeking out the friction from his body against the most sensitive parts of me. He pushes deeper and I moan as he hits the center of my core, letting free that deep sensation, ecstasy raging through me. He captures my mouth once more, sinking his tongue deeper as he drives into me.

He rocks his hips like that again and again until the pressure building up inside me has nowhere to go. I feel as though I might break in two. Each thrust sends pleasure rippling through my body until it surges, a cry tearing from my lips. Shadows pour from my fingers, wind whipping around us as they coil and twist through the air. Evander tenses and shudders over me, freeing a low growl as he goes over the edge with me and my body clenches around him, warmth spreading through me with his release.

Evander kisses me fully, passionately after, and pulls my body against his as he rolls to the side, slipping easily out of me. We stay like that for some time after, facing one another, neither willing to move. I stare at him as he peppers kisses along my neck and jaw and my body calms.

My entire being cools with his touch, settling as he seems to smother the flames inside while stoking the warmth between my legs. How he cooled me and caught me on fire with the same touch is unbelievable. And when the shadows had surged forth, my body felt more at ease, the release of my magic colliding in space with the release of pent-up desire for him. Now, the shadows have dissipated, fading into a cool mist of gray around us.

I stroke my hand across his chest, letting my fingers trail further down and over the ridges in his stomach. I eye the scars that decorate his skin and the deep V of muscles that taper down. It should be a crime to have muscles like this.

"I would caution you against moving that hand any further unless you're ready for more," he warns, his voice low and unbearably sexy.

Despite what we just did, and the fact that I am bare-ass naked next to him, my thighs slick with both our release, his words still elicit a flush. One that runs from my chest up to my cheeks in a heated wave. I pause my exploration of his body, not sure if I'm ready to push him when the look in his eyes tells me he's not kidding.

"What exactly should I expect tomorrow?" I ask, shifting the subject even though I know it will likely irritate him.

"Bria," he grumbles, his tone firm as he skates his hand across my hip, fingers tracing the edges of my body until he hits the curve of my ass.

I frown. "I need to know, don't I?"

Evander forces out a heavy breath. "You really want to talk about this now?" he asks, his gaze wandering over my exposed body as he speaks and squeezes his fingers into the flesh of my ass.

I swallow and nod my head, wanting to take him up on his offer to go again but also needing to hear more about what will happen with the high priestess.

"She's going to take energy from you, your magical energy. I'm guessing it's like what you did with Silas, but she never refers to it as *feeding*." The last word is nearly a growl, and I recall the way he reacted when he found out about Silas. Jealous Evander is high up on my list of infuriating but unbearably hot things. "Nor has she ever discussed a bond or connection. They are going to want you sedated so that you don't fight back or remember much about it." He brushes his fingers back and forth over my hip, sending a shiver up my spine.

"She pulls it all into this orb, the blue orbs they use to harness and trap magic. You've seen them, the ones in the symbol of Vaohr and that the priests in the temple had with them." He hesitates and looks as if he's about to tell me more but stops.

"What do they do with the orbs?" I query, hyper focused on him as he talks.

"You saw yesterday during the rite. The priests say some spells and somehow make the magic work for them. I'm not entirely sure about the spells and how they work, but I know they got them from the witches. And I believe the first high priestess helped them with that, she was a witch from what I understand."

"And no one notices they're using spells? Wouldn't that break this whole charade if people knew the truth?"

Evander smirks, letting the side of his mouth quirk up. "It would, but the priests use magic very sparingly. It's rare to see them wield it outside of the rite and various demonstrations by the king throughout the year, mostly holidays and such. And they say prayers, not incantations, according to them."

"So where does it all go? If they are using it so sparingly." I have so many questions I want to ask, so many answers that require fulfillment.

"That, my love, is not something I can answer," he responds, rolling onto his back and stretching his arm out for me. I scoot toward him and nestle into his shoulder, resuming my act of running my fingers down his body. "The priests keep everything inside the temple very guarded. No one goes upstairs, no one knows where the magic is kept. Not even those of us who helped retrieve it and deliver it to them."

I think for a moment about why the king and the priests would keep collecting more magic if they weren't using it. What could the purpose be? Were they building up a store for something bigger, and if so, why? King Braddock holds control over the entire Kingdom of Azudora, the whole world.

Evander tenses and a low growl rumbles from his chest before he yanks my arm, sliding my body up on top of his. I squeal, not expecting the movement, and he buries his face in my neck, nipping and kissing along it. His cock, already rock solid again, slides against my body still dripping from before.

"What did I just tell you?" he mutters against my skin, and I realize then how low my hands must have been when lost to my thoughts. I smile, letting my head fall to the side as he trails kisses along my collarbone and lower, letting the smooth, lush skin of his lips grace my body. I let myself go, getting lost in him and the sense of being alive.

CHAPTER 60

Evander

The next morning, I wake in a tangle of limbs. Bria's body is wrapped around mine, her ivory leg stretched across my hips, her skin flush against mine. Her long, toned arm is slung over my chest. I tilt my head back to see golden and bronze hair splayed over my arm and chest, rippling across the pillows behind us.

I lift the arm that's under her to graze my fingers along her upper arm, over her shoulder, closing my eyes and reveling in the feel of her next to me. I breathe in the scent of her hair, her skin, and beneath it all, the sweat from the night before.

Her body stirs and she shifts her leg directly over my still very exposed groin. My eyes flare open, pleasure flooding over me and straight to my already hard cock. She moves again, her leg rubbing against me, and I know this time she does it on purpose.

"Awake, are we?" I ask, rolling her onto her back and pinning her beneath me.

She hums in affirmation and looks up, the fire still there. Still burning but with less intensity than the night before. Mere flickers of sapphire and cobalt instead of raging wildfires of blue and black. She quirks her brow and I splay my mouth over her neck, peppering her with kisses and grinding my hips, letting my cock push hard against her.

I'm ready for more. To take in as much of her as I can before... No. It hurts too fucking much now to even think of her not being here. I want to spend every waking moment with her. To fill our time with this. And with so much more than this.

She kisses me deeply. And I come undone as her tongue brushes across my lips. As she curls her legs around me, there's no urgency, no flames to extinguish, no surge of magic to be released. Just us. I slowly move myself inside her and feel her body wet and ready for me, taking my time and soaking up every second with her.

"You're perfect," I murmur against her, watching as she throws her head back, a husky moan escaping when I'm seated to her core.

The world around us melts away as I drive myself in and out of her.

Being with her makes me feel whole. I love her with every piece of myself. Every inch of my body and soul. And I plan to show her that, to make her aware of just how much I love her. Until her dying breath I will be here, with her. There will never be anyone but her.

CHAPTER 61

Bria

After the events of last night and this morning, breakfast is underwhelming. We passed Luthais guarding Nimai's door, and it made me wonder if she was still sleeping off the drugs or if she was being held in there—a regal dungeon of sorts. His face was drawn, gripped with worry, which didn't sit well with me and still doesn't. There is no good reason for that man to worry about my sister.

Aamon took Evander somewhere after breakfast, leaving me utterly alone in this palace full of enemies. I yearn for him to come back, unsure of what to do or where to go. I wish we could have left last night but I was in no shape. I lost control of myself, of my magic. And he brought me back to my body.

But today I feel wholly different. I am in control. And we *are* leaving tonight, Evander and I discussed it last night. When night falls and the shadows creep around the castle, I plan to cloak us all and we can finally be rid of this godless hellhole.

As I walk the seemingly endless corridor to my bedchamber, the deep navy gown I donned for the day trails behind me. I glimpse Luthais far ahead of me, but I continue moving slowly, picking up my skirts so that I'm making nearly no noise at all. With no one around, he's slumped his shoulder against the side of the door. His face is pressed to the wooden edge, hand pushed flat against the door, and his mouth is moving. *What is he doing?*

I stop, forcing my body to still. He's talking, whispering through the door to her. I'm so curious to know what he could possibly be saying to my sister, the girl he captured. But if I draw closer, he will absolutely hear me. As of now, he has yet to look up, focused solely on Nimai.

Luthais drags his fingers down the wood and they settle on the metal handle. He jiggles it to no avail. She's locked him out. Joy and something more, maybe pride, well up inside me, spilling out in a full grin along my face. She's still in there. They haven't fully broken her yet.

I'm not too late.

I let down my skirts and pick up my pace, walking toward him. Luthais hears the rustling gown and lets his hand drop. He replaces the concern on his face—the warmth I saw just mere moments before— with a scowling mask of irritation. It drops into place easily, as if he learned, as Ev had, never to show his true emotions here. He folds his arms across his massive chest, still leaning against the door, and his lip curls up at me.

"I would like to see my sister," I say, trying to keep my face neutral as I look up at him. My voice is still a bit raw from last night and gods is he huge. He stands taller than Ev and he's just *big*.

"Well, she locked the door, so good luck with that," he snaps back, rolling his eyes. The irritation may be real, but the concern is as well. I haven't a clue why he isn't running off to Aamon or the king if she's locked him out, but he must have some reason.

My nostrils flare and I bite down on my lip to keep the grin from spreading across my face once again. But Luthais catches it and snarls at me, removing himself from the doorway.

I lean into the door and knock softly, letting my knuckles rap against the heavy wood. I open my mouth to speak, but the door flies open in front of me. Stumbling forward, I see the floor rising up. But the air around me seems to slow, wavering and shimmering before an arm sweeps around my middle, catching me before I slam to the ground in a tangled heap of my gown.

Luthais has one hand pressed to the doorframe, his fingers curled around it to steady himself as he catches me mid-fall. The other is around me, hauling me back to my feet. Nimai stands before us, and her pure beauty makes my heart twist in my chest.

I straighten my gown, smoothing down the silk as he releases his grasp. The air seems to shift again once he lets go and the coolness of it makes me register just how warm his hands were. My thoughts cloud for a moment as I sweep forward into the room without speaking so much as a "thank you" to the man behind me. There is something strange about the air, almost staticky now, and I want to ask Nimai if she feels it too, but I'm wary with Luthais around. Wary to divulge anything that may indicate a change in our magic or our bond. I wish even more to slam the door in his unfairly beautiful face and block him out so I can speak with my sister alone, but he's at my back, moving into the room. His presence is annoying and causes the hair on the back of my neck to stand at attention. I should have known he wouldn't let me see her alone.

Warmth seeps into my pores, heating my body like a match being struck when I get closer to her. The bright floral scent of roses fills my nostrils. I surge forward, encompassing myself in Nimai's embrace, letting her light and love wash over me. I shudder as a sob breaks free from my lips and I smother my face into her shoulder, wrapping my arms tightly around her, refusing to let her go.

I hear a hiss escape her and step back, holding her arms and examining her face to determine the cause.

"What is it?" Pain grips her features, stretching her pouty pink lips thin and pinching her brows together.

Shooting a glance behind me, she straightens her shoulders, stacking her spine up to her full height. She's taller than me now—a full head taller—and so graceful. She may have the features of our mother, but her tall, thin body has come from our father.

"It's nothing," she assures me softly, her eyes focused on Luthais.

Had he done it or Aamon? How much did they hurt her before we got here?

Nimai breaks free from my grasp and nearly stumbles to the bed before climbing up onto the mattress. It barely moves beneath her weight. She's thin. Not terribly thin, but she could stand to gain a bit of weight, to fill out the curves she should have. She moves to the middle, crossing her feet beneath her. Her movements are slow but these are not lingering effects from the drugs she was given last night. This is utter exhaustion and crippling pain that's stifling her young body.

If I close my eyes, I might be able to feel her, to see if she could show me what pains her. To see who did this to her. But I stare at her instead, worried about what Luthais may make of our connection and taken aback by her sitting just as she used to when we were younger. My heart aches when I think of her before all of this happened. When she would curl into me and I would stroke her midnight hair back from her face and read to her. She stretches a hand out to me and I follow, climbing up onto the bed and pulling my gown along with me.

Luthais watches us closely from the door but makes no movement further into the room. He leans back, raising a booted foot to rest against the wood with a soft thud. I see it again only for a second as his eyes linger on my sister—a flash of something in his features, but I cannot put a name to the emotion. I don't know him well enough. Perhaps it's guilt for the beatings she's clearly sustained at his hands.

My eyes narrow on him, and he catches my stare but gives no reaction, just wearing his cool, calm demeanor. I will kill him for it. I feel the itch in my palms, my fingers prickling at the thought. Nimai holds my hand tightly as if urging me to keep calm, as if she can feel my power reaching out. And perhaps she can now. But he holds my gaze only for a moment before returning it to Nimai. His features soften when he looks at her and rage boils inside my veins, setting my blood on fire.

"I've missed you, B." Her voice is breathy, quiet, and soft, as if it floats on air.

The words tear my gaze from Luthais and back to her. She is achingly beautiful. She always has been, but something has shifted since the last time I saw her. Likely the same things that have shifted in me—the changes you go through when you're forced into a life you didn't choose. When you have your reality torn from your grasp too early. Too young.

"I've missed you too, Mai." Just as I had not heard my own nickname in years, I let hers escape my lips, but it's painful to say it. Makes her more real. It had been easier for me to forget when I was training my life away. I squeeze her hand, holding it so she cannot disappear again. So she can stay.

"Is mom—" I try to ask but am unable to finish the sentence, too aware that Luthais is in the room, watching us, and that I am supposed to believe Nimai traveled here with him of her own volition. I am not supposed to know what really happened in the rebel camp.

Her face breaks, shattering into a thousand pieces, terror and agony pushing into all the space that's left. Glistening tears roll down her rosy cheeks. I raise my hand to wipe them away, wishing I could take away all the pain she has suffered in this lifetime.

"I don't know." The words come out fragmented in a jagged sob, and I wrap her in my arms, holding her as I did when she was younger. It doesn't matter that she's taller and older now, she's still my little sister. My little Mai.

I catch Luthais's stare from where he stands and glare back at him, letting the flames flare in my eyes. His eyes widen as he takes me in. He knows. He can see it in my eyes that what he did is something I will never forget.

"Do *you* know?" I question, forcing him to recognize he's to blame if my mother has not survived.

He shoves his hands deep in his pockets and grits his teeth before speaking to me. Will he tell Aamon or even the king that I know more than I have been letting on? After all, it doesn't matter if I stay here. They are already drugging me, or so they think. And I'm set to meet with the high priestess. They needn't keep up pretenses for much longer anyway.

"I heard many of the rebels got away. I have no idea how many or if your mother was with them." He sighs and I see something flicker in his eyes, a flash of something within. "Rumor has it some made it to your other camp."

"And how did my sister make it out? I don't think I got the whole story from you regarding that. Did I?"

My insides are a mess, swirling with fury, heat building up a firestorm within me. I can contain it now, after the release from last night. But I won't need to contain it for long.

His eyes narrow, and he opens his mouth to speak but Nimai beats him to it.

"He saved me." A quiet lie, one that barely makes it past her lips. Her head is still tucked into my chest. She lifts her chin toward him as she talks.

But I'm not taking the lie. Not now. Not when we are so close to leaving. Maybe I could just kill him now, get Evander, and we could be gone. Though I need the dark of night to cloak us all in shadow.

Still. It doesn't mean he has to leave this room again.

"Is that so?" I ask, my lip curling back to bare my teeth in a snarl. Heat pours into my fingers as I caress my hand down her silky blue-black waves.

His nostrils flare. He senses the fight coming. But he doesn't move, not an inch from where he's reclined against the door. He doesn't shift under the weight of my burning stare.

Nimai's head snaps back, out of my grasp, and her green eyes sear into me. "Leave it, Bria," she whispers, and I feel her fingers intertwine with mine.

Luthais remains watching us, his gaze floating to our intertwined hands then back up to me. He's trying to figure us out. *Let him keep trying*, I think. We will be gone before he understands what either of us are capable of.

"So, you and Ev?" Her question jolts me from my anger, and I glance back at my sister and see her gleaming smile. Her eyes sparkle like fresh dew strewn across blades of grass, her pink lips turned up in joy. Oh, how I've missed that smile. She is the embodiment of pure happiness, which is what makes it even more painful to realize what has been done to her. To this pure soul.

She's changing the subject on purpose and I let her. I let her calm the roaring in my ears and block out the hulking figure at the door. I focus my thoughts and my energy entirely on my sister.

"I suppose so," I say, letting a smile creep across my face.

She squeals in delight. It's a noise I have not heard in so long that it warms my heart over a thousand times. I think I might faint from the exhilaration I feel just being near her again.

"I can't believe it!" she exclaims, her voice an uncomfortably high pitch. "You know Dad would have approved."

My heart twists in my chest when she mentions our father. But she's right. He always had a soft spot for Ev as a boy. It's probably why he let me play with all of them, why he let me become so close with them despite the ludicrous rules placed on us by our roles. Then again, maybe he knew that, with my destiny, those roles and rules would never matter.

"I know he would."

"I never would have believed it if someone else had told me," she teases.

"What is that supposed to mean?" I ask, though I know too well what she means.

"You made quite a reputation for yourself as a heartbreaker, aside from Cedric. I don't think anyone expected Lady Bria to be captured by anyone. But Ev makes sense to me."

There's a snort from the door but I don't bother acknowledging it.

"Mmmm, you know I never broke any hearts. Especially not Cedric's. I just had no interest in those other boys," I say by way of an explanation, my lips turning up despite my attempt not to smile.

The boys who had shown interest in me often did so because of my status, not because they saw me for me. Cedric wasn't like them. He was drawn to me because of lust but remained with me for love. And Ev is an entirely different story. He's the only person who has ever seen the real me and still wants me for it.

She laughs, a full laugh that echoes in my bones. Her head tips back, throwing gleams of violet into her waves. It feels like we're back home for an instant, but I remember too quickly that Luthais is here, lurking by the door, watching his captives.

"You're in love." It's a statement. She's not asking.

And in that moment, I admit to Nimai what I have not yet admitted to myself. Or to Evander, for that matter.

"Yes," I confess, letting the truth of it wash over me, pulling me down into the depths of elation. "I am in love."

We stay like that for hours, talking about our mother and our friends who also fled to the southern camp. Nimai gives me all the details she can about what life was like there for her—far less stressful than the last five years were for me, but she has changed a great deal, grown into the role she was meant to play. The southern camp continued to thrive after they'd arrived. Much like my own camp, it was a well-functioning community, accepting new individuals to the rebel forces over the years. I only hope enough of them made it out when Luthais and his lackeys torched the place.

Luthais. He remains the entire time, watching us throughout the conversation. He moves at some point from the door to the small table across the room, making himself comfortable by kicking up his legs and grazing on the tray of food left out by the servants. But he never speaks to us, just stays. Watching and listening.

Nimai doesn't speak of her capture. Nor does she say anything of her time in the dungeons. But here, so close to her, I can see the blue and purple blooming under her eye. I take in every wince and grimace she makes when she moves her shoulders and back, the glassy look in her eyes that takes over when the pain hits as she relives some horrible nightmare. The ginger way she walks to the washroom and climbs back onto the bed to avoid aggravating her injuries. Was her back beaten? Burned? Lashed? Any positive answer is unacceptable. And no matter the answer, they will all pay.

And it kills me how Luthais appears comfortable. Far too comfortable for someone who hurt her like this. To remain calm in the presence of a person you captured and beat... I don't understand how a person becomes that way—so callused and jaded with such disregard for human life.

A knock at the door brings me back to reality, makes me remember where I am and who I'm with. Luthais moves to open the door, revealing Evander pressed against the frame. His eyes dart around the room until his gaze settles on me. My core tenses as a smirk twists the corner of his mouth.

"What do you want?" Luthais snarls at him, stepping to block him from entering.

But Evander is having none of it and he pushes past the man, no small feat given he's a few inches taller and broader than Ev. But he comes in anyway, striding into the room as if he owns the place.

"The high priestess is waiting for you," he informs me, the smirk abruptly falling from his face.

Fear tightens my entire body, pulling a dark shroud over me. *Already? How long has it been? What time is it?*

"Now?" I gasp, eyes searching the mantle for the clock. It's four. We've talked for hours upon hours. I'm distraught that it's already time for me to go see her, but even more shocked that Luthais let us be together for so long. He never once interrupted our discussion or bothered to tell us what the time was, just leaving us alone to spend time with one another.

Sadness ripples across Evander's face and my stomach nearly drops out of my body. "Now," he answers, and I think I might vomit.

I feel wholly unprepared for this.

CHAPTER 62

Evander

There needs to be more time. More time for me to explain what I know of the high priestess, to tell Bria who she is before we see her. I've been avoiding it and now it's coming back to bite me in the ass. I've had the time, but I'd just found every reason within me, every excuse not to tell her.

And when she finds out, she's going to kill me. Or leave me. I'm honestly not sure which is worse.

I kept telling myself I couldn't bear to see the flames in her eyes flicker with hatred toward me. Couldn't stomach the thought. Not again. But now, I'm determined. I'll tell her on the ride to the temple, away from the prying ears and eyes of the castle.

At least that's what I think until Bria and I descend the stairs hand in hand and see my father waiting for us. And he doesn't offer us horses. Instead, he motions for us to follow him. He leads us back, far back, into the deepest corner of Castle Eccleston. Past the kitchens, the servants' rooms, and the guards' quarters. To a small room.

A room I know like the back of my fucking hand.

It's all dark gray stone, no windows, no furniture, just a large tapestry with the symbol of Vaohr emblazoned on it. This isn't a room you relax in or entertain people in. It's not even a room that's used at all by the servants or the guards. This room is merely a distraction—a bleak, miserable little corner of the castle that draws no attention. Because behind that gaudy tapestry lies the entrance to the dungeons.

And he is leading Bria and I right for it.

"What the fuck is going on?" I ask, trying to keep fear from clamping my vocal cords tight.

There is no good fucking reason Aamon would lead us down into the depths of the castle. We are supposed to be heading to the temple. My jaw clenches as I look at the wall holding the large tapestry and my mind begins to race. Had he figured it out? Does he know we aren't here to help him at all, but to rescue Nimai and betray him again?

Fuck. Me.

"Watch your tongue, Son. The high priestess is a very busy woman. She does not have time today to travel to the temple. She still has much work to do this evening after she meets with you," he remarks, not bothering to look at me.

I shake my head. "I understand she's busy, but does she really want Lady Bria to go down there?" I gesture toward the ominous wall.

My father turns to look at me then, anger turning his eyes nearly black. It's foolish to question him, and more so to question *her*. But my stomach is twisting into knots, telling me that we might not return if we follow him down those stairs right now.

"Evander," he warns, snarling my name. "You know better than anyone to question the high priestess and her methods." He spins on his heel and strides toward the tapestry, pulling it aside to reveal the door. "And besides, do you think your betrothed should go into this blind? This new role of hers? Or should she know exactly what she's getting into?"

His words strike me. They want her to know what's happening? They have no intention of making this easy on her, making her comfortable or pulling the wool over her eyes. Not anymore. They are looking for her to suffer. I'm not sure what changed for that to happen.

Bria's body stalls, staring ahead at the door like her feet have grown roots and embedded themselves into the stone floor beneath her. The iron door is imposing, a heavy latch keeping it in place with a large lock. I have to yank her arm to get her to move forward because Aamon is pushing through the doorway ahead of us and I know hesitating will just be worse than facing who waits for us in the dungeons.

The stairs are made of ancient uneven stone, steep and shallow, making for a slow descent into darkness. Aamon grabs a lantern hanging at the doorway and begins to make his way down the steps ahead of us. I move to throw the drawbar in place behind Bria and her eyes lock on me as I barricade us in. Fear possesses her features.

"Just in case anyone gets too curious," I explain, aware Aamon can hear me from where he stands a few steps below.

Aamon grunts from below, "Vaohr help them if they do."

Bria grabs ahold of the long, navy-blue skirts in her hand as she picks her way down the steps. I take her other hand in my own, staying ahead of her to keep her steady on the stairs. The air starts to become thick and damp, sticking in my nose as we creep our way down. I know we are nearing the long hall of cells when the stench hits me. I hear Bria suck in a breath behind me as I switch to breathing from my mouth, bile threatening to surge outward.

"Breathe through your mouth, not your nose," I whisper to her, Aamon now quite ahead of us, not slowed by the rippling skirts of a gown.

I catch a glimpse of her face in the dim light and can see she's ready to heave if she continues to breathe in the potent smell. She nods and parts her lips, twisting her fingers tighter with mine.

"What is that?" she asks as we near the end of the stairs and the opening that leads to the source.

I don't risk glancing back at her as I answer, not needing to see her reaction. She doesn't recognize this smell because she has never needed to know it, to have it haunt her. I desperately wish that I could tell her I don't know, that I have no idea the horrors that could be behind a stench like that. But this is a smell I became far too accustomed to in my time here.

"It's the smell of rotting," I say, letting loose a long sigh, thinking I never had to speak of this place or return to it again. But here I am, stomach turning with the knowledge of what we are about to come face to face with.

"But rotting what? I've smelled this before, in my visions." She still doesn't get it. Doesn't understand what she is about to see. Though to be fair, I've had no chance to fully prepare her for all of this.

The stairs end and my boots hit the old dirt floor, kicking up a swirl of dust around my knees. I look up, holding her hand tightly as I meet her wide gaze.

"Flesh," I manage through gritted teeth, and watch as her eyes flare and disgust grips her features, making her mouth go slack.

Leaving Bria with that horrid reality, I turn back around, pulling her along with me. We breach the low archway and Bria tucks in beside me, her fingers pressing into the back of my hand, squeezing the fine bones hard enough that it feels she may break them.

She's terrified, and rightly so, but relief hits me like a fucking brick when Aamon opens the door to the first cell with a loud scraping noise and slips inside. It means we aren't trekking through the maze of barred rooms that runs the length of the castle. There are far more dank cells under the palace than the wing we are currently in. So many more than she probably knows. And I'm aware some hold the living, some the dead, and some who waver halfway in between—in another realm where their magic has been drained and they long for death, but the high priestess has yet to give it. Not until they fulfill their destiny. Not until they have given everything back to Vaohr.

The urgency increases as we round the corner to the cell. I have to tell her. There's no more time left. She is seconds from finding out anyway and now it probably won't matter, but I stop in the entryway, blocking her view of the dirty, barred room. I drag a hand through my hair, tugging at it, and Bria's face blossoms with concern when she observes my distraught reaction.

"Bria, there's something I need to tell you," I quickly begin, the words tumbling out.

But it's too late, I know it before I turn. All the blood drains from Bria's already pale face as she stares over my shoulder, making her a ghostly white. She looks as if she might faint, and I wouldn't blame her at all if she did.

"Hello, Bria." The voice drifts out from behind me. It's a soft whisper, gentle across your skin. Not at all what you would expect from the high priestess, the woman known to tear people apart through their minds.

"Bria, I'm so sorry," I choke out.

My heart feels like it's being cleaved in two when she tears her gaze away and lets it land on me. Her eyes flicker with flames, magical cobalt and sapphire rippling through them. I struck the match that started that fire. I brought her down here and let her come face to face with my worst nightmare. My secret, my shame.

Bria says nothing. She just glowers at me like I've locked her in this dungeon and hurt her, like I did those unspeakable things to her sister. She stares at me like I'm the villain. And I suppose, right now, I am.

I turn away from Bria, even though it pains me to do so. And there she is. The long, royal blue robes she dons flow over her ethereal body. Her hair falls in light chestnut waves around her face and shoulders, pouring out from beneath the hood she wears. She still looks as I remember from when I was a child, her aging halted by magic. Her eyes lock onto me, flames of gold and brown dancing within, and a beautiful smile breaks out across her face.

No matter the circumstances, I cannot help the responding smile that explodes across my own.

"Hello, Mother," I say softly as she extends her arms.

Her embrace is tight and full of warmth. She is so strong now, surprisingly so after all that has happened to her. After all *he* did to her. My father stands off to the side, watching the two of us, examining the interaction and likely making notes in his head regarding what to do with us. The soft fabric of her robes ghosts over my skin as I pull back.

"Hello, Ev. Oh, how I've missed you." Her voice is a welcome sound. I really have missed her too, despite everything.

My mother never chose this. And I never told anyone. And now as I step back, I can see the terror seizing Bria, her expression frozen in shock and horror. It's awful to see her like that and my hand flies to my chest, expecting my heart to tear from my body. It's breaking with the fear that she will never look at me the same. Not now.

I reach my hand out to her and she recoils. I won't pretend that doesn't sting in the worst way and I drag in a breath, trying to steady myself from her reaction.

"Don't," she hisses back at me. "Don't touch me."

Fuck. I've royally screwed everything up.

"Bria, dear. Don't be angry at Evander. If he told you it was me, would you have come willingly?" My mother speaks directly to her, golden eyes warm when she looks upon Bria, her words breathy, airy. She always did love Bria fiercely.

Bria's eyes slice back to my mother, finally taking in the scene of the crumpled form in the corner, barely remaining between life and death, and the staff clutched in my mother's long, lithe fingers. The staff is gold, crafted from a tree in the Gilded Forest. It's knotted and curved, winding at the top around a mystical crystal orb that glows a luminous white-blue.

All pretenses are gone now. I can tell just by looking at Bria. She's done pretending and gods damned over playing this role. I'm not convinced she won't kill us all in her efforts to get her sister out alive. Me included.

"Never," she seethes, her words dripping with disgust.

Aamon slowly but surely moves to the other side of my mother, assuming a protective stance not for the woman he married—he doesn't give a shit about her—but for the priestess.

"I thought as much. He did what he had to do, Bria," she responds, and Bria's body stiffens, her limbs going rigid.

"Olaphina, how could you?" she questions, disbelief apparent in her tone. "How could you hurt innocent people like this?"

Just like the mask I wear around my father, I see the mask of the capital, the role my mother has to play, slip back into place easily, as she has done for many years. Ever since he broke her. Her features smooth over, the fire darkening to a deep gold in her eyes.

It used to disturb me before I found my own walls to put up. It doesn't bother me anymore though, not after what she's been through.

"Dear girl, your powers are stolen. They do not belong to you, nor do they belong to any of these others. None of you are innocent," she explains, waving her hand in a wide arc, gesturing to the slumped body in the corner and the expanse of cells disappearing down the dirt corridor.

"You will give your power back, whether you choose to do so or not.

Vaohr will take what is rightfully his. If you comply, this will be easy. Your life can be your own, you can live with Evander and be married. Have children and let them be raised by the priests and myself. They could be raised by their own grandmother. Don't you see how lucky you are?" Her voice hitches the smallest bit when she says the word "grandmother," and I wonder if Bria notices. If she has any idea how my mother really feels and how much this must be killing her inside. "I love you, Bria, but if you fight me, child... You will suffer a great deal."

I move closer to Bria, expecting she might run but she remains, and I should have known better. She was nervous before, but she is determined now, her eyes fixed on the high priestess.

"Is this necessary?" I ask, trying to calm the situation, unsure of how we ended up here. Unsure of why we aren't in the temple and instead in these dank dungeons. And unsure of why my mother is provoking her so.

"You would be wise to watch yourself, boy." Aamon's lip curls up, an amused sneer on his face. There's no love lost between he and Bria and he's keen on letting that show. "The king wants her power more than anything, and by any means."

I clear my throat, trying to dislodge the lump that's forming there. As I thought before, something has changed. They have new information or have figured something out to be acting this way, to be trying to scare her, to intimidate her and trick her into using her magic.

"You said we were to be married, have children and live here, serving Vaohr. Then you take us to the dungeons and treat her like-like she's some petty criminal?" I shake my head. "I don't understand."

My mother speaks again, to my father's clear irritation. "That dose of belladonna should have been lethal to a normal person." My stomach nearly drops out of my body, my blood running icy cold at the memory of Bria almost taking it. She came so close to dying and we didn't even know. "And yet from what Aamon says, she was barely phased. We cannot tread lightly here, Evander. Bria needs to understand her role, understand her service."

So that's what this is.

They believe her to be so powerful that she overcame a dosing that should have been deadly to a petite girl like herself. That kind of power could help them exponentially and in the king's eyes, there is no time to waste. Now that they know, he doesn't need to wine and dine her. There's no need to have her give power willingly...or even have children willingly. All his plan requires is my mother overpowering her, subduing her, and then Braddock can do whatever the fuck he wants. Like he always does. The dinner was just so they could scope her out, analyze her, and determine her strengths and weaknesses.

And I am a gods damned idiot. I missed all of that and we were fooled. My gut told me we were walking into a trap, and I didn't believe it.

My mother takes a step toward Bria, and I throw myself in front of her, pushing her back behind me and using my body to shield her. My mother may care for Bria and may wish that no harm comes to her, but that doesn't mean she won't hurt her. It doesn't mean she hasn't caused harm to hundreds of people who did nothing wrong, just like Bria. Aamon is here, and she will do whatever is expected of her while he's present. And I refuse to let Bria be another one of her victims.

I clench my jaw and slam my teeth together. "You're not touching her," I grind out.

The gold in my mother's eyes flickers and I hear a small sound come out of her, a quiet hum. Her lips move wordlessly, and though I abruptly recognize what she's doing, it's too late for me to stop it. She lifts the staff and my body collapses to the ground, pain searing through my head as I crash into a world of darkness.

Watching him crumple to the ground in the flash of white that bursts from Olaphina's staff is agonizing, but I remain standing, not yielding to the urge to help him. It appears to be the same occurrence as yesterday—the blinding light the priests used to knock him out cold.

Yesterday, however, he was taking the rite. This time makes no sense. He may have been protecting me, but the Olaphina I knew would not attack her own son like that. Why didn't he tell me she was still alive? That she was the high priestess?

He lied to me. Just like his father lied to my family.

I'm livid, so angry I think the heat in my eyes could sear him from where I stand. And my body is in complete and utter chaos. A storm of emotions brews throughout: my heart crushing from the weight of betrayal from the man I love; fear coursing through my veins with the knowledge that I am alone with these monsters; anguish at seeing him hurt like this.

Not moving. He's not moving.

From where I stand, it's impossible for me to tell if he's still breathing and I don't dare go check on him. There's no option for me to leave myself vulnerable around these two, and there's the matter of vengeance to deal with. Both of them deserve to die for hurting my family, Evander, and all of the innocents across the years. The desire to inflict the same pain upon them, the same torture, far outweighs the other emotions warring inside me.

My palms itch, and without looking, I'm aware the shadows are creeping around my fingers. I loose the grip I have on them just a bit, letting fire surge through my veins, heating my body from the inside out. From the corner of my vision, I observe the curling tendrils whipping out from my arms and hands. But my eyes remain on Olaphina.

How Evander, the man I love, could have come from these two baffles me. Olaphina was a wonderful mother, but now? Now I cannot stand the sight of her, knowing who she has become. And Aamon has always been a horrible excuse for human life. Neither of them deserves to have a son like him. Shadows lick my palms as the anger rises, and both sets of eyes on me widen. Not in fear, but eagerness. Eager to see my display of power.

"You need to relax, Bria. It will be easier this way," she coos. They're words that are meant to soothe but instead turn to kindling for the blaze, making it rage even higher.

Her lip quirks, the slightest hint of a smile before she closes her eyes.

And there it is.

Like hands closing around my head, fingers prying into my skull. I feel a pull from deep within my core, tugging upward like there's a string tied around my middle, connected to those invisible fingers on my brain.

She's trying to take my magic, to pull my energy. To drain me. It's the feeling from my visions. This is what she did to Nimai. The fire turns wild inside me now, stoked by fury and ire and blazing out of control.

The fingers tighten on the invisible thread and yank, sending a shooting pain straight through my spine and feeling like a heavy punch to the gut. From top to toe it aches, and I would not be surprised to see real, visceral wounds sprouting up along my abdomen and straight up through my chest. I cry out in agony, the sensation shocking me and bringing me to my knees.

This wasn't what happened with Silas. I never hurt him like this. This is different. Dark and wretched and awful.

My hands slam into the dirt floor beneath me, fingernails clawing into the soft ground. I try to ease my breathing around the pain and a shudder breaks across my skin, goosebumps sprouting up and beads of sweat forming at my brow as I fight through the anguish. The dark, shadowy mist swirls further around me, and the dirt stirs beneath my fingers.

Stirs. Why is it stirring?

For just a moment, I turn inward, away from the pain and to that odd and familiar sensation. Because there's something here. Something that is teasing my magic, calling it out to play.

Bones.

"You had better rein it in, girl," Aamon warns from beside the priestess, but I ignore him.

They feel my power and they see it. Aamon's eyes are dark, his hand on the hilt of his sword, ready to kill me if he needs to.

"They were fools thinking you could be tamed. You've always been a wild card, even as a child. Your power is the only way to keep Azudora safe, girl. There are threats beyond your imagination. Back. Down." He's nervous now, making up excuses to keep me in line.

There are no threats to Azudora. Azudora is the world.

A smile pulls the corners of my lips up, a deadly smirk that I hope is the cause for the fear I see in Aamon's eyes. He looks scared and he fucking should be.

Because this dungeon is a place of death. And I am born of the god of life and death.

Beyond the shadowy figure in the corner who hovers between the realms, there lay others who met similar fates and crossed over. I've found my way out. And it seems only fitting that these monsters in front of me end up slain by those they've murdered, brought back to life if only for a moment.

A moment to seek vengeance.

I keep my mind open and call to the bones, just as Cato taught me. I urge them to move, sewing them together until the bones stack on top of one another, quickly forming into a lurking figure behind Aamon.

Whoever they killed was big, taller than Aamon. The skeleton looms above him.

Those fingers are still digging in my mind the whole time, trying desperately to get a solid grip on my gifts. Searing pain splits through my skull and I'm vaguely aware of the garbled scream that tears from me, but I fight for focus. I fight to keep the shadows swirling, not just around my body, but in my mind. I force my power to slip through her fingers again and again, so she is unable to grasp the darkness, unable to pull and suck my power out.

Quiet. It's so quiet.

Honestly, I'm in awe of that part. As my dead companion rises, straightening his spine behind Aamon, there is no sound. No creak of joints or clack of bones hitting together. Just the fire roaring in my ears, drowning out the world around me. No one will ever hear my shadows or bones coming for them. Not until it's too late.

I concentrate nearly all of my energy into the skeletal figure, allowing the dark shadows to spiral through the room. They pick up dirt from the floor and whirl it around as if a storm is forming right here, just in this one cell, a confined tornado that whispers the promise of death.

The deep mist swarms, making it difficult to see. I can barely make out the glowing blue orb through the sheen of darkness. So when her staff comes for me through the shroud, I almost don't see her. Olaphina is quick on her feet, but unfortunately for her, I'm quicker. Ebony tendrils surge from my hands, entangling her arms and staff in vines. They snatch the weapon of pain and destruction and send it clattering to the ground. The thud reverberates through the room, but the orb remains glowing, the crystal staying strong and withstanding the impact.

At the same time, Aamon must have made a move, but I cannot see him through the cloud. The only indication is the skeletal warrior readying. I can feel it bend its joints before I get sucked in. Suddenly, I'm able to see through its eyes as it watches him. Aamon draws his sword, lunging, likely readying to deal a deadly blow. To me.

We dive for him, digging the fingers of jagged bones deep into his neck. A sickening symphony of popping rings out as each finger shoots through the skin into the hollow near his collarbone, to his vocal cords. Blood bursts from each hole, showering through the mist and splattering in a hot spray across my face, a copper tang flooding my mouth. Aamon claws at his throat, a wordless scream trying to escape as he's strangled by his own blood pouring out. His eyes dart around wildly as he catches mine.

No. Not mine.

His own gaze catches empty sockets of the dead I summoned. The satisfaction I feel at finally seeing the man who betrayed my father, the man who had him killed, meet his own demise... It is unlike anything I have ever felt—a mix of elation and sickness forces bile up the back of my throat. My stomach clenches and tenses, feeling like it's somersaulting in my body and threatening to betray me.

Aamon goes down in seconds and the bones collapse to the ground beside him. My vision snaps back to my own body, sending me reeling back onto my ass. The slam to the dirt floor is jarring but I manage to maintain the shadows. It's too difficult, too draining to keep the dead moving without Silas.

Olaphina remains tangled in the web of obsidian that twists around her arms and legs. My vision blurs—from rage, or the mist surrounding me, or possibly the magic pulsing through my veins, it doesn't matter. My eyes are on her.

Trained on the real mistress of nightmares.

She isn't fighting the vines, even with the thorns and spikes that drive into her flesh with every flick of my fingers. Olaphina keeps her composure, her lids heavy as if the shadows are draining her, causing her to fatigue quicker. It's good, but not good enough. I lift my hand to move the vines. She clearly is not in enough pain. And I can change that.

I shove myself to my feet and spit on the floor, Aamon's blood flying from my mouth. I twist my palm out toward her and Olaphina goes flying back against the wall, pinned. A small noise is forced out of her as the breath is knocked from her lungs, the impact stunning her body. The intricate web of dark cages her in, wrapping around her middle and squeezing tight. So tight. The deep blue hood slips off her head and that cascade of warm chestnut waves falls about her face. I go to take a step toward her but feel him. His presence. Even before he places a hand on my shoulder, I know Ev is there.

He's alive.

Comfort and relief race through my body. Solace. That's the best description of what I feel as I heave a ragged sigh and press my eyes tight against the tears fighting to spring free.

Alive. He's alive. The words keep repeating in my head.

"Please, Bria." His voice is pleading, begging me not to hurt the woman who raised him. Not to kill her.

The loving mother he grew up with, the sweet and gentle Olaphina. The one who read to him, told him stories of the magical creatures of the world. Who prayed to the old gods and kept magic alive. Who believed in the protection of crystals and the power of a prophecy. The one who showed him what a mother's love could be, who showed him that he could be a strong and kind and gentle man.

But where is that woman now? All I see is the king's bitch, the one who murders innocent people in cold blood. The one who drains their magic until they are merely shells of humans, holds them prisoner in between the realms of life and death like the tortured soul in the corner of this cell. The woman who tormented and abused my sister. Who sacrificed all those lives...for what? There is no excuse for what she has done, no cleaning the blood off her hands.

My body wars with itself as his fingers slide down my arm, trying to grasp my hand. My teeth clench. I want to pull away, to run from him because he lied to me. And at the same time, his fingers intertwine with mine and I feel the heat radiating through them, instantly cooling with his touch. I feel complete with him next to me.

He lied to me. He kept the truth from me, and I easily could have died here. Maybe I shouldn't give in to him so easily. But then again, I just killed his bastard of a father, and he's still here, still reaching out to me. And not just to keep me from killing his mother, but to comfort me.

Olaphina's eyes jump to our hands, to the ring I wear, and a smile creeps along her beautiful face. She's so young, bears no sign of the lines of age his father did.

"My ring," she remarks softly, the sound of that smile slipping into her voice.

I glance down at the beautiful golden vines as Ev turns our clasped hands toward her, letting her see. The dark crystals gleam brightly even in the damp, dark air of the dungeons.

"Evander, you gave her my ring." She sounds surprised. And happy. Why is she happy? Olaphina may have liked me as a child, even loved me, but that love is gone. She just tried to kill me, so what the fuck is going on?

Ev slips his body behind, pulling me close to him and curling his other arm around my waist. I don't pull away. I just narrow my eyes on his mother and let him encompass me in his warm embrace, ready to pull the vines tighter if needed, prepared to drain the life from her as she has done to so many before.

"Of course I did," he answers, as if there were no question in his decision. "She's the love of my life."

The words tighten my chest, a vice gripping my heart, halting the breath in my throat. My eyes sting as he speaks, and I'm trapped. Unable to move, unable to breathe.

He lied to me but here I am, letting him hold me and comfort me.

I killed his father and here he is, embracing me and calling me the love of his life. Speaking as if nothing has changed between us. But everything has changed. Hasn't it?

The love of his life.

"The betrothal may have been a ruse, a ploy to get us into the castle for Nimai. But the ring wasn't, we weren't. We aren't."

She nods, a small movement acknowledging his words. "Nimai. Once I saw her here, I knew Bria would come. But I didn't expect you, my son."

Evander sighs behind me, shifting on his feet but not letting go of my waist. "Bria began having visions over the last week or so. She could see Nimai. She could feel her and knew that Nimai was in pain. Bria took off after her."

"And you followed," she finishes. "I didn't think anything would drag you back here, but I suppose I was wrong. And yes, they are linked. The priests were hoping for that when they took Nimai, hoping to lure

Bria here." Olaphina's voice is strained. Despite her casual tone, the vines are tight against her chest and neck. "Your father didn't expect you, nor did he expect the betrothal."

More shocking revelations. We did fall into a trap. I acted like a child and brought Evander into this mess. And now there's a chance we might never get out. Because even now, even if I kill Olaphina, there will be no escape. There will be no way out after killing the captain of the guard and the high priestess. Maybe I could hold them off long enough for Nimai and Evander to escape. Maybe.

I turn my body in his grasp, unable to keep from him any longer. His gaze is soft, the golden flecks in his irises warming the chocolate brown. His expression is pained, though, lacking its usual teasing nature, and I instantly miss the way he typically looks at me.

This fucking hurts.

"Bria," he breathes, so quiet I can barely hear him despite how close we are to one another. "I meant what I said, and I need you to know that."

I have this insane longing to hug him, to kiss him, to wrap my body around him and apologize for what I've done and what I'm about to do. Because I can see the sorrow in his eyes, and I understand he had a reason for lying to me. I can forgive that, but his mother is still here—the beast that remains in this cell before us—and I cannot risk anything else with her.

She has to be dealt with, and I don't think we can come back from that. No matter how much I may want us to. I choke on my words, hardly able to speak.

"I can't," I say finally, my voice strained and cracking with the effort. "I'm so sorry, Ev."

He drops his hands from me, confusion and hurt rippling across his features. I've wounded him with my words, and I know that. But what I'm about to do to the high priestess will be so much worse.

"Bria, would you mind releasing the binds?" I hear Olaphina's words ghost over my skin, and I spin on my heel toward her, letting my hands shoot from my sides.

The living shadows tighten around her hands. Sharpened spikes from the mist of black fly out and crash into her palms, blood spurting from her hands in a rain of deep red all around the cell.

She flinches but the smile never leaves her face. It makes my stomach drop as crimson runs down her arms, staining the deep blue of her robes a dark and ghastly color. And she still smiles, her eyes filling with warm golden flames as she watches us.

"Bria, stop!" Ev roars from behind me.

I can't help it, but I laugh when he screams—harsh and high-pitched, depraved. "Give me one good reason why. She's tortured hundreds. She tortured my sister. She's a fucking monster."

Olaphina glances from me to her son, her gaze flickering but softening. "She's not wrong, Evander. I did all those things. And more."

Evander shifts behind me, his form stepping into the blur of shadows swarming between his mother and me. His chestnut hair lifts with the breeze as he trains his gaze on me, the pleading gleam back in his eyes.

"Bria, I promise you, it isn't what you think."

I scoff, unsure of what lie the two of them would make up now, what he might say to keep me from harming his flesh and blood.

"She was just trying to pull from me, Ev. Before you woke up. She tried to drain me," I explain, unsure if he even knows what she tried to do.

Evander's eyes dart from me to his mother before falling to the body of his father on the ground. Still. Unmoving. A muscle along his jaw flexes.

"But am I now, Bria?" she asks quietly.

Bitch.

She isn't. And I don't know why. She dropped the grip on my mind and my body the second Aamon's hit the ground. I narrow my eyes at her, refusing to respond to what I assume is some scheme.

"I was not and am still not trying to pull your magic from you. I only intended to provoke you."

"Why would you provoke me?" I shriek, incredulous. She's making no sense. She dug into my fucking brain and came after me, yet she claims she wasn't trying to take my magic. I just need to get out of here and get Nimai. To get away from this wicked place.

Evander dips his head toward his father, apparently understanding far more about what she's saying than I do. His calm demeanor throws me off even more. How can he be so calm right now? "Because he never would have let you leave alive." I watch as Ev drags a hand through his hair, tugging it by the roots, only for a tangle of chestnut to be rustled back up by the swirling shadows. But Olaphina finishes for him.

"He saw your power, Bria, and there is no way he would have trusted you. No matter what the two of you did to try and convince him. I knew you would have to kill him, so I let you. I provoked you, knowing you might well kill me too, but that you would be safe. Both of you."

So many emotions course through my veins, anger and sadness and confusion all topping the list. I dampen the black mist, allowing the shadows to curl at my feet and hands. I relax my grip on Olaphina but do not release her.

"Why would you care what happens to either of us? You nearly killed Evander!" I snap at her.

She closes her eyes for a moment, breathing in through her nose as the grip of the binds loosens. "And I would do it again without a thought. Aamon always used Evander as a threat. It's why he kept him around me when he was here in the capital, made him torture people, made him watch me. All so he could hold him over me. The one person I loved with all my heart. My son." Tears perch in the corner of her eyes, making the gold twinkle like falling stars.

"He beat me, burned me, starved me, and whipped me all in an effort for me to say I was unworthy. Say that I was not a true wielder of magic but a cursed bitch who stole from Vaohr. Yet somehow, I resisted. I tried to be strong for my son, to show him there was nothing unworthy about us, about him." She takes a long, steady breath, tears coursing down her cheeks, drawing bold lines through the dirt that now sticks to her skin.

"Having magic in your blood does not make you a wretched thing that deserves this and I needed Evander to know that. That was, until he told me he would kill Evander. He would murder our only child if I did not submit to his will and agree to become the high priestess."

The rage within me subsides as the words pour out of her, as she lets every detail spew forth from her lips, from her soul. I knew she survived torture, but I never knew why or what happened to both of them. The shadows curl back into my body, receding to the far corners of the room and dissipating. I let the flames calm and release her because she's speaking the truth, and there's no way I can kill her now. No way I can murder the woman who did what she had to in order to keep her son, the man I love, safe and alive.

"And I knew that he would do the same today. He would use Evander to get to me. To get to you. He would have killed my son. And for that I will forever be in your debt." She tugs her arms down from the wall, the wounds in her hands already starting to heal, the blood drying in a deep wine across her wrists and arms.

"Why not just kill him yourself?" I question. She is clearly powerful. A different type of magic than I had seen in Silas, something stronger.

"Ah, that," she says, pulling her hands together and rubbing where the wounds are.

"He has a protection spell against my magic," she explains.

I shake my head. "But how? I killed him with magic. How could he be protected from yours but die by mine?"

"Our magic is not the same, Bria. Like you, it's in my blood, runs through my veins and sparks in my system. It didn't take long for the priests to learn that it lives in blood, the witches helped with that little sliver of information. They have taken my blood for years, beaten me until I could no longer stand and drained vials upon vials of it to keep for their spells. And to keep me from killing them all." She slides up the billowy sleeves of her robes and the insides of her arms are covered in scars.

Long marks carve up her skin, puckered and pocked from burns, and up near her elbows are small slashes, all along the inside.

"I imagine they would have done the same to you. And as far as I know, they already took blood from your sister in preparation for her birthday tomorrow, knowing she would become a threat." My heart sinks with the mention of Nimai and what they must have done to get her blood.

"I had—" My voice stalls, lodging in my throat. "I had no idea what happened to you. What happened to either of you." I feel horrible, knowing what I do now. She may be a monster, but she was forced into it. She was made into it.

Nothing can change what she did—to my sister, to the hundreds of others she harmed and killed. Olaphina has so much blood on her hands that she will never be clean of those sins. But I've also never experienced what it feels like to have your child threatened, to have to choose between their life and the life of innocent people. To feel useless, hopeless, and alone for years. And deep down inside I know that if I were in the same situation, I likely would have chosen the same.

Evander rubs a hand across the back of his neck. "I didn't want you to know." The shame in his voice is tangible and it twists my insides up like someone wringing the last drops of water from a towel.

I look at him and stretch out my hand, feeling pulled to him, no matter what lies between us. No matter what lies ahead. The need to touch him is overwhelming.

"No more lies," I order.

He grasps my hand and walks toward me. "No more lies," he agrees.

We stay there, watching each other for a few seconds, absorbing all that has happened and all we still have to do. But for this one moment, I have the slightest hope that it will be alright. That we will be alright. In this one moment, I feel forgiveness and understanding flood over us, washing away what each of us has done and replacing it with respect. And love.

Olaphina's movement toward us jolts me from the precious moment, and I recoil, moving back a few steps from where I stand, my hand still clasped within Evander's. I understand why she did what she did. But understanding her is a far cry from trusting her. Especially while we are still in the capital, and they still have her blood.

The energy thrumming from her is intense. *Not like Silas*, I think again. It feels raging hot, like the fire of magic that burns inside of me. She said it was different, but how? It has this feeling, like it's something old and ancient and from the earth. Olaphina tilts her head as if assessing me and continues to move closer, closing the gap between us as her robes softly swish around her.

"You feel it, Bria, don't you?" she asks, her voice soft and ethereal.

I nod, though I'm unsure what *it* is. Old magic, maybe. But how?

"How can you do that? I've never heard of someone with power like mine," I question, needing to know how she pulls energy like I do. I thought it a power of the gods if it had been passed down to me, but clearly it isn't.

She smiles, a small and graceful movement of her full lips.

"That is a story for another time. But you can do more with it, Bria. You can pull energy from those without magic too, feed from their life energy. It's a different sort of draining, and it's deadly to the mere mortals you may use it on. Though that may prove useful when you go up against the king."

Drain energy from those without magic. Life energy, she said.

"I could kill people?" I shake my head. It seems impossible. Too powerful, even.

"Yes, remember that the next time you come up against someone who wishes you harm, Bria," she remarks, glancing down at my healing wrist.

I open my mouth to ask her more questions. I have a feeling she could answer so many things I yearn to know about my magic. About where it comes from and about the old gods and the Forsaken Woods. But her mood shifts, as if sensing something around us.

"You need to listen to me. There is not much time before they come looking for Aamon. Before they come looking for all of us." Her face is pained as she reaches out to touch my hand, the one that bears her ring. She grasps it tightly and the golden flames in her eyes burn brightly as she speaks. The simmering energy in my core springs to life with her touch, heat rising through my spine, pulsing through my bones and blood.

"They are running out of people to take magic from in the capital. They have been searching further and further from Easthallow, as I'm sure you've noticed. And that means the world is changing. If they lose this power, everything will change." Her voice is tense now, different from the airy, soft tone she held only moments before.

"You need to get Nimai and run. Get to the Forsaken Woods and seek out the Guardians and the Ancients. Go *now*." Her words are rough, as though she is scraping them out of her throat. As if it hurts her to say them.

My body tightens, every muscle clenching in fear. What is she talking about?

"What Ancients?" I ask hurriedly.

She squeezes my hand and I feel it heat more. I shoot a glance down and my fingertips are dark again, hers faintly glowing.

"I don't have time to explain. Evander will know what to do." She presses a kiss to my forehead before doing the same to Evander and then shoves us out of the cell.

Evander tugs me along, grasping the intensity of his mother's words. I crane my head around to watch her as we rush from the damp, dirt-filled dungeon room and her lips part in a smile, revealing the same dimple in her left cheek that her son bears.

"I'll be here when you need me, Prophecy." The whisper creeps up my spine, sending goosebumps across my arms and legs.

"Let's go," Evander commands as he begins hauling me behind him up the steep stairs. Up to the castle. To get Nimai.

And run.

CHAPTER 64

Evander

We storm up the stairs as quickly as possible. Bria has her skirts pulled high up on her waist as I nearly drag her behind me. I have my sword strapped to my side and I can see from here that my dagger is still sheathed to Bria's upper thigh. There will be no time to grab the rest of our weapons, our armor and clothes. There's only time to get out.

Bria killed the captain of the guard. They will find him soon enough. And my mother, the high priestess, will be expected to explain, to provide some sort of excuse for what happened in the dungeons. Knowing her, it will likely be the truth—that Bria was too powerful to contain. And then she will be hunted.

Again.

And so will I.

We hit the landing and I slam my hands into the drawbar, jerking it out of the way and spilling us out into the empty stone room. The light from the sconces hits Bria. She's splattered in blood, her dress covered in it. A spray of crimson freckles decorates her face, her chest, and her upper arms. Dirt is jammed under her fingernails and covers the skirts of her gown, the edges of it nearly black. I imagine I don't look much better.

We stealth out of the room, and I lead her quietly down the hall to a back staircase. I recall from my time here that this stairwell holds the servants' access for the various floors of the castle. We will draw far less attention here than going through the grand foyer looking like this. There's a fleeting moment when I wonder if she could cloak us in shadow but think better of it. Whatever strength remains in this fierce girl at my side will be needed for us to get the fuck out of here.

The stairwell is quiet. It's now past dinnertime and the servants have cleaned and retired to their own quarters. I breathe out a heavy sigh of relief at that. There's a chance we will be leaving a sea of bodies in our wake, and I would rather avoid killing as many innocents as I can. I'm sure Bria would agree if I asked her.

As we slowly make our way up the stairs, I turn to Bria. The dim light makes it difficult to see her, but she clasps my hand tightly.

"Keep your hand on your dagger. Be ready to kill anyone you see," I say, making sure she understands that we can have no witnesses to our escape. The further we get ahead of the king and his men, the better. We cannot risk it. "Don't hesitate."

The servants' stairwell opens to the alcove behind our rooms. I move my finger to press against my lips, urging Bria to be silent. Without a doubt, someone will be guarding the door that leads to Nimai and I hope it is anyone other than Luthais tonight.

I drop her hand and grasp the edge of the doorframe, peering out slightly and catching a glimpse of blond hair. I yank my head quickly back to not be seen.

"Shit!" I curse under my breath.

"Is it Luthais?" Bria questions, keeping her voice a low whisper.

I nod. Does he never fucking sleep?

"It's okay," she breathes, her eyes flickering. "I can handle him. You get Nimai."

She's right. She can handle him and at some point, I need to trust her to do what we both know she's capable of. I've witnessed firsthand what her shadows warp into and even more so what she can accomplish with the dead. And after what my mother said, there's a chance she can kill him in other ways too.

"Kill him if you need to. Don't hesitate, Bria. These people are our enemies."

She lurches onto her toes and slams into me, my back thudding into the cold stone wall. She kisses me forcefully but rips back before I can dive into her and wrap her up in my arms. Her smile is brilliant, all gleaming teeth and blazing eyes. We are getting her sister. And going home.

Bria disappears from my view, her skirts swishing around her. When Luthais spots her, I hear him utter a string of curses, no doubt shocked by her appearance.

"What the fuck happened to you?" he yelps, fear and concern flooding his voice.

But Bria gives no response, and the air begins to thrum, the buzz of her energy rippling through the hallway. Black mist shrouds the space outside the alcove, drawing a sheer midnight curtain that mutes the light and throws the area into darkness. I wait and listen until muffled screams indicate it's time for me to move and I swing around the corner.

Luthais is pinned to the wall, ensconced in a cage of shadow, his mouth bound along with his limbs. Those gray eyes narrow as he watches me move past him to the door. Fury radiates from him and the air around his body seems to shudder, though I imagine that must be the swirling mist. We fooled him, and his rage is palpable even through the dark depths of the shadows.

Bria is barely visible through the ebony whorls around her, only noticeable by the wildfire of her eyes flickering through the shadows. She has this, but I need to be quick about it. She'll be drained too soon if she continues to use her power like this and we still need to get to the Gilded Forest and Quinn before we can get out.

I move my hand along the door, gripping the handle and slipping inside, letting it shut quietly behind me. Nimai is lying on the bed, a book propped in her hands while her head hangs to the side. I chuckle at the sight. She fell asleep reading a book, completely unaware of what was occurring outside her door, something I can easily see her sister doing as well, if her life were not the shitshow it currently is. I stride quickly to her to wake her, placing my hand on her shoulder and gently shaking her body.

Nimai groans and my hand stills when I hear it—the scream that pierces my heart. It makes my blood run cold and every hair on my body stand at attention, my limbs freezing for a moment. I've heard it before even if I don't want to recognize it. Too many times to count now.

Bria is hurt, and badly.

Nimai's eyes flare open and lock on to me. But I'm already moving, turning on my heel and running back to the door, flinging it open to reveal my worst nightmare. The shadows are fading around her, pulling back.

Blood.

There's so much fucking blood.

It's pooling around her body as she kneels on the floor in her gown. Bria's hands are clutching at the wound, trying to stifle the crimson flow of life pouring from her middle.

My eyes fly to Luthais, who is still caged, his eyes wide, his face a pained grimace. Quickly searching the dark mist for who attacked her, I see the body—a guard on the ground behind her, not moving. His body is littered with gaping holes, but I see no weapons aside from his own. He was killed by blades made of dark and destructive shadows that dissipated once their job was done.

But they weren't quick enough to save her. I wasn't quick enough to save her.

CHAPTER 65

Bria

I had it under control. Or at least I thought I did. But now, as blood pours into my hands and seeps between my fingers—my feeble attempts to staunch the wound in my abdomen doing nothing—I realize I had been too focused. Once again, I'd let anger cloud my vision and was entirely set on Luthais. There was something about him that kept me from killing him. Maybe it was the way he looked at Nimai, or the way the air around him rippled in waves, seeming to manipulate around his body. Some weird energy, old energy, even. But whatever that something was, it made me feel like I couldn't kill him. Not yet, anyway. Perhaps it was just my realization that he actually has a soul. Somewhere.

So instead, I trapped him without injuring the man. Gagged and bound, he'd glared at me as I'd waited for Evander and Nimai. Then through the shadows, his eyes had widened, fear settling in the slate gray depths that seemed to flicker with something more, though I could not pinpoint what it was. While I'd concentrated on those eyes, I'd heard a cracking noise and the back of my neck prickled. Luthais thrashed against the onyx cage, slamming his body into it and causing the mist to undulate, making it look as if he could actually break free of it. But before I could find out why he was fighting so hard or understand how he was cracking through the shadows, looking so shocked and scared, a blade was shoved straight through me. From my back through my stomach.

I've never experienced pain like this before—sharp and blinding, all-consuming pain. When the scream came ripping from my throat, I felt as if I would shatter into a thousand small pieces. Vicious ebony blades formed of mist had slammed into the guard behind me, killing him instantly. But they did nothing to quell what I felt. What I still feel.

Death. I'm dying.

The fire burning in me is beginning to gutter, the mist subsiding, receding to the crevices and cracks in the castle. I hold on to the cage around Luthais but have no idea how much longer I can contain him. Or how I can cloak us out of here now.

Luthais stares at me, unable to speak through the shadowy fingers clamped on his mouth. He's stopped fighting the shadows now, maybe realizing it's useless. No sense in fighting it and exhausting himself when I won't be able to hold them soon anyway. I cannot tell but it looks a lot like sadness in those deep gray eyes. Part of me hopes it is. That he really does have a soul worth saving. That maybe my choice had not been in vain.

Evander's voice flits in and out of my brain as my vision blurs further. I'm unable to concentrate on anything other than the pain and the blood that seems to be a raging river running straight out of me. Pooling beneath me and soaking every inch of my gown.

"We need to get out. Now." He's speaking to Nimai. When my slow-moving gaze makes it to her, she's frozen in shock, watching my hands pressed to my belly, blood creeping between my fingers and running in rivulets of wine down my hands and arms.

Evander bends down to grab me, placing one strong arm under my shoulders and one under my knees, lifting me against his chest. I reach my arm up, hissing at the sharp ache it causes in my abdomen. But I cling to him, digging my fingers into the neck of his tunic with all the strength I have left. He presses a kiss into my hair as he begins moving.

"We're leaving, Bria. I'm going to get you home." *Home.* The word echoes in my brain.

My next breath holds the smell of sandalwood mixed with sweat and the metallic tang of blood. My blood. Closing my eyes, I let Evander carry me down the servants' stairs. He moves so fast, far quicker than I would imagine possible while holding another person, having them weigh you down. I can only tell because we are on level ground now, no more jostling from the steps. But I can't manage to open my eyes.

I try to hold on as long as I can, but I drop the shadows containing Luthais when I know we are on the first floor, moving to escape through the back of the castle. I can only hope we are far enough from him that it won't matter. That by the time he manages to sound an alarm or catch up, we will be gone.

The warm night air hits my face, telling me we've made it outside. Evander brings his face close to mine, whispering to me, panic surging though every word he speaks. He knows I'm dying, too. He can tell.

"Bria, I need you to stay with me. I need you to stay. Please." His words are broken, barely escaping his lips, getting stuck and cracking in his throat, splintered by panting breaths.

Outside. I'm putting so much energy into focusing, just concentrating on what his words mean, trying to grasp that outside, I have things to do. Outside means more guards. Outside means I need to cloak us, to gather the shadows around us. I can't get pulled under by fatigue or blood loss or even death. Not yet.

Using every shred of energy I have left, I summon the shadows, calling forth darkness to mold around us, trying to maintain that small flicker of light within me that is seeping out of my core at an ungodly rate. Trying to pull it back into me. It aches and I truly worry the wound might rip my entire body in half. But I hold on to it anyway, feeling my body heat and my palms tingle the tiniest bit. I still don't open my eyes when I sense them. I sense the darkness, enveloping us in the shadows and hiding our escape from view.

The blaze inside starts to sputter almost immediately, my dying body revolting at my use of power. Evander is running now, holding me tight against him, clinging to me as my head drops back. I pass out for a few seconds, maybe minutes. I'm not really sure how long, but when I come to, the shadows are disappearing. No matter what I do, I cannot get a firm grip on them. They slip through my fingers despite my begging and pleading for them to stay with me, to save my sister and my love even if they cannot save me. I try my damnedest to reignite that magical fire inside, to will it back to life, but the smoldering embers have nothing left to give.

I have nothing left to give.

My eyes spasm and I catch a glimpse of gold in the distance, sparkling with the light of the full moon. The Gilded Forest. He's going make it. Nimai is going make it. Quinn can get them back to the camp and to the Woods.

They must go to the Woods. That's what Olaphina said.

"Ev," I rasp, trying to force his name past my lips.

He pulls me tighter as his boots hit the ground harder, moving as fast as he is humanly capable of toward the forest. The warmth in my abdomen starts to subside then, a coolness spreading across my body. The fire and heat of my magic is disappearing and with it, the pain seems to be diminishing. *That's good*, I think. Less pain will be good.

"Get Nimai to the Woods," I gasp, sucking in as much air as I can. My lungs feel full, something sticky and warm beginning to coat the inside of them. They aren't working quite right now.

"I will, Bria. I promise you," he chokes the words out, panting as he runs.

We break through the edge of the forest, gold gleaming and glinting on every surface. I manage to keep my eyes open for a few seconds longer but they flutter, heavy, too heavy to watch. It's colder here, within the forest. So cold that my teeth start to chatter, clacking together violently. My arm slides from my grip on Evander's tunic. I attempt to keep my fingers clasped on to him, but the effort is futile. All the strength I have left goes flooding out of my body through the gaping hole.

"What the fuck happened?" I hear Quinn's voice through the cool haze settling in around me as Evander stops running, his chest heaving against me.

"Bria!" another voice screams. I know that voice. It sings through my bones and they ache to be with it but there's no way for them to move toward it.

My sister's beautiful sound travels through me when she answers. "She was stabbed as we tried to flee. A guard caught her with his blade."

Her voice is shaking but she's fighting back the tears. I can tell and I'm proud of her. She's being strong when she needs to.

That's my girl.

My limbs start to shake too now, uncontrollable shivers coursing through my body. Evander slides down a tree and settles us in a heap on the ground. There's no pain now, just cold and calm. His body presses in around me, trying to warm me, trying to stop the shaking.

I manage to pry my eyes open, just for a moment, and I see him. Tears glisten in the corner of his eyes—those beautiful molten chocolate eyes, burning with gold, silhouetted from the full moon so bright above us.

So fitting, I realize, that I will die by the light of the moon, just as I lived.

"It's the prophecy," Quinn says, his words barely audible.

Evander tightens around me, burying his face in my hair. He rocks our bodies back and forth, and I can hear him whispering over and over again into my ear. What is he saying? There are too many voices swirling around me now and my brain cannot manage to focus on all of them at once.

"No. It can't be," Nimai replies, pleading. "Our mother said we needed to be in the Forsaken Woods. That she wouldn't die before I came into my gifts."

"It is. This is her destiny, Nimai. This is *your* destiny." Quinn's voice is rushed and firm, urging the two of them to listen to him. "You both need to let her go. Guards will be on us soon if what you say is true."

The sounds dim around me. They are still speaking but I have no energy left to hear them. The moon shines on my face and I wish I could smile back at it. I feel it though my heavy eyes have slipped shut once more. And I know now that they will not open again.

A whisper pushes through, a soft breeze whisking me away into the darkness beyond.

"I love you."

CHAPTER 66

Evander

I just keep rocking, willing life back into her. Her chest isn't rising anymore. There is no heartbeat thudding against my own chest. No thrumming of energy coming from her. Bria's arms hang limp in my grasp, her head tipped back, ivory skin gleaming in the moonlight.

"I love you." The words I had tried not to say, the words I had kept locked up tight to not distract her, to not keep her from her destiny. They now flow out of me, and I cannot stop them even if I wanted to. I whisper over and over to her, hoping she can hear me, that she will come back to me. That she will let me love her the way I've always tried to.

Nimai sinks to the ground, her knees slamming into the roots of the trees a few feet away. The scream of anguish at losing her sister tears from her throat and echoes off the gilded trees around us, sending a sharp jolt up my spine. I yank my head from Bria, staring at her sister. Her dark hair sparkles blue and violet in the moonlight, making it look as if stars are glimmering all around her.

That's when I feel it. The thrumming.

I glance back down at Bria, but she's still. Too still. Too quiet.

The thrumming is coming from Nimai. She throws her head back and her skin starts to glow. Her whole body glows, all at once. She becomes a golden star, burning from the inside out.

Quinn runs toward her, but something is happening, something he cannot help her with. He stops short when he realizes it too, not daring to touch her. He looks at me, eyes wide in terror. My brain scrambles, trying to determine what this is, but then it hits me. It's late, the moon is perched high in the middle of the sky. It has to be midnight.

Her birthday. She's come of age.

Quinn was right, it's the prophecy.

I hold tight to Bria, watching as her sister pulses. Waves of energy wash over us, making my hair stand up on end, goosebumps pebbling across my body. She stays like that for a moment, energy swelling inside her, the dress pooling around her in a glowing ring of white and gold. Then her head snaps up, her eyes locking on her sister.

Flames of emerald and forest green flare inside her eyes.

Fuck. She looks terrifying and unbelievable at the same time.

Nimai stands, raising herself from a seated position with otherworldly grace, as if the forest has lifted her to stand. She takes the few steps over to us and I freeze, unable to speak or move. Unable to do anything but just watch her in utter shock and awe.

At first, I'm not sure what she plans to do. But the look in those magical eyes tells me everything I need to know. She has her power now.

She drapes her body over her sister, covering her completely while Bria is still in my arms, and I absorb the weight of her, the weight of both their bodies against mine. She cries then. Sobs finally escape and wrack her glowing body as she slams her hands into Bria—one hand on her heart, one hand on the bloody hole in her middle.

My body is pushed back against the golden tree, forced into it from the surge that roars from Nimai. The bark bites into my skin and blood trickles down the flesh of my back as her power traps me there. A blinding white light bursts from her, encompassing the area around us, flooding my eyes with such intensity I have to squeeze them shut for fear they may burn out of the gods damned sockets. Stars sparkle on the inside of my lids, a fiery heat sweeping over me. I suck in a hot breath and feel it searing against my lungs.

I'm gasping, panting for air, but I stay clinging to her, my fingers digging into her body, warm with the heat that rushes out of Nimai and into her. I've absorbed Bria's heat before, and I focus on that now, letting Nimai's power surge over me and allowing myself to take it in, not letting it burn me or hurt me in any way.

This is it, I think. This is what the prophecy foretold. Bria, the descendant of Lilith, would die. Struck down in the kingdom she was meant to overthrow in order to save our world. And Nimai, the descendent of Kiara, would bring forth a new day. That has to be what the searing light and heat are. Her powers are growing. The power of the sun, light, and all things pure and good in this world—that is what Kiara held and that it what Nimai will hold.

The daughters of the Keeper will rise, the moon shall die, and the sun shall give birth to a new day. The world will thrive under the reign of magic once more.

Bria is gone. Nimai is the one who will lead us forward now.

I have to let her go.

But there is no forward for me. She's gone, and my heart is broken.

The world is black. Everything is dark. But the pain is gone. And everything else has gone along with it.

I know what this is. I'm hovering between life and death. I'm in the in-between like that body in the corner of the damp, dark dungeon cell. A tiny thread still holds my soul to my body. But that thread is fragile and frayed, ready to snap in an instant and send me tumbling down.

There are voices, and there is light, and sound, and movement. But it's too far away, I can see none of it. Cannot hear, smell, or feel any of it. At least not at first.

But after a while there's green, a sea of pine trees, green grass, and moss. Slate mountains and a crystal-blue river that stretches along lazily, one that cuts right through the thriving forest. A living forest. Filled with magic. And there are people, lots of people, who buzz—magic filling their veins, emanating from them. An electric wind swirls and whips around the entire area.

Something in me stirs with the wind and there it is again. That old, earthy feeling of Olaphina's magic. Something deep and true, from the world before.

The Ancients.

But as soon as I see them and feel them, they disappear, darkness cascading over me again. Pulling me down, out of the in-between. And to what lies beneath, whatever that is.

It's not that I want to go. In fact, I would much rather stay. I want to live and be with my sister, my friends, my love. But I accepted long ago that this was my fate, that one day I would die and that there was no way to keep it from happening. I understand most people come to terms with their ultimate demise at some point. I'd just come to terms with it a lot sooner, knowing it would hit me when I was young and vulnerable. So now, I just let the darkness grasp me, twist its long fingers around my own and drag me deeper. Away from the warm body that surrounds me, away from the world that I know and love.

All sensation leaves as I sink further and further into the nothing that awaits me. I can't help but wonder if this is it. Will I be like this forever? Sinking and swirling through nothing, or will it all suddenly stop, and I will finally cease to exist?

I'm not really sure what to expect. How can anyone know exactly? It's not as if death comes for many who then live to tell the tale. So, when warmth spreads throughout my body again, tingling through my veins that once pumped with blood, I assume it's happening—that I'm finally gone, my soul leaving and moving on. To wherever it goes.

Perhaps to reside alongside Lilith and Kiara's. Maybe in the Woods with the Ancients. I don't know if they are alive or dead waiting to meet me. But they are waiting for me, nonetheless.

And I will wait for them. For my friends and family. For Evander. I hope the prophecy comes true and they all have the chance to live in a world where magic reigns, where there is truth and happiness and joy. Where no one is hunted, and they can be themselves. There will always be conflict, no matter who rules. I'm not naïve enough to believe otherwise. But I need this sacrifice to be worth it. I need the loss of my life to allow them to experience this new world.

That heat radiating from the wound in my abdomen spiders along my veins and surges through my body. It spreads across my skin like the moonlight that had poured down upon me just minutes before, seeping into my bones and pulsing through where my heart once beat. Making it feel as if it beats again.

But that's impossible. I'm dead.

A sharp pain shoots through that wound. It stretches through the space created by the sword, gouging along the edges of the hole, a thousand tiny fingers ripping and pulling at the pieces. They tug the edges of the gaping wound and sew them back together, forcing the muscles and sinew to bind. To heal.

A thud in my chest resounds in my ears. I can hear it. But how?

Then again.

Fuck. What is it?

A steady beating now. Picking up speed as the heat surges along every single pore of my skin, every inch of my being. And that smell. I can smell. Roses and sandalwood.

My eyes snap open.

Everything is golden and white and glowing. A shocking difference to the inky depths of darkness I was just experiencing. There was nothing but cold and unknown there, but now there is nothing but warmth and light. And as the glow starts to fade, I watch, training my tired eyes on where it's coming from, to find the source of the ethereal light.

Ebony waves peek through the glow, beams of light sparkling along the violet hues embedded in the strands. They shine and shimmer like stars come to light on a dark night. And eyes filled with flickering green and gold stare back at me. Her whole body vibrates with energy and life.

Nimai.

I'm not dead. How in the fuck am I not dead?

She has the power to heal just as Cato thought. The living embodiment of Kiara. But I *was* dead. Not just broken. Dead. How did she heal me from that? As far as I know, Kiara had no ability to bring life back into the lifeless. And I had been clinging to a thread, my soul tethered to my still, lifeless body by one fraying tendril.

I drag a ragged breath into my lungs, filling them with air, no longer struggling through the thick, sticky blood that settled there. She sits back on her heels and looks at me, her eyes dazzling with the radiating light. Blood stains my hands, my abdomen, most of my clothes and hers as well, the tear in my gown exposing the pink flesh she has sewn together. There's no longer a gaping hole pouring my existence out onto the forest floor, but new skin bursting with life.

A smile spreads across her beautiful face. She is striking. My heart clenches at the sight of her, and I register once more that it's beating.

My heart is beating.

My chest is rising and falling. I reach a hand to touch her and feel as her hand moves to mine. Her skin is hot, and a jolt of energy zips through my arm and to my core with her touch. My face breaks into a similar smile, crinkling my eyes as tears flow freely from them, pouring down my face and tickling my neck as they pool on my gown.

"Mai." My voice is ragged and cracks as I whisper her name.

"Hi, B," she says back.

My gaze slides to Evander. I'm still locked in his embrace and his eyes are glued shut, his head thrust against the golden bark of the tree. His hands cling to me, gripping me tightly, his face streaked with blood and tears. Locks of chestnut fall across his handsome face, riddled with agony. He's too paralyzed by his own grief to realize I'm not gone.

I lift my hand up, wincing at the pain, the aching I feel throughout my entire body. I brush my hand down his cheek, seeing Olaphina's ring glinting in the moonlight, the crystals shining brighter than they ever have before. There's something magical about them.

Evander opens his eyes and I think he might drop me. Shock consumes his features, turning his tanned skin stark white as he scans my face and my body.

"You—" He chokes on the words, tears glistening in his eyes once more.

"I'm here. I'm alive," I whisper as he buries his head in my hand.

Evander dips his head, pressing his forehead against mine and holds me tightly, causing my wounds to scream despite their healing. His breathing comes in ragged pants. He pulls back to look at me, the gold in his eyes sparkling, captivating as always.

"How?"

I shake my head, moving gingerly as the pain creeps into my bones. I don't know how, and I plan to find out. But right now, it doesn't matter. What matters is that I'm back. I'm alive.

"Gods above!" Quinn gasps, and I crane my neck to see him past

Nimai. He's standing, staring at us, his eyes widened pools of gold and green, one hand tangled in his long hair as if he had been tearing it out. "Fuck, Bria. I'm so sorry. I thought you were dead."

Oh. He means when he told them to leave me. *Bastard*.

He's not wrong though, they should have left.

A pair of icy blue eyes watches me from beside him and I finally recognize where that voice I heard had come from. The scream that danced along my skin and called to my soul as I died. *Silas*.

Seeing the two standing there makes my heart twist deeper. The thought that I had lost them all is making it hard to breathe. I want to drown myself in all of them, to never let them go.

But it's then that I notice Quinn's other hand is occupied. His sword is drawn and there's another person. A figure on his knees in front of the men. I struggle to sit up so I can see the figure, pain still radiating through my core. Evander aids me, never letting go of his grasp. I sit across his lap and look toward the kneeling guard, a gash across his brow that still seeps blood down his forehead. His mouth is slack, awestruck. His slate gray gaze is fixed on my sister, who is still glowing an ethereal gold.

My mouth tugs up at the corner despite my attempt not to smile.

"I imagine seeing someone brought back to life without your god present must be a bit...shocking," I say, my voice raspy and low.

Luthais slides his eyes to me and there's that flicker again, just a flash of something like lightning before it's gone. A loud alarm rings from the kingdom, a bellowing sound that reverberates off the golden trees and makes the ground shake.

"You need to run," he demands, his eyes frantically darting between Nimai and me, the air rippling around him for a second. I swear I see it, but it's gone before I can fully register the movement. Dying is a bitch and it does weird things to your mind.

Quinn quirks a brow at me. A small gesture with a larger question attached. A question of whether we should leave Luthais alive or not. Silas's hands are glowing that cold white, itching to blast a hole in his chest if I say yes. There's no need for the sword with Silas there, but Quinn is a warrior and gods be damned if he lets himself be unarmed.

"Thank you," I offer. Speaking to the guard on his knees before looking at Quinn. "Don't let him follow."

Before Luthais can utter a word of disapproval, Quinn lifts the sword. He brings the hilt down firmly, dealing a harsh blow to the side of Luthais's skull and he crashes forward onto the rooted ground, his face bouncing off the hard surface. Fuck if that won't hurt when he comes to.

"Are you sure?" Evander asks from behind me.

I nod. "We have enough blood on our hands and—" I don't know how to express what I feel from him. "I think he was trying to warn me about the other guard." There's more than that in terms of what's going on with Luthais and I feel a twinge of guilt at not sharing it with Evander. But this isn't the time nor the place for that conversation. We have no time.

Nimai remains staring at him splayed out across the golden roots, moonlight making his blond hair gleam nearly silver. And the thought occurs to me then that she may feel differently than me about this. He is her captor, after all. Her abuser.

"Mai. Did he—"

"No," she says curtly, cutting me off before I can finish the question. She's watching his chest heaving as he lies there. "He never laid a hand on me, that was all Aamon and ..." she trails off.

Evander tenses behind me at the mention of his father, and I wonder just how far Aamon had taken his torture of my sister. But we both know he will never harm another person. Not in this life. And her story is one she should *choose* to share in time with me, I will not push her. Not now and not ever.

"But he did nothing to stop it," Quinn responds, more a statement than a question. The picturesque warrior is waiting, ready to kill Luthais if Nimai wishes.

Nimai moves to Luthais on the ground and brushes a still-glowing hand across his blood-streaked face before pulling herself up to stand. Looking at Quinn, she shakes her head and her lustrous hair shines violet in the moonlight.

"He did nothing to stop it, but he didn't help them either."

Quinn grunts in dismissal of her defense but gathers that Nimai is not out for blood here. Silas disappears behind a cluster of trees and comes back with the horses, pulling them over to us by the reins.

"We need to go, now. You heard the alarms. Whatever you did in there...they know." Those icy blue eyes are flooded with pain, his face tense.

Oh gods, I can only imagine what my dying felt like for him and Nimai.

"And they will be looking for us," Evander states in agreement.

We hurry from the ground to the horses as the alarm sounds again. The steeds stamp as the earth quivers beneath them. Evander never lets go of his grip on me as we mount and ride through the Gilded Forest. His arms wind tightly around me as if he thinks I may stop breathing again. As if he doesn't quite believe I'm really here and if he doesn't hold on, I may just disappear from his side.

I guess I can understand that. It still doesn't feel real.

His grip is calming, and I too fear that this is all a dream, and I'm still floating through the nebulous space between life and death, just waiting for it to crash down on me and rip my loved ones away once more.

I've already forgotten how slow the trek was through this forest with its golden roots tangling around every step. But Evander and Quinn push forward, making the best progress they can. It's still a safer route for us than the main roads out of Easthallow. We're ahead of them, and if they decide to follow, we will stay ahead of them. Silas remains behind us on his horse, unwilling to move far from my side, and I welcome the closeness, wishing I could nestle my body between his and Evander's. I need them both so much in this moment.

"We have to get back to the northern camp and evacuate them all," Evander says, breaking the silence between us.

Quinn darts a glance back to us before turning his attention ahead once more and picking his way across the forest. Nimai is folded into him, silent. I imagine she might be sleeping, knowing how exhausted she must be from that display of power.

"What did you tell him?" the warrior's voice is rough and gravely.

Evander lets loose a long sigh. "Enough. I tried to be vague, but he pushed me for an exact location."

Quinn grunts in response. Evander revealed too much information about the camp. About our home. And Braddock and his men will be heading there soon.

"I told him it's in another part of the Kaanos but they will find it eventually. It's only a matter of time. My mother said they were running out of gifted people, running out of power. So they will be looking. And his commanders were there. All of them."

Even without Aamon we cannot be free of them. They will find us. We will still be hunted. Unless...

"We need to bring them to the Forsaken Woods."

Quinn rears his head back, his eyebrows shooting up as if I've said something insane. I suppose it may have sounded that way. But I think it's the only choice we have. There is nowhere left that is safe in Azudora for us or for the rest of the rebels. Our entire world is owned by the king. Except for the Woods.

"How can we do that? There are Guardians. There are protections around the area..." Quinn replies, frustration filtering through his words. "Not all of us have magic in our blood, Bria."

Nimai speaks from in front of him, shocking me that she's awake and listening. But her words barely carry back to us through the thick trees. "The Guardians will let us pass."

Quinn faces forward and I'm guessing he's giving my sister the same incredulous look he gave me as she sits in front of him. "How do you know? Can we risk the entire camp for this?"

"They are looking for me. I can feel them." Her voice is light and breathy. I wonder what happened when she came into her magic earlier. How could she feel the Guardians? I didn't even know they truly existed, but she's somehow connected to them.

Evander presses a kiss to the top of my head. "Kiara had a way with animals from what I remember. It makes sense that Nimai would too. We wondered when we saw the Guardian a few days ago...we wondered if it would let us pass."

I tip my head back, trying to look at his face. "You saw them?"

He nods. "Just one. It was magnificent."

"So, we head to the Woods," Quinn states, a firm direction that we all agree upon.

Everyone falls back into silence, the weight of all that just happened and all that remains ahead heavy. Suffocating. Someone will need to go back to the camp, but none of us are ready to make that decision just yet. We've had no time to process it all—the trauma behind us and the uncertainty ahead of us.

I let my body relax back against Evander, allowing him to wrap fully around me, breathing in the scent of sandalwood and remembering what I heard as I died. What he said over and over to me, whispering in my ear as I left him. I tilt my chin up to brush a kiss across his jaw.

"I love you too," I breathe, and his arm tightens against me.

We are here. We are alive. And we are in this together now.

I may not have all the answers. In fact, it feels as if I have none. I have no idea whether my dying fulfilled the prophecy. Or if it will come for me again, taking what had slipped from its grasp by that thin, fragile tether that held me in this world. But I have a feeling who does know.

The Ancients.

Acknowledgments

First of all, I want to thank you for reading this.

Writing this book was an escape for me. An escape from the deep trenches of post-partum anxiety and panic disorder. I suffered from near constant racing thoughts and frequent panic attacks after having my son and writing became a much needed reprieve from that, an outlet for my non-stop brain, a way to focus my energy and thoughts into something productive. I never knew I would fall so in love with it. With writing and the story and the characters I created.

So thank you, from the bottom of my heart, for taking the chance and reading my book.

There's no way I would have made this happen without my husband. He supported me throughout it all, no matter how ridiculous this pipe dream I had was. Not once did he tell me he thought it wasn't possible, in fact, when I wanted to give up, he's the one who pushed me to get out there. To get on social media and start promoting it, to publish it. Not to mention, he put up with me for hours to make my cover art and map. He's truly my best friend, he's my Ev and I wouldn't have it any other way.

To my test readers – Danni, Sommer, Sarah and Georgia. Thank you for taking the time to get immersed in my world. Even if the slow burn of it killed you (Sommer) or the constant texting from me made you want to scream. You have no idea what it means that you helped me and were there for me through it all.

To my editor Alex, thank you for your guidance and your feedback. Your comments helped me push through when I worried it wasn't good enough. Your love of my characters and story made me so happy.

And thank you to Marcia for formatting this all for me, to Hannah for being the most supportive person I've never met and to my niece Kate for believing in me and lending her Gen Z prowess to help me.

This world wouldn't be possible without you.

Second Edition

I need to add that this version was given updates by both Rachel and Courtney, my amazing team that works on alpha reading, editing, and proofreading (see that Oxford comma in there?). You've made sure I could create a second edition that is truly mine and you've worked so hard to make book two even better than it was. I can never thank you enough.

The new cover is also thanks to my phenomenal husband, yet again. Who, despite hating working with me, helped me make this the cover I wanted it to be.

And thank you to Millie, because I never would have gotten the courage to reformat this on my own and push forward without your guidance and support. You've become such a good friend and I'm lucky to have you!

www.ingramcontent.com/pod-product-compliance
Lightning Source LLC
Chambersburg PA
CBHW061857310726
48972CB00004B/1070